SUCH A NICE GIRL

www.penguin.co.uk

Also by Andrea Mara

The Other Side of the Wall
One Click
The Sleeper Lies
All Her Fault
Hide and Seek
No One Saw a Thing
Someone in the Attic
It Should Have Been You

SUCH A NICE GIRL

Andrea Mara

bantam

TRANSWORLD PUBLISHERS

UK | USA | Canada | Ireland | Australia
India | New Zealand | South Africa

Transworld is part of the Penguin Random House group of companies
whose addresses can be found at global.penguinrandomhouse.com.

Penguin Random House UK, One Embassy Gardens,
8 Viaduct Gardens, London SW11 7BW

penguin.co.uk

First published in Great Britain in 2026 by Bantam
an imprint of Transworld Publishers

001

Copyright © Andrea Mara 2026

The moral right of the author has been asserted.

This book is a work of fiction and, except in the case of historical fact,
any resemblance to actual persons, living or dead, is purely coincidental.

Every effort has been made to obtain the necessary permissions with
reference to copyright material, both illustrative and quoted. We apologize
for any omissions in this respect and will be pleased to make the
appropriate acknowledgements in any future edition.

Penguin Random House values and supports copyright. Copyright fuels creativity,
encourages diverse voices, promotes freedom of expression and supports a vibrant culture.
Thank you for purchasing an authorized edition of this book and for respecting intellectual
property laws by not reproducing, scanning or distributing any part of it by any means
without permission. You are supporting authors and enabling Penguin Random House
to continue to publish books for everyone. No part of this book may be used or reproduced
in any manner for the purpose of training artificial intelligence technologies or systems.
In accordance with Article 4(3) of the DSM Directive 2019/790, Penguin Random House
expressly reserves this work from the text and data mining exception.

Set in 11.5/15.5pt ITC Giovanni Std
Typeset by Six Red Marbles UK, Thetford, Norfolk

Printed and bound in Great Britain by Clays Ltd, Elcograf S.p.A.

The authorized representative in the EEA is Penguin Random House Ireland,
Morrison Chambers, 32 Nassau Street, Dublin D02 YH68.

A CIP catalogue record for this book is available from the British Library.

ISBNs:

9780857505897 (cased)
9780857505903 (tpb)

Penguin Random House is committed to a sustainable future
for our business, our readers and our planet. This book is made
from Forest Stewardship Council® certified paper.

For Nia, with love

1

On the day it all begins, Siobhán wakes with a sore head, a dry mouth and a whole host of hazy memories of the night before. Anxiety kicks in immediately. Why did she drink so much, what did she say, who did she offend? *It was a wedding,* she answers herself, *you drank champagne just like everyone else, and you didn't say anything to offend anyone.* This is just how it is after any night out now – the joys of middle age. Plus it was her first time drinking in months. Still. She can't help feeling that something happened. That something is wrong.

Bit by bit, the images filter back – the cocktail bar by the pool, the DJ, the non-stop nineties, the guests still dancing at 2 a.m. Dear, lovely Charlie and slightly less lovely Emma-Rose had the happiest day of their lives, and there's something unfailingly joyful about weddings. The hangover, Siobhán decides, is worth it.

The muslin curtains in Charlie's guest room are pretty but not functional and the July sun pierces her eyes when she sits up.

Feeling for her phone, she blinks to clear her vision as she checks it. Her eyes widen at the screen. Four missed calls from Ré.

Her daughter never calls her. Why did she phone four times at . . . 4.27 a.m.? Maybe she just wanted to see where Siobhán was, to say goodnight? Nevertheless, a small current of unease runs through her. Somehow, even though Ré is now twenty-four years old, a fully grown adult, and even though Siobhán prides herself on not worrying (excessively) about her daughter, she is now worried. She slips out of the bed, hits the call button and pulls on a white T-shirt and jersey shorts as she waits. But it rings out. Ré will be asleep, of course. It's only five past eight. Ré was up partying just as late as she was. Though now that she thinks about it, she didn't see her during the last part of the evening. When *did* she see her? She was there for the cake-cutting for sure. And they were chatting just before someone dropped a tray of glasses, interrupting everything. Ré was asking her something, though she can't recall what. She tries to remember: did she see her after that?

Siobhán pads across the sun-dappled carpet, out to the landing, and makes her way quietly downstairs to the kitchen.

Grace is there already, attempting to make a coffee, hunched over the machine, her long hair half hiding her face.

'Morning,' Siobhán says to her oldest friend. 'Have you seen the girls yet today?'

Grace turns, grimaces, touches her temple.

'I am *way* too old for this. What time did we get to bed and why do my eyes ping open at 6 a.m. no matter how late I'm up? And no, I haven't seen the girls, but I imagine they're still sleeping in the pool house.' She nods towards the kitchen window, the pool beyond the patio, and the guesthouse where their daughters are staying for the three-day wedding extravaganza. Siobhán struggles to call it a 'pool house'; it sounds so notion-y and American. This is Dublin, for goodness' sake, and it's only warm enough to use the pool for three days each summer. But Emma-Rose, Charlie's new wife, likes to call it a pool house. And Grace, being American, doesn't find it notion-y at all.

'Ré phoned me four times last night after I fell asleep. I think I'll pop out and check what's up.'

Grace stiffens. 'That's odd . . .'

'I'm sure they're fine,' Siobhán says. Grace is the most relaxed person she knows, often annoyingly horizontal, except when it comes to her daughter. 'How about I check on them while you put a coffee on for me?'

'I'll come with you.' Grace abandons the coffee machine.

The pool house, a cute bungalow nestled in the thick trees on the far side of the pool, gleams in the morning sunlight. It's small, with just one bedroom, a bathroom and a living room that doubles as a home office for Emma-Rose, but it's perfect for Ré, and Grace's daughter, Luna, who don't mind sharing. Like their mothers, they've been best friends for ever. Unlike their mothers, they're happy to crash wherever they lay their heads.

It's when Siobhán raises her hand to knock that the first frisson of real worry sets in. The door isn't locked. It's not even properly closed. Siobhán pushes it, glancing back at Grace, and steps inside.

The blinds are drawn and it takes a moment for Siobhán's eyes to adjust, to take in the scene. A bottle of beer upended at the foot of the sofa, its contents pooled across the wooden floor. An empty glass, sticky with fingerprints, lying on the rug. Beside it, a familiar bronze compact in two pieces, the powder in crumbs either side. A brass lamp lying flat on the desk. Couch cushions scattered on the rug. A trophy, one Emma-Rose had won for her business, on the floor by the window. The smell of the spilled beer, stale and sickly, turns Siobhán's stomach, amplifies her hangover, as she tries to make sense of it. Did the girls leave this mess? She moves towards the only other room in the pool house, the twin bedroom, and knocks gently on the door. No reply. They'll be asleep, of course. She knocks again, feeling Grace's breath on her shoulder.

'Just go in.' Grace's voice has a trace of urgency.

Siobhán opens the door and peers in, squinting against the bright sunlight that streams in through the sliding doors. One suitcase, one holdall. Clothes on the floor. Twin beds, side by side. Empty. Siobhán frowns. Would they really be up this early? Gone for coffee, gone for a run? Not after a wedding, surely. Not after such a late night.

'Weird,' she says out loud, trying Ré's number again.

And at first, she thinks the call has connected. Because she can hear a response. But then her brain processes that the response she's hearing is not the one she wants. Because what she's actually hearing is Ré's phone ringing. Here in this bedroom. This empty bedroom. Grace pushes past her, reaching under the bed on the right. In her hand is a familiar purple phone case. Ré's phone. Siobhán's stomach drops a notch. Why would she go anywhere without her phone?

'Try Luna,' she says to Grace.

'I already did, but I'll keep trying.' Grace moves back to the living room. 'They're clearly not here. Let's go search the main house.'

They cross the lawn quickly and enter the kitchen – it's quiet; the bride and groom still asleep, no doubt. There are two coffee mugs on the draining board, both used, one with pink lipstick stamped on the rim. Mugs used by the girls, maybe? But if so, Siobhán wonders, where are they now, and why doesn't Ré have her phone? The whirr of the dishwasher is the only sound as she and Grace leave to check the other downstairs rooms.

The living room, not as neat as the kitchen, shows more evidence of the wedding – half-full champagne flutes line the mantelpiece. Cake plates sit on the hearth and the coffee table. A wad of napkins soaks up a red wine spill on the wooden floor. But there's nobody here. The dining room, the den and Charlie's home office are empty too. As they move through the house, Grace continues to try Luna's phone, and Siobhán, her breath quickening, tries calling some of the girls' mutual friends. No answer anywhere, but then it's not yet nine on a Sunday morning.

They search the utility room, the catering kitchen and the garage. Nothing. Nobody.

Upstairs, they start on the top floor, checking the guest room in which Grace had slept, though of course it's empty.

'That's Xavi's room, right?' Siobhán whispers to Grace, pointing at an open door across the landing.

Charlie's son from his first marriage is a few years older than the girls and has been living here since his mother sold her Dublin home and moved back to Portugal.

'Yeah.' Grace steps forward to peer around the door, and Siobhán follows. The empty bed is a crumpled heap of sheets and clothes, one pillow on the floor.

'Maybe they're all together somewhere,' Siobhán says. 'They might have gone to a party with Xavi?'

'That could be it,' Grace agrees. 'But let's keep looking.'

Down on the next floor, after checking Siobhán's room, they stand outside Charlie and Emma-Rose's bedroom, debating interrupting their hosts' first morning as a married couple. Siobhán is reluctant. Grace, never one to let etiquette stand in her way, has raised her hand to knock when a woman's voice stops her.

They turn to find Charlie's elderly mother eyeing them.

'They're not there. Charlie's gone for a run and Emma-Rose went to pick up yet more flowers.' A sniff of disapproval.

'Oh, right,' Grace says. 'We're actually looking for Ré and Luna. You haven't seen them, have you?'

'No.' Mrs Caine purses her lips, zeroes in on Siobhán. 'I noticed that Réiltín wore a black dress to the wedding.' Charlie's mother is one of the few people who insists on using Ré's full name. 'Odd choice. Luna looked lovely in her turquoise, though. She really is such a nice girl.' She bestows a smile on Grace. 'Anyway, I've just been in to Margaret.' She nods towards the bedroom her sister, Charlie's aunt, has been assigned. 'She didn't sleep a wink with all the noise. So don't go disturbing her now.'

Charlie's mother lets herself into her room and closes the door.

In silence, Siobhán and Grace make their way downstairs and back out to the pool house. Together they survey the living room. The upturned lamp. The scattered cushions.

Siobhán's gaze lands on the rug as something catches her attention. Something dark. She hunkers down. A smear in reddish brown. Camouflaged until now by the red oriental rug.

'Is that . . . is that blood?' Grace's voice is a hoarse whisper.

'I . . .' Siobhán's role in their friendship is to calm Grace when she gets worried about Luna. To reassure her that everything is OK. But right now, staring at the dark stain, she can't find the words. Her heart hammers in her ribcage as she tries to make sense of what she's seeing. *Is it blood?* It can't be. It's a spill of some kind: pizza sauce or make-up.

'OK, that's it,' Grace says. 'We need to call the police.'

Siobhán hesitates, torn between that Irish thing of not wanting to overreact and the very real worry about the state of the pool house and the absence of the girls. They're twenty-four, they can go where they want, of course they can. And they don't live with Siobhán and Grace. They don't even live in Ireland. If this was any other day, Siobhán wouldn't know whether or not Ré had stayed in her own bed in her London flat or slept somewhere else. But . . . She googles the number for Cabinteely garda station and hits call.

It takes a minute to explain what's going on to the guard who answers and, understandably, he doesn't seem particularly worried.

'Have you checked with their friends? Could they be sleeping it off somewhere?'

'We've tried, but no one's answering. It's too early,' Siobhán says, hearing how obvious it must sound to him – of *course* they're probably sleeping it off somewhere. 'But where they were staying is a bit of a mess, and there's this stain on the rug, and the pool-house door wasn't locked. And—'

'Sorry, did you say "pool house"?'

She flushes. This is where the notions come in. 'It's a guest house, you know, one of those garden cabins.'

'Tell me the address?' There's something different in his tone now. Concern? Urgency?

'Forty-six Kensington Road.'

'OK. Hang on.' Muffled background noise suggests he's turned away to speak to someone. Grace raises her eyebrows at Siobhán. *What's going on?*

The guard is back.

'Right, there's a car on the way. Sit tight.'

This change of approach should reassure Siobhán, but instead . . . it makes her feel sick.

While they wait for the gardaí, Grace and Siobhán search the expansive garden – the area around the pool house, the loungers around the pool – the road beyond the gates, and back inside to search the house once more.

Then the doorbell rings and the gardaí are here.

Siobhán watches them – two plain-clothes detectives – look

around the pool house, at once comforted and alarmed that they've turned up so quickly. Two grown women who had perhaps become bored at a family wedding. Who had friends all over Dublin with spare beds and couches. And that stain on the rug – pizza sauce, no doubt. Yet here they are, two detectives, examining the pool house as Siobhán and Grace wait outside.

One of the detectives, a woman in her thirties with dark hair and dark-framed glasses, comes to the doorway and clears her throat.

'Could we go somewhere quiet for a moment and take a seat?'

A cold shiver runs through Siobhán.

'What is it?'

'Could we go inside there?' The detective points and begins walking towards the main house, crossing the garden in quick strides. She enters through the patio doors. Siobhán and Grace follow without speaking.

Inside the house, they take seats in the living room.

Siobhán swallows, her throat dry. Grace perches beside her, still in her pyjamas.

'Could I ask you both to listen to this?' The detective holds up her phone. There's something unreadable on her face, and Siobhán feels a sudden lurch of terror.

She nods. Grace is frozen, eyes wide. Siobhán moves to comfort her, to reassure her. But, she realizes, she can't. She doesn't know what's coming.

The detective presses play and they lean in close.

A hushed voice. A whisper too low and quick to make out who's speaking. The rapid words just about audible:

'I need police, help me, my room-mate has a knife, we had a fight, she said she's going to kill me, please send help, I'm in the pool house out behind forty-six—' Then the call cuts off.

Siobhán stares at the phone, white noise roaring in her ears.

'Obviously, this is forty-six Kensington Road, and you've told us the cabin they were staying in is called the pool house,' the detective says. 'Is that one of your daughters on the audio?'

Grace puts her hand to her mouth. 'Oh my god, that's Luna.'

Siobhán startles, stares at her friend, then back at the detective. 'No, I . . . I think that's Ré.'

2

When it's clear that Siobhán and Grace can't agree who is on the audio, the detectives move outside to confer. Siobhán is numb, the recording playing over in her mind. Why did Ré call the police? What did Luna do? She sits for a while longer, trying to take it in, then stands to move into the kitchen. Grace stands, too, following wordlessly. Why did Grace say it was Luna in the recording? Surely it was Ré? Wasn't it? Siobhán replays the call again in her head. What does Ré sound like when she whispers, when she's stressed? She glances back at Grace. Maybe, to Grace, it really does sound like Luna.

The two detectives are on the patio, speaking in low voices, replaying the audio. Siobhán can't hear it from inside the kitchen, but she knows it by heart already. *My room-mate has a knife . . . she said she's going to kill me.*

The door from the hallway bursts open and Charlie bustles in, his face flushed from his run, beads of sweat on his forehead. He makes a beeline for the coffee machine, smiling hello at Siobhán and Grace. His smile fades when he sees the two strangers enter through the patio doors.

He straightens. 'Everything OK?'

Siobhán and Grace look at each other. Where do they even start?

SUCH A NICE GIRL

One of the detectives steps forward and saves them from trying.

'I'm Detective Aisling O'Connell. And you are?'

'Charlie Caine.' Charlie, ever affable, stretches a hand to shake the garda's, but his forehead creases in a frown. 'What's going on?'

'Do you live here?' Detective O'Connell asks him, then turns to Grace and Siobhán. 'Do you all live here?'

Charlie shakes his head. 'No, just me and my wife and son. We hosted my wedding here yesterday. Grace and Siobhán are very old friends of mine, and they're here as wedding guests, along with their girls.' He touches Grace's arm. 'Grace and I used to be married, and Luna is our daughter. Can you tell me what's happened?'

O'Connell nods. 'There was an emergency call made last night from a landline with a withheld number – the caller mentioned a "pool house" and the number forty-six, but the call cut out before they could give the full address.'

'Did they trace the call to here?' Siobhán asks.

O'Connell shakes her head. 'Not yet – withheld numbers take a bit longer to trace, but Command and Control – where the calls go – figured there couldn't be many areas in Dublin with pools and pool houses, so they contacted Cabinteely because we cover Foxrock.' That Foxrock is one of a handful of areas in Dublin where houses might have pools is left unspoken.

Charlie nods, his face slack with confusion.

'When this lady' – O'Connell gestures towards Siobhán – 'phoned the station about two possible missing persons from forty-six Kensington Road, we made the connection.'

Charlie's jaw drops. 'What do you mean, "missing persons"?'

'It's Luna and Ré, Charlie,' Grace says, panic in her voice. 'They're missing, and the pool house is a mess, and there's something that looks like blood on the rug. And Luna made a 999 call to say Ré was going to . . . going to . . .'

Grace's words hit Siobhán like a punch. Grace is her best friend, she's known Ré since she was born – how can she think Ré would hurt Luna? But then, isn't Siobhán the same, believing it's Ré's voice they heard, that Luna is the threat?

She aims for diplomacy. It won't help if she and Grace fall out. 'Well, we don't really know which of them is on the call.'

'I think it's Luna,' Grace says in a whisper. 'I'm scared it's Luna.'

Detective O'Connell interjects. 'I don't think we can definitively say whose voice is on the audio, but our priority is to find both girls and ascertain they're safe.' She addresses Charlie. 'Did you see the girls this morning?'

Charlie shakes his head slowly. 'Not this morning. I went for a run at half seven, though, pretty much straight out once I woke up, so I didn't see anyone.'

'And what about last night, Mr Caine? Can you tell us when you last saw your daughter and her friend?'

'I remember seeing them when we were cutting the cake. And they were dancing with Xavi a bit later.'

'Xavi?' the detective asks.

'My son. My eldest.'

The detective glances at Grace, and Charlie picks up on it.

'From my first marriage, before Grace and I got together. He lives here.'

'OK, could we speak to him?'

'Sure. He's gone to get a matcha something or other. Doesn't like any of the drinks we have here, apparently.' Charlie nods towards the coffee machine. 'The coffee shop's just up the road in Foxrock village – he'll be home any minute. But back to this disappearing act – did someone say there was blood on the rug?'

'We don't know if it's blood,' O'Connell says firmly. 'We'll have to test it.'

Charlie lets out a breath. 'So, maybe it's food or nail varnish and the place is a mess because the girls are messy, and they've gone to hang out with friends?'

Siobhán looks at Grace. This is entirely plausible. The girls are messy. Well, Ré is. And they absolutely might have gone somewhere for a better party.

'And even if it *is* blood,' Charlie says, 'couldn't it mean that one of them cut their finger or something? I cut myself shaving yesterday and got dots of blood all over the towel.' An attempt at a grin. 'Emma-Rose was fit to kill me.'

'But what about the emergency call?' Grace says, her voice shaking.

'Could I hear it?' Charlie asks.

O'Connell takes out her phone and plays it while her colleague steps towards the patio doors to take a call.

Siobhán's headache pulses as she strains to listen, to *really* listen, to the audio. Is it Ré? Could it be Luna? But Ré wouldn't hurt Luna. She's impulsive, temperamental, flies off the handle. But that's not this. She wouldn't take a knife, she wouldn't threaten Luna. They're best friends.

'It's Luna,' Grace says, more to herself than anything, and Siobhán bristles.

'Charlie, it's Luna,' Grace repeats. 'You hear it – you know your own daughter's voice.'

Charlie lifts his hands, helplessly. 'I . . . I can't tell. It could be either of them. Is that all there is?'

O'Connell nods and writes something in her notebook. 'I'm afraid so.'

Siobhán watches Grace wringing her hands. She's so chill generally, but now she's spiralling.

'This is just like when Arabella went missing.' A sob breaks up her words. 'It's happening again.'

Oh Grace, don't do this. Siobhán stifles her irritation and rubs her friend's back. 'It's not the same. Arabella was a baby; the girls are grown adults. And Arabella was found – that's the most important thing. Her parents got her back within an hour, remember?'

O'Connell looks up from her notebook, her grey eyes alert behind her glasses. 'Arabella?'

Grace's shoulders shake with silent sobs, and Siobhán steps in to explain to the detective.

'Grace used to nanny for a family in Ballsbridge, and the baby she looked after was snatched one day. It was extremely traumatizing for her, as you can imagine, but it was more than thirty years ago.'

The male detective – Dunleavy is his name – has finished his call and joins the conversation now, looking puzzled.

'Sorry, I just caught the end of that, but I don't know this case – are you certain the victim's name was Arabella? I'm pretty sure I know all of our missing-child cases?'

Siobhán nods. Ireland is small, and the few desperately sad open missing-child cases are known to everyone in the country. She rushes to clarify.

'No, everything was fine, it's not an open case – Arabella was found literally ninety minutes later. Everything turned out absolutely fine,' she repeats, though this is whitewashing, for Grace's benefit. Grace, who has spent Luna's entire life worrying that history will repeat itself, coddling and cotton-woolling her daughter, spoiling her. Grace's back is tense under her hand as she continues to rub and soothe, and a small, shameful part of Siobhán wants to shake her, to say *Stop dining out on that story, this is not that.* But of course, that's not even true. Because the one thing Grace has always feared has come to pass – her daughter has disappeared. And here is Siobhán, irritated, exasperated, when she should be focused on finding the girls.

'I'm going to play the audio again,' O'Connell says, directing her words at Charlie, perhaps in the hope that he can be more objective than Siobhán and Grace.

'I'm sorry.' Charlie shakes his head when the clip stops. 'I still don't know which of them it is. But surely there's some kind of explanation?'

There must be, Siobhán thinks. There has to be. Only right now, she can't work out what it is. Right now, it seems that their daughters are missing, and one of them has threatened to kill the other. *Or worse.* The thought comes before she can stop it. *One of them is already dead.*

3

THE TWO DETECTIVES MOVE out to the patio again, both speaking on their phones, just as Emma-Rose, Charlie's new wife, comes into the kitchen, pristine in a cream Celine tracksuit, an enormous bouquet of pink roses in her arms. She stops dead when she sees them all gathered, and the two suited strangers outside.

Her eyes widen. 'What's going on?'

Charlie fills her in. Without responding, Emma-Rose begins the process of snipping the twine that binds the flowers. Slowly she places them one by one in a vase at the centre of the huge oak kitchen table.

'I'm sure they'll turn up, a little hung over, with a good explanation.' She turns to face them, switches on her trademark smile, the gap between her front teeth making her seem suddenly sweet, as it always does. 'You'll be laughing about this by the time the guests arrive for the Day Two lunch. Which is at one p.m.' Her smile tightens. 'As you know.'

She looks Siobhán and Grace up and down. Siobhán is still in shorts and T-shirt, her hair mussed from sleep. Grace is in striped pyjamas and flip-flops.

'Plenty of time to get ready,' Emma-Rose adds, glancing at her watch.

Ben, the catering manager who had overseen yesterday's

wedding, comes in from the hall, a crate of glasses in his arms. Siobhán sees Grace's cheeks pinken visibly, and an image flashes back: Grace and Ben sharing a cigarette in a dark corner of the patio late last night. Grace leaning close, pretending to be drunker than she was, claiming to be cold. Ben rubbing her arms to keep her warm. Siobhán smiling to herself as she drifted past. Something else flits back now, too ... something about Ré trying to speak to her? It's all so hazy, and Siobhán wishes she hadn't had quite so much to drink. On top of the fear and panic, guilt over how little she can remember about late last night is eating into her.

'Emma-Rose, shall I start setting these up outside?' Ben asks in his soft Scottish accent, then stops short, no doubt taken aback by the relatively crowded kitchen and the serious expressions. 'Oh. Shall I come back later?'

'Come on in, Ben.' Emma-Rose's tone is businesslike. She throws a defiant glance at Detective O'Connell, who has just stepped inside again. 'Yes, please set the glasses up where we had the cocktail bar last night. We'll stick to champagne and wine for lunch, then reopen the bar at four. You have a barman coming to set up at three, yes? Robert again?'

Ben nods, still looking unsure, clearly more in tune with the atmosphere than Emma-Rose, Siobhán thinks. He'd been there quite late, she knows; maybe he saw the girls ...

'Ben, could I ask you something – you were here last night, and—'

She catches his glance at Grace, his worried expression.

'Helping at the bar and with the clean-up,' she adds quickly. 'You might be able to shed some light – we're looking for our daughters, Ré and Luna.'

'The girl in the blue dress and the girl in black, yes?'

'Yes – did you see them in the later part of the evening?'

Ben's forehead crinkles. 'I think the last time I saw them they were dancing by the pool, with Emma-Rose's son?'

'Xavi isn't my son,' Emma-Rose says crisply, before softening it with a smile.

'Oh, I'm sorry. I just thought . . . but yes, dancing with that young man and some others. That must have been midnight?'

Siobhán nods, trying to focus, to remember. Ré talking to her, asking her something. Just before the tray of drinks fell. What was Ré asking her? A swell of nausea rolls through her, as though reminding her that if she'd had a little less to drink, she might be better able to recall all of this. Where did Ré go after the tray fell? They need someone who saw the girls later. They need someone to fill in the gaps between the midnight dancing and the 999 call. And, Siobhán remembers, four missed calls from Ré at 4.27 a.m. A cold sweat breaks out over her skin. Was her daughter calling her for help, for protection from her friend, or calling to confess?

4

As OTHER OFFICERS ARRIVE, O'Connell proceeds to take their official written statements and personal details. They tell her about the girls: where they live in London – both in Deptford – about Ré's job in a laboratory and Luna's upcoming relocation to South Carolina.

'She leaves next month, so the wedding was the last time the four of us would be together for a while,' Siobhán explains, and Grace begins to cry.

O'Connell asks for names of friends, and Siobhán and Grace do their best to supply contact details and phone numbers, starting with Kayla, who was close with both girls in secondary school, and Prisha and Abbey, a couple who hung out with the two of them in UCD.

O'Connell asks about boyfriends or girlfriends. Both girls are single, their mothers confirm. Luna had a boyfriend, Theo, but they broke up and he now lives in Canada.

O'Connell requests photos of the girls, then asks about cameras, directing this to Charlie, who is standing by the counter, his coffee still unmade.

'There's a camera at the front of the house and another at the back,' he tells her. 'Both linked to my phone. I've had a look already, but there's no sign of either girl leaving.'

O'Connell gives him an email address so he can send her the footage. She looks around the kitchen, then gets Charlie and Emma-Rose to show her the rest of the house. Siobhán lets out a breath as they depart, relieved that the detective is making decisions, driving the search. She and Grace stay in the kitchen, sitting at the bleached-oak table, thumbing through contacts, making unanswered calls until O'Connell comes back and asks about passports.

'They'd probably be in the pool house, in their luggage,' Siobhán says. 'The girls came straight here when they flew in.'

Grace jumps up and moves towards the patio doors, perhaps to check for the passports, but O'Connell stops her. They'll search the pool house for passports and anything else they need, she says. For now, it's off limits.

Siobhán swallows against rising nausea.

'What about your own homes?' O'Connell asks. 'Would the girls have gone there if they were injured or hiding?'

Injured or hiding. Oh god. But this also gives Siobhán a sudden burst of hope. That's exactly where Ré might have gone if . . . if she and Luna had a fight. *A fight that involved a knife? A 999 call?* Siobhán bats away the thought.

'Ré might. I'll go there now and check,' she says to O'Connell. 'It's only fifteen minutes away, I'm in Dalkey.'

'No, no, we'll send a car,' O'Connell says.

Siobhán tries again. 'Not at all, I'll go—'

O'Connell holds up a hand. 'I'm sure there's a simple explanation for all of this, but in light of the emergency call, we have to treat this as a potential crime.' She turns to Grace. 'Your house is in Greystones?'

'Yes,' Grace says. 'They could have gone to either one. They'd have keys. Or . . .' She stops. Wondering, no doubt, if their keys are in the pool house with everything else. Everything including

Ré's phone, Siobhán thinks. Everything except Luna's phone. *What does that mean?*

'We'll search for keys and passports,' O'Connell says, reading Siobhán's thoughts. 'But in the meantime, if you could each give me your house keys, that would be useful.'

A small cough from the other side of the kitchen pulls everyone's attention to Emma-Rose.

'Could I just check, will the police tape be gone by one o'clock when my guests arrive?'

She points out through the patio doors, and Siobhán sees it. Distant but unmistakable – white tape across the door of the pool house with 'GARDA NO ENTRY' in blue letters. A uniformed garda at the door, standing sentry. Like a crime scene. Like you see on TV.

Siobhán's legs weaken. Is this really happening? Where the hell is Ré, and why doesn't she have her phone, and what did Luna do to her?

Or . . . or, just as bad, what did Ré do to Luna?

5

WHEN EMMA-ROSE'S QUESTION ABOUT the police tape is answered with nothing more than a withering look from Detective O'Connell, her cheeks colour.

'Sorry. That sounded insensitive. It's just that it's my Day Two, and, well, as everyone knows, it's almost as important as the wedding day itself. It's like an episode of *Kin* out there.' A little laugh. 'I really can't have guests here if it looks like there's a crime scene in my garden.'

'It may well *be* a crime scene,' O'Connell says evenly. 'And I'm afraid, to that end, we'll have to ask you to cancel the lunch.'

Emma-Rose's mouth drops open. 'But I have twenty-three guests who'll be here in less than four hours. The invitations went out months ago!'

'I really am sorry,' O'Connell says, though she doesn't sound too sorry. 'But we have garda technical team officers examining the pool house right now, and they'll need to do the same for the garden, unless the girls are found in the meantime or we can rule out foul play.'

Foul play. A heavy dread settles over Siobhán.

'We may need you to vacate the house, too, depending on what we find,' O'Connell adds.

'Surely this is an overreaction?' Emma-Rose lets out an exasperated sigh. 'They're two fully grown adults. They're probably sleeping off hangovers somewhere. They certainly made the most of the champagne last night,' she adds under her breath.

Siobhán and Grace exchange a glance. Emma-Rose has been on the scene for a few years now and has always come across as a little self-absorbed, in a way that seems obvious to them but to which Charlie is oblivious. A little cool towards Charlie's old friend and Charlie's ex-wife. Siobhán has never fully warmed to her, but this is a whole new level of self-absorption. She opens her mouth to speak, but Charlie throws her a small, pleading look as he walks over and puts his arm around his wife. Siobhán sees Emma-Rose wince slightly and check her clothes, maybe for sweat transfer from Charlie's running top.

'You're right, they're adults, but the guards know what they're doing.' Ever the diplomat, he kisses the top of her head. 'I know it's awful, but I think we have to cancel the lunch. I'm sorry. I'll make it up to you.'

Speechless now, Emma-Rose gestures around the kitchen, at the flowers, the cases of wine, the stacks of gleaming white plates. She points through the kitchen window, where Ben is visible, laying out glasses on a pop-up cocktail bar by the pool.

'Are you serious?'

O'Connell jumps in. 'Very serious. Please take some time to contact your guests, and we'll get on with our questions.' She turns to Charlie. 'Could I see your son, Xavi, please? We'll need to speak with everyone who stayed in the house overnight.'

As Charlie lifts his phone to call his son, Xavi walks into the kitchen, car keys in one hand, matcha tea in the other. His hair is tousled, his eyes red-rimmed, stubble dark against pale skin. Yesterday's excesses have taken their toll on all of them, Siobhán thinks, her head still pounding.

Xavi looks around. 'What's going on?'

Charlie explains, and O'Connell jumps in to ask him when he last saw Ré and Luna.

'Uh . . .' He runs a hand through his hair and takes a sip of his tea. 'We were dancing? I think? Yeah. And there was something—'

'Something?' O'Connell prompts.

'The girls had an argument. I can't remember the details.'

Siobhán's stomach plummets. Somehow, despite all evidence to the contrary, she still hoped there was a mistake. A simple explanation.

'About?' O'Connell asks.

'I'm not sure.'

'Please try,' O'Connell says. 'Anything at all will help. Do you remember where they were when they argued?'

'Uh . . . I need to sit down. I feel a bit queasy.' Xavi pulls out a kitchen chair and flops into it. Charlie eyerolls a little, shakes his head.

'I remember they were deep in conversation down by the far side of the pool,' Xavi says. 'On two loungers. I didn't hear what they were talking about. And I was pretty well on, to be honest. Then later, near the pool house, I heard shouting. I thought it was the TV. But . . .'

'But?' O'Connell nudges.

Charlie says quietly: 'There's no TV in the pool house.'

'Yeah. It was Luna and Ré.' He turns his drink in his hands, twisting it on its spot on the table. Emma-Rose deftly slides a coaster beneath.

'And do you remember what they were arguing about or what time this was?' O'Connell asks.

A helpless shrug. 'I reckon I went to bed around three or four, but I was pretty wasted, so I don't know. Sorry.' He sits up straight as something seems to strike him. 'Oh, Jasmine might know!'

The mention of Jasmine sends a tinge of unease through Siobhán.

'Who is Jasmine?' O'Connell asks.

'My wedding planner,' Emma-Rose explains. 'I don't know what time she left, but I can't imagine she was still here when you were going to bed, Xavi?'

Xavi's face flushes. He takes a sip of his drink and clears his throat. 'She, like, stayed on for a drink after the DJ finished. And we ended up, well, you know.'

Emma-Rose's eyes widen, and Charlie tsks.

'Don't be mad at her, Emma-Rose. She did a great job on the wedding and, once the catering was done, I mean, she's a grown adult . . . so . . .' A shrug finishes the sentence.

'A grown adult due back here at nine forty-five this morning to run Day Two. Day Two that's not actually happening now. I can't believe this.' Emma-Rose puts her hand to her forehead. 'I've got a headache coming on. I'm going to lie down. If you need me, I'll be in my room.'

'Wait, what about the guests, the cancellations?' Charlie asks helplessly, eliciting a glance from O'Connell. Siobhán gets it, though. Charlie likes to throw parties – to chat and open wine. The consummate *bon vivant*. He does not, however, enjoy the administrative side. Not of parties, not of anything. No doubt Emma-Rose organized everything for the Day Two, just like she did the wedding.

'Get Jasmine to do it,' Emma-Rose says over her shoulder, as she heads for the stairs. 'If she shows up.'

Jasmine. Siobhán's mind goes back to Friday, to Jasmine's arrival and the ripples it caused. The chat with Grace on Friday night, sitting by the pool. The things they said about Jasmine. And about Luna and Ré.

O'Connell has stepped outside to talk to a colleague, and now she comes back in. Stares at all of them for a moment before speaking.

'The stain on the rug will have to be analysed in a lab, but' – her eyes rest on Grace and then Siobhán – 'preliminary tests indicate that it is indeed blood.'

6

The day before the wedding

EARLY FRIDAY MORNING, WITHIN an hour of arriving at Charlie's house, Siobhán and Grace are lying by the pool on wide rattan loungers with soft cream mattresses, as comfortable as any bed. They're debating the wisdom of Mimosas before ten. *Start as you mean to go on* is Grace's mantra.

Siobhán, who has an eleven o'clock business call ahead, is less certain about the Mimosas but willing to have her arm twisted.

'You're the boss,' Grace points out, 'and the meeting is on Teams. Nobody will smell the alcohol.' She's already mixed a jug of champagne and orange juice that sits surrounded by six champagne flutes on the rattan table between their loungers.

Siobhán rolls her eyes. Grace has always been the bad influence – in a good way, of course. Maybe everyone should have one friend who is a bad (but good) influence. The friend who orders champagne when Prosecco would have been fine. The friend who suggests the nightclub after the pub. The friend who invites everyone back to theirs *after* the nightclub. The irreverent friend with the cutting remarks. Not always sweet, but definitely fun. The one you hope will turn up, because it's just more craic when she's there.

That's Grace.

That's how she'd been in UCD when Siobhán first hung out with her – mostly in the café, the bar or Dunkin' Donuts, not so much at lectures. And later, not in college at all, when Grace dropped out, unbeknownst to her mother. She could get away with it, though. Her mother owned (still owns) a paper business in South Carolina. Not a newspaper, but paper production, and neither Grace nor Luna, nor perhaps the next eight generations, will have to work for a living. Grace doesn't work outside the home and is very happy to live off her monthly income from the family business. Luna, to her credit, started as a junior accountant at a firm in London, determined to work her way up. Then her grandmother offered her a too-good-to-turn-down position in the paper business in South Carolina, so in three weeks, Luna will relocate there. Grace has half talked about *maybe* getting a job now that Luna's flown the nest – something 'interesting', she said to Siobhán, something that would utilize her talents but not take up too much time. Siobhán told her there are thousands of jobs like that out there, and Grace was delighted, oblivious to both the sarcasm and the eyeroll.

Then a month ago, Grace's father's estate came through probate, giving her an additional lump sum of almost six million euro in her bank account. To Grace's public horror and private delight, the figure was reported in the media, under the guise of 'public interest', because her estranged father was an Irishman who had gone to the States in the sixties and made a huge amount of money in property. Siobhán, on the other hand, comes from a very normal family with very normal jobs, and back in college, Siobhán *did* go to her lectures. She worked hard at her commerce degree, her business masters, and the founding of Scorch Cosmetics – not quite a global empire, but doing pretty well, especially in recent months. And she loves her work. She loves the products, the design, the planning, the expansion.

Even the 11 a.m. Teams meetings when she'd rather be drinking Mimosas.

When Ré arrives at the house, holdall in hand, Charlie sends her through to the pool deck. She emerges, flushed from the heat, her pale cheeks red, her forehead glistening. Siobhán jumps up and hugs her tightly, holding on for longer than usual. It's been a while since she's seen her. Siobhán's been so deeply immersed in expanding her business she's had space for little else in recent months. She and Ré still text regularly, but when is the last time they had a proper chat, she wonders? She takes her in now – the asymmetric bob, back to its original dark brown after teenage dalliances with pink and bleach. The wide blue eyes, always darting, always curious. The sardonic grin, ready for a cynical take. Is she thinner than usual? Anyway, Siobhán thinks, giving her daughter one more hug, this will be the weekend to make up for it.

Grace takes her turn for a hug, then sets about pouring drinks, the Mimosa decision now firmly made.

'So how are you, how's London, are you excited for the wedding?' Grace asks, handing a glass to Ré.

'Good, fine, and no, not really, in that order,' Ré says, lowering herself to perch on a lounger beside Siobhán's.

Grace is arranging herself back on hers, rolling up the waist of her tank top for maximum tanning and to show off her belly-button ring. Siobhán is fit and strong and not particularly body conscious, but she is *way* beyond belly-button rings.

'Oh, come on, we're all dying to see Bridezilla in action. It'll be fun.' Grace settles back, pulls her sunglasses over her eyes.

'Yeah, fun until one of us says the wrong thing.' Ré sips her drink. 'I honestly don't know what Charlie sees in her.'

'I do,' Grace says. 'Someone beautiful and charming who

does all the things he doesn't want to do, like running the house and paying the bills? Someone who looks good on his arm, treats him like a king and basically makes his life easier – what more could he want?'

'Jeez, that sounds like hard work for Emma-Rose.' Ré rummages in her handbag, a battered leather satchel she's had for a decade, and pulls out a pair of scratched sunglasses. Siobhán has bought her new bags and new sunglasses over the years, but Ré is a creature of habit.

'Let me tell you this.' Grace sounds like she's making a speech. 'I was married to the man for ten years, and he is charming and kind and great company, but after a while, being in charge of everything wore me down. Charlie is ruthless in business and works too hard, then has nothing left for home.'

Siobhán nods, though she's conflicted on this, aware of just how hard business owners *must* work. And Grace benefited from that effort, before and after the split. But at the same time, having to do everything on the home front – especially the emotional labour of parenting – is hard. Siobhán knows that well: she's always done it alone.

'Of course, *they* don't have kids. That makes it easier.' Grace lifts her sunglasses, arches a brow at Ré. 'No offence.'

'None taken.' Ré laughs. 'I know I was hard work.'

Grace wriggles further down on her lounger and her belly-button ring glints in the sunlight. She and Luna went together to get the piercings when Luna turned sixteen. 'My daughter, my BFF' Grace's Instagram caption read. Siobhán has heard all the advice about not being your child's best friend, you're there to parent, to set boundaries, and so on. But sometimes – especially when she's worrying about feeling disconnected from Ré – she wonders if she should be more like Grace. Grace and Luna chat all the time by phone, and Grace always seems at ease with their relationship. Siobhán, on the other hand, has been struggling since Ré's move to London. Reassessing her life, missing her daughter. What does she have, really? A successful business, yes, and a daughter in another country. No other family. Some good friends, one great friend. Is that enough? The business keeps her busy, but sometimes it's . . . lonely. And you can't tell anyone you're lonely; nothing sends people running faster.

'Oh, Mum, did you remember the wedding card?' Ré asks. 'Can I sign it?'

'Of course.' Siobhán slips the straps of her top off her shoulders, conscious that tomorrow's dress is a halter-neck and last-minute tan lines won't enhance the look. 'And incidentally, when will you be old enough to buy your own cards?'

Ré grins. 'Better for the environment if we do one card between us, and better for my empty bank account if you cover the present.' She takes another sip of her drink. 'Also, I wouldn't be getting all "of course" – you're not exactly famous for remembering things.'

'Says the person who almost booked flights for the wrong weekend.'

'Says the person who forgot to submit my secondary school application.' Ré smirks over the rim of her glass.

'You can't keep bringing that up,' Siobhán says, grinning, but inside, her stomach clenches just as it always does, remembering the sick feeling the morning she realized she'd missed the deadline; that her application form, so carefully filled out, hadn't arrived at the school office, and she hadn't checked to make sure it had. It was Grace and Charlie who pulled strings to get Ré her place in the end. Somehow, the laser-sharp precision with which she runs her business evades her at times in everyday life. A little like Charlie, perhaps, now that she thinks about it, only she doesn't have a spouse to fall back on.

Ré is scanning their surroundings. 'God, I'd forgotten how gorgeous this place is. Though I don't get why they're having the wedding here – I thought Emma-Rose would be more of a four-hundred-guests-in-a-castle type.'

'Usually, yes,' Grace says, 'but her mom passed away last year, so they're keeping it small.'

'Ah, of course. Sorry.' Ré's cheeks redden.

'Small and low key,' Grace adds. 'You know, ten cases of vintage Dom Pérignon, a seven-course meal and an ice sculpture of Emma-Rose back in her prime.' She grins, and Ré laughs.

'Excuse me, she's *still* in her prime, she's the same age as us.' Siobhán whacks Grace gently on the arm.

'Vintage Dom Pérignon, of *course*,' Ré says, with what sounds like sarcasm but might be admiration. 'Those two are made for each other. Where did they actually meet?'

'The golf club – where else?' Grace sprays sun cream on her legs. 'At a party there. Parties are how we all met, back before the apps, Ré. The good old days. Parties and snogging people on the dancefloor of Copper Face Jacks. Speaking of which, I hear you've been seeing someone?'

Siobhán sits up straighter on her lounger. Why doesn't she know Ré's seeing someone?

And even in the bright morning sunlight, it's clear that Ré has reddened.

'No?' The strap of Ré's vest top slips over her shoulder and she flips it back up. 'I'm not seeing anyone.'

There's something slightly defensive in her tone. Or is Siobhán imagining it?

'Oh. I guess I picked it up wrong.' Grace is busy rubbing in sun cream. 'An older man? Guy in his forties?'

What? Siobhán splutters her drink.

'Mum. Grace. I'm not seeing anyone in their forties, or anyone at all.' Ré stands up from the lounger and tugs down her black denim skirt. 'Now, where am I staying – the garden house, right? Is it unlocked?'

Siobhán nods. 'I think so. Emma-Rose has moved all of her work stuff to a spare room in her grandparents' house to make space for you.' Emma-Rose runs a one-woman events management business so her 'work stuff' tends to include anything from boxes of fairy lights to pink feather boas. 'She said the WiFi code is on a sticker on the underside of the desk phone and to make yourselves at home.'

She watches as her daughter lugs her weekend bag off the lounger and skirts around the pool towards her accommodation.

'What was all that about?' she asks once Ré is out of earshot.

'Luna said she saw Ré out one night with this older guy.' Grace begins rubbing sun cream on her arms.

'In London?'

'Yeah, she was on her way home in an Uber and saw them at a table outside a bar near where she lives.'

'I guess it must have been a friend or work colleague.'

'Indeed,' Grace says in an exaggerated drawl, eyeing Siobhán over the top of her sunglasses.

'OK, spill.' Siobhán sips her drink. It's warm now, and slightly sickly in taste. 'What's your point?'

'Just that if it is true, Ré should be careful.' Grace lies back. 'Older men are bad news.'

'Well, first of all, apparently it's not true. But also, maybe you're seeing this through the filter of your own mistake?'

This is something Grace does. Siobhán adores her, but Grace can be judgemental and blinkered, projecting her own experiences on to everyone else. When of course most people are not trust-fund babies, most people do not live in beautifully refurbished seaside cottages, most people *do* have to work for a living. And most people did not date older men who turned out to be drug dealers. This long-ago error of judgement is a big part of why Grace has helicoptered Luna, Siobhán suspects.

Grace turns on her side, leaning up on her elbow. 'You mean Anthony? He wasn't even that much older than me, when I think back. He was twenty-two, and I was eighteen. Eighteen, and an idiot.'

Is that all it was, the age gap? Siobhán is surprised. For some reason, at the time, it had seemed much bigger. Grace was eighteen, taking time out of college to work as a nanny, barely a legal adult. Anthony had a flashy car. A nice house. A well-paid job. Or what they thought was a well-paid job. All these years later, it's like a made-up story. A weird mirage. But it has shaped the mother Grace has become – the hypervigilant, hear-no-evil, blinkered defender of her daughter.

Siobhán sighs. 'I always thought we could stop worrying about our kids once they turned eighteen. It's like a universal myth to get parents through the teenage years.'

'Ha. I thought we could stop worrying once they slept through the night.' Grace turns her head. 'Oh, here's Luna!'

Luna swishes out to the deck, cool and groomed, in a bright white broderie anglaise camisole top and bleached denim shorts. Her long blonde Sabrina Carpenter hair, unfrizzed and unfazed by the heat, cascades in waves over tanned shoulders. Poor Ré will be comparing herself again, Siobhán thinks, as she stands to hug her best friend's daughter, inhaling expensive perfume and salon shampoo.

Luna takes a seat on the lounger beside Grace, filling them in on her journey and her upcoming move to the States.

Side by side, Grace and Luna look so alike, Siobhán thinks as

Luna chatters. It's not just appearance; they're alike in personality too, something that's made Siobhán see Grace differently in recent years. She'd always thought *she* and Grace were similar – similar values and views, even if they came from very different backgrounds. But somehow, in recent years, seeing Grace and Luna together has heightened the sense that, actually, that's not so true any more. Or maybe it never was. And maybe the fun side of Grace blinkered Siobhán to her less appealing traits. Grace can be a little entitled, a little self-absorbed, a drama queen. *Everything* is about her. A news story about a bombing? Grace was in that exact spot four years earlier; it could have been her. A pointed comment in a WhatsApp group? Definitely directed at her. Siobhán often thinks of one particular night out, when she and Grace were crossing the road after a meal, and a car went by a little too fast. According to Grace, the driver had aimed for her, was deliberately trying to run her over. And of course, as always, it was Siobhán who had to talk sense into her, calm her down.

In spite of all this, Siobhán loves Grace. There's something about longevity that makes everything more tolerable. And it's been so busy in recent years with Scorch that she hasn't had quite as much time for her best friend – this weekend will be good for reconnecting with Grace as well as with Ré.

'Luna,' Siobhán asks after a bit, 'your mom was saying you saw Ré with some older guy?'

Luna smiles as she pops open Grace's sun cream. 'I did! Pretty fit older guy, I might add.'

'Happily, he's not her boyfriend,' Grace chips in.

'Oh. It's just . . . they seemed . . . close. But I guess I got it wrong. And Ré can fill you in when she arrives.'

'She's here already. She's in the garden house if you want to go say hi?'

Luna hesitates, then begins spraying sun cream on to her shoulders. 'I'm going to soak up the sun while I can. I'll catch Ré at some point.'

At the time, it seems like nothing. But when Siobhán thinks back on it later, there's something in that moment – the first hint that between their girls, all is not as it seems.

7

Now

IT'S BLOOD. THE STAIN on the rug is not pizza sauce, not blusher, not bronzer. Blood.

The kitchen blurs and tilts. Siobhán needs to sit down. *Please let Ré be OK.* She'll do anything. She just needs Ré to be alive. *And not a killer.*

'Can . . . can you tell whose blood?' Grace asks as she follows Siobhán's lead and lowers herself on to a chair.

O'Connell shakes her head. 'Not right now. The on-site test just determines that it *is* blood. The lab analysis will give us a DNA profile, and if we have DNA from the girls, we can check for a match.'

'DNA?' Grace's voice is a hoarse whisper. Siobhán's head is swimming. *DNA from what? Surely not from . . . do they mean a body?*

'We'd need blood, saliva, hair with a root, or skin cells,' O'Connell explains. 'Obviously, as they're not here, we can't easily get this, but a hair from a hairbrush is our best bet. We'll go through their belongings.'

Siobhán closes her eyes. Christ almighty. This is real. She's sitting in Charlie's south Dublin kitchen on a beautiful sunny Sunday morning and she's being asked to provide DNA for her only daughter. Her only living relative. Her entire world.

'Does it take long?' Charlie asks.

O'Connell purses her lips. 'It's quicker than it used to be, but a number of days at least.'

Days not knowing whose blood it is? Siobhán bites down on her knuckles, stemming tears, trying to think straight.

'It could be from a cut finger or something,' Charlie points out, downplaying in a way that's well intentioned but frustrating.

O'Connell nods. 'We're keeping an open mind.'

Siobhán lets out a jittery breath. *But what about the knife? The whispered, panicked call?* Her eyes go to the knife block on the granite counter. O'Connell follows her gaze.

'Emma-Rose has confirmed none of the knives are missing.'

Siobhán nods. And there's no kitchen in the pool house. So maybe this is all some kind of mistake.

Xavi clears his throat, flashes a glance at Grace, then Siobhán, before addressing O'Connell. 'I know nobody wants to imagine it, but is there a chance someone else was involved – someone took the girls?'

It takes Siobhán a moment to process this. The horror that one of their girls hurt the other superseded by an even worse horror.

O'Connell is measured in her reply. 'We're not ruling anything out, of course, but at this point, based on the evidence we have, it doesn't appear that anyone else was involved.'

Siobhán exhales. The fear of a faceless, nameless stranger is too much to bear. *But is the idea that either Ré or Luna hurt the other any more bearable?*

'We'll also carry out voice analysis,' O'Connell is saying, 'although whispered speech is much harder to analyse than normal speech. We'll need reference samples if you have them – maybe voice notes the girls have left you?'

Siobhán nods, dazed. 'I can do that now. How do I get them

to you?' She wonders if there's some high-tech way the gardaí gather this kind of thing. There isn't, it turns out. O'Connell writes down an email address, and asks Siobhán and Grace to download some voice notes and send them on.

Siobhán looks at her chats with Ré, tears blurring her vision. Mundane messages from a time – only yesterday – when everything was normal. When everything was perfect and she just didn't know it. A message with a photo of Ré dressed for the wedding; a black prom-style dress she'd worn with Docs. A snarky text during the ceremony about the vows Emma-Rose had written. A 'where are you now?' message just after ten. No voice notes yesterday. She scrolls further back. There's one from the day before. Feeling oddly self-conscious, she presses play. Ré's voice sounds out in the kitchen:

'Hi, Mum, just running out to get coffee. I can't stand the stuff in Charlie's machine. Want anything?'

Siobhán grimaces at Charlie. 'Sorry.' She swipes at a tear.

He smiles. 'I'll take it up with her when she's back.' He puts a hand on Siobhán's shoulder and she closes her eyes to stem more tears.

'Yes, that's the kind of thing we need,' O'Connell says. 'Send three or four more if you have them. You too,' she says to Grace.

'Will it take long? The analysis?' Grace asks.

'Hard to say. But our main concern is to find both of your daughters as quickly as possible, to have any injuries treated and' – she clears her throat – 'to stop things before they go further.'

8

O'CONNELL LOOKS LIKE SHE'S about to say something else, but the doorbell rings and she waits silently for Charlie to go out to answer. Hushed voices from the hallway tell Siobhán that Charlie is explaining what's going on to whoever is at the door.

Beside her, Xavi straightens, smooths down his hair. Siobhán checks her watch. Nine forty-five on the dot. Jasmine must be here.

Moments later, Charlie ushers Jasmine in. Like yesterday, she's groomed to perfection, in a royal-blue dress and demure court shoes, put together like someone far older than her twenty-five years. Ré would never wear something like this, Siobhán thinks. But then Ré is a lab assistant, usually in a lab coat, and favours a palette of black and only black.

Jasmine looks around the kitchen once Charlie does introductions.

'I'm so sorry,' she says. 'My god, I can't believe it.'

O'Connell asks if she saw the girls late last night.

Jasmine's eyes flick to Xavi, then immediately away. Of course, Siobhán thinks, she doesn't know he's just told everyone they were together.

'The last time I saw them was at about one a.m.' She hovers near the door. The rest of them, apart from O'Connell, are seated around the table, looking up at her. 'They were deep in conversation in two loungers at the far end of the pool.'

This tallies with what Xavi said, but Jasmine seems much surer in her response, Siobhán thinks. Then again, unlike the rest of them, she hadn't been drinking all day.

'And you didn't see them after that?' O'Connell asks.

'No, but I did hear them,' Jasmine says. 'They were in that little house they're staying in, arguing. Raised voices, though I couldn't make out what it was about. It was late, at least three a.m., but I'm not sure of the exact time.'

'You couldn't make out anything?' O'Connell asks.

Jasmine shakes her head apologetically. 'I heard the word "Marrakesh". That's it, really.'

Marrakesh.

Siobhán looks at Grace. The girls had taken a trip there in the spring. Had something happened? Now that she thinks about it, Siobhán can't remember hearing much about the trip. The girls had flown to and from London, so Siobhán hadn't seen Ré when she got back. And it had been in the lead-up to Siobhán's pitch to a giant pharmacy chain, the next-level deal that would – and did – change everything. So maybe she hadn't asked as many questions about the trip as she normally would.

What had Ré said on text about it? As O'Connell continues her questions to Jasmine, Siobhán searches for 'Marrakesh' in WhatsApp and finds a message she sent Ré asking how the trip was.

'Hot, busy, different' was the reply. And looking back now, she realizes that Ré hadn't said anything more specific since. Nothing about how she enjoyed it, how she felt, what she thought. This is something Siobhán does, too – maybe everyone does – focuses on factual responses if she doesn't want to give emotional responses. *Hot, busy, different.*

She looks to Grace, inclining her head to see around the giant vase of pink blooms Emma-Rose had placed in the middle of the table. 'Did anything happen in Marrakesh?'

Grace shakes her head. 'No. Not that I know of.'

But Siobhán has known Grace for more than thirty years, and one thing she knows for sure is that Grace is lying.

9

THE CONVERSATION KEEPS GOING, swirling around Siobhán as she watches Grace's face, looking for a clue. *What is she hiding?* O'Connell, standing at the foot of the table, is asking her something.

'Sorry, I missed that?' Siobhán says.

'Could you tell me about Marrakesh?'

'They went in April, with their friends, Prisha and Abbey. I think they just pottered around Marrakesh for a few days then went to the coast. Do you know more, Grace? Did something happen?' Siobhán watches for a reaction.

Another headshake. 'Same as you. They travel so much, we hear so little. I follow Luna's Instagram Stories to keep up.'

As O'Connell picks up a pen, asks for their social media details, Siobhán keeps scrutinizing Grace. There's something she's not saying. Maybe it's not important and maybe she won't say it in front of Detective O'Connell? Siobhán makes a mental note to ask her later.

'And do the girls argue a lot?' O'Connell asks.

'No, not at all,' Siobhán says. 'They've been best friends since they were born.'

O'Connell tilts her head, waiting for more.

And it's only now, watching O'Connell's reaction, that Siobhán wonders about this, about how it sounds to other people – or perhaps, how it really is – did Ré and Luna choose to be best friends, or did their mothers create that narrative and make it true? Siobhán more than Grace, perhaps, because of Ré's lack of wider family?

'What I mean is, Grace and I met in college and became friends very quickly. A decade later, when we both found out we were expecting babies at the same time, and that they were both girls, we were thrilled. The girls have grown up together. Same primary school, same secondary. They both went to UCD, though Ré did science, and Luna did commerce. So they've been best friends since they were babies, literally.'

'We gave them matching names,' Grace adds. 'Luna means moon, and Ré is short for Réiltín, Irish for little star.'

O'Connell looks bemused, and Siobhán gets it. It seemed like such a good idea when the girls were born. Now, a quarter of a century later, the matching feels a little twee, and Ré goes by a short version pronounced like the man's name Ray, causing all sorts of confusion.

'So this argument last night was unusual?'

'Yes,' Siobhán and Grace say in unison. Charlie nods. Xavi is focused on finishing his tea.

Jasmine, now standing at the head of the table, the opposite end to O'Connell, frowns.

'You don't agree?' O'Connell asks, fanning herself with her notebook. She's still wearing her suit jacket.

'Oh. It's not that I don't agree, and their mothers know them best. But they argued a lot back when I knew them.'

'You knew them before the wedding?'

'In secondary school. We were friends.' Jasmine looks at Siobhán, and her cheeks redden. 'For a while.'

'And did you stay in contact?' O'Connell gives in to the heat and slips off her jacket.

'No, we lost touch. I was surprised when I turned up on Friday and found them both here.'

'And the arguments back then?'

'Oh, the usual stupid teen stuff, you know.'

Siobhán does not know. As far as she was aware, the girls had had a pretty easy friendship throughout school and college. Nothing beyond the usual bickering you'd get between two quite fiery people, anyway.

'One thing I noticed, though,' Jasmine adds, 'they didn't seem as close any more. They didn't hang out much at the wedding.'

Siobhán is about to object. Then she remembers Luna's hesitation to join Ré in the pool house. Remembers them sitting with and chatting with other people all weekend, not so much each other.

Grace pushes back her chair, startling Charlie beside her. 'Look, this is all very well, but shouldn't we be out searching for them? How does this help find my daughter?'

My daughter. Siobhán bites down frustration. Grace is so certain Luna is the victim. But she has a point about wasting time.

'Grace is right. I think we need to get out and look.'

'We have a search underway, and we're checking CCTV in Foxrock village and the wider area. But until we narrow it down, it's difficult to know where to start,' O'Connell says. 'All of this information helps.'

It doesn't, though, Siobhán thinks. Because none of it makes sense, and they're wasting time.

'Should we look at the security camera footage?' Charlie suggests, holding up his phone.

This sounds like an attempt to give Siobhán and Grace something useful to do, and for that, Siobhán is grateful. She nods.

'I've looked already and emailed it to your colleagues, but no harm in all of us looking together?' He directs this at O'Connell, and she nods.

He lays his phone at the centre of the table, moving the flowers out of the way, and everyone leans in as he presses play.

'This is the back camera. It's a motion sensor so it shows pretty much the whole evening.'

'Does it capture the pool house?' Grace asks.

But Siobhán can already see that it doesn't. Onscreen, there are people dancing, arms in the air, gold bangles glinting in the glow of overhead lanterns. The DJ, the cocktail bar, the crowds around it. You're never too old or too rich for a free bar, as Charlie likes to say. Behind the swaying bodies, the pool glimmers. And beyond that, the ends of four white loungers are just about visible. But then nothing, just shadow and darkness. The garden house is out of scope of the camera.

'What about the bit where Xavi and Jasmine saw the girls on the loungers? Can we find that?' Siobhán asks. It might not tell them anything, but if she could just see Ré . . . Just know she was there at a point in time. She swallows a lump in her throat.

Charlie fast-forwards, picking up the phone to scrutinize the screen.

'OK, got it.' He lays the phone down again, and Siobhán cranes her neck.

And there they are. Or at least, part of them, illuminated to a small extent by the pool lights. A shape that looks like Ré's Dr. Martens boots at the end of one lounger, and what might be Luna's feet, encased in strappy gold sandals, on the other. Siobhán blinks back more tears.

'How long are they there – what time is it when they move off the loungers?' Grace asks.

Charlie moves the video on again, and stops at 3.11 a.m. 'Here.'

Onscreen, there's movement. The sandals disappear first. Luna exiting towards the pool house. Not stalking off, but . . . purposeful, Siobhán thinks. And then she disappears beyond the camera's scope, into darkness. A minute later, Ré moves off, following her friend. Slowly. Cat-like, almost. Into the darkness, too. And that's it. The last sighting of Ré McKenna and Luna Caine.

10

It's just after ten now, and only Grace and Siobhán remain in the kitchen. O'Connell has gone to take statements from Charlie's mother and aunt, Xavi has gone for a shower, and Charlie has gone to placate Emma-Rose, who is no doubt still upset about her cancelled Day Two.

Siobhán and Grace have been asked to stay indoors, away from the patio area and garden. Through the window, Siobhán sees two figures in white suits conferring. Her stomach churns. Did they find something? She cranes her neck, watching as another officer comes around the side of the pool house and beckons. On her phone, notifications begin to light up. People tagging her on Facebook. Suddenly fearful, hopeful, she clicks into one. But it's an appeal. A picture of the two girls with an appeal for information on the Garda Síochána Missing Persons page. Siobhán follows this page. She never imagined being part of it. It suddenly dawns on her that Grace's mother might wake up to news that her granddaughter is missing. She nudges the phone across the table to Grace and says, 'Your mom might hear.' Grace nods and makes a call, leaving a voicemail to tell her mother what's happening. To her credit, she keeps her voice calm, telling her mom not to worry, that she'll call her later.

'We can't just sit here,' Grace says when she disconnects. 'We need to use every contact we have, find someone with high-up garda connections.' She pushes back her chair. 'And we need to be out there searching.'

Siobhán hesitates. Normally, she's a rule-follower, and Detective O'Connell had been clear in her instructions. Grace generally bends the rules to suit herself. She's a queue-jumper, a string-puller; using connections to get Luna into over-subscribed sports clubs or, in earlier years, to get herself into already full nightclubs. And occasionally, it annoys Siobhán. But Grace is right this time – they have to search.

Siobhán stands, her head still pounding. 'Where, though?'

'What about asking their friends? We could start with Kayla? Maybe she can shed light on what's going on between them, something to point us in the right direction?'

Siobhán picks up her phone. 'Will I ring her?'

'No, it'll be easier in person,' Grace says. 'Just text to say we're calling over.'

Fifteen minutes later, they're in Charlie's driveway, getting into Grace's car.

Grace, now in jeans and a T-shirt, had said she'd let O'Connell know they were leaving. This communication had taken Grace longer than Siobhán expected, and when she asks, Grace explains that she couldn't find O'Connell at first. There's something faux casual about the way she says it and, for the second time today, Siobhán has the sense that Grace is lying.

'Anyway, I found her, and she nodded and waved me on,' Grace says as she puts on her seatbelt. Siobhán wonders how explicit Grace was with O'Connell, and what O'Connell thought she was nodding to . . . But Siobhán is also reasonably sure that O'Connell would have stopped them if they shouldn't be doing this. And what harm can it do, anyway?

The radio blares a song from the nineties as soon as Grace

turns the key in the ignition, and she jabs a finger at the button to turn it off. The song reminds Siobhán of something. Something about last night? She tries to remember, but it won't come back. Something and nothing, maybe, but she'd feel better if she could recall. Memories of last night are still hazy, fragmented.

As Grace indicates to pull out on to Kensington Road, Siobhán turns to her.

'When they asked about Marrakesh – was there something you weren't saying?'

Grace keeps her eyes on the road, craning her neck to check for traffic. 'No?'

'It's just . . . I don't know. The way you answered . . .'

'No . . .' A shrug. With feigned nonchalance? Or is Siobhán seeing things that aren't there?

Eight minutes later, they pull up outside Kayla's Blackrock house – well, Kayla's family home, where she grew up. According to Ré, Kayla can't afford to buy (nobody in their twenties can) but refuses to waste money on exorbitant Dublin rent, so continues to live with her parents. A tinge of envy had crept over Siobhán when she'd originally heard that. Much as she wants Ré to be independent, she misses her now that she doesn't live at home in Dalkey. It's a very large house for just one person, beautiful sea views notwithstanding.

Kayla is at the door as soon as they get out of the car, waving them inside and through to the big, old-fashioned pine kitchen. The first few minutes are spent filling her in on what they know, as Kayla sits, elbows on the table, hands over her mouth.

'And you really can't tell whose voice is on the audio?' she asks when they've finished.

Siobhán and Grace exchange a glance and shake their heads. And in that moment, an unspoken agreement is formed. However much each of them believes their own daughter made the call, they'll get nowhere by arguing each time it comes up.

'Should I go out searching?' Kayla pushes back her chair. 'Just tell me where to start. What do the guards think – like, is it that one of them has taken the other at knifepoint?'

Siobhán swallows against a tightness in her throat. Kayla has never had a filter. She's loud, lacks self-awareness, speaks without thinking. But maybe she's just saying what the rest of them are avoiding.

'Or' – Kayla continues her mile-a-minute stream of questions – 'do the police think one stabbed the other and then took the body away to dispose of it?'

Siobhán freezes. In the hours since this nightmare began to unfurl, that thought has not crossed her mind. But of course, now that she considers it properly, now that Kayla has put it so baldly, there's no getting away from it: either one of the girls made the other leave the house at knifepoint, or . . . or one stabbed the other and took the body off the premises to hide it. *Jesus Christ.* The room begins to spin. Siobhán grips the table, knuckles white, stomach sick.

'Are you OK?' Kayla leans across. 'Will I get you a water? A tea? A brandy? I don't know if we actually have brandy. Sorry, I shouldn't have said that about a body. I'm really sorry, I wasn't thinking.'

Grace reaches a hand to grab Siobhán's while Kayla gets up to fill two glasses of water.

'That's . . . that's not it.' Grace's usually confident voice is low and shaky. She turns to her friend. 'Siobhán, listen to me. The only way we can get through this is if we believe both girls are alive. Something has gone very wrong. But they're out there, and we *will* sort this out. OK?'

Siobhán nods. There is nothing in the world to suggest this

is true, but the alternative is too horrific. And she's relieved, comforted by this reconnection with Grace, this united front. Whatever chance they have of finding the girls, they're better working together.

'So, let's focus on what we can find out. Kayla, have you noticed anything up with either of the girls recently?'

Kayla places the glasses of water on the table, shaking her head.

'Not really. Ré hasn't been in touch as much, but you know what she's like.' She sits back down, tucking a sandy curl behind her ear. 'When she gets into a project, she focuses on that and forgets about the rest of us. Remember that business she set up in TY? And the time she got really into sailing and all her sailing friends? Anyway, yeah, of course you know what she's like.'

Siobhán does know. When Ré is into something, she's really, really into it.

'We heard they had an argument last night, something to do with their Marrakesh trip,' Siobhán says. Beside her, Grace stiffens. It's true, then. There *is* something Grace isn't telling her. 'Do you know anything about that?'

'Well, obviously, the mugging shook them up, but, like, nothing that would still cause arguments months later. Not really. Though I know there was a bit of blaming at the time.'

Siobhán stares at Kayla, her mouth suddenly dry. 'The mugging? What mugging?'

Confusion washes over Kayla's face. 'When the girls got mugged? In Marrakesh? Oh god, I've done it again, haven't I. I'm so sorry.' Her cheeks redden and she pulls a fruit bowl towards her, picking up an apple, twisting the stem in her fingers. 'My mother keeps telling me to think before I speak. I do this kind of thing all the time. I was bitching about my boss on the bus on Friday, said his name on the phone to Prisha *multiple* times, then realized when I was getting off that Garvin – that's my boss's PA – was on the bus, too.'

Siobhán stares at her. 'Kayla, the mugging. What happened, exactly?'

'OK, so Ré and Luna went to visit some little art shop that was in an area they'd been told wasn't quite as safe as the rest of the city.' Kayla puts down the apple and picks up her phone. She scrolls for a moment. 'Look, here it is.' The phone screen fills with Luna's familiar Instagram grid. The first image is a photo of a pretty pink building with colourful paintings on display outside. 'Ré was adamant that they'd be OK – it was during the day, they'd stick together, and so on. Luna agreed to go with her – she wanted photos for her Stories.'

Siobhán nods. Grace is quiet.

'Anyway, they copped at some point that they'd taken a wrong turn. The area they were in was pretty crowded and then they realized they'd been steered in different directions, deliberately separated. Each of them was kind of herded into a different side street, you know? Two guys robbed Ré and the other two robbed Luna.' Kayla puts down her phone, looks from Siobhán to Grace. 'God, sorry you're hearing it like this.'

Siobhán is reeling. 'Were . . . were they hurt?'

'No. Terrified, like, but they weren't hurt. They just handed over their stuff. Money, credit cards. Ré's phone, Luna's bag. Jewellery from both of them, every piece they were wearing. That's why Ré doesn't have her grandmother's ring any more.'

Siobhán shakes her head. She had no idea the ring was gone. God, has she been that caught up in her business that she didn't notice something had happened? And what else did she miss – in recent months, this weekend? Her mind rolls back over all of it, like a timelapse video – what has she overlooked?

'And Luna's Tiffany necklace you got for her twenty-first,' Kayla is saying to Grace. 'The one with the crescent moon and the diamonds,' she adds, as though Luna might have received more than one Tiffany necklace from Grace for her birthday.

Grace sucks air through her teeth. 'This is just *awful*.'

Siobhán turns to look at her. Grace often spins stories to suit her own narrative, firmly believing what she's saying. And she gets away with it with most people, but not the friend who knows her best.

Siobhán's eyes narrow. 'You knew.'

'What?'

'Don't even try. You knew they were mugged.'

Grace sighs. 'OK, yeah. I knew.'

'What is going on?'

'It's like Kayla said: they were mugged. Luna called me from the hotel, but she asked me not to say anything to you. It was the week before your pitch meeting and Ré didn't want to worry you. And she felt awful about the ring because you'd told her not to bring it.'

Siobhán lets out a breath. *Oh god. Poor Ré.* As if Siobhán wouldn't have dropped everything for her. But of course that's exactly why Ré didn't tell. And on a day that didn't feel as though it could get worse, Siobhán's heart cracks.

'Sorry,' Kayla whispers. 'People always tell me I should think before I speak . . .'

'No, it's fine.' Siobhán swipes at her eyes as more tears threaten. 'It's better we know, especially if that's what they argued about. Grace, shouldn't you have said? When Detective O'Connell asked?'

Grace examines her hands. 'I did. After, when I went to let her know we were coming here. I didn't want to worry you.'

You didn't want to get caught keeping secrets from me, Siobhán thinks uncharitably, turning back to Kayla.

'Was there something else about the mugging, something that would cause an argument?'

'Well, as I said, Ré felt guilty because it had been her idea to go to that area.'

'Exactly.' Grace rubs her hands up and down her lap. 'Luna had pointed out that it was dangerous, but you know Ré, once she gets an idea in her head . . .'

'Sure, but from what we've heard, Luna wanted to get photos – presumably she chose to go there?' Siobhán keeps her tone light, trying not to sound defensive.

'Of course, yes,' Grace says in a way that does not mean 'Of course, yes' at all and leaves Siobhán feeling uncomfortable. They never fall out and, really, in the midst of all this, it's the least of her worries, but somehow, not having Grace onside makes everything worse.

'Anyway, no matter what happened,' Grace adds, 'would this really lead to an argument at four o'clock this morning, and this . . . this knife and the blood and the call for police?'

Kayla picks up the apple again, and this time takes a bite. 'Were they drinking at the wedding?'

'Well, of course they were drinking.' Again, Siobhán tries to keep a defensive tone at bay, but it slides in anyway. 'It was a wedding.'

Kayla bites her lip. 'I know. It's just . . . they haven't really seen each other since Marrakesh, and they're always arguing when they're drunk and sometimes it gets out of hand.'

Siobhán frowns. 'What do you mean, "always arguing"?'

Now Kayla looks genuinely perplexed. 'You know. Just, Ré and Luna. That's what they do?'

'Well, it's news to me. Did you know this?' Siobhán turns to Grace.

'No. I mean, they're best friends. I imagine they squabble a little. But surely not full-blown arguments?'

'Oh god, you have not seen *anything* like those two when they're at it, especially on a night out. I suppose you don't see them when they're out all that much,' Kayla concedes. 'But honestly, they can be pretty horrible to each other.'

11

IN THE CAR OUTSIDE Kayla's, a sick feeling rolls through Siobhán's stomach. Nothing that's happened this morning makes any sense, but one thing is clear – she and Grace don't know their daughters as well as they thought they did.

They debate what to do next. Siobhán wants to call the girls' friends Prisha and Abbey – they'd been with them in Marrakesh and might be able to shed some more light on the mugging. Grace is straining at the leash to do something more useful – to search.

'But we don't know where to start, and we're just two people,' Siobhán points out. 'We don't have the ability to search all of Dublin between us.' The sheer weight of this, the enormity, stops her for a moment. She swallows, gathers herself. 'I think our best bet is to speak to people, find out what's going on, narrow down the search that way.'

An exhale tells her Grace has capitulated, so Siobhán phones Prisha first and arranges to call to her house.

Just like Kayla, this is Prisha's home-house, where she grew up, where she still lives with her parents and sisters. She and Abbey are saving for a deposit on a flat, both living at home until they do.

'Are our girls the only ones who've moved out?' Grace mutters as they walk up the driveway to a large redbrick house in Carysfort Downs.

And Siobhán can't help wishing now that they hadn't. Maybe if Ré still lived at home, Siobhán would know what was going on in her life, in her head. That's not how it works, she knows that, you have to let go, but still, right now she'd swap with Prisha's parents or Kayla's parents or any other parents in the country.

Prisha is just awake, her hair tousled, her eyes bleary. She was out last night, she explains, and is catching up on texts, trying to process the news that her friends are missing. She leads them to the kitchen and gestures for them to sit, then fills herself a pint of water and drinks half of it in one go.

'I got a text from Luna last night.' Her voice is croaky.

Grace sits forward in her chair. 'When? What does it say?'

Prisha sits, squinting at her phone. 'I replied to a picture she put on Snapchat, asking how the wedding was going. She said a bit weird, because she'd just found out something from Ré.'

Siobhán's stomach drops.

'Can we see?' Grace sounds breathless.

Prisha pushes her phone across the table and, heads together, Siobhán and Grace take in what's onscreen:

A selfie of Luna, a huge wine glass full of what looks like champagne.

A reply from Prisha: **Love that for you. Wedding good?**

And then from Luna: **Ish. Good earlier. Just found out something from Ré that's upset me. Long story best told over drinks x**

Siobhán stares at the screen, her skin prickling.

She looks up at Prisha. 'That's it?'

Prisha nods. 'I was asleep and didn't see her reply till a few minutes ago.'

'And do you have any idea what it could be about?' Siobhán asks.

'No clue. But also, you know Luna.' A glance at Grace. 'She can be dramatic.'

Grace frowns, as though this is a surprise, though surely it's not – she knows Luna better than anyone. Ignoring this for now, Siobhán asks Prisha to send her a screenshot she can forward to the gardaí. She scrutinizes the message as she saves it to her own phone, then attaches it to an email. Grace is asking Prisha about the mugging. But Prisha's version tallies with Kayla's; she doesn't seem to have any additional details.

'How did they seem after?' Siobhán asks.

Prisha darts a glance from one to the other, chews her lip. 'They were both pretty shaken, and they argued about it later that night. Luna was pissed off that Ré had brought them there, a little off the beaten track. Ré pointed out that Luna is a grown adult with free will, and so on. I think they were both just stressed and lashing out.'

'And Kayla said Ré's phone was taken?' Siobhán asks.

'Yes, she had to buy a new one the next day. They were both most upset about the jewellery – Ré's sapphire ring and Luna's moon necklace.'

Siobhán nods. With both her parents gone, mementos like her mother's ring have always held huge sentimental value for Siobhán, and Ré knows that. But right now it seems like the most unimportant thing in the world.

'And what did the police say?' she asks.

'They were looking at CCTV from near where the girls were separated, and they seemed to take it very seriously,' Prisha says. 'But they hadn't caught anyone, last I heard. Ré would love that ring back, that's the main thing.'

Of course, Siobhán thinks, and she doesn't want to admit what happened until she has it.

'The police were great right from the start, in fairness,' Prisha continues. 'Luna still had her phone – it was in her pocket, not her bag – and she was trying to figure out how to call the police when she saw one and ran over to him. They couldn't find Ré at first, but then Luna spotted her on the way back to the hotel. Ré was devastated about the ring. And shook. Both of them were. Like I say, they argued about whose fault it was.'

'Was the argument unusual?' Grace asks. 'Or do they argue a lot?'

'They argue,' Prisha says, nodding as she speaks. 'They get on each other's nerves. It can be quite stressful for me and Abbey being around them. Sorry,' she adds, as though just remembering who she's speaking to.

Siobhán frowns. 'I don't understand. Kayla said the same. But how have Grace and I never known about this? Never seen it?'

Prisha looks from one to the other. 'Well, because you're best friends,' she says simply. 'And you always thought they were, too. Sometimes they are. But often they're not. And I think, consciously or not, they didn't want you to know that. So . . .'

A sound from outside pulls Prisha's eyes to the open kitchen door. A car engine.

'Who's that?' she mutters, mostly to herself, craning her neck to see out to the hall.

And Siobhán has the crazy idea that it will be the girls, somehow turning up here, with a perfectly good explanation for everything.

But then there's the sound of a key in the door. And a voice.

'Just me, I finished early because Sonia wasn't there this morning and, honestly, I couldn't be arsed bobbing around in the sea with only teenage boys for company. Oh!'

A wet-haired woman in a dry-robe arrives into the kitchen and stops short when she sees Siobhán and Grace.

'Sorry, excuse my language, I didn't know we had guests. I'm Shiva.' She stretches to shake hands.

When Prisha explains who Siobhán and Grace are and why they're here, Shiva's smile vanishes.

'I'm so sorry, this is awful. Is there anything I can do?'

Siobhán shakes her head. That's just it. There doesn't seem to be anything anyone can do.

They leave Prisha, asking her to keep thinking about what Luna's late-night message may have meant, and drive back to Charlie's house. When they pull into the driveway, there's a small group huddled there. Every face turns to look at them – Detective O'Connell, Charlie, Emma-Rose, Xavi.

Charlie straightens, as though bracing himself to say something. Emma-Rose is biting her lip. Xavi looks down at his shoes. Only O'Connell remains completely neutral. Inscrutable.

Siobhán and Grace are out of the car in an instant.

'What is it?' Siobhán's limbs are loose.

Charlie glances at O'Connell, then back to Siobhán and Grace. 'Detective O'Connell will tell you.'

12

The day before the wedding

SIOBHÁN SLIPS ON FLIP-FLOPS, stands up from her lounger, and stretches. Grace and Luna remain prone, side by side, soaking up the morning sun. They're like peas in a pod, with their long, blonde, beachy hair and matching Nina Ricci sunglasses. Luna's suitcase sits by her lounger still. Unable to resist the lure of the sun, she hasn't made it to the pool house yet. Meanwhile, Ré has not re-emerged.

Siobhán makes her way down the garden, skirting around the pool that glistens and dazzles under the sun. Only Charlie could manage to have his wedding on the warmest, most glorious weekend of the year. But then Charlie has always been lucky. Or maybe it's his charm, his ease with people, smoothing his way in life. And money, she thinks pragmatically. Money certainly brings luck, and since his construction business took off in the early two-thousands, Charlie has never been short of it. She thinks to when she first met him, when they were both broke students in UCD, working part-time jobs in a nearby pub. Grace used to beg them to come to parties, to call in sick. She worked during the day and was free every night and could never comprehend that they didn't have the same capacity for socializing. And Grace never understood what it was like to have no money. Charlie, on the other hand, has never forgotten what it's like to have no money and has always been scrupulously fair with his ex-wives and his children. Sometimes to Emma-Rose's dismay, Siobhán thinks, with a wry grin to herself.

There's a noticeable change in temperature when she steps off the sandstone deck that surrounds the pool and on to the flagstone path that leads to the pool house. The shade from the tall fir trees gives this spot a fairy-tale feel. Like the cabin is a Hansel and Gretel cottage, nestled in a tiny forest. A shiver runs across her skin and she has a sudden and eerie sense of being watched. She looks around, looks behind her, but all she can see are empty loungers on the far side of the pool. Luna and Grace must have gone inside.

Arriving at the pool house, she knocks softly.

'Ré?'

'Yeah, in here,' comes Ré's voice.

Siobhán pushes open the door and steps inside. She hasn't been here much. These days it's mostly used as Emma-Rose's office for EROS, her event management business. Charlie had built the house for Xavi when he was a teen, to give him somewhere to hang out with his friends, but would then chastise him for spending too much time here with those same friends. Xavi and Charlie's relationship hasn't always been great. It's better now than it used to be, but Charlie still treats Xavi like a child at times, and Xavi tends to lean in to the charming layabout persona, perhaps because that's what his father has decided he is.

She looks around now, taking it in. The wooden floors and walls, the criss-crossed ceiling beams, the faded oriental rug that covers most of the living-room floor, the wide L-shaped couch on which Ré now lounges. Emma-Rose's desk, clear but for a phone, a laptop and a neat set of filing trays. On the wall behind the desk there's a giant poster with 'EROS' in pink letters and an image of pink and gold balloons. A background for Zoom calls, presumably. The room is bright and pretty and soothing, and it strikes Siobhán that it will suit Ré to have this quiet spot to retreat to during the busy three days ahead.

'Are you coming out to the pool?' Siobhán sits beside her daughter.

'Soon. Just tired after the journey. And I keep getting this weird thing where I can't see properly, kind of at the sides of my vision. It's really odd. I have to just sit. And then it goes away and I can see again.'

'You need to go to the optician. Are you wearing your contacts too much?'

'I don't think that's it. It's been happening since I was in Marrakesh.' Something crosses her face then and her eyes dip down. 'Anyway, it's also because I was up at five a.m.' A grin. 'And out last night, so I'm a little fragile.'

'Ah, OK. Who were you out with?' Siobhán asks lightly.

'Just some friends.'

A beat passes.

'From work?'

'No, two friends from Dublin who're living in London.'

'Do I know them?'

Ré sits up. 'Why the twenty questions?'

'I wondered if it was someone you were seeing, maybe.'

'Is this about what Grace said?''

'Well yeah . . . Luna apparently saw you with a guy and told Grace?'

Ré's brow creases. 'OK, that doesn't sound weird and stalkery at *all*. Where did she see me?'

'Outside a bar in Deptford.'

For just a second, Ré freezes. Then she laughs.

'Jesus, is she spying on me?' She laughs again, but there's

something forced about it. Siobhán scrutinizes her daughter's face. Her deep blue eyes, wide with incredulity. Her freckles crinkling across her nose. Her mouth, open in surprise. Is she genuinely taken aback at Luna or is there something else going on here?

'Nope, she just happened to be going past in an Uber and saw you.'

'*God*, she's nosy. But I'm not seeing anyone. Maybe she saw me with someone from work. Or it wasn't me at all.' A shrug. 'Anyway, how are you doing? How's Scorch going?'

Siobhán fills her in – the big contract with the pharmacy chain, the new concession in Dublin Airport, the talk of UK expansion. Ré asks all the right questions, genuinely interested. She's always been like that, though, interested and curious about her mother's work. When she was small, Siobhán worried about how much time Ré spent with babysitters, but Ré never seemed to resent it, no more than she had ever been bothered by not having a dad. Or at least, not that she'd ever said, and Siobhán, admittedly, had avoided probing too deeply.

They chat about the upcoming wedding, then Siobhán hauls herself off the unexpectedly comfortable couch, wondering if it's a waste to have such good furniture in what is essentially a log cabin, reminds Ré that lunch is at twelve thirty and heads back to the main house for her meeting.

Just after half twelve, Siobhán emerges from the house to find everyone already seated around the large patio table. Luna and Xavi sit either side of Grace. Ré is opposite, beside Charlie. And Emma-Rose is hovering, unsmiling, agitated about something, it seems.

'Oh, there you are, Siobhán, I wondered where you'd got to. We're just about to serve lunch.'

'Sorry, the meeting ran on.' Siobhán wavers for a moment, unsure whether to take the spare seat beside Charlie or to sit at the top of the table. Either one has the potential to annoy Emma-Rose.

'Sit here, Mum,' Ré says, patting the chair at the top of the table, and Siobhán does.

Emma-Rose sits beside her fiancé, as a man in a black apron with an 'S' logo on the pocket appears from the kitchen. His left leg is encased in an orthopaedic boot and he hobbles slightly, prompting a small look of distaste from Emma-Rose. It can't be easy working for her, Siobhán thinks, especially when her own business is event management.

'Ben, great, we're all here finally,' Emma-Rose says to the man in the apron. 'Please go ahead with drinks.'

Behind Ben are two girls aged about eighteen or nineteen. All three carry bottles of champagne.

Only Emma-Rose and Charlie would have catering staff for the lunch on the day *before* the wedding, Siobhán thinks. Then again, they're probably right – why not, when they have the money? Flutes filled, the guests clink, and soon, crab salad starters are placed in front of each person. Siobhán takes a sip of champagne and sinks down in her chair, enjoying the babble of chatter, safe in the knowledge that there are no more work meetings until Monday. There are always emails, of course, and there'll be a few phone calls this afternoon. But perhaps, for the next three days, she can relax with some of her favourite people in the world. Xavi and Ré banter back and forth across the table. Charlie chats to Grace and Luna. Only Emma-Rose is quiet, her eyes darting around the group. A hostess who wants to host but is never quite able to relax into it.

Just as the two young catering staff begin to clear plates, Ben shows someone out to the patio. A woman in a structured red dress. A blonde woman with a pretty face. A familiar face. It takes a moment for Siobhán to work it out. The woman is speaking to Emma-Rose. Apologizing for interrupting the lunch. A clipboard in her hands. She's the wedding planner, it seems. Emma-Rose says her name. Jasmine Whitaker. The familiarity is not imagined. The woman looks at Grace, who has pushed her sunglasses up on her head. At Luna, who is staring back. At Ré, who is staring at her plate. Ten years peel away in an instant. Jasmine. Siobhán's heart sinks. This is not good. Not good at all.

13

Now

SIOBHÁN STANDS BESIDE THE car, staring at Charlie, then at O'Connell, her legs weak, Grace's fingers digging into her arm. Holding each other up.

'What is it?' she manages in a whisper.

O'Connell steps forward. 'We found blood on the ground behind the pool house, below the back gate that leads to the lane that runs behind the house.'

Siobhán takes this in. No more clinging to theories about cut fingers.

'You think that's how they left, through the back gate?' Grace asks.

'We do. The camera at the front of the house didn't show them leaving, and the camera at the back doesn't capture the pool house or the gate behind it. So this is the mostly likely exit point, and the bloodstain would seem to confirm that.'

The bloodstain. Siobhán's head begins to swim, and she grips Grace more tightly. If only she could start over. Go back twelve hours. Stay with Ré. Talk to Ré. Find out . . . find out what? Again something flutters close to her memory and just as quickly disappears.

'They need us to leave now,' Charlie says quietly and, for the first time, Siobhán notices the bags at the doorstep.

'I'm afraid so,' O'Connell says. 'We have to treat the entire house as a possible crime scene. If you ladies could gather some belongings, my colleague here will go with you. After that, we can't allow anyone back in the house until this is resolved.'

'Where will you go?' Siobhán asks Charlie, still in a daze. 'Emma-Rose's house?'

'There are tenants in hers – I don't think they'd be too happy to have us land on their doorstep.' A wan smile. 'And obviously Xavi's mother's sold her place in Deansgrange, so the three of us will book into a hotel. We'll stay nearby, don't worry.' He picks up a bag, and Siobhán has a sudden urge to beg him not to leave. Somehow it makes everything worse if it's just Grace and Siobhán left alone trying to figure this out.

'Don't go yet. Please. We should . . . we should talk some more about everything we remember from last night, right?'

Beside her, Grace nods. Maybe she feels it, too, a visceral need for help. For someone to fix this. For safety in numbers.

'Of course, we're all in this together – we'll meet up again as soon as we've found a hotel and checked in. Say in two hours?'

Emma-Rose chimes in, her eyes on her phone screen. 'It may take longer, Charlie. I'm googling hotels, and there's nothing yet. July isn't the easiest time to find accommodation in Dublin.'

Charlie lifts his hands. 'As soon as we can, then.' He turns to Siobhán. 'You head home to yours and, if it suits, we'll meet you there later?'

The thought of rattling around her house on her own, sick with worry, fills Siobhán with dread. Charlie reaches to pick up his bag. Emma-Rose is still frowning at her phone.

'Stay in mine. Please.' The 'please' comes out in a whisper.

Siobhán clears her throat. 'There's plenty of room, and it's easier than trying to find a hotel. And . . . I don't want to be on my own while all this is going on.'

'We couldn't impose like that, you've enough to be worrying about . . .' Charlie says, but she can already hear the capitulation.

'I mean it. You'd be doing me a favour. And there's no point wasting time trying to find a hotel – it could take ages.'

'OK, then . . . if you're sure?'

Siobhán nods, a small weight lifting.

'Right, and we can try to work out together where they might be,' Charlie says. 'The more we talk, the more likely we are to find them.' He puts a hand on her shoulder.

Siobhán nods, unable to speak over the lump in her throat. Grace's fingers grip tighter, and she sags against Siobhán.

'I still can't believe this is happening.' Grace sounds so lost, unlike any version of her Siobhán has ever known. 'It's just like back when . . . the one thing I always worried—'

'You come too, stay in mine.' Siobhán says it because she means it, but also to cut Grace off, to stop the spiral. 'We should all be together.'

Grace nods against Siobhán's shoulder, then they straighten and walk together towards the door to gather their things.

A shout from behind stops them, and they turn.

Ben, the catering manager, is hurrying up the driveway, trying and failing to run in his boot, his face red, beaded with sweat.

'Sorry, hi, sorry.' He stops, catching his breath. 'My van. It's gone.'

O'Connell steps towards him. 'Where was your van?'

'Behind.' Another stop for breath. 'I had to run all the way around – the gate at the back is cordoned off.'

'OK, take your time. Your van was where?'

'There's a little circular cul-de-sac at the end of the lane that runs behind the house. It's so cars can turn, but Charlie said it's never used. So Robert – the barman – parked there on Friday to carry glasses and tableware in.'

'And that van is gone?'

'Yeah. We went to get it just now, to collect what we could before you close up the house.' A glance at Emma-Rose and Charlie. 'Sorry. That probably seems insensitive. It's just I have another wedding tomorrow . . .'

'Don't worry, we understand,' Charlie says.

'And then the van wasn't there,' Ben says, still breathless.

'Do you know the reg plate?' O'Connell asks. 'What does the van look like?'

'The reg will be somewhere in insurance documents at the Sage office. But it's a distinctive van. Green with "Sage Catering" inscribed on the side in white lettering.'

O'Connell notes the details, energized, it seems, by what must feel like a first lead.

'Both girls can drive?' she asks Grace and Siobhán.

They nod.

'But how would either of them take the van, if they don't have the keys?' Emma-Rose asks, her tone sceptical. Siobhán looks over at her. It's as though she's downplaying it to salvage her wedding, holding out hope that this is all a misunderstanding.

You and me both, Siobhán thinks.

'Good point.' Ben holds up his hand. 'I have the keys here.'

'Are there spare keys?' O'Connell asks.

'Yeah, I have a second set so the staff can get stuff from the van or nip off to pick up supplies.'

'So your staff have those?'

'Well, no. We used a shelf in the catering kitchen, so anyone who needed them could grab from there.'

'The *catering* kitchen?' O'Connell's eyebrows almost reach her hairline.

Emma-Rose interjects. 'The smaller kitchen off the garage, so that catering staff can work uninterrupted.'

O'Connell shakes her head ever so slightly. She turns and calls in through the open front door, where her colleague is on his phone. 'Did anyone see keys in that other kitchen off the garage?'

They don't hear the reply as O'Connell steps inside and out of sight.

'You should gather your stuff, I guess,' Charlie says after a moment. 'While we wait for them.'

'I think we're supposed to be accompanied,' Siobhán says. Though, really, she can't trust her legs right now.

Charlie nods. Beside him, Emma-Rose is on her phone, and Xavi is on his. Ben stands a little bit away, no doubt wondering how he got caught up in all of this. Grace is still gripping Siobhán's arm, her fingers frozen.

O'Connell arrives back, her face serious.

'The keys appear to be missing,' she says, addressing Ben. 'And there's something else we noticed. Could you come to take a look?'

14

The day before the wedding

SIOBHÁN STARES. JASMINE WHITAKER. It's definitely her. How is she all grown up and dressed like an adult and holding a clipboard? *There's this thing called time, Mum?* says Ré's voice in her head. And yes, it's been ten years. But still. The last time they saw Jasmine, Siobhán was calling the gardaí. A shudder runs through her at the memory. Looking back, she hadn't handled it very well. Looking back, Jasmine was only fifteen. Fifteen had seemed so grown up at the time, but now . . .

Jasmine smiles around as Emma-Rose makes introductions. Her eyes land on Luna and her smile fades.

'Oh.'

Luna bites her lip.

Jasmine's eyes flick to Grace, then Siobhán, then Ré. Her mouth drops open, but just as quickly, she switches back to a smile.

Emma-Rose smiles, too, the little gap in her front teeth showing, oblivious to the tension. 'Jasmine is my wedding planner. She's been an absolute godsend. She'll be here today, all day tomorrow, of course, and on Sunday for the Day Two. So just carry on as though she's not here, and don't be surprised if you find her in all sorts of unexpected corners of the house – she's very thorough!'

I'll bet she is, Siobhán thinks, remembering finding Jasmine rummaging through her bedside drawer. It's hard to stop staring – the transformation is so complete. Back then, Jasmine lived in crop tops and shorts, thigh-high boots and chokers. Fifteen-year-old Jasmine wouldn't be caught dead in today's structured dress.

Her face is the same, though. Her eyes – minus the flicked eyeliner – are the same. And right now, her eyes are anxious.

Grace smiles. 'Hello, Jasmine. How lovely to meet you.'

And just like that, the decision is made for all of them. Today at this lovely lunch, nothing will be said.

Jasmine smiles back, looking relieved. 'And you.'

Siobhán scrutinizes her from behind her sunglasses. She still looks worried, as well she might. Emma-Rose is not the kind of person who'd respond well to knowing that fifteen-year-old Jasmine had been reported to the gardaí for stealing prescription meds, a watch and a credit card from Siobhán.

Luna smiles, too, now. 'Hi,' she says, a greeting that refrains from expressing whether or not she already knows Jasmine. Nicely done, Siobhán thinks.

Ré follows suit. A lower-key mumble of a 'hi'.

And now it's Siobhán's turn. Grace was there back then. Grace was part of it, to a large extent. It was Grace who made the call to Jasmine's mother. And Grace who stipulated that the girls – Luna and, by extension, Ré – should no longer engage with Jasmine. But it was Siobhán who called the gardaí. On a teen who was still grieving the dad she'd lost just a few years earlier. And right now, facing Jasmine, she feels awkward and guilty and sad.

'Hi, Jasmine,' she says, forcing brightness into her voice.

'Hi.' Jasmine's tone is warm, her smile wide. But her eyes are still anxious.

SUCH A NICE GIRL

Siobhán watches as Jasmine turns to speak to Emma-Rose, something about tonight's dinner. Her demeanour is poised and professional, but her fingertips tap silently on the underside of the clipboard. Luna and Ré stare, then exchange a glance, and Siobhán feels every inch of it. The title of an Agatha Christie book comes to mind. *Cat Among the Pigeons.*

15

Now

Siobhán watches as Ben from Sage Catering follows O'Connell inside Charlie's house, the detective's words echoing in her mind.

There's something else we noticed.

What does that mean? Her feet move of their own volition towards the front door, but another guard, a young woman with blonde hair and kind eyes, raises her hand, then steps in front of the doorway.

'I'm sorry, Ms McKenna, but we can't let anyone in. We'll have to ask you all to leave the premises now.' A nod towards the cars, the gate. 'I'm Garda Stephanie Harrington – I'll be working with Detective O'Connell on the investigation.'

'But what did they notice? This is my daughter we're talking about.' A glance back towards Grace. 'Our daughters.'

'I understand, but we can't say right now, and we do need you to leave. As your liaison officer, Detective O'Connell will be in constant contact.' Her face softens. 'I promise. We're doing everything we can, but you have to let us do our job.'

'Detective O'Connell said we could gather our things?'

'Oh right, of course. I'll come with you.'

And that's it, it seems. They are chaperoned while collecting their belongings, then chaperoned back outside. Garda Harrington watches while they get into their respective cars. They leave in convoy, with no idea what the gardaí have found in the catering kitchen.

Siobhán is first to pull in through the gates of her home, the others following like a funeral cortège. She gets out to unlock the front door.

Her keys clatter in the silver dish on the hall table, and she lets out a breath. Her house is her sanctuary. Normally her happy place. Years of hard work embedded in every stone. Discipline and determination bought her all of it – the four bedrooms, the four bathrooms, the airy kitchen-living area with the glass back wall and the sea views. That last part was the most important for Siobhán, having grown up within a stone's throw of Sandycove beach. What she couldn't have imagined was the cosmetics business she'd create and the sea-view villa she'd end up in. Built by an architect who then relocated to the States, it's the dream home of her imagination brought to life. And she knows better than to take it for granted.

She walks through to the kitchen-living area, breathing in the view that never gets old: the sea, dotted with small sailboats, glittering under a cloudless sky. She keeps going to the bifold doors and opens them. With sun on her face and sea air in her lungs, there is a brief respite from the panic. A two-second break. Then it's back. The sick feeling in her stomach, the roaring in her ears. Where is Ré, where is Luna, and whose blood is on the ground? Kayla's words replay in her mind. *Do the police think one stabbed the other and then took the body away to dispose of it?*

Oh god. She desperately needs Ré to be alive, but she also needs to know that Ré is not a killer.

Ré can certainly be impulsive, with a tendency to lash out when she's angry. At four, this meant throwing things. At fourteen, it meant screaming things. And at twenty-four? Ré is mostly pretty stable but can still fly off the handle when she's mad. When things go wrong, when she gets stressed. Not like this, though. Siobhán sinks into a chair on the deck. Not blood and knives.

Behind her, a low hum of voices tells her the others have made their way inside. Exhaustion hits, and she wonders now why on earth she invited them to stay here; playing host is the last thing she wants to do. But when she stands and moves from the deck back into the house, Charlie is boiling the kettle and Grace is showing Emma-Rose upstairs to one of the two guest rooms. They don't expect her to host. This is the base, the trench, the war cabinet. This is where and how they'll stick together and figure out what's going on.

Resolute now, she smiles at Xavi and beckons him to follow her to the second guest bedroom. Grace can take her room, she decides, and she'll take Ré's.

When she comes back down, Charlie is standing at the island whisking eggs. On the hob, a pan heats.

'Scrambled eggs and toast for everyone,' he says, looking up. 'Quick and easy, and, let's face it, one of only two dishes I can make. Hope you don't mind?'

'Thanks, Charlie. I don't think I could eat, but you guys should. Xavi must be starving.'

'Yeah, especially with a hangover. I'd say he's desperate to get out for a breakfast roll, but even Xavi knows that would be insensitive.'

'Is he living with you permanently now?'

A nod. 'When I think of all the years I spent trying to connect with him, make the house an appealing place for a kid to stay. Now I can't get rid of him.' He shakes his head. 'Twenty-eight years old and no sign of him getting a place of his own.'

'But he works, I presume?'

'If you could call it that. He's an actor. And as everyone knows, acting jobs are not an easy way to pay the rent. So he does some investing in currencies and whatnot – his own money, I should add, he's not getting any of mine for that – and he's also a consultant.' Charlie lowers the whisk to make air quotes when he says 'consultant'. 'Helps people find their dream home.'

'That's pretty cool,' she says, on autopilot.

'It *would* be if people couldn't do it themselves by clicking into MyHome or Rightmove and if I didn't have to give him a monthly allowance while he gets on his feet for the last two years.' A sigh. 'Ah, he's not the worst, a product of his upbringing, I suppose.' He seasons the eggs with a small amount of salt and a good grind of black pepper. 'How's work going for Ré?'

Siobhán swallows. This attempt at normalcy is well intended, but she can't do it. Her eyes brim and she lowers herself into a chair.

'Sorry,' Charlie says, his voice low. 'We'll find them. I know we will.'

'I just . . . I'm so scared something's happened to Ré. But also, that she . . .'

'That she did something to Luna?' he asks. 'Do you really think Ré would hurt Luna?'

'No.' She shakes her head. 'But also, I don't know . . . And then I feel guilty for even entertaining that idea.' She lays her hands flat on the table, staring at her nails, the polish that had mattered yesterday. 'The thing is, we'll always believe the best of our own kids. And that's as it should be. We're their most important advocates, so it's our job to believe in them. To defend them. And realistically, what parent thinks their own child will do something terrible? But obviously that's what the parents of the people who do terrible things think, too. We can't all be right.' She looks up at Charlie. 'My heart says no, she didn't do anything bad. My head says maybe she did. I want to be wrong, but also, that the doubt even exists says something, doesn't it? My child is not perfect. Nobody's child is perfect.' She exhales slowly, a long, shuddery breath. 'Every bad deed ever is carried out by a person who was once someone's child.'

The plate of eggs and toast is warm and almost comforting in her hands, but the smell makes her feel sick. The others stand around the island eating. All but Grace, who, like Siobhán, just stares at the food.

'What do you think it was?' Xavi says after a bit. 'The thing the guards noticed in the catering kitchen?'

'O'Connell will let us know when we see her, I guess,' Grace says dully.

'I don't know if she will.' Charlie butters more toast. 'There's a limit to what they'll tell us.'

Xavi puts his empty plate down on the island. 'What, like we're suspects?'

'No, Xavi,' Emma-Rose interjects, her tone patient but condescending. 'Since either Ré or Luna called the police on the other, there aren't any additional suspects involved.'

Siobhán flinches.

Charlie jumps in again. 'Xavi, the guards don't know what went down, and any one of us could be hiding something. *We* know we're not, but obviously they don't know us from Adam.'

'OK, guys, it was just a question.' Xavi sounds tetchy. He's probably still nursing a hangover, wishing he was in his own bed.

Charlie takes a bite of toast. How is he eating, Siobhán wonders? How is he so calm?

Emma-Rose looks up from her phone. She's already set her plate aside, eggs eaten, unbuttered toast untouched. 'I could text Ben to ask if he knows what they found?'

They all look to one another, as though waiting for someone to give permission. Siobhán bites her lip.

'Good idea,' Grace says. 'Go for it.'

Emma-Rose types on her phone, and they wait in silence. A buzz tells them there's a reply, and Emma-Rose reads it out loud.

'Ben says, "There was a knife missing from the set I brought with me and left in the catering kitchen. I hadn't even looked until the police asked. And the spare keys for the van weren't there either."'

Siobhán tries to take it in, to process. Missing knife, missing keys, missing van. Two missing girls. One missing phone. And Siobhán can't help thinking, that last part – the presence of Ré's phone, the absence of Luna's – must mean something more?

16

As the others to and fro about the missing keys and the missing knife, Siobhán paces, trying to order her thoughts, to stay calm, to think things through. One fact keeps jumping out: Ré's phone was left behind. Does that indicate she's the victim? She *is* scatty; she often forgets her phone. Especially when she's stressed, rushing. Luna is more organized. Ré used to call her Little Miss Perfect when they were small. Not meanly, just . . . *observationally*. Or was it? This news that the girls argue a lot has shaken Siobhán. They're 'horrible' to each other, Kayla had said. Siobhán doesn't like to think of Ré being horrible to anyone. That she can more easily imagine Luna being horrible doesn't paint her in the best light. She's always been irritated by parents who believe their own child can do no wrong, that someone else's child must be at fault, the bad influence, the antagonist of the story. Yet isn't that what she's doing right now? And isn't that what they did ten years ago, during Jasmine's fall from grace? There are two sides to every story, and the truth usually lies somewhere in between.

'Siobhán?' Grace's voice interrupts her thoughts. 'Is there something else?'

'I'm just still trying to think of anything that might have caused a fight between the girls,' Siobhán replies.

'What if we look at the photos from last night?' Charlie suggests. 'We've looked at the security camera footage, but shouldn't we check through any photos on our phones?'

Siobhán nods. How did she not think of this sooner? She still has a nagging sense that something happened over the weekend, something she's not seeing that might provide a hint to what's going on. She begins scrolling through her photo gallery, and the others follow suit, all five of them clustered around the island, thumbing through pictures. Pictures from a time that seems a million years ago, Siobhán thinks, her heart contracting. A photo of Ré filling a plate at breakfast, wearing the T-shirt she'd worn to bed and an oversized cartoon grin for her mother's camera. A selfie when they were ready for the ceremony. Then a full-length picture, this time taken by Xavi – Ré and Siobhán, side by side, arms around one another. Siobhán in a jade-green halter-neck, Ré in her black prom-style dress. Everything so bright and sunny and perfect. She stares at Ré's face, her expression, looking for something – *anything* – that could hint at what was about to unfold. Tears brim as she scrolls on through photos of the bride and groom, the pretty white chairs laid out for the ceremony. The sky changing colour, the dancing, the glasses of champagne. A selfie at the cocktail bar, a clink of margaritas. Ré still smiling, less cartoon, more real now. A picture of the crowded dancefloor – Charlie, Ré, Emma-Rose, two of Emma-Rose's friends, Xavi, Charlie's next-door neighbour and, to Siobhán's surprise, even Charlie's mother. In this photo, Luna appears for the first time. It strikes Siobhán that Jasmine is right. Ré and Luna weren't together much at the wedding. Luna is in the background, looking over at the group. And it's just one photo, a snapshot of a moment. And a camera can capture an expression that's fleeting in real life and give it permanency. And it might mean nothing, but there's something about Luna's stare.

Siobhán glances at Grace, who has her head over her own phone.

'Grace.' She holds up her screen. 'Was Luna OK last night? She looks kind of pissed off in this one.'

Grace rears up. 'What – she failed to smile for the camera so she's a murderer?'

'God, no!' Siobhán lifts a hand. To placate her friend, to defend herself. 'I genuinely just wondered if she was OK? She's not in any of my other photos.'

'Well. She's in mine, and she's fine in all of them.'

There's no rulebook for this kind of conversation, and Grace's retort has a justifiable snip to it. Then again, Grace did lie to her about the mugging, so maybe she could climb down from her high horse for a minute . . . That lie still feels disconcerting, even if it was for good reasons. Grace is many things, and she's not everyone's cup of tea, but she doesn't usually lie to Siobhán. Up until today, Siobhán would have said she trusted Grace implicitly, trusted her with her life.

She pushes on, holds up her phone to Xavi. 'Do you remember anything from this bit – how Ré was then?' She checks the time the photo was taken. 'Just after one?'

'Only that we were having fun, dancing, drinking.'

Charlie cranes his neck to see what's on Siobhán's screen. 'Am I in the photo? I barely remember that. God, I'm too old for day drinking.'

'You can say that again,' Xavi mutters.

Charlie looks at him. 'What's that?'

'You don't remember?'

'Remember what?'

'You got really annoyed with me soon after that.' Xavi's

handsome face settles into a slight sulk. 'Sent me inside to sober up, even though you were the one who had clearly overdone it.' His lips tighten. 'Like I was a teenage kid who'd nicked a bottle from the drinks cabinet.'

Charlie scratches his head. 'Jeez. Sorry, Xavi. I don't even know what that was about.'

'Yeah. That makes two of us.'

Siobhán files it away. It's probably not relevant, but the questions are worth asking.

'Is there anything else we can think of?' Siobhán looks around. 'Anything to suggest the girls weren't getting on?'

Emma-Rose looks up. 'There is one thing. When I emailed both of them about sharing the pool house, I don't think they were too happy.' She shakes her head. 'I thought they'd be pleased.' A glance at her husband. 'We had to let Charlie's mother have Luna's room, obviously, but Luna knew that in advance. I think she was fine until she realized she'd have to share. And they both asked if there were any other options.' Emma-Rose tucks her hair behind her ear. 'I thought it was a bit cheeky, to be honest.' She stops. 'Sorry. Anyway, I assumed they just wanted their own space, didn't want to share with anyone. But maybe they didn't want to share with each other?'

Siobhán nods slowly at this new information. Perhaps it's time to speak with Abbey, their other friend who was in Marrakesh. She glances at Grace. The words are on the tip of her tongue – an invitation to come with her – but she stops. Maybe this would be easier on her own . . . Grace is her oldest friend. She loves her. She'll never fall out with her, not over this, not over anything. But this situation is hard to talk around. Keeping things on an even keel is difficult. Nerves are frayed. Maybe it would be good for both of them to have half an hour's breathing space. They're still on the same side, and this . . . this will help keep it that way.

17

The day before the wedding

EMMA-ROSE IS IN FLYING form at dinner on Friday evening. She keeps calling it a rehearsal dinner, as though they're on an American TV show. And to be fair, it's a pretty spectacular spread, Siobhán thinks, looking around. The patio and pool deck have been transformed with twinkling lights and lanterns and a long table around which they sit at carefully inscribed place names. Candles flicker along the length of the table, casting a soft glow. The catering staff – the same three people who had served lunch – are placing scallop starters in front of each guest. The champagne has already been poured.

Emma-Rose stands, bright and shiny in her gold sequin dress and blonder-than-ever hair, tapping a teaspoon to a glass.

'Before we begin, I'd like to thank you all for being here. Tomorrow will be busy – we have forty-five friends joining us for the wedding party, but tonight is all about family and' – a glance at Siobhán and Ré – 'old friends.'

There is just the slightest emphasis on the word 'old', and Siobhán fights an eyeroll as they stand to clink glasses. Emma-Rose has never said as much, but Siobhán suspects that Charlie's bride-to-be cannot fathom why she is such an integral part of his life.

'Everything is so lovely, Emma-Rose,' Siobhán says when they sit again. 'Your wedding planner seems great. Where did you find her?'

'Through Charlie, funnily enough.'

This is not what Siobhán was expecting. Surely Charlie remembers what happened with Jasmine?

Emma-Rose must see the surprise on Siobhán's face.

'I *know*. Charlie's not the first person you'd task with sourcing your wedding planner. And it's about the only thing he's done so far, but I guess when it's your third wedding . . .' Emma-Rose grimaces, and Siobhán feels a tiny moment of connection in that little chink in the armour.

'Anyway, to be fair, she was a brilliant find. David in his golf club recommended her – she's his niece or godchild, I think. Blooms Day is her business name. She's on Insta.' She arches a brow. 'In case you ever decide to tie the knot with someone.'

Siobhán makes a mental note to grab Charlie to ask what on earth he was thinking, and changes the subject.

'Your family couldn't make tonight's dinner?' she asks Emma-Rose.

Ré, beside Siobhán on her left, inclines her head to listen. Grace, on her right, is busy chatting across the table with Luna.

'Oh, it's just me.' Emma-Rose smiles, but her eyes glisten suddenly. 'It was only my mum and me growing up, but as you know, she passed away last year. That's why we kept the wedding small, avoided the traditional head table.'

'Oh god, of course,' Siobhán says. She knew this. Why did she ask such a stupid question? 'It must be hard not having your mum here. I'm so sorry. Do you have any extended family?'

'Not really – a heap of first cousins, but' – she rolls her eyes – 'most of our interactions are through solicitors, arguing over crumbling properties and old wills. So no, it'll be mostly friends tomorrow. Found family, isn't that what they say.' She clears her throat, her eyes still glistening. 'Anyway, tell me more about your family.' She addresses Ré. 'Charlie tells me your dad – Aidan, is it? – lives in Australia. That must make it hard to see him?'

Siobhán feels Ré stiffen beside her and jumps in to answer.

'Oh, they don't . . . Ré hasn't met Aidan.' *Fuck.* Does Emma-Rose not know?

'Oh really? Wow, I hadn't realized. So, he just lives too far away, or?'

Siobhán's skin prickles with heat. They never talk about Aidan. Is Emma-Rose doing this on purpose?

'He doesn't know about Ré. He and I were together only very briefly.'

On her right, Grace appears to have just tuned in to the topic.

'Now that's *one* way of putting it,' she says with a wink.

Shut the fuck up, Grace, Siobhán says with a nudge of her elbow. Grace, to be fair, does not know the truth; does not know why she doesn't talk about Aidan. A sliver of unease sets in.

'This is fascinating!' Emma-Rose says. 'So you've never met him, Ré? He genuinely doesn't know you exist?'

A tiny nod from Ré.

'Siobhán, you dark horse!'

Siobhán has a sudden sense that this is an attempt at bonding. One Emma-Rose is going about very badly . . .

'Where did you meet him?' Emma-Rose goes on, clearly not picking up on Siobhán's discomfort.

'A concert. Robbie Williams in Lansdowne Road.' Siobhán forces a stiff smile.

'Oh my goodness, I was there, too!' Emma-Rose lets out an uncharacteristic squeal. 'Imagine. We might have passed each other, not knowing we'd end up here a quarter of a century later.'

'Yes. I mean, there were thousands of people there, but . . . sure. Anyway, it's an old story, it's not something we keep hidden.' Siobhán works to keep her voice even, her tone casual, conscious that Ré is right beside her. Hoping, as ever, that Ré never actually meets Aidan.

18

Seven months earlier

THE IDEA HAD POPPED in and out of her head sporadically during her teens, but until last year, Ré hadn't done anything about it. She'd never needed a dad, never missed having one. Siobhán was everything to her, and Ré often felt that, as an only child, the parent–kid ratio was as good as that of any of her friends. But something had changed last year. Something Luna had said one night over drinks: she'd been banging on about how great a boyfriend Theo was, how glad she was to find someone she could imagine introducing to her dad.

Luna's words echoed that night as Ré fell asleep. *Someone she could imagine introducing to her dad.* Ré would never get to do that. She'd never even met him herself.

Her mother had been matter-of-fact on details: Aidan, an Australian lecturer who had spent a term at UCD School of Business – they'd met on a night out and Aidan had ended up back in her flat, before flying home to Melbourne two days later. Nine months after that, along came Ré. Siobhán said she didn't know Aidan's surname and hadn't asked for a number – there was hardly any point when they lived on opposite sides of the world, and it was never intended to be anything more than a bit of fun, a one-night stand, no strings attached. Ha. Famous last words.

When Ré was small, she'd asked her mum once or twice if they should try to find Aidan. She only knew his first name, Siobhán had explained, and Melbourne was a big city. There was no way to track him down. But even at a very young age, Ré couldn't help thinking there was something more to this.

When Ré turned eighteen, she asked again, and her mum told her the bit of the story she'd left out – Aidan had been married. Siobhán didn't know this until his wedding ring slipped from his jeans pocket when he picked them off the floor the following morning. He didn't try to cover it up, she said. He tucked it back in his pocket, dipped his head, and said goodbye.

So best we don't go searching for him, Siobhán had said. Let sleeping dogs lie.

But last year, maybe prompted by Luna's comments, it began really nagging at Ré. What was he like, this Aidan from Australia? Would she look like him? Did she get her clumsiness, her impulsiveness, from him? If Aidan was in her life, would she understand herself better? Maybe none of it mattered. But still, she was curious. And she began her own quiet search.

She hadn't confided in her mother; she couldn't. Siobhán had expressly told her not to do this. And she wouldn't do anything to jeopardize Aidan's marriage, no way. She just wanted to know a bit more.

She started asking her mother some casual questions (Which university in Melbourne? What was his area of study, exactly?) and she began searching online. It took time and effort and some false leads, and soon the project consumed her, occupying every waking minute. She was laser-focused, energized. Finding Aidan was in that moment her only goal.

And then, one day, she did.

Aidan Kiely, economics lecturer at the University of Melbourne, had mentioned in an online interview for the college that he'd spent time on sabbatical at UCD in Dublin. It *had* to be him. Ré thought for a minute about how best to approach it, then sent an email to the university, asking to interview Aidan for a blog – a flimsy fib, but hopefully enough to get his email address. That's when she found out Aidan had moved to another university, this time in London. It was a sign from the universe. She was doing the right thing.

After that, it was easy. She contacted him through his college email address, explaining she was reaching out to people who may have known her mother, Siobhán McKenna. It struck her that it might sound like Siobhán was dead, but she'd worry about that later. At first, she heard nothing. She paced and fidgeted for three days, waiting and wondering if she should try again.

Then, on the fourth day, Aidan replied. A friendly three-line response to say he remembered Siobhán fondly. If he suspected Ré's real reason for getting in touch, it didn't show. Then again, she hadn't mentioned her age. The next step was asking to meet for coffee. She wasn't sure he'd go for it, but it turned out that Aidan was a pretty outgoing, easy-going kind of guy who didn't hesitate to say yes to meeting Siobhán McKenna's daughter.

And so here she is, at a window seat in the Alfred Tennyson bar, waiting to meet her father for the first time. Outside, Belgravia twinkles with Christmas lights. Inside, it's warm and buzzy. A group of women at the table beside Ré's clink champagne glasses, bunching together for a selfie. Ré hasn't ordered anything yet. What do you even drink in this kind of situation? Empty-handed, she watches the door.

She recognizes him as soon as he walks in – his picture on the college website is clearly recent. Tall, dark hair turning grey, black-rimmed glasses and a pleasant smile. A little like Hugh Jackman. Or maybe that's just because he's Australian. Does he look like her? Around the eyes, maybe? Or is it only that they both wear glasses? She watches as he glances around. He doesn't know what she looks like, of course. God. Is she really doing this? Her hand is raised, waving. She is doing this, it seems.

'Ré?' He walks over to her table, and she stands to greet him.

'Yes, hi, Aidan. Thanks for meeting me.'

He takes her in as he sits, curiosity on his warm, open face.

'I'm sorry to hear about your mother. I didn't know her well, but she seemed like a great person.'

Of course that's what he thinks.

'I . . .' The right words are not coming now. Why hadn't she scripted this?

'I hadn't actually realized she had children when I met her,' he adds.

'Child. It's just me, no siblings,' Ré says.

'She must have been very young when she passed. I'm so sorry.'

Oh god, she has to fix this.

'The thing is, she's not dead, and this is completely my fault. I confused you. My wording was badly chosen and, well . . . I looked for you because' – *don't say it, it's too soon, break it more gently* – 'I think you might be my dad.'

Jesus. Did she really just blurt that out?

Aidan's mouth drops open.

'Oh. Oh!' Realization dawning in real time.

A server arrives at the table to take their order. On autopilot, Ré asks for a cappuccino.

'I'm going to need something stronger,' Aidan says, though he's smiling. He turns to the server. 'Could I have a gin and tonic?'

'You know what? Me too, please,' Ré says. 'Cancel the cappuccino.'

'So.' Aidan stares at her. Taken aback, she thinks, but . . . not in a bad way?

'So.'

'Sorry, I'm kind of stuck for words.' He shakes himself. 'God, that sounds bad – please don't take it the wrong way.'

'I've just ambushed you with some fairly substantial news. Feel free to be speechless.'

'Let me start over. It's lovely to meet you, Ré McKenna. I . . . I don't have any children – well, any other children. My wife and I split long ago, and I never met anyone else. So this is . . . it's a pretty big deal!'

'Yeah. For me, too. And just to say, I'm not, you know, looking for anything. And my mum doesn't know I'm here.'

'You didn't want to tell her?'

'She asked me not to look for you.'

'Right.'

'Because you were' – her cheeks heat up – 'well, because you were married and she didn't want to do anything that might cause trouble, you know?'

'Ah, OK. My wife had moved in with her boss before my trip to Ireland and we divorced soon after I got back, but it's quite possible I told your mother I was married.' He picks up a beer mat, tears a little piece off. 'I was still holding out hope that my wife would see her boss for the smarmy git he was, but . . .' A small shrug, a wry smile.

'No, you didn't tell her you were married, but your ring slipped out of your pocket.'

'Oh. That's embarrassing. Anyway, thank you for reaching out. I'm really happy to meet you.'

'Don't you want to know if it's, like, I don't know, definitely true?'

On any TV show Ré's ever watched, the newly informed dads never believe it at first.

He arches his brows. 'Why would you make it up?'

So easy. So straightforward. This is not what TV told her to expect. This guy is almost too good to be true, but maybe she needs to drop the cynicism.

Two gin and tonics arrive and he lifts his towards her.

'Cheers to you, Ré McKenna. It's a pleasure to meet you.'

They clink, and she feels warm and fuzzy inside before taking even a first sip.

'So.' Small talk with her new dad . . . where to even start? She goes for something basic. 'You live here now?'

'Yep. My parents were Irish and English – the name Kiely probably gave the Irish bit away. They moved to Australia when they got married, and that's where I was born, but I've always felt a strong connection to this side of the world. A post came up in the London School of Economics two years ago and I jumped at it.'

Two years. Her dad's been just a few miles from her for the last two years.

'Oh wow. And where do you live?'

He tells her he's in Herne Hill, and that he's got a good circle of friends through the university and a triathlon club he's joined. They chat easily, and at the end of their drink – he's going to a dinner party; she's meeting friends – he asks if she's planning to tell her mother. She's not. For now, at least. She can't. Siobhán had said not to search for him, and she'd done just that. She will, though, in due course, she thinks. Once she's met with him a few more times. What could be the harm in that?

19

Now

SIOBHÁN WALKS OUT TO the hall and picks up her keys.

'I'm going out for a bit,' she calls back to the group in the kitchen. 'To clear my head.' Already it sounds false.

Grace looks puzzled. 'Are you going out to search?' She moves to stand. 'I'll come with you.'

'I'd search if I had the first clue where to start.' Siobhán's shoulders drop. 'Sorry, I don't mean to sound snappy. I'll be better able for this after a half-hour on my own.'

Grace stares at her a fraction longer than necessary. Siobhán's cheeks heat up. Why doesn't she just tell Grace she's going to speak with Abbey? It's not too late to say it now . . . But she doesn't. She turns and leaves.

Abbey is at work in Indigo Bean, a café in Dún Laoghaire – a weekend job that helps supplement her earnings from her day job. It's become a meeting spot for all of them, with Abbey doling out about-to-be-binned pastries at the end of the day and occasional free refills of coffee. Ré and Luna don't get to hang out here often, but they still come in whenever they're home, and suddenly, as Siobhán pushes through the door, she imagines finding them here, sitting at their usual corner booth, chattering over iced lattes and cinnamon rolls. The familiar interior, buzzing with Sunday brunchers, is a gut punch in this new world where Ré is missing.

Abbey is apologetic – she has only five minutes to spare for Siobhán while her co-worker covers her tables. She beckons Siobhán back out of the café.

'I'm so sorry,' she says, pulling a vape from her apron pocket. They've moved down the street from the café now, to stand in the doorway of a solicitor's office. 'I feel like I should be doing something to help, but I'm stuck here till four. Or will I just tell them I have to go? It feels so wrong to be working when this is going on . . .'

'No, that's OK. We're the same. We don't know where to start. That's why we're trying to find out everything we can about what was going on with those two. Do you know of anything – any arguments?'

A gentle shrug. 'I mean, they argue.'

So it seems. 'Anything worse than usual – something about Marrakesh?'

'They were both upset, for sure. But, like, it was three months ago.'

'Can you tell me what happened?'

Abbey does, and the story matches with Prisha's, giving Siobhán no new clues.

'OK, is there anywhere you can think of that they might go? Like, somewhere someone could . . . hide out?' Her stomach knots at the words.

'Not really . . . oh, wait! I just thought of something. Theo's family home. It's empty a lot because his parents are in Marbella most of the time and, obviously, Theo's in Canada.'

'OK – go on?'

'Theo's been pretty free and easy with the keys over the years, getting extras cut for people who're visiting or just want somewhere to crash, a place to stay while they're between apartments. His parents wouldn't be *hugely* aware of this.'

'Right. Would Ré or Luna have a key?'

'Definitely Luna. She had one when they were together. She and Theo used to stay there a bit when she was home from London, especially during cold weather, because the heating in his flat was crap.'

Siobhán's heart leaps. This could be it. This could be where they are.

'And would Ré have a key?'

A shrug. 'Maybe? And there's one in the key safe at the side of the house. Theo gave us all the code; it's 2221. God, Theo's parents would go ballistic if they knew. But they're in Marbella and, also, Theo's always been good at hiding things.'

Siobhán phones Grace from the car, tells her she'll pick her up in ten minutes, that she might have a lead.

'So you *did* go searching without me,' Grace says, an edge to her voice. 'What's going on? Is this because you think Luna is the one who did something? You don't trust me? You're—'

Siobhán cuts in. 'No, absolutely not. I was out driving and I passed Indigo Bean and remembered Abbey worked there. That's all.' It's a lie that's almost true – she *could* have thought of Abbey while she was out driving. And it will keep the peace.

Grace says nothing for a moment, then, in a slightly clipped tone, tells Siobhán she'll be waiting in the driveway.

Ten minutes after Siobhán collects Grace, they're standing outside Theo's family home, a decaying Edwardian house in Glasthule. There's a sense that it was once as well kept as its neighbours either side, but perhaps with Theo's parents away, it has deteriorated. The long, narrow driveway is bordered with shrubs, half hiding a tangle of weeds and calf-high grass behind. The house has an austere, unfriendly feel, maybe because most of the time nobody lives here. The windows are dark, like eyes watching Siobhán and Grace. Side by side, they stare at the front door. The woodwork around it needs a coat of paint and the tiled porch step is dusty. Siobhán swallows. Could the girls be inside?

She looks at Grace, and Grace nods. Siobhán tries the bell, in case Theo's parents are not actually in Marbella. In case her daughter answers the door and has an explanation for everything. But there's no answer, only silence.

The key safe is exactly where Abbey told Siobhán it would be – around the side of the house behind the green bins. Back at the front door, her stomach in knots, Siobhán inserts the key and turns it. Beside her, Grace's breath is audibly short.

They step inside the house.

The hall is wide, with yellowy pine floors and a faded runner leading to an open kitchen door. Wordlessly, they move to the kitchen. Oak cupboards, dark green walls, flagstone floor. A large, well-worn table, six chairs. Siobhán opens a door off the kitchen that leads to a dining room and on to a sitting room.

'Upstairs?' Grace whispers. Siobhán nods. They should have told O'Connell they were doing this. What if there's . . . what if . . . She bites down on the thought and climbs the carpeted steps.

The first bedroom looks like it must be Theo's parents' room, its only furniture a double bed, two bedside tables and built-in sliderobes. It has an underused, dusty feel. Next to it is another double bedroom. White furniture, pink lamps.

'Theo has an older sister,' Grace whispers. 'She's moved out.'

The next bedroom is smaller, but only just. A double bed with a dark blue duvet cover. A desk. A bookcase with a mishmash of books, a web of tangled phone chargers, a tattered pencil case, a yellowing newspaper, a can of Lynx and a cross-country trophy lying on its side.

'This feels wrong,' Grace whispers. 'Snooping in Theo's old bedroom.'

Siobhán deflates. She'd been so sure there'd be some kind of answer here. Not *sure* so much as hopeful – clinging to driftwood in a sea of unknowns.

She follows Grace to the door, instinctively reaching to upright the cross-country trophy, and in doing so, she knocks the newspaper to the floor. When she bends to pick it up, a Polaroid photo slips from beneath the pages, and she picks that up, too, then freezes, staring, as her brain takes a moment to process what her eyes are seeing.

20

THE PHOTO IS OF a couple, faces turned towards each other, lips touching. The boy is Theo. And the girl is Ré.

Siobhán is reeling. Theo and Ré? Why would Ré not tell her this? And what was Ré doing with Luna's boyfriend? Ex-boyfriend?

An intake of breath at her shoulder reminds her Grace is here, too.

'Did you know about this?' Grace's tone is knife-sharp.

'No. Maybe it's just something . . . I mean, they're friends?'

'This looks like more than friends,' Grace snaps.

It does. Sure, they all hung out together when Theo was seeing Luna, but there's no obvious explanation for this photo. Siobhán is reeling, trying to make sense of it, and somewhere at the edge of all of this, although it shouldn't matter, Grace's coldness stings.

'So Ré was seeing Theo behind Luna's back.' Grace says it more like a statement than a question. 'That's why they fought? That's what Luna's text to Prisha meant? "Just found out something from Ré that's upset me"?'

'No . . . this must be from a different time. Before or after Luna and Theo were together.' Siobhán peers at the photo. Ré's hair is similar to how it is now, the asymmetric bob she's had for years, trimmed to precision every six weeks. She's wearing a black sweatshirt that could be one of any number of black sweatshirts she's owned since forever.

Grace points at the photo, at a tiny dot on Ré's nose. 'When did Ré get her nose re-pierced? After it closed up?'

'Last summer some time. July.'

'Which is about a month after Theo and Luna got together,' Grace points out.

'But this could be from any time since they broke up, too. Honestly, Ré wouldn't do that to Luna. You *know* that.'

'But we *don't* know that – we don't know anything with certainty.' Grace's voice goes up a notch and Siobhán steps back, uneasy, uncomfortable. She knows this side of Grace, she can see the warning signs – her voice going up, her cheeks blotching red. But Siobhán has never been on the receiving end of Grace's bite. Various teachers, coaches, mechanics, retailers have, for sure, but never Siobhán.

'There's blood, a missing knife, a 999 call. You can't honestly say, "Ré wouldn't do that." Maybe you don't know her as well as you thought you did.'

The words sting, and Siobhán digs her nails into her palms, trying to quell the hurt and resentment that bubble up in response. She keeps her voice low, her tone even, pushing down what she'd really like to say.

'I suppose neither of us knows them as well as we thought.'

Grace looks frustrated. 'But it's . . . look, it just feels like Ré is the loose cannon in all this. The powder keg. I was there, remember? The tantrums. Throwing things. Flying off the handle over the smallest stress. I'm the one you confided in when you thought there was something wrong with her. When you were googling psychiatrists.' Grace's face crumples; she reaches for Siobhán's arm. 'I'm sorry, I know this is awful, I hate saying it, but what if she lost it? What if she . . .'

Siobhán's face heats up. Is Grace really saying these words? *Isn't it possible, though?* Isn't it true that Ré can be impulsive, lash out when she's angry? A memory surfaces. One of the worst days of Ré's time in primary school, back when she was seven or eight. A call from the principal, a summons for Siobhán. Ré had pushed Ava Sheeran, a classmate, and Ava had sprained her wrist in the fall. *Mr and Mrs Sheeran are not best pleased*, she remembers the principal saying. It turned out that Ava Sheeran had been throwing conkers at Ré and had refused to stop. Eventually, Ré saw red and pushed her. This was always the problem. The provocation and the taking things too far. And all focus was now on the sprained wrist and the possible legal action that Mr and Mrs Sheeran might take. This was one of the few moments – facing this alone – that had made Siobhán wish she was part of a Mr and Mrs, too.

She had dreaded pick-up that Tuesday afternoon, feeling the collective gaze of the other parents. They were a pretty nice bunch generally, but sprained-wrist drama brings whispers. Siobhán had stood there, a little apart, pretending to look at her phone, her face hot, wishing she wasn't on her own. Wishing Grace was there. But Tuesday was Luna's after-school violin class, so Siobhán stood there alone.

Except, then, Grace *did* arrive. She'd forgotten it was Tuesday, she said. She'd forgotten about violin, that Luna wouldn't finish till later. She'd stood chatting to Siobhán until the class came out. When Siobhán took Ré's hand, Grace took her other hand. And as a trio they walked back to Siobhán's car, chattering, ignoring the looks.

Now, in Theo's room, Siobhán turns to her oldest friend.

'Grace, I—'

Siobhán doesn't really know what she's going to say next, but Grace's phone pings with a text just then, giving her time to think. Grace pulls her phone from her pocket, glances down. Then her face changes.

'Oh god.' Grace stares at the screen, sagging against the wall of Theo's bedroom.

Siobhán grabs her arm. 'What? What is it?'

Grace puts one hand to her mouth, still leaning against the wall. 'A text. A text from Luna.'

Everything hits Siobhán at once. Hope. Terror. *They're alive. No,* Luna *is alive.* And now she's jealous and relieved and heartbroken and confused.

Her throat works to get words out. 'What does she say? Where are they?' Siobhán hears from her voice that she's crying.

Grace turns the phone to show Siobhán, her hand shaking.

There it is, stark and clear and life-shattering:

Mom I'm sorry I messed up

21

The day before the wedding

RÉ LOOKS AROUND THE table, enjoying the warm evening light and the buzz of the champagne. Other than being stuck so near Emma-Rose, Ré reckons she's going to enjoy this pre-wedding 'rehearsal' dinner. Charlie and Emma-Rose have gone completely over the top with all of it. A beef fillet main course, a pecan cheesecake dessert, and champagne with everything. She's lost in thoughts of food and drink when Emma-Rose zeroes in on her, catching her off guard.

'Charlie tells me your dad – Aidan, is it? – lives in Australia. That must make it hard to see him?'

Ré tenses.

Siobhán jumps in, and as she explains that Ré has never met Aidan, heat flames in Ré's cheeks. She is absolutely definitely going to tell her mother about Aidan, but tonight is not the night. Emma-Rose begins grilling Siobhán about the long-ago one-night stand and, however irritating this is, now that Ré has met Aidan, it's interesting hearing her mother talk about him. The picture she's always had in her head has been replaced by the real Aidan, though her mother's words remain the same. Siobhán's talking now about meeting him at a concert, and Ré listens more avidly. She'd known it was a night out, but not what kind of night out. A Robbie Williams concert, of all things. She can imagine Siobhán at a Robbie Williams concert, but not so much Aidan. This secret thought makes her smile. Now Emma-Rose is banging on about being there as well.

'Speaking of concerts,' she says to Ré, 'will you go to Electric Picnic this year? Luna was so sad to miss it last year. Seems like she missed *all* sorts, she was telling me after.'

Siobhán gives Ré a questioning look, perhaps hearing the emphasis on 'all sorts'.

'Yeah, I think so. Not sure if Luna's going, though . . .' Ré trails off as Emma-Rose is distracted by Jasmine's arrival.

Beside Emma-Rose, Xavi is looking at his phone. He glances up, mouths something that looks like 'Sorry' and darts his eyes towards his new stepmother.

Ré smiles at him. It must be tough going living with Emma-Rose. Then again – Ré looks around at the house, the pool, the garden – it certainly has its upsides.

An hour later, the cheesecake has been consumed and the catering staff are beginning to clear the plates. More drinks are poured, with Charlie, in his element, playing cocktail maker. He has every spirit and liqueur known to humankind and is kept on his toes with requests for ever more obscure cocktails, particularly from Ré and Xavi. Luna, who spent most of the day on a lounger and threw on a kaftan at dinner time, has gone to change. Jasmine is a constant presence in the background – hovering, making sure everything's running smoothly. Ré still can't get her head around it, this transformation. Jasmine looks like a different person entirely. Back then she was spiky. Electric. Like if you touched her, you might burn. They could never quite relax around

Jasmine, but god, she was fun. Life was always more interesting when she was there. And now . . . it's awkward. The way they ghosted her. The way they followed their mothers' instructions. Like sheep. Snapshots of that last night sear Ré's mind now as she watches Jasmine speak with the catering manager. Should they talk to her? Clear the air? Maybe Luna will know what to do.

Luna is in their shared bedroom in the pool house, steaming the dress she'll wear to tomorrow's wedding.

'You actually brought a steamer with you?' Ré says, flopping on her bed.

'Yeah. How do you plan to get the creases out of your dress?'

Good question, Ré thinks, eyeing up her weekend bag, which still contains tomorrow's outfit. That was probably a mistake. Then again, she can always borrow Luna's steamer . . .

'Oh – Mum was saying you saw me with some guy?' Ré says, carefully, casually.

'Yes! Who was that – your boss? A sugar daddy?' Luna winks theatrically.

'Just a work colleague. But now my mother thinks I'm seeing some older guy. For whatever reason, your mom said it to her.' Ré tries to keep a hint of accusation out of her voice.

Luna tosses her hair. 'Oh, you know what those two are like. They have no love lives of their own so live vicariously through ours.'

This is true. Ré's mum has been on about three dates that Ré can remember, but has never been able to really devote the time to meeting someone. Her priorities, she always says, are her two babies – Ré and her business. Ré has a feeling her mother is trying to model singledom as a good life choice, trying to resist admitting to Ré that, actually, yes, sometimes she wouldn't mind a person in her life. And Ré would be quite happy if Siobhán met someone, not least to stop her worrying that her mum is lonely with her gone. She wonders if that's selfish, and decides it's just human. Grace, on the other hand, dates regularly, but prefers not to get into any kind of serious relationship. Ré had spotted her eyeing up the Scottish catering guy over dinner and wonders, but doesn't ask, if Luna saw it, too. Luna can be funny about her mother's flings, mostly pretending they're not happening.

'Speaking of love lives,' Ré says, 'have you heard anything from Theo?'

'No, why would I? He lives in Canada.' A telltale flush tinges Luna's cheeks and Ré changes the subject.

'So, pretty weird seeing Jasmine.'

Luna's eyes widen. 'I know. Awkward. Have you spoken to her?'

'Nope, but our paths haven't crossed, so I haven't *not* spoken to her. I guess I'm hiding here to ensure the continued non-crossing of paths . . . What do you think we should do?'

'I honestly don't know . . .' Luna turns back to her dress, running the steamer down its length again. It's a beautiful shade of turquoise that will be stunning with her colouring. Ré wonders if she should have broken away from her lifelong uniform of black.

Luna steps back to admire her work. 'Maybe we just front it out, say nothing.'

'We were pretty shit to her, though.' Ré leans to unzip her holdall. She should maybe hang up the dress, at least. 'We probably owe her an apology.'

'Stop,' Luna scoffs. 'We don't! She *stole* from you.'

'Oh, come on, Luna.' Ré sits up to shake out the dress. It is indeed fairly crumpled. 'It was ten years ago.' She would dearly like to point out that Jasmine isn't the only teen who ever stole, that Luna, of all people, should get off her high horse, but it's easier to say nothing and keep the peace.

'Whatever you think,' Luna says, in that annoying way that sometimes means 'I don't agree with you' and sometimes means 'Ré, you're a fuckwit'.

A familiar bristle uncurls inside Ré, and she works to tamp it down. She lays the dress across the end of the bed, smoothing it with her hand.

'I just think people change from teens to adulthood.' Ré watches as Luna hangs her dress in the wardrobe and unplugs the steamer. Maybe she can use it when Luna leaves. If she can figure it out. 'And Jasmine was fun,' she continues. 'Well, when she wasn't busy rummaging through my mother's medicine cabinet. And her jewellery box.' That last part brings a little lurch of sadness – Siobhán hadn't been too worried about the stolen credit card, but her deceased mother's watch, never recovered, had caused deep upset.

'Well, exactly.' A sigh. 'Listen, you do you, Ré, but I'm keeping my good jewellery in the safe in my dad and Emma-Rose's room.' Luna juts her chin at a pair of hoop earrings on the little night stand that sits between their twin beds. 'If she comes snooping in here, she's welcome to my Lovisa hoops, and that's it.'

She picks up a navy velvet pouch that presumably contains her good jewellery, then moves to check her hair in the full-length mirror, turning one way then the other, tucking a corner of her white shirt into the waist of her shorts. A trio of gold chains glints at her neck. She pulls sunglasses from the night-stand and puts them on the crown of her head, though it's dusk now and they're hardly necessary.

'God, I've missed this weather. I feel like I haven't had a drop of Vitamin C since . . . when – Marrakesh, I guess?'

Marrakesh. Just the word makes Ré feel cold. And she thinks again of the unopened email burning in her inbox.

22

Now

THE WORDS OF THE text swim as Siobhán re-reads them.
   Mom I'm sorry I messed up
   'Ring her, Grace, now!'
   Fumbling, Grace hits the call button, and they wait. The phone on the other end, wherever that might be, rings and rings, and then it rings out. She tries again. Siobhán can't breathe. Still there's no answer.
   'We need to tell the guards. They can try to find where she is. Oh god, Grace, what has she done?'
   Grace shakes her head, no words coming. Siobhán grabs her own phone and hits the number for the station. Grace sinks to the floor, her head in her hands. Siobhán stares at her, then walks out of the bedroom to make the call from the landing.

Siobhán and Grace arrive back at Siobhán's house in Dalkey just before O'Connell pulls up with Detective Dunleavy.
   As soon as the guards come into the hall, Siobhán points at Grace's phone.
   'There's the text. Luna has . . . we don't know . . . maybe done something—' Her voice cracks, words failing to make it past the tightness in her throat. She swallows.

Grace lets out a whimper, like an injured animal, and Siobhán is aware of how horrific this is for her friend, but there's no room for that feeling now. Now is for finding them. Now is for saving Ré. *If it's not too late.*

O'Connell is reading the text, typing something on her phone. 'OK, the message tells us the phone was switched on, if only for a moment.' She looks up. 'It's been switched off again, and we don't know if it was on for long enough to get a location, but we're working on it. In the meantime, I'd like to speak with each of you again, in case there's anything at all we've missed.'

Siobhán nods silently, unable to get words out.

Mom I'm sorry I messed up.

What does it mean? What has Luna done?

Siobhán leads the way to the kitchen. On the counter, the kettle boils, with Charlie standing, watching, his expression calm. Why is he not falling apart? Does he still think there's some simple explanation? That they're overreacting? She wants to shake him, to wake him up.

'I need to speak with everyone,' O'Connell is saying to Charlie, briskly but not unkindly. 'Are your son and wife here?'

Charlie shakes his head. 'Xavi went out to buy milk.'

'And your wife?'

Now his face colours. 'She's gone for a hot-stone massage.'

'I'm sorry?'

Charlie reddens further. 'She was a bit stressed, and her salon was able to fit her in. She won't be long.'

O'Connell's face is a picture of disbelief.

Charlie dips his chin, a chastened schoolboy. 'I'll text to see if she's on her way.'

'And please ask your son to hurry back. Right, let's get started with those of you who *are* here.'

Siobhán and Grace sit at the table. O'Connell shakes her head.

'We need to speak to you separately.' O'Connell is already moving towards the door. 'Siobhán?'

Siobhán stills, glances at Grace. Grace stares at her hands.

Why do they want to speak to them separately? An answer comes unbidden: *Because you're not on the same side.*

23

The day before the wedding

SIOBHÁN IS ON HER third and definitely final post-dinner margarita. *Almost* definitely. Luna and Ré have gone to the pool house, and Xavi has disappeared, too. Charlie's mother and aunt have retired indoors. Siobhán and Grace are side by side, their chairs turned to face the pool, its gently rippling surface pink and purple under the evening sky. Emma-Rose and Charlie are speaking to Jasmine by the cocktail bar, as Ben and the catering staff set up clean glassware for tomorrow.

'No matter how cool we think we are,' Siobhán says, 'we're not actually so fun that the younger ones want to hang out with us, are we.'

Grace tosses her hair in mock indignation. 'Speak for yourself, McKenna.' She grins. 'Also, there's free drink – they'll be back.' She swivels in her seat to face Siobhán. 'Did you ask Ré again about the older man?'

'She swears she isn't seeing anyone, that it must have been a work colleague.'

'Oh, good.' Grace curls her legs underneath her, tucking her pink pleated skirt around them. 'Older men are a goddamn disaster.'

SUCH A NICE GIRL

Siobhán grimaces, studies her glass for a moment. 'Do you ever think about him and what happened? Anthony?'

'As infrequently as possible.' Grace sips her drink, a Hugo spritz. Her plan is to try every spritz in the alphabet over the weekend. 'I just hope our girls have a better radar for spotting trouble. God, I was an idiot.'

'You were eighteen – don't be so hard on yourself,' Siobhán says. 'I didn't see the red flags, and I don't have the excuse of being madly in love.'

'You didn't like him, though. I do remember that.' Grace tugs at a pleat, smooths it. 'That should have been a sign.'

Siobhán plants a hand on Grace's shoulder. 'Eh, not the first or last of your boyfriends I didn't like, so probably not a useful litmus test.'

Grace snorts a laugh. 'Fair.'

They sit for a moment in silence, the soft lap of the pool the only sound. A small evening breeze wisps at Siobhán's hair, and she adjusts her hair claw.

'Did you ever tell Luna,' she asks, 'about what happened back then?'

'No way. She'd freak out.' A shudder. 'And it would be too upsetting. She's quite sensitive.'

Siobhán doesn't reply. Realistically, Luna might be curious, fascinated, shocked even, but hardly upset over something that happened before she was born. Then again, Grace has always been overprotective. And although she couches it in coded *oh wow, that's so* brave *the way you let Ré do xyz* remarks, it's clear that Grace thinks Siobhán is under-protective. Under-careful to the point of carelessness.

'Anyway, enough about all that.' Siobhán finishes her margarita. 'Will we have one final, final drink?' She cranes her neck back towards the bar. But it's just Jasmine there on her own now. 'God, I don't know what to say to Jasmine,' she murmurs to Grace, sinking lower in her chair. 'Maybe I should be the bigger person and acknowledge it?'

Grace glances back, too. 'The last thing she'll want is you ambling over to be fake nice just to make yourself feel better,' she says dryly.

'Harsh.' *But fair*. She looks over at the bar again. Jasmine is engrossed in her phone.

'Apparently it was Charlie who hired her, by the way,' Siobhán says, making sure Jasmine can't hear her.

Grace sits up straighter, almost spilling her drink. 'What?' Her voice gets louder. 'I mean, first of all, when has the man done anything as useful as hiring a wedding planner, but what was he thinking?'

'I know.' Siobhán gestures to Grace to lower her voice.

'And now there's a literal *thief* working here,' Grace whispers. 'Shouldn't you warn Emma-Rose?'

Siobhán baulks at this. 'Grace, Jasmine was just a kid back then.' She glances at the bar, but Jasmine has disappeared inside.

Grace sips her Hugo spritz. 'Well, I might lock my room.'

'Oh, come on, she's a grown-up, a professional doing a professional job.'

Grace arches a beautifully defined brow. 'Or a thief whose business gives her licence to roam inside rich people's houses.'

Siobhán shakes her head, but not without affection. Grace is all talk, always, and quick to skate over the truth when it suits her – the only reason she's taking the moral high ground now is to stir trouble.

Turning again, she sees that Charlie is back, fiddling with something on the cocktail bar. He once told her if he hadn't gone into construction he'd have loved to be a barman and that he might buy a pub when it's time to retire. Something for Xavi to run, maybe. Siobhán's not sure how Xavi feels about this plan, or if he's even been consulted, which would be standard Charlie. Grand gestures, well intentioned but not quite thought through. He looks up and she beckons him.

'I don't normally do table service, but I'll make an exception for you two,' he says as he ambles over, a picture of relaxation in his white linen shirt, red wine in hand – not a man remotely stressed about hosting a wedding tomorrow. 'What'll you have?'

Siobhán narrows her eyes. 'What were you thinking, hiring Jasmine Whitaker?'

His brow corrugates in confusion. 'What's wrong with Jasmine?'

'Don't you remember? When she was in school with the girls? The whole thing with the stealing?' Siobhán turns to Grace. 'You told him back then, right?'

Grace nods. 'Absolutely. Luna was furious about it, and I remember warning you, Charlie, when she was coming here one weekend.' A pause. 'I'm almost certain I said it.'

Siobhán looks at Grace, puzzled. Ré was the one who was furious. Luna had been reasonably accepting; unexpectedly mature – Siobhán remembers being envious. In fact, against her better judgement, she'd compared Ré and Luna, something she was usually careful to avoid. *Look at Luna – she understands it's not OK to hang out with Jasmine. Surely you can see that?* To nobody's surprise, that made everything worse, and Ré punctuated her response with a slammed bedroom door.

A rustle from the garden snags her attention, and she turns to peer into the dusk. Her eyes scan the lawn, the shrubs that line the path towards the pool house, the trees at the back, but as far as she can see, there's nobody there.

Charlie is scratching his head. 'I remember something about a friend who wasn't allowed to call around any more, but that's a long time ago.' He glances back at the kitchen. 'Are you sure it's the same Jasmine?'

'Definitely. She doesn't look that different,' Siobhán says. 'And obviously, her name rings a fairly loud bell.'

'I only heard her first name and her business name.' Charlie drags over a third chair and sits down beside Grace. 'And I never met her back then – I honestly don't know if I ever knew her name. Shit. Sorry. The guards were involved, right?' He runs a hand through his hair.

'Yup.'

Charlie looks perplexed. 'But, like, David Kearns at the golf club recommended her; she's his niece. And he's the vice principal of the school. Why would he do that if he knew she was a troublemaker?'

It's clear from his reaction that he genuinely had no idea who Jasmine was. And it doesn't surprise Siobhán, really. One of the reasons Grace and Charlie broke up was because she got tired of begging him to carry some of the emotional labour of child-rearing, or even tune in more; to know Luna's friends, her teachers' names, her favourite books. At the very least, Grace used to say to Siobhán, to stop picking up his BlackBerry whenever Luna was trying to tell him a story. He was at a key stage in building his business, he used to say to Grace, and Siobhán understood that – she was at the same key stage with her business. The late nights working on pitches after Ré was asleep. The meetings she did while using TV as a babysitter. The first shop and the bank-holiday launch that none of her friends could make. Grace quickly rounding up her book club and her tennis pals and her art-class friends to fill the room. The highs and lows of working for yourself – Siobhán knows *all* about building a business. But she had to be there for Ré, too, and she did that as best she could; dropping balls all over the place, but trying all the same.

'Perhaps David's a loyal uncle trying to help her establish her business?' Siobhán says. 'And feeling bad because she had to leave the school?'

David Kearns had managed to keep it pretty low key at the time, but there was no question – the niece of the vice principal couldn't be seen to get special treatment, so another school was quietly found.

'Maybe he thought I knew already, since I met him through the school originally?' Charlie suggests. A worried look crosses his face. 'What am I going to tell Emma-Rose?'

It strikes Siobhán, not for the first time, that this man who makes million-euro decisions at work every day is like a child when it comes to real-life decision-making. She shakes her head. 'You don't tell Emma-Rose a thing, not the night before her wedding.'

'I can't say I agree.' Grace shrugs, looks at her ex-husband.

Charlie is affable, charming and warm. A life-size teddy-bear with greying curly hair and a middle that's a little rounder than it used to be. He always stayed well clear of the various teenage dramas Luna brought to Grace's doorstep, much to Grace's frustration. He's not above fibbing to others or even to himself to keep things running smoothly. So it's highly unlikely, Siobhán reckons, that he's going to tell his fiancée that her wedding planner was once in trouble for stealing.

And indeed, it only takes a moment for Charlie to acquiesce.

'Maybe let sleeping dogs lie.' He drains his wine.

'On your head be it,' Grace says archly. 'Now, what about those drinks you offered?'

Grace and Charlie stand and amble together towards the bar, chattering about the merits of an Aperol versus a Campari spritz. Siobhán stays on her chair, watching the ripples cross the pool. Another rustle pulls her attention to the garden. Is there someone there after all? She holds still, listening. Then another sound, like a light scrape on concrete. It comes from the patio area around the corner, where a terrace stretches the full width of the back of the house and the garage. Siobhán stands, moves slowly around the corner on to the terrace to look. It's shadowy now, dusk melting into dark. Is there someone there? She senses movement before it happens. A sudden flurry that makes her jump, her heart in her throat. Then she laughs. A pigeon. Good god, she's just been stalking a pigeon.

There's nobody here, nobody eavesdropping on her conversation.

And anyway, even if there was, what would they hear?

Everything, she realizes, when it's too late.

They would hear everything.

24

Now

IT'S HER OWN LIVING room, but Siobhán feels like a stranger. A suspect almost, sitting here, being asked questions by O'Connell while Grace stays in the kitchen.

Siobhán passes on the new information: that Ré might have been seeing Luna's boyfriend. She doesn't have Theo's contact details, but Grace might.

Now O'Connell is pushing. Is there any reason for Luna to hurt Ré? Any history of instability, temper, violence? Siobhán wonders if something new has come to light, something additional to Luna's text. Or is Grace being asked exactly the same questions about Ré? Is this divide and conquer – do the detectives think if they separate Siobhán and Grace, one of them will divulge a secret, betray the other? There *is* no secret; there's nothing to betray. Not as far as Siobhán knows, anyway.

But then again, Grace went behind her back this morning to tell O'Connell about the mugging . . . Maybe she has other stories she wants to tell?

O'Connell leads her back to the kitchen. She and Grace lock eyes, and Grace looks away first. O'Connell and Dunleavy exchange quiet words, then O'Connell asks Grace to tell her again about Theo, about the theory that Ré was seeing him. Is she trying to trip Siobhán up, to see if Grace says something different? Siobhán shakes herself. She's not under suspicion; this is just what police do.

Grace is answering. 'Like I said, we don't know if he was with Ré when he was going out with Luna or afterwards, but we know it was within the last year because Ré's nose is pierced in a photo we spotted, and she only got that done' – Grace turns to Siobhán – 'when?'

'Last July.'

Siobhán notes Grace's choice of words. 'A photo we *spotted*.' As though they happened across it on one of their phones. Not 'a photo we found when we let ourselves into a house without the owner's permission'. A tiny but effective skate across the truth. This is the kind of thing Grace has always been good at. Harmless shortcuts to save hassle. Siobhán has a sometimes ruinous instinct for honesty, and now the Polaroid is burning a hole in her pocket, but she can't bring herself to hand it over. It would mean admitting where they were. But more than that, she wants to keep the photo. *What if she can never take another?*

'Luna and Theo got together last June,' Grace is telling O'Connell. 'A year ago.'

'OK. Do you have contact details for Theo Hogan?' O'Connell asks.

Grace pulls out her phone, scrolls, then swivels it to show O'Connell.

'I don't think Luna's been in touch with him, though, not since they broke up.' She stops, as though something has just dawned on her. 'You – the gardaí – have Ré's phone, right? The one that was found under the bed?'

O'Connell nods. Grace darts a glance at Siobhán. 'Maybe check that, to see if there are messages between Ré and Theo?'

And somehow, even before O'Connell nods, before she picks up her phone, Siobhán knows. Instinctively, she knows there will be messages between Ré and Theo.

She stands, dizzy.

'I think I'm going to be sick.'

25

The day before the wedding

GRACE IS BACK IN her seat sipping an over-full strawberry daiquiri when Siobhán returns from the terrace.

'Where were you?' she asks, eyeing Siobhán over the rim of her glass.

'I thought someone was eavesdropping. I was afraid they'd heard us talking about Jasmine.' Siobhán grins. 'Turns out it was a pigeon.'

A small drip of daiquiri lands on Grace's skirt, blending seamlessly into a raspberry-pink pleat. 'You didn't say anything that wasn't true,' she points out, running her finger along the glass to stop further drips.

'Mm, but *you* called her a thief,' Siobhán points out.

Grace shrugs. 'Still true. Jasmine took your Valium, your credit card, and your mother's watch. She's a thief.'

Siobhán marvels often at her friend's straightforward take on life. Grace never ties herself up in knots overthinking, the way Siobhán does. It would make a pleasant change to glide through life like this.

'I still feel sad about my mum's watch.' She lets out a sigh. 'I'd love to ask Jasmine if she could return it, but I don't think I could.'

'I'll do it if you want . . .' Grace is trying to tuck her feet under her skirt again when somehow the daiquiri slips from her hand and smashes on to the patio. Before either of them can react, Emma-Rose is out of the house and rushing towards them, heels clacking.

'Is everything OK? Oh.' She surveys the shattered shards, the river of pink. 'It's fine. Don't worry. But we'd better get it cleaned up. We don't want any of the guests to cut themselves tomorrow.'

'Sorry about that,' Grace says. 'I'll clean it.'

'Not at all. Ben can do it, or one of the girls.'

Siobhán looks around. Surely the staff who served them lunch and dinner aren't still here?

'They're in the catering kitchen, prepping for tomorrow,' Emma-Rose says, reading Siobhán's thoughts.

'There's no need to call anyone,' Grace says. 'Where do you keep the dustpan and brush, and maybe some kitchen roll?'

With a small shake of her head, as if to say guests cleaning up is going to ruin the aesthetic, Emma-Rose clacks back to the house.

Siobhán and Grace lock eyes, trying not to laugh. Together they gather the larger shards of glass and take them inside to the bin. Then as Grace continues the clean-up, Siobhán plays bartender, making two uncomplicated gin and tonics before returning to her seat by the pool, vowing to go to bed after this. Once Grace has finished sweeping and soaking, she pops the dustpan and kitchen roll under her chair and drops into the seat. She has a piece of kitchen roll wrapped around a cut on her index finger, bright red blood seeping through as she pulls it tighter. Siobhán's about to tell her to get a plaster when another rustle from the garden draws her attention there. Then light footsteps. And she sees now that it's Luna, making her way towards them. Sunglasses high on her head, golden hair flowing over her shoulders, wide mouth painted pink, she's her mother's twin. People say Siobhán and Ré are like twins, too, and they *do* both have dark brown hair and deep blue eyes, though Siobhán can't always see the similarity beyond that. That's how it goes, she supposes: it's hard to spot it yourself. Mostly she's just grateful that Ré doesn't look like her dad.

Luna's on her way to leave her jewellery in the safe in Charlie's room, she says in a stage whisper. Grace announces she's planning to put her Van Cleef earrings there, too. Siobhán thinks but doesn't say that they're both being a bit neurotic, while at the same time wondering if she's being a bit naive *not* using the safe, and if she might regret that in due course.

As Luna heads into the house, the catering manager, Ben, arrives out with a sweeping brush in his hand and Emma-Rose trailing behind.

'That took longer than expected. Sorry, ladies,' Emma-Rose says, looking flustered. 'I got waylaid by Charlie's aunt asking me all sorts.' Her eyes flick to Grace, then, just as quickly, she looks away. Siobhán can't help wondering what that's about. Something that's left Emma-Rose feeling . . . embarrassed?

'Right. Ben, if you could do a little once-over to be on the safe side. We don't want any guests to end up in A&E.' A sigh. 'But look, these things happen. Don't be worrying, Grace.'

'Thanks, Emma-Rose,' Grace says. 'I'll try my best.'

Siobhán spots Grace's smirk, and a smile twitching at the corner of Ben's mouth.

Grace stands and reaches for the sweeping brush that Ben's holding, her hand touching his. 'Let me do that.'

He shakes his head. 'Not at all. Part of the job.'

He's really quite attractive, Siobhán notices, with a kind of

Ewan McGregor look about him, or maybe it's just the Scottish accent making her think that. Grace is smiling at him in a way Siobhán recognizes. Oh, how Emma-Rose will freak out if one of her guests – her husband's ex-wife, no less – hooks up with her caterer. Now *that* would liven up the wedding.

'I see you've cut yourself.' Ben points at the kitchen roll wadded on Grace's finger. 'I'll grab the first-aid kit from the cocktail bar.'

'Oh, would you? That's so kind,' Grace says. 'It's actually quite sore now.'

Emma-Rose's hand flutters to her mouth. 'Oh dear.' Her eyes dart to the patio surface, and Siobhán realizes she's probably worried about blood dripping on the ground.

Ben arrives back with a box of plasters and gauze, then sets about gently unwrapping the crimson kitchen roll from Grace's finger.

'It's not too deep, but we don't want to take risks,' he says, spraying it with antiseptic then wrapping it with gauze before sealing it with a plaster.

'Thank you. I feel better already.' Grace smiles. 'Would you like to join us for a gin and tonic when you're done?' she asks, standing closer to him than is strictly necessary. They would, Siobhán thinks, be an objectively good-looking match.

Emma-Rose lets out a huff of surprise.

'Oh now, I don't think Ben will have time, Grace. There's a lot left to do. And you ladies must surely be finishing up soon. I know you like your drink, but we don't want the place awash with the smell of booze when I'm walking down the aisle tomorrow!' She laughs to show she's joking, though she's absolutely not joking.

Ben is still busy with the brush, hiding another grin, as Emma-Rose prattles on. 'And the girls, too, they won't overdo it, will they?' She addresses Grace directly. 'I know Luna's been raised around drink from a young age – Charlie told me about the call from the school counsellor when you used to buy vodka for her. But hopefully they'll be sensible? Anyway, I'd better get back to it,' she says, without waiting for an answer, and bustles up to the house.

'Well, that's us told,' Grace says, eyebrows arched, grin extra wide.

Siobhán can see through it, though; the high colour in Grace's cheeks gives her away. She was mortified over what happened back then – the school counsellor contacting her on behalf of another parent over buying drink for sixteen-year-old Luna. Grace had been indignant – if she didn't buy it, Luna would have stood outside the off-licence asking strangers. And she's not the only parent who did, either, but she is the only one who got a rap on the knuckles. Charlie could have done without telling Emma-Rose that particular secret.

'Ben, we won't tell if you fancy a sneaky G and T. Surely you must be nearly finished work?' Grace nods towards his injured leg. 'And you must need to sit down by now. What happened there?'

He leans on the brush. 'Ha. I wish I had an interesting story about skydiving or skiing, but I fell off a bar stool and broke my ankle.' A sheepish laugh. 'Doesn't paint me in the best light, and nobody believes I'd had only half a pint.' His accent is pure Alan Cumming, and Siobhán can see Grace melting. 'Not the best timing.' Ben darts a glance towards the kitchen.

Grace nods understanding. 'I take it her highness wasn't too happy about the injury?'

'I didn't think to say it, because it doesn't interfere with the job – I can manage the staff same as ever and there's always someone on hand to drive the van, but I didn't think about how unattractive it might look.'

Grace's eyes are saucers. 'Oh my god, did she *say* that to you? That the boot is *unattractive*?'

'Her wedding.' A small shrug. 'She's entitled to have it just so.'

'Well,' Grace says, her voice lowered, 'you know what Charlie told me?'

Siobhán leans closer. Ben, charming and professional, but clearly not beyond a little conspiratorial chat about his exacting client, leans closer, too.

'The catering company asked Emma-Rose if she minds if any of the staff have what they called "strong accents",' Grace tells them. 'Apparently they always ask, but generally the answer is "No, not at all, any accent is perfect."' Her eyes gleam. 'Except Emma-Rose. She said she'd prefer if they used "local staff with south Dublin accents" so her guests could understand them more easily.'

Ben's eyes widen. 'Ha, not sure how I got in the door.'

'Ah, but your accent is beautiful.' Grace touches his arm. 'It's like audio butter.'

Siobhán suppresses a grin. *Oh Grace, you never change.*

'Are you sure you won't join us?' Grace is practically purring.

Siobhán glances up to the house. If this keeps up tomorrow, Emma-Rose will have a conniption. Emma-Rose is nowhere to be seen right now, but Charlie is standing by the patio doors, staring across at them, his mouth set in a tight line. Maybe Emma-Rose isn't the only one who doesn't like guests and staff fraternizing?

'I'd love to, but I'd better finish up inside,' Ben says. 'It was good to meet you.'

He's speaking to both of them, but his eyes are on Grace.

'Yes, see you tomorrow, unless we've taken to our beds with our chronic hangovers.'

Ben smiles once more and departs, and Grace turns to Siobhán.

'"I know you like your drink, ladies." The absolute cheek of her.'

Siobhán holds up her gin and tonic. 'We *have* been sitting here having "one last drink" for an hour, like.'

'You know something? Emma-Rose doesn't deserve to know anything about Jasmine. I'm telling her nothing, and if the Artful Dodger in there hasn't changed as much as her clipboard and court shoes suggest, Emma-Rose can find out the hard way.'

'Ben seems nice,' Siobhán says with a smirk.

'Mm.'

'Imagine her reaction if you end up with "the staff".'

An impish grin breaks across Grace's face. 'Imagine.'

26

Now

O'Connell phones someone, stepping to the other side of Siobhán's kitchen to do so, but Siobhán can hear snippets, mentions of 'Theo Hogan' and 'messages'. So they're rechecking Ré's phone in light of the news about Theo. The sick feeling in her stomach intensifies.

'Would they usually use iMessage?' O'Connell asks over her shoulder. 'Snapchat?'

'Both,' Grace confirms.

'Instagram?'

'Maybe,' Siobhán says, thinking of her own phone, the conversations she has with the same people across various social media and messaging apps. Even with Ré, it's a mix.

O'Connell finishes her call and rejoins them at the table.

'We're currently trying to contact Theo Hogan.' She addresses her next question to Grace, her grey eyes probing. 'Was the break-up amicable?'

Grace shakes her head. 'No. Luna was heartbroken. The trip to Marrakesh was supposed to cheer her up.'

'So if she found out Ré had been seeing Theo, she'd be upset?' O'Connell looks from one to the other. 'Angry?'

'Well, sure, but nobody threatens to kill someone over a boyfriend,' Grace says.

Siobhán stares at her. *What planet is she on?* 'Grace, they do. Think about it. When you hear about stabbings in the news, whenever it's not street crime or domestic violence, it's drunken arguments late at night where it gets too heated and someone grabs a knife.' The words send a fresh bolt of anxiety through Siobhán. But they have to face reality; it has to be said.

'Not our girls.' Grace is resolute. Blinkered, as always.

Siobhán wants to shake her. Inwardly, she does. Outwardly, she stays calm. 'But why not? Because they're from a nice part of Dublin? Because they went to a fee-paying school? Grace, this could happen anywhere, even on Kensington Road.'

'No, it just . . . no.'

She's so sure of herself. Always. For better or for worse. Siobhán tries again, conscious that O'Connell is watching their interaction with interest.

'But then what does Luna's text mean?' Her throat is tight.

Grace puts her head in her hands. 'You keep blaming Luna.'

Siobhán is crying now. 'Whatever she did, Grace, I know she didn't mean it. I've known Luna since she was born. But *something* happened.' The words choke out between sobs. She reaches for Grace's arm. 'We just have to find them.'

O'Connell, interested, watchful, but unfazed by this display of emotion, holds her hand up, indicating that she's taking a call. Moments later, she's back. She clears her throat.

'There are messages on Ré's phone with Theo Hogan.' She looks at Siobhán. 'Including one from late last night that reads "Luna knows."'

27

The day of the wedding

THE DAY OF THE wedding dawns bright orange and gold, though Siobhán is not aware of this, sleeping as she does until after nine. Her head is clear, and she has a sudden urge to show Emma-Rose how wrong she was, worrying about hangovers. Then again, it *is* her big day. Siobhán promises herself she'll be nice to Emma-Rose. She'll do it for Charlie.

Breakfast is indoors today, laid out as a buffet in the big kitchen-dining space that looks out on to the patio. Outside, an army of event staff, caterers and florists are busy setting up pretty white chairs in rows across the lawn, tying bunches of pink roses to the back of each one, and installing a floral arch where the bride and groom will stand for the nuptials. As Siobhán watches, granola pot in hand, a cello is placed beside four chairs. For a string quartet, no less.

Grace is outside, Siobhán sees now, chatting with Ben. Yesterday's black T-shirt has been replaced with a crisp white shirt, and it suits him. Siobhán can see why Grace is interested. Ben is holding a clipboard and looks like he's trying to check off a list while Grace tells him some animated story with lots of hand gestures and a little hair-tossing. Go Grace, Siobhán thinks, watching as her friend touches Ben's arm.

She wanders out to the patio now, too, and, hearing voices, turns the corner on to the terrace, where she finds Charlie and Luna sitting side by side on the low windowsill of the catering kitchen. Charlie's cradling a tiny espresso in his large hand, the picture of relaxation. Luna, in oversized sunglasses and an oversized T-shirt, looks a little glum.

'So, the big day is finally *here*.' Siobhán scooches in beside them on the windowsill.

'Mm.' Charlie grins. 'Don't tell my lovely fiancée, but I can't wait till the formalities are done and it's all about the party. It's a *lot* of work.'

Siobhán can't help thinking Charlie has done precious little to prepare for the 'formalities', and she feels a pang of sympathy for the bride-to-be.

'I can imagine,' she says, with mild sarcasm that Charlie more than likely misses. 'So, around forty-five guests? Anyone we know?'

'Oh yeah, you'll have met lots of them at parties here over the years,' Charlie says. 'Friends and neighbours, mostly.'

'Are the Egans coming?' Siobhán asks. The Egans are neighbours from nearby Mart Lane, a couple she's always got on well with, particularly Lynn, the wife, who loves a glass of champagne and a dance.

'No, they're in Perth visiting their son, who's doing some kind of horse-trainer course there. Terrified he's going to love it and settle on the other side of the world.'

'What, and leave all this behind?' Siobhán waves her hand around. The Egans' house and garden are much like Charlie's. 'Then again, they don't have a pool.'

'They will soon. They're getting one put in while they're away. Concrete is being poured as we speak, I believe. And much to Emma-Rose's disgust, it's bigger than ours.' He grins.

Charlie nudges Luna, who's been quiet so far.

'You used to babysit him, didn't you? The son? And now he's nineteen and living on his own in Australia.'

Luna nods but says nothing.

'Hey, why so glum? What's up?'

A sigh. 'I'm just tired.'

'Come on,' Charlie presses. 'I know there's something. What is it?'

Another sigh. 'I guess everything changes after today, doesn't it? It's not just you and me and Xavi any more.' She gives herself a little shake. 'It's fine. I'm overthinking. Ignore me.'

Charlie puts an arm around his daughter's shoulder. 'Sure Emma-Rose and I have been together for four years – a piece of paper doesn't change that. Nothing will change for you and Xavi.'

Siobhán listens quietly. It's not entirely true that it's just a piece of paper or that nothing will change, and she wonders if that's what Luna's thinking about. About the long-term down-the-line implications. About what might happen to the house and the business if something happens to Charlie. She shakes herself. These are very morbid thoughts for a wedding day.

Ben and Grace make their way over, and Ben greets all of them by asking if anyone needs anything. Luna requests an iced latte. Siobhán smiles and says she's fine. Charlie doesn't say anything at all. He gives Ben a long, hard look, then his eyes flick to Grace. For a moment, it's awkward, and Siobhán can't work out what's going on. Is Charlie annoyed that Grace is commandeering Ben's attention? That she's flirting? Surely he can't imagine he can sit in judgement over Grace's dating choices? And certainly not on his wedding day. The silence is broken when Jasmine strides out from inside, phone pressed to her ear, lips pressed tightly together. She disconnects the call and puts on a bright smile for her unexpected audience.

'Sorry, I didn't realize you were all here.'

'Is something wrong?' Ben asks.

Jasmine glances at Charlie and perhaps decides he's not as scary as his fiancée. 'The tables for the meal were delivered yesterday, but they were one short, four instead of five. And now they're saying they can't deliver the fifth, I have to pick it up. I drive my mother's Micra, not known for its table-carrying capacity,' she says with what sounds like forced levity.

Siobhán can't work out if it's the admission of fallibility or the mention of the Micra that catches her, but suddenly she feels a pang for Jasmine.

'I could drive,' she offers. 'I have my car here. I'll collect the table.'

Ré arrives up from the pool house just as her mother says this and throws her a surprised look.

'Thanks, but it's not going to fit in any car,' Jasmine says, clearly trying to keep the anxiety from her voice. 'It's too long.'

'You can take the Sage van,' Ben says. 'It's parked out back, the laneway behind the house. The spare keys are on the shelf in the catering kitchen.'

Jasmine's eyes widen. 'Are you serious?'

'Have you driven a van before?'

'I have. Oh my god, Ben, you're a lifesaver, thank you so much.'

Siobhán bites her lip. Jesus, she's only twenty-five, doing her best, doing a job that requires a pretence of constant perfection, and now Siobhán feels horribly guilty.

'Of course, go ahead,' Ben says. 'Let me know if you don't see the keys.'

Jasmine makes a praying motion with her hands, then flashes a wary glance at Charlie.

'Emma-Rose never needs to know.' He grins, back to his old self.

'I think it's in all our interests to keep things running smoothly today.'

Upstairs, as Siobhán makes her way towards her room to get ready, she hears a noise coming from inside Charlie and Emma-Rose's room. A mutter of frustration and then something that sounds like a whimper. Torn for a moment, she hesitates. The next sound is a sob. She steps forward and peers around the open bedroom door, where she sees Emma-Rose at a vanity table, staring at a tube of some kind.

Siobhán hesitates again. She really doesn't know her well enough to intrude like this. But she can't leave a woman crying on her wedding day.

She knocks lightly on the open door. Emma-Rose looks up, startled.

'Are you OK? Can I help?'

'Oh, god, this is so . . . silly.'

Is she having cold feet? Siobhán steps into the room, wondering now who is helping Emma-Rose to get ready. She's wearing a white tank top and shorts that might be pyjamas. Her dress hangs on the outside of her wardrobe door. There are no bridesmaids or groomsmen in the wedding, but surely one of her friends could have come early to be with her?

Siobhán crosses the room. 'What is it? Let me help.'

Emma-Rose closes her eyes. 'Sorry, I'm being ridiculous. I just . . . Weddings are so much work. And then the big day comes, and little things go wrong, and you can't control them, and Charlie, I love him, but he is zero help.' She shakes her head. 'Sorry.'

'I get it.'

'And then, last night, he got annoyed with me. Who gets cross with their bride-to-be on their wedding weekend? You just leave it till after, right?'

Siobhán nods. 'Absolutely. Do you want to talk? If it helps . . .' It strikes her that she's genuinely keen to help but also curious as to what might have annoyed Charlie.

'It was so . . . *nothing*. You know? Basically, I was telling his aunt about Grace's inheritance, and the catering staff were there, too, and Charlie took me aside – like, literally, steered me by the elbow – and told me not to talk about it in front of strangers. As if the staff care.'

Siobhán nods. Charlie's glare suddenly makes sense. 'Ah. Was it the Scottish guy, Ben, who was there?'

'Yes, I think so.' She shakes herself. 'I don't know why I just told you all that, or why it's upset me. Charlie's great. I'm very lucky. I think I'm just stressed and getting upset over small things.' She stares at the tube in her hand. Make-up, Siobhán sees. And if it's make-up that's the problem, she can definitely help.

'Is there something wrong with your foundation? Can I do anything?'

'You're going to laugh.' Emma-Rose hesitates then slips down the strap of her tank top. On the back of her shoulder is a smudged . . . butterfly? A tattoo of a small blue butterfly, partially and not very well blotted with foundation.

'I'm trying to cover it because the dress is backless, but I can't reach properly. I really didn't think this through,' she adds ruefully.

Siobhán smiles, holds out her hand for the tube.

'Here, let me.'

'I love the tattoo,' Emma-Rose adds, 'but it doesn't *quite* go with today's look.' A grimace. 'And I feel so stupid, sitting here, having organized this entire wedding by myself, and falling at this, of all hurdles.'

Siobhán nods. Carefully, she squeezes a tiny amount on to a

sponge and rubs it on to the little blue butterfly. Like magic, it disappears.

Emma-Rose twists to see in the mirror.

'Oh! It worked!' A smile breaks across her face. 'Thank you. Siobhán—' Emma-Rose stops. Starts again. 'I know I'm a bit much. I feel ridiculous about last night, the broken glass, fussing and fretting. I know you and Grace must think I'm desperately annoying—'

Oh god. Siobhán tries to interrupt. 'Not at all, honest—'

Emma-Rose holds up a hand. 'You don't have to say anything. I don't mean to be the way I am. It just comes out. And the last few days have been stressful. Turns out event planners are not great at stepping back and letting other people help.' A shaky laugh.

'Emma-Rose, I get it, and if you need anything else at all, just let me know.' Siobhán meets her eyes in the mirror. 'And I wish you the very best for today. It's going to be amazing.'

Emma-Rose's eyes glisten. She blinks and clears her throat.

'Thank you. I . . . I'd better get on with it. And of course, no need to mention any of this to anyone. Or what I said about Charlie and the inheritance stuff either.'

'Of course.' Siobhán smiles and leaves her to it.

Forty minutes later, make-up done and dress on, Siobhán realizes she's left her heels in her car and goes downstairs to get them. Out in the driveway, the sun beams down, glinting on Charlie's Porsche – he is nothing if not a middle-aged cliché. Siobhán retrieves her shoes from her more modest Audi and takes a minute to sit on a long wooden bench beside the front door to put on her sandals and enjoy the sun. Charlie's home-office window is a little further along and, as she sits, face turned to the sky, she realizes Charlie is in there, talking to someone on the phone, his voice wafting out through the open window. There are no days off for the self-employed, she knows this, and it doesn't surprise her that Charlie is making work calls even on his own wedding day. Then she hears him say Grace's name, and without consciously or deliberately doing so, she tunes in.

'Grace doesn't always think before she acts. It'd be just like her to run off with some waiter and, next thing you know, he's entitled to half her inheritance.'

Siobhán stiffens, torn between wanting to leave before she hears more but also curious as to what on earth Charlie is playing at.

'Yeah, so just check into him, will you? Text me back. The wedding's in less than an hour so I won't be able to take a call. Right, so.'

Charlie seems to have disconnected. Siobhán stays on the bench, afraid to move now, in case he hears her through the open window. Is it weird that he's worried about Grace and Ben? Or maybe he's like this with everyone Grace dates, and neither Siobhán nor Grace has ever known about it before? Either way, on the day Charlie is marrying Emma-Rose, a woman they have all suspected of gold-digging tendencies, this seems – no pun intended – a bit rich.

28

Now

LUNA KNOWS. A TEXT from Ré to Theo.

Another dizzy spell hits Siobhán. 'What . . . what time did Ré send the message?' she asks O'Connell.

'At 4.08 a.m., about half an hour before the call to emergency services.'

'So . . . Luna found out Ré had been seeing Theo, Ré told this to Theo. And then an argument broke out. And then . . .' Siobhán trails off.

'Did Theo reply?' Grace's head is in her hands, her shoulders slumped, her voice muffled.

'Not yet, and it looks like it's not been read,' O'Connell says. 'We're still not able to reach him but if he lives in Canada, he may not be awake yet.'

Emma-Rose arrives in, still in her cream Celine tracksuit, mouth still pursed, despite her massage. In whispers, Charlie fills her in.

'I just can't understand why they haven't been seen,' he says, out loud now. 'If they went to a hotel, we'd know. If they went to someone's house, we'd hear. It makes no sense.'

He winces suddenly, closes his eyes.

'Migraine?' Emma-Rose asks, stepping closer to him, her voice softer than usual.

Charlie nods. 'I'll be fine. It's just the stress.'

Siobhán watches, wondering if he's perhaps not as together as he sounds.

Palms at his temples, he lowers himself into a chair. 'Unless . . . maybe they're in someone's summer house or mobile home?'

Emma-Rose's eyes widen. 'Actually, that's just reminded me of something – when I messaged the girls about sharing the pool house, neither of them was keen on the idea, as I told you. Luna called me and said she could book into an Airbnb that's walking distance from our house. She'd looked it up already. I told her Charlie would be disappointed and that if anyone should stay somewhere else, it should be Ré.'

Charlie puts a hand on her shoulder. 'Emma-Rose.' He looks at Siobhán apologetically. 'She doesn't mean to sound so—'

Siobhán waves it away. She's way past taking offence.

Emma-Rose looks at her. 'Sorry, Siobhán, that sounded rude. I just meant – anyway. The Airbnb she mentioned – I suppose that might be empty, right?'

O'Connell buzzes to life. 'OK, did she say the name? The address?'

'It's across the road from Foxrock Church. Not far from Xavi's mother's house, actually. I'm not sure what number, but there can't be many Airbnbs there, right?' She gives a hopeful smile, happy to be of use, perhaps, and Siobhán is grateful.

Grace is already on Google. 'I got one. Bella Vista, opposite the church, on Kill Lane, available for short-term rental and . . . it's available tonight. So it's empty.'

O'Connell stares.

'Did you say Kill Lane?'

'Yes, why?'

O'Connell is back on her phone. The rest of them wait. Then she moves away, makes a call, her back turned, and still they wait, silent.

Finally she faces them again. 'We've had calls in, sightings, responses on social media. We always do. As you can imagine, we note them all, but many are false alarms.'

Siobhán nods; they all nod, waiting.

'There was one call about a house on Kill Lane,' O'Connell says slowly, carefully, as though considering how much to tell them. 'Someone on their way home from a party around five a.m. who heard a door bang and thought they heard a shout. They waited for a minute but there was nothing else.' Her eyes are watchful behind her glasses, looking at each of them in turn. 'When they saw our appeal for information, they phoned the Garda Confidential Line.'

Siobhán swallows as she pushes back her chair. Could this be it? And what will they find when they get there?

'Slow down.' O'Connell waves Siobhán back into her seat. 'It might be nothing. We'll send a car. You wait here.'

'Please. I know it might be nothing, but they're our daughters.' Siobhán is already moving towards the front door, a dizzying mix of hope and terror coursing through her. 'We can't stay here, not knowing.'

29

The day of the wedding

RÉ LETS OUT A sigh and flops back on her bed. Luna is taking forever in their shared bathroom. It's after twelve and the ceremony begins at one, with clear instructions from Emma-Rose to be seated no later than twelve forty-five. This is very Luna, though, always putting herself first. When they were small, Ré could never see it – Luna ditching her for other friends hurt, but only ever made Ré think badly of herself. Luna borrowing her things without reciprocating left her believing it was because Luna's clothes wouldn't suit Ré, when actually loaning out her belongings didn't suit Luna.

As ever, hindsight is in sharp focus. And it doesn't matter these days, when their lives aren't quite so intertwined.

Except now, when Luna's still not out of the bathroom.

And while not quite as high maintenance as Luna, Ré likes her hair sleek and her eyeliner just so, and neither of these things is achievable without access to her make-up and hair wax, all of which are in the bathroom.

'Are you nearly done?' she calls.

'Five minutes.'

Five minutes. OK, she can work with that. She pulls out her phone while she waits, checks her messages and ignores a chirpy 'we haven't seen you in a while!' email from the gym she keeps paying but not attending. The other email, the one from Marrakesh, the one she hasn't opened yet, sits further down her inbox, as it has done for two weeks now. Her thumb hovers over it. Maybe it's time to rip off the plaster. A sick feeling rolls through her. If there was someone she could send it to, that would help. Someone who could open it for her, screen it, let her know if it's safe. But the one person she'd normally go to for anything like this is her mother, and her mother doesn't know what happened in Marrakesh. For someone who's always been pretty open with her mum, it feels odd to be keeping two significant secrets. Odd and unnecessary. She should really just tell her she was mugged, but as time passes, it feels harder to bring it up, to relive it, to answer inevitable questions about it. So she keeps promising herself she'll tell Siobhán at some point, but definitely not while they're at this wedding. And of course there's the Aidan secret, too . . . That's a little trickier, admittedly. The sound of the tap tells her Luna is still primping and preening, so she googles 'Robbie Williams Lansdowne Road Concert' and clicks on the Images tab, where she finds photo after photo of the crowd and the stage and Robbie himself. The first site she clicks into turns out to be a review of a 2017 concert, but the next one is a Facebook page for the 2001 concert, complete with crowd photo. Ré zooms in on the sea of raised arms. Imagine if she saw them. Obviously, that's ridiculous, but still. Imagine. Who was her mother there with, she wonders now? And who was Aidan with? And look at all those people . . . Imagine if they hadn't met that night – Ré wouldn't exist. Of course that's true of every human, really. But still, a chance meeting for one night only at a long-ago concert feels very sliding doors . . . Then the bathroom latch unlocks, jolting her back to real-life doors.

Luna looks exquisite in a turquoise dress that's beautiful on her golden skin but would wash Ré out completely.

'What do you think?' She does a twirl.

'Gorgeous.'

'OK, phew. Right, I need my heels and bracelets. Oh shit, I just remembered the jewellery is in Emma-Rose's room.'

Ré smirks. 'That'll teach you. You can't really invade the bride's bedroom on her wedding day.'

'No . . . I'll sneak up just before one.'

'Or do without the bracelets.'

'No way! It'll be fine.' She looks Ré up and down. 'You'd better hurry, it's nearly time.' With that, she swans out of the bedroom. Ré lets out a sigh and heaves herself off the bed. She glances at her inbox one more time, then resolutely closes her email. Tomorrow.

Just as Ré's finished getting ready, her mum arrives at the garden house to admire her outfit and to take a selfie together. With ten minutes to spare, they sit for a bit, and Siobhán fills Ré in on last night's drinks on the patio, the broken glass, Grace's dramatic 'injury' and her interest in Ben. Ré finds herself wishing the story was about Siobhán and Ben, that Siobhán could have some fun instead of watching Grace from the sidelines. But that's never how it's been. As Siobhán talks, Ré considers for a moment that this could be it – the time to tell her mum about Aidan. *Speaking of love interests, Mum . . .* But before she can brave getting the words out, Siobhán is off again, telling her about Charlie's reaction to Ben and Grace, and a phone call she overheard outside his home office. Ré is as surprised as Siobhán – Charlie doesn't seem the jealous type, so maybe this is genuine; he truly thinks Ben might be after Grace's inheritance. And of course, maybe he is, Siobhán concedes, but Charlie should have more faith in

Grace's ability to judge character. If Ben is faking interest to get at her bank account, Grace will be the first one to spot it. She's a lot of things, but she's not stupid, Siobhán points out. And if she wants to flirt with Ben, she's a grown adult woman who can make her own decisions.

Yeah, on that topic . . . Ré opens her mouth, truly ready to tell her mum about Aidan, but then Siobhán jumps up, shocked at the time, and they have to go. Tomorrow, Ré thinks. She'll tell Siobhán tomorrow.

30

Now

THE AIRBNB ON KILL Lane looks just like all the other houses beside it: large, detached mid-century homes with well-kept gardens, long driveways, floor-to-ceiling windows and converted garages. Bella Vista is pristine white with a green apex roof and a light grey front door. Pink hydrangeas bloom in terracotta pots either side of the tiled porch and the blinds on the front windows are drawn halfway. Rose bushes form a border between the driveway and the front lawn – blooming bright despite the warm weather. It has a well-cared-for, welcoming sheen to it. It doesn't look like somewhere bad things happen. But still. Bad things can happen anywhere, Siobhán knows that.

She and Grace have come here in the back of a garda car, with Dunleavy driving and O'Connell in the passenger seat. Siobhán's first attempt to open the car door fails, her fingers shaking badly, then she's out on the path, staring at the house, Grace right behind her.

O'Connell is already moving towards the open gates at the end of the driveway.

Siobhán finds she can't move, can't put one foot in front of the other. Thoughts ricochet around her head – it could be nothing. It's probably nothing. The caller to the garda station was on their way home from a party and might have been drunk. Emma-Rose might have misremembered the location of the Airbnb. It might all be a coincidence that the street name and the phone call match. But then again, what if they're here? . . . What if it's too late?

The front door opens. Siobhán's breath is caught inside her throat.

But it's not Ré or Luna who comes out of the house, it's a garda, her phone clamped to her ear. Garda Harrington, who was at Charlie's earlier. O'Connell glances back from the gateway.

'They got here a few minutes before we did, got the lock box code from the owner,' she explains. 'Wait here.'

For what feels like eternity, Siobhán and Grace stand frozen, staring at the house. O'Connell stops to speak to Garda Harrington, but they can't hear what she's saying. O'Connell continues to the front door, steps inside, out of view now.

'We're grasping at straws,' Grace says in a whisper.

Siobhán takes her hand. 'I know. But we only have straws to grasp.'

O'Connell appears in the doorway again and begins to walk back down the driveway, her expression unreadable. She has something in her hands. A plastic bag, transparent, with blue writing printed on it. And something inside. O'Connell holds up the bag as she draws near.

'Do either of you recognize these?'

Now Siobhán sees what's inside. Familiar Nina Ricci sunglasses. Identical to the pair on the crown of Grace's head. O'Connell is looking at Grace, too.

'They could be Luna's,' Grace says in a shaky voice. 'Were they inside the house? Did you find anything else?'

'Not inside,' O'Connell says after a pause. 'In the corner of the porch, outside the front door. We haven't found anything else.

We'll do forensic tests on these, but for now, do you think they belong to your daughter?'

'She's not the only one with those, of course, but on balance . . .' She pulls her own pair from her head and looks up at O'Connell. The rest is left unsaid.

They're back in the garda car now, side by side, while O'Connell, out on the footpath, takes another call. Siobhán sits silently, staring straight ahead. What does it mean if they were here? It's not the full picture, but it's a piece of the jigsaw. Perhaps they came here and realized they didn't have the code for the key safe? And by 'they', doesn't she mean 'she' – Luna – the person who texted 'Mom I'm sorry I messed up'? The person who messaged Prisha that she'd found out something from Ré that upset her. The person who had considered booking the Airbnb.

At this, something jabs at Siobhán's mind, the sense that she's overlooking a key piece of information. She closes her eyes, trying to get there, but is interrupted by O'Connell when she bends to speak to them through the open car door.

'We're going to finish up here now. The house is clear and undisturbed. There's no evidence that anyone actually made it inside. The owner has confirmed that she did receive a query from Luna, but she didn't book it in the end. There were no bookings at all, and the owner confirmed that nobody could get in without the code for the key safe.'

Again, something nudges at Siobhán's thoughts. Something about a key safe?

Not a key safe. She remembers now. A key.

31

The day of the wedding

BENEATH A CLOUDLESS BLUE sky on a July afternoon, Charlie and Emma-Rose are married.

Siobhán, who cries easily, dabs at her eyes. Grace, who never cries, hides a rogue tear, pretending to scratch her cheek.

With a watery grin, Siobhán hands her a packet of tissues, whispering, 'I won't tell.'

They're in the front row, flanked by Ré and Luna. Across the aisle, Charlie's mother sits with his aunt. There's no tear-dabbing there, but perhaps that's how it is when you attend your son's third wedding. Siobhán has always been a little bit afraid of Mrs Caine – ever since their very first encounter back when Siobhán and Charlie met in UCD. They'd gone back to Charlie's to hang out one afternoon and Siobhán had asked if she should go outside to smoke. Charlie had told her with cool nonchalance that it was fine to smoke in the house. Mrs Caine had arrived in from work to find Siobhán perched on her kitchen counter, tapping ash into a brimming ashtray. It soon became clear that smoking was not in fact OK in the Caine household. Neither was it OK in Siobhán's house, and she should have guessed Charlie was shortcutting the truth. After that, Mrs Caine assumed every time Charlie got into trouble – out late, missing lectures – it was down to Siobhán. It strikes her now for the first time that maybe she was the Jasmine of that story. The handy scapegoat. It's always easier to believe someone else's child is in the wrong, leading your child astray.

Siobhán watches Emma-Rose's face while the celebrant speaks. Her mouth is technically smiling, but there's a tautness there. Perhaps she never fully relaxes. And it must be difficult to let her hair down with all of this self-imposed perfect-day pressure. She does look good. Fabulous, in fact, in a Vera Wang backless dress and crystal-encrusted heels. Her tattoo, Siobhán observes – with a note of self-congratulation – is nowhere to be seen. Her normally severe blonde bob is pinned back from her face, giving her a softer look, despite the taut smile. And her make-up is, as ever, flawless. She doesn't use Scorch, Siobhán's make-up brand, because 'cheaper cosmetics' make her break out. Siobhán had been indignant at that, not least because her products are at the mid-range stocked-in-Space-NK end of the scale, and Grace, who knows her make-up, uses Scorch products *all* the time. Charlie says Emma-Rose sometimes speaks without thinking and doesn't mean to cause offence. Siobhán has always been sceptical about this, but today, at least for one day, she'll give Emma-Rose the benefit of the doubt.

The meal is magnificent. Jasmine's fifth table had arrived earlier, with the help of Ben's van, and was quickly set up by efficient staff, while guests drank champagne on the patio and lawn. Now they're seated at the five long tables, tucking into a prawn and lobster bisque starter. Ben is overseeing the serving of food, and if Grace isn't careful, she's going to get him fired – each time he passes their table, she stops him for a chat, making him laugh, touching his elbow. Siobhán finds herself wishing for the first time in a long time that she had that ability, that ease. She's never been able to flirt the way Grace has, and until recently, it hadn't really crossed her mind. Now perhaps she's left it too late. Emma-Rose glances over at one point and, if looks could kill, Grace and Ben would be six feet under. Siobhán tries telepathically telling Emma-Rose not to take it seriously. Grace loves the chase, but since she and Charlie split she hasn't had any kind of serious relationship and seems to be happier single, realizing she very much likes having her own space. As soon as Luna moved out, Grace sold her Killiney house and bought an old fisherman's cottage with a sea view about a mile outside Greystones in Co Wicklow. At first, Siobhán couldn't imagine her glamorous friend roughing it in a cottage, but her first visit to the house set her straight. On the outside, it's like something from an old Irish postcard, with original whitewashed walls and a low peaked roof. Inside, it's been refurbished with white oak floors, gleaming white walls, a top-of-the-range kitchen and huge windows looking out on the Irish Sea.

For Siobhán, *her* single status has been less about enjoying solitude and more about the busyness of building a business and raising a sometimes tricky daughter. Secretly, she's always thought she'd like to meet someone. She tends not to admit it to Grace, like it's letting the side down to confess she doesn't want to stay single for ever. And now, with the business and Ré both more stable, maybe there will finally be time for romantic pursuits.

Siobhán lifts her glass to sip her drink, enjoying the brief respite from conversation as the guest on her right steps away to make a call, and Ré, to her left, chats with Xavi. When the starters are being cleared and with her neighbour not back, Siobhán decides to pop to her bedroom.

She perches on the side of the bed and answers two emails, enjoying the peace. Three-day weddings are wonderful, joyous, et cetera, but there's very little alone time and a *lot* of small talk. On autopilot, she clicks into Instagram for a scroll, then stops and types 'Jasmine Whitaker' into the search bar. Two accounts come up – one personal, but not private, and one business: Blooms Day Wedding Planning by Jasmine. It's all very pretty, very well put together, with admirable engagement. One particularly enthusiastic follower called Laura has commented on every single post, and the more Siobhán reads, the more something about Laura rings a bell – maybe she's someone who follows Siobhán's Scorch account, too? Laura's profile picture looks vaguely familiar – a silver starfish brooch on a green background. Siobhán keeps scrolling. Jasmine's business account goes back three years, the personal account much further. Siobhán has scrolled back past lockdown before she acknowledges to herself that she's not just being nosy – she's looking for her mother's watch. But Jasmine typically wears something similar to Siobhán's own Samsung smart watch on one wrist, and stacks of gold bracelets on the other. No sign of the Chanel watch with the octagonal face that decorated her mother's wrist throughout the eighties and nineties. Feeling voyeuristic and foolish, she clicks out of Jasmine's account. Her existing theory makes most sense – the gardaí never recovered the watch because Jasmine, off her face on vodka and Valium, lost it.

Realizing she's been gone longer than intended and the main course is probably being served, she closes Instagram and hurries back to the landing, where she almost collides with someone coming out of Emma-Rose's bedroom.

Jasmine.

'Oh, hi,' Jasmine says. 'I was just picking up earrings for Emma-Rose. The ones she's wearing are hurting.'

It strikes Siobhán that this would, under ordinary circumstances, be an unnecessarily detailed explanation. Is it because of Jasmine's history with Siobhán and Grace – is she worried Siobhán will suspect her of stealing? *God, poor Jasmine* . . . The next words are out before Siobhán has time to think: 'Jasmine, look, I want to say – I'm sorry about everything that happened back then. You were so young, and I was heavy-handed.'

Jasmine colours. Her eyes are bright with what might be tears.

'I . . . I'd better get these to Emma-Rose.'

Flustered, she turns to walk down the stairs, and Siobhán is left feeling unsure about all of it. Though one thing is certain, she thinks, mentally rolling her eyes. She should probably tell Grace and Luna that the safe is not quite safe.

Back downstairs, passing through the kitchen, Siobhán spots Grace and Ben standing at the sink. Heads together, Grace seems to be holding her finger in the running water as Ben turns the tap. Their shoulders are just a hair's breadth apart. Their forearms touching. Skin to skin. Siobhán can feel the tingle as though she's there in Grace's place. Busy with the first-aid operation – Grace's cut from last night re-opened, presumably – they don't notice Siobhán. She watches for a moment more, with a sudden wistfulness. A pang. A wish to have someone who's just for her. To run water on her cut. For twenty-five years, she's never felt she missed out, not really. She was too busy. But now . . . A movement pulls her attention towards the patio doors, where she sees that Charlie's watching, too, a hard-to-read expression on his face. A sudden shiver runs through her and, without being able to pinpoint why, she can't help thinking that perhaps, today of all days, Grace might dial it back.

32

Now

SITTING IN THE BACK seat of the garda car outside the Airbnb, O'Connell's words tumble in Siobhán's head. Key safe. Key. Somewhere the girls could access.

'Grace.' Siobhán turns to her friend. 'Charlie's neighbours on Mart Lane. The Egans. Luna used to babysit for them, right? Charlie mentioned it yesterday.'

Grace nods. O'Connell perks up.

'Would Luna have had a key to their house, or the code for their key safe?'

'You keep making it sound like Luna did this. It's—'

'Please, Grace, it's not about blame. Did she have a key?'

'I don't know. It's a few years since she babysat for them. The younger ones are all teens now.'

'I know, but just think. Didn't she use to collect the youngest from school and bring him back to their house? Wouldn't she have needed a key?'

'Oh yeah . . . so maybe she did have a key. Or maybe they used to leave one under the mat. But even if she did have one back then, I don't think she'd still have it now?'

'Like we said, everything's worth a shot.'

O'Connell interjects. 'Could you give me the Egans' address? We can go now to check it out.'

Siobhán and Grace spend an interminable twenty minutes in the back of the garda car, first driving from Kill Lane to Mart Lane, a two-minute journey, then sitting outside the Egans' home waiting while O'Connell and Dunleavy search the grounds.

Grace is rocking back and forth, muttering about always knowing something bad would happen. Siobhán tries to tamp down her frustration, aware it's born of stress, but all she wants to say is: Of course you *worried* something bad would happen; you didn't actually *know* something bad would happen. Good god, that's what motherhood is – imagining the worst-case scenario every single day until you die. But because Grace has always panicked out loud, and so *loudly*, Siobhán must take the role as the 'calm' one, and worry only in her head. She pats Grace's hand now, tries to comfort her. Grace, who just a couple of hours ago called Ré a 'loose cannon'. Grace, who threw years of confidences back in Siobhán's face. Grace, whose daughter 'messed up'.

Five more minutes tick by, and the detectives still haven't come back. Waiting is excruciating, and Siobhán can't bear sitting doing nothing.

'Would you have a number for Lynn Egan?' she asks Grace.

Grace shakes her head. 'I only know her about as well as you do – I never lived in the Kensington Road house.'

Siobhán had forgotten that.

'I'll ask Charlie,' she says, typing a message.

'I guess the police will call them anyway? To ask about keys and whatnot?'

'I know. But I can't just sit here. Maybe Lynn will be able to think of something we can't.'

Grace looks at her watch. 'It's about one in the morning in Australia.'

God, and nine hours now since the 999 call.

While she waits for Charlie's reply, Siobhán forces herself to think back over the night. Surely there's something they've missed. Some clue. What was that last conversation with Ré about? Just before the girl from Sage dropped the glasses? Siobhán remembers going to get a sweeping brush, helping to clean up . . . no, actually, she realizes now, she didn't clean up. She told Ré she was getting a brush because . . . because she wanted to end the conversation.

And suddenly, it comes back. She knows what they were talking about. A little chill settles over her. It couldn't be linked to this, though, could it? It *couldn't*. But still. She'll find a quiet moment to say it to O'Connell, she decides. Out of earshot of the others. *Just like Grace did earlier,* a little voice reminds her. *This is different, though.*

She cranes her neck to see if she can spot the detective just as a text arrives from Charlie with Lynn's number. Siobhán calls it immediately, despite the late hour in Australia; she can at least leave a voicemail. To her surprise, Lynn picks up.

'This is Lynn?'

'Lynn, hi, this is Siobhán McKenna, Charlie Caine's friend. This is going to sound weird, but—'

Lynn interrupts. 'It's OK. The guards were in contact already. I told them – there's a key to the side gate in a hideaway rock in the front garden. That gets you into the side passage, where there's a toolbox with a back-door key in it.' She takes a quick breath and keeps going, speaking rapidly. 'Luna knew that when she used to babysit.'

So the guards are inside. Siobhán can't wait any longer. Dropping the phone on the back seat, she gets out of the car and races through the gateway on to the grounds of Lynn's house with Grace following just behind. Siobhán runs to the front door and bangs on it. No response. There are no windows to the hall, no glass panels at the front door, no indication of what or who is inside. She runs across to the nearest window – what might be a living room – but the curtains are drawn. Grace is still at the door, ringing the bell, again and again. Then Siobhán hears a movement, a click.

But it's not the front door that opens, it's the garage. As she watches, the corrugated door begins to lift, creaking slowly upwards. Heart in her mouth, Siobhán looks back at Grace and runs towards it. The door is fully up now; she can see inside.

And what she sees stops her cold.

33

The day of the wedding

Ré's cynicism about the wedding, her worry about the unopened email and her awkwardness around Jasmine have all dissolved in a white-wine haze. Ré doesn't even drink white wine, but it came with the meal, and with every glass she drank, it became more and more delicious. Actually, she thinks, nodding to herself, nothing tastes as good as free wine. The tables have all been cleared now to make room for dancing, and the DJ is playing nineties music – the kind her mother loved first time round and she loves because twenty-first-century music is truly weird. Opposite her, Xavi dances, bottle of beer in hand, a grin on his face. The bride swishes by, graciously chatting to all her guests. She looks happy, glowing, and finally relaxed. To Ré's surprise, she stops to chat to them, too.

'You two are super cute together,' Emma-Rose whispers to her, with a smile and a wink.

Ré's eyes widen. Did she really just say that? Did Xavi hear? Also, since when did Emma-Rose pay Ré any attention ever?

'We're just having fun,' Ré says, keeping it neutral. 'Such a nice wedding. Love the music.'

'Ah, I remember when I first met Charlie. I called it just having fun, too!' Another wink.

Good god. Maybe she's drunk. Or actually . . . happy?

Emma-Rose glides away to her next guests and Xavi leans in.

'What did she say? You looked kind of . . . horrified?'

'Oh, nothing. Just checking we're having fun.'

'Wow, the fun police herself checking up on us.' He grins. 'Want another drink?'

'My round,' Ré says magnanimously. 'I'm very generous at free bars. I'm just going to run to the loo first.'

Xavi lifts his beer bottle in salute, still dancing, as she weaves her way through the guests, around the pool, and down to the garden house. Inside, it's quiet, and warm, with evening sun streaming through the huge windows, and she takes a moment to catch her breath, fix her hair. That's when she notices Luna's velvet jewellery pouch on the night stand. So Luna must have changed her mind about using the safe. Some of the jewellery has spilled out on the surface of the night stand, like Luna rifled through it in a hurry. Ré hasn't seen Luna in a while, now that she thinks about it. Maybe she should look for her. As she lets herself back out of the garden house, the opening bars of Robbie Williams' 'Rock DJ' start up. Ré grins to herself, thinking of Aidan and her mum, twenty-five years ago, on a warm July night, dancing to this same song. She makes her way back to the patio-dancefloor, singing along, remembering at the last minute her promise to bring back drinks. At the cocktail bar she asks for a beer for Xavi and a white wine for herself. The bartender, a guy in his thirties with a professional smile and a cute dimple, cups his hand to his ear but can't hear her order above the volume of the song. He leans in and she repeats it, still swaying to the music. He snaps the cap off a beer, and she has the sudden, surprising sense that she's holding a jigsaw piece that's about to slip into place. And as the song comes to an end, it does exactly that.

34

Now

SIOBHÁN STANDS AT THE open garage door, her hand over her mouth. The missing Sage Catering van. Somehow, even though it's been clear all morning that the girls are missing; even though the blood and the emergency call are evidence that something's gone wrong, until now, looking at the van, it still seemed like there'd be an explanation, like none of it was real.

'Stay back, Siobhán.' O'Connell is in the garage, beside the driver's side door. 'I've called the Garda Technical Bureau. You can't come in here.'

'Are they . . . ?' Siobhán can't finish the sentence. Grace is beside her now, holding on to her.

'The house is empty. But there are signs that someone was here.'

'What . . . what signs?' Grace asks.

O'Connell moves towards them, her face lit by sun now.

'I can't give specific details. I'm sorry.'

Siobhán is numb. 'And the van?'

'The van is empty, but there's evidence to suggest one or both girls were in it. We need to examine it.'

Evidence. Does she mean more blood?

'How are they not here?' Grace sounds anguished. 'Where could they have gone?'

'My colleague is contacting Mrs Egan again, to see if there was a car on the premises.'

'You mean they might have taken the Egans' car? Can you put out a search for it?'

O'Connell makes a 'slow down' motion. 'That's what my colleague is checking right now.'

'It means we've lost hours chasing the wrong vehicle, though, doesn't it?' Siobhán whispers. 'Everyone's been looking for the Sage van, but they've gone in some entirely different car. To god knows where.'

O'Connell nods. 'True, but this also explains why there were no sightings of the Sage van. Now that we'll have the details of the vehicle they might actually be in, it will be easier to find them. This is a good thing,' she adds in a gentle tone Siobhán hasn't heard before. 'You've really helped by suggesting we search here.'

'I should have thought of it sooner. Charlie was talking about it yesterday morning . . . that the Egans are away. Telling me and Luna.'

At that, Grace turns. 'You keep doing that, making pointed comments to remind us you think Luna did this. Ever since the text.'

'That's not what I—'

Grace cuts her off, raising her voice. 'You don't have to keep saying it. I know this is shit and terrifying for you, but it's shit and terrifying for me, too, and believe me, I am desperately sorry. If Luna has done something to Ré, I will never, ever forgive myself. I'll wonder for ever what I did wrong, how she ended up here. But please, please don't say it every time.' Grace puts her hands over her face. 'Please don't keep blaming her. I can't take it.'

Siobhán sucks in a steadying breath. A breath to stem the tide of everything she wants to say right now. Everything she wants to scream. It's not a competition. It doesn't make a difference who has it worse, who's suffering more. If one daughter is dead and one is a murderer, they've both lost their children.

From the back seat of the car comes the sound of Siobhán's phone ringing. She runs out through the gateway and makes it just in time to pick up.

Charlie. She answers in a rushed breath.

'What is it? Did you find something?'

'Siobhán, I think we'd better have a talk.'

35

The day of the wedding

RÉ STANDS STARING AT the barman, staring but not seeing. How had she not worked it out sooner?

'Would you like the Albariño or the Piquepoul?' the bartender asks a second time, half shouting.

'It . . . it doesn't matter. Whichever you have,' she says, still stunned by her own stupidity. The song, mocking her now, comes to a close.

If Aidan and her mother met at a concert in July 2001, and Ré was born in June 2002, it was either a *Guinness Book of Records* pregnancy or her mother isn't telling the truth. Has she spent all this time finding Aidan and connecting with him for nothing? But maybe that's not it. Maybe her mother is just wrong about where they met? It was a long time ago . . . It seems like a pretty big deal – surely a person should remember the one time in their life they met the father of their only child, but maybe . . .

She pulls out her phone and texts Aidan.

I hear you met my mum at a concert! (I haven't told her I found you yet, she was just chatting to someone about it last night.) What was the concert, she was cagey so thinking it was someone cringe!

Is it believable? It'll do. She hits send, then gulps down half a glass of wine.

Now, to find Siobhán.

Siobhán is nowhere to be found. Ré makes her way across the lawn, down as far as the garden house, then back up to the kitchen. Inside, a few guests cluster around the coffee machine, taking a break from wine, but her mother is not one of them. She steps out to the hall, where it's quieter, and now she hears a voice from the room at the far end – Charlie's study. Her mum? She walks towards the room and puts her hand on the door, ready to push it open, but it's not Siobhán's voice, it's Jasmine's. Ré is about to step away when she catches her own name. Now it's impossible not to stay to listen. Ear against the door, she holds her breath, hoping nobody catches her.

'. . . same as ever, Luna too. But god, so awkward. I'd never have taken the job if I'd known. I'd better hang up, Emma-Rose will kill me if she catches me. She's a stickler for, like . . . every fucking thing. That's me being nice.'

Ré should leave. This is none of her business, even if it is secretly enjoyable, listening to Jasmine complain about Emma-Rose.

'Yeah, I'll be over tomorrow.' Jasmine's voice is alarmingly close now, and Ré realizes she's about to exit the room. She steps back, just as Jasmine opens the door.

'Uh, sorry, Mum,' Jasmine says into the phone, 'I have to go.'

Ré holds up her hand in a gesture of apology mixed with *don't hang up on my account*, but Jasmine has already disconnected.

'Just had to give my mum a quick call.'

'Is she OK?'

'Oh yeah, not a bother. But she's fascinated by this wedding and the house and keeps texting, begging for pics and updates.

She's unreal. So I called her to fill her in. I know I shouldn't be on the phone . . .'

'God, surely even Emma-Rose wouldn't mind a quick call to your mum.'

They lock eyes and laugh. Emma-Rose absolutely would mind, and they both know it.

'Um, since we're here . . .' Ré says when they stop laughing. 'Look, obviously it's awkward, but I'm really sorry about what happened. Back then.'

Jasmine waves it away, her pink acrylic nails glinting in the hall lamplight. 'You didn't do anything wrong.'

'Cutting you out like that, though.' Ré puts a hand on the newel post at the end of the banister, conscious that the all-day drinking has left her unsteady. 'I feel horrible.'

'OK, but I was off the rails.' Jasmine lowers her voice to a whisper. 'Jesus, I took your mother's credit card, her pills. It was a horrible thing to do.'

'You were fifteen. And my mum cancelled the credit card, got a new prescription. There was no harm done.' *Apart from the watch.* Her mother still feels sad about that.

'Even so,' Jasmine says, 'I don't blame your mum and Grace for stopping us hanging out. I'd do exactly the same.'

'You made a few bad decisions when you were dealing with your dad's death. We should have stuck by you. Me and Luna, I mean.'

Something flashes across Jasmine's face, and her lips tighten. Even through her white-wine haze and in the low hall light, Ré sees it.

'What is it?'

Jasmine looks down the hall, then up the stairs. When she answers, she's whispering again. 'Let's just say I think Luna was perfectly happy to be asked to cut contact.'

This throws Ré. 'What? No. Come on, we were all such good friends.'

A pause, as though Jasmine is considering her words. 'That's not what I mean.'

'OK, then what do you mean?'

'Best ask Luna. But if you really think about it, about everything that happened or supposedly happened, ask yourself, what would I have done with—'

The living-room door opens suddenly, interrupting Jasmine. Grace peers out, then stage-whispers, 'The coast is clear,' to someone. She crosses the hall and opens the front door, followed by Ben from the catering company. He glances at Jasmine and Ré, gives them a sheepish smile.

'Just taking a small cigarette break,' he explains, following Grace out. They can hear Grace laughing as the front door closes.

Jasmine and Ré exchange a grin, and the tension breaks.

'An unlikely couple, but cute all the same,' Jasmine says.

'Well, Charlie is apparently worried he's after her money,' Ré says, and immediately regrets it. Why does she never think before she opens her mouth? *Because the lure of connecting over juicy gossip is always too great.*

'Nah, I've known Ben a long time on the events circuit,' Jasmine says. 'He comes from money. He doesn't need anyone else's.'

This surprises Ré. 'Why does he do this?' She waves a hand around, gesturing to the general running of a wedding. 'I don't know if I'd be interested in making iced lattes for Luna whenever she wants one if I was rich.'

Jasmine types something on her phone. 'His family used to run a meat production business – big money, been around for generations.' She's still searching for something on her phone as she talks. 'Ben's dad ran it with Ben's brother.' She glances over her shoulder, but the front door is still closed.

Ben and Grace won't hear her. 'Then Ben joined the business and found out they were using migrant workers, paying them a pittance, and putting them up in overcrowded accommodation that was little more than a barn. Ben blew the whistle and the business folded when they lost half their customer base. Here.'

She holds up her phone. The screen is filled with news articles about a company called Foxborough Foods.

Ré takes the phone, her eyes skimming the headlines. Slave labour. Rat infestations. Malnutrition. Children as young as fourteen working in the factory.

'Jesus.'

'Yeah. Grim. The dad and the brother don't speak to Ben now. They blame him for bringing down the business.'

'They sound delightful.'

'Yep. Anyway, I don't think Charlie needs to worry about Ben. There's still money—'

Jasmine stops as light spills into the hall through the opening kitchen door and Emma-Rose appears.

'Oh, there you are, Jasmine. The catering girls are finishing up soon – do you have the tip envelope?' Emma-Rose pauses. 'Are you on your phone?'

'Just checking emails about the table return tomorrow,' Jasmine says with a professional smile.

'Great. Once the tips are sorted, could you tweak the Day Two table plan? Charlie's mother never actually replied – of *course* – but apparently she'll be here.'

Emma-Rose nods at Ré, then holds the kitchen door open so Jasmine can get on with her work.

Back out on the patio, Ré spots her mother by the bar and makes a beeline for her.

The dimpled bartender is filling a glass of champagne for Siobhán and holds up the bottle to offer one to Ré.

She nods, and thanks him. When on Kensington Road, et cetera. On Tuesday she'll be back in her tiny London flat, drinking own-brand tea. They take their glasses and step to the side, leaning against a trellis fence, watching the dancefloor. They chit-chat about the day, how good it's been. Ré tells Siobhán about Jasmine – about Ben and the family money, about Grace and Ben's sneaky cigarette break, and Jasmine's belief that Luna was happy to cut contact. That, Siobhán says, tallies somewhat with her recollection, and she seems pleased to have been proved to be right.

'Mum,' Ré says after a moment, 'I was wondering about something. You were telling Emma-Rose last night about meeting my dad at a Robbie Williams concert in Lansdowne Road?'

'Oh god, yes, the interrogation.' Her mum is swaying slightly, her cheeks flushed from ten hours of champagne.

'It's just, that concert was in July 2001, and I was born eleven months later, so . . .'

Ré waits for her mother to catch up.

'Oh.' Siobhán blinks. 'Are you sure it was July?'

Ré holds up her phone to show her the picture from Facebook.

'Wow, I've mixed it up, then.' Siobhán takes a sip of her drink. 'It was obviously a different concert. Maybe it was Harry Styles? I always mix up Robbie Williams and Harry Styles.'

Ré laughs. 'Mum, are you on drugs? Harry Styles was a child in 2001!'

Siobhán shakes her head. 'God, how could I forget this?' She nods at the glass in her hand. 'This isn't helping. Um. A U2 concert, maybe? Sorry, Ré, it probably sounds awful that I don't know.' She smiles, but there's something not quite genuine about it. 'I'll remember in the morning.'

You mean you'll google in the morning, to find a concert in September 2001. The thought slips into Ré's mind, fully formed. She stares at her mother. Is she lying about all of this? Is Aidan not her dad?

'The thing is, Mum, I've—'

A crash interrupts as one of the girls gathering empties drops an entire tray of glasses. Everyone stops, and a shout goes up from the small cohort who think cheering someone's humiliation is a reasonable response. The girl hunkers to gather the glass, immediately cutting herself. The dimpled barman dashes over to help, and Jasmine and Ben are by her side in seconds, too. Siobhán, all action, despite her champagne blur, says something about getting a sweeping brush, and makes her way to the kitchen, swaying in her heels as she goes.

A genuine impulse to help or a useful escape? Ré can't help thinking it's the latter. What her mother doesn't know is that Aidan's response will come tonight or tomorrow. And then Ré will find out the truth.

36

The day of the wedding

RÉ FINDS XAVI AGAIN, remembering she'd promised to get him a drink and then left it on the bar. He passes her one of the two bottles of beer he has in his hand.

'I saw you got sidetracked with your mum so I took the initiative.' A lopsided grin. 'My dad's always at me to take the initiative.'

And my dad's probably not even my dad, she thinks, as a wave of sadness descends.

'You OK?' Xavi asks, tilting his head.

She shakes herself. 'Sure. Let's dance.'

TLC's 'Waterfall' is playing, and the dancefloor is full. Charlie and Emma-Rose are nearby, and Ré is surprised to see that Emma-Rose is actually not a bad dancer. So she *can* let loose. And she's really properly beaming now, truly relaxed, eyes locked on Charlie's. Perhaps she's human after all. '(I've Had) The Time Of My Life' from *Dirty Dancing* comes on, and Xavi grabs Ré's hand to go full-on Patrick Swayze and Jennifer Grey. Other people around them begin to clap, and it reaches a crescendo when they attempt, and – to Ré's surprise – successfully achieve the famous lift. Charlie joins them and, at first, Ré thinks he wants to dance, but then she sees his face. Eyes narrowed, mouth tight.

He's swaying, and his words are not quite clear, but Xavi looks crestfallen and surprised. Ré leans in discreetly to try to hear.

'Fuck's sake, Xavi, go inside and sober up. You were raised like brother and sister. It's inappropriate.'

Xavi throws a confused look towards Ré but doesn't resist when Charlie propels him off the dancefloor and through the patio doors.

Ré stands staring, watching them disappear into the kitchen. She blinks. *What the—*

Oh.

Of course.

37

Now

'Siobhán, I think we'd better have a talk.'

The phone is so tight against her ear it almost hurts. Her jaw hurts. Everything hurts.

'What is it, Charlie?'

Somehow, though, she knows what this is. The thing he tries to bring up every now and then. The thing she denies, fobbing him off. The thing Ré asked her last night. The thing she'd just decided she'd tell O'Connell.

'Could you come back to your house? Xavi's been filling me in on some stuff I said last night.'

Siobhán closes her eyes. Opens them. Glances at Grace, who has walked out towards her, as far as the Egans' gateway.

'OK. We'll ask O'Connell to drive us.'

She disconnects, feeling Grace's eyes scrutinizing her.

'Siobhán, what is it?'

'Charlie wants to talk to me.' She pockets her phone. 'I don't think it's going to shed any light on where the girls are, but we should probably get back to the house.'

A puzzled look settles over Grace's features.

'Is there something you're not telling me?'

'No, of course not.' It's a struggle to keep her voice even.

'Siobhán, you wouldn't keep anything from me, would you?'

In lieu of replying, Siobhán addresses O'Connell, who is making her way towards them.

'Is Lynn's car missing?' Siobhán asks.

'Yes. A black Qashqai, and we're searching for it now.' Wisps of hair frame O'Connell's face, escaped from this morning's neat ponytail, and behind her glasses, her eyes look red and tired. 'You're better off at home until we have news.' It's a dismissal, but her tone is kind.

Siobhán nods, a weariness coming over her. 'Would you mind dropping us back to my house?'

In Siobhán's kitchen, Xavi and Charlie wait, their expressions taut. Numb with dread, Siobhán's eyes flit around the room – anywhere but Charlie's face.

Emma-Rose is at the kitchen counter, busy with something. She turns, and Siobhán sees she's wearing an apron, an old one Siobhán used to wear when Ré would talk her into baking.

'I rummaged through your cupboards. Tuna sandwiches is all I could come up with,' Emma-Rose says. She grimaces, but her eyes are soft. 'You might not feel like eating, but I really think you should.'

And it's this – high-maintenance, difficult Emma-Rose making tuna sandwiches – this is Siobhán's undoing. Head in hands, she bursts into tears.

Immediately, they cluster. Steadying hands rubbing her back, soothing her. Charlie, Emma-Rose, even Grace, who is in this as much as Siobhán is, leading her to a chair. A cup of tea is set in front of her. There's an offer of something stronger, but no, a clear head is needed.

'Sorry, sorry.' With the heel of her hand, she wipes away tears. Charlie clears his throat. 'Are you OK to . . .?'

Siobhán raises her hand, spreads her fingers. Just a little, just enough to stall him.

'I wouldn't mind getting out to the garden for some air.'

Charlie nods. 'I'll come with you.'

Grace is busy now with her phone and doesn't seem to notice. Emma-Rose is back at the counter, buttering more bread. Xavi watches but says nothing.

Outside, Siobhán steps down from the wooden deck and on to the lawn, leading the way towards a wrought-iron bench by the shed at the end of the garden.

The metal is warm with afternoon heat, burning the backs of her legs. It's just after three and the sun is still high in the sky. The seat shifts slightly as Charlie sits beside her. On autopilot, she reaches to unbuckle her sandals, slips them off. The grass is cool and welcome on the soles of her feet.

'So,' she says finally.

'So you know what I'm going to say, I think.' Charlie's voice is soft.

'I suppose I do.'

He lets out a sigh that sounds so wistful, so sad.

'God, this is . . . In one way, I always wondered. And yet now it feels like a shock. Almost like I *didn't* know it, really. It's . . . wow. A lot.' He shakes himself. 'In a good way, I mean. Ré is incredible.' He sounds genuinely awed. 'And she's my daughter.' His eyes glisten.

Siobhán pats his hand, wishing with all her heart that Ré was here, that the circumstances of this conversation were different.

'Why would you never admit it?' Charlie asks. 'The times I asked you over the years?'

Her throat is tight. This day was always going to come.

'I'm sorry, Charlie. I really am. But Ré is the most important person in my world, and Grace is second, a very close second. I couldn't admit I'd kept this from her for over two decades.'

Silence now. Her eyes still shut. The sun on her face feels good, and for the briefest moment it's almost possible to forget everything.

'Grace would have understood,' Charlie says eventually. The hesitation tells her he isn't sure this is true. 'I wasn't properly in a relationship with her when you and I . . . you know?'

She opens her eyes, turns and smiles.

'You can say it. "Slept together". And I know you weren't properly in a relationship yet. But you were moving in that direction. "Talking", as Ré would say. Unbeknownst to me, obviously, or I'd never have gone there.' She wonders about that for a second, just as she does in her more honest moments. Didn't some part of her suspect Grace and Charlie, her two best friends, had a connection? Wasn't that at least a little factor in her drunken decision that night, a subconscious bid to get in the way? And isn't that a little part of why she's never told Grace?

The sun beats down, hot on her face, the familiar heat of yesterday and the day before, and she aches for that near but faraway time when everything was OK.

'And then,' she continues, 'within weeks, you *were* properly in a relationship. And she was pregnant, and you were talking about getting a place together, about rings. I could hardly say, "Oh, Grace, your new husband-to-be? I've just found out I'm pregnant and he's my baby-daddy too."'

Charlie nods slowly, then shakes his head.

'All this time. I could have been a dad to Ré.' His voice is hoarse, claggy with emotion. 'A proper dad.'

'No, you couldn't.' The words sound hard, but she keeps her tone soft. 'You were married to my best friend, and I never wanted her to know, and that's it, full stop. Being a dad to Ré wasn't an option.'

'But what about after Grace and I split?'

She stretches her hands in front of her. Her nails, bright coral to contrast with the blue dress she wore to the wedding a million years ago. The sapphire ring to match the one Ré wore until it was taken in Marrakesh.

'I thought about it. But I wasn't sure we could move past a ten-year lie. I don't know if our friendship would have survived. And it's selfish, I know, but I valued Grace above you in all of this. Sorry, that sounds harsh.'

His eyes are trained on a rose bush at the other end of the garden, giving nothing away. But the flush in his cheeks tells her he's stung.

'What about Ré? Did she not matter?'

It comes out sounding sharp. She can't blame him for that.

'Ré never needed for anything,' she says simply. 'And I made sure she knew you, she's always been part of your life – in and out of your house, best friends with Luna. That's not an accident. I've always worked so hard to keep their friendship strong.'

Is that part of what's led to this, she wonders suddenly? Her pushing their friendship over the years – did she put them in a place where they had to hide their differences from their pushy mothers?

'Doesn't she have the right to know who her dad is?' Charlie's voice is strained.

'I wrestled with that for a long time, Charlie, but like I say, Ré was happy. Lots of kids don't have dads. And . . .' She stops.

'And?'

'She would always have been second to Luna.'

Siobhán knows this with every fibre. Luna was his daughter from the start, the child he had with his wife. If Siobhán had suddenly announced Ré was Charlie's, too, ten or fifteen years in, it would have upended everything, but she'd still always have been second. The late entry.

'And maybe if Luna and Ré weren't friends,' she continues, 'that wouldn't have mattered. But they are.' The words jolt her back to now. 'God, at least, I thought they were friends.' A tear spills down her cheek and she puts her face in her hands.

Charlie says nothing for a moment, then he wraps his arm around her shoulder and pulls her close. He clears his throat.

'There's a reason I'm bringing it up now.'

Pulling away from his embrace, Siobhán looks at him. 'What do you mean?'

'I was talking to Xavi. Apologizing for telling him to sober up last night, since, ironically, I don't even remember doing so. I forget sometimes he's not a kid any more. Anyway, he told me what I said. Apparently, I told him the way he was dancing with Ré was inappropriate, that they were raised like brother and sister.'

'Oh fuck. Charlie.'

'I know. The drink talking, obviously. You've never admitted it, but deep down, I knew. I just knew. Something about her mannerisms – I don't know. Or just the dates, the timing of everything.'

He looks up towards the house, and Siobhán follows his line of vision. A figure hovers just inside the patio doors. Grace. She disappears back into the kitchen.

'OK. Go on.'

'Well, as Xavi quite rightly pointed out, they *weren't* raised like brother and sister; it was a nonsense thing to say. Ré was his half-sister's friend who he bumped into occasionally.'

Despite the heat from the sun, a chill sweeps across Siobhán's skin. 'OK. And did Ré hear you say this?'

'Xavi reckons she did. He was mortified at being ushered away like a child; he didn't pick up on what the words might really mean because, obviously, he didn't know.'

Siobhán sits up straighter on the bench. 'But maybe Ré did?'

A helpless shrug. 'She's a smart girl. And there was all that talk Friday night about you meeting her so-called dad at a concert, and . . . I don't know.'

Siobhán bites down on her knuckles. It *was* on Ré's mind. She *did* ask about the concert, right before the girl dropped the glasses.

'And you're wondering if it has something to do with the fight?' she asks, her voice small.

'I honestly don't know, but if she *did* put two and two together, it's pretty big news for both of them,' Charlie says heavily. 'It means she and Luna are not just friends or frenemies, they're sisters.'

Siobhán nods slowly. And that might have gone down just fine . . . or perhaps spiralled into a fight.

38

THEY SIT ON THE bench in silence, the implication of what Charlie's just said ricocheting around Siobhán's head. A lifetime of lies. A lie that has gone on so long it's become true, to Siobhán at least. She never thinks of it. Never looks at Charlie and thinks, there's Ré's dad. But for Ré? Discovering it out of the blue last night . . . what might that have done?

And suddenly, Siobhán is overwhelmed with panicked guilt. How did she think it was OK to keep this secret all this time? How did she make her peace with her decision? She knows how. By burying her feelings and putting her head in the sand. And she knows why. She did it for Grace. *And for yourself, so Grace wouldn't be mad.* A sick feeling spreads. Was her decision a huge mistake? And is it what caused the fight?

Charlie sighs. 'Maybe it has nothing to do with it . . .' he says, answering his own question. 'God, this whole thing's a nightmare, whatever caused it.' He squeezes her arm. 'How are you holding up?'

'Not good. I honestly don't know how you're so calm, Charlie. Sorry, that's not a criticism. It's good that one of us is.' She faces him. 'You know when the girls were small and they were in crèche and preschool?'

'Yeah.'

'Sometimes the crèche manager would call us over at pick-up. Not just me – any given parent. We used to talk about it. Laugh about it. If you were called over, it was usually because your kid had been bitten, or your child had bitten another kid. You know?'

'Yep,' he says, though really, he rarely did crèche pick-up.

'And the consensus back then was always that it was easier to be the parent of the bitten child than the biter.' Siobhán smiles through a fresh film of tears. 'Nobody wants to hear their child is the instigator. The culprit. It sounds awful, but we meant it in a jokey way.' Another smile. 'Ish.'

'I get it.'

'And now, I don't know any more. In the grown-up world, both prospects are awful. I don't want Ré to be bitten, but I don't want her to be the biter.' A sob escapes.

'I understand.' Charlie speaks gently. 'But Siobhán, that's why we have to tell the guards that they're sisters, and we have to tell Grace.'

Siobhán's stomach drops. She stares at him.

'Oh, Charlie, I don't know. We're jumping to very quick conclusions here. We don't know if Ré picked up on the real meaning behind what you said last night.' She faces forward again, kicking gently at the grass, nudging it with her toe. 'And . . . And we certainly don't know if she told Luna.'

'Siobhán . . .'

'And on top of that,' she rushes ahead, 'I genuinely don't know how the girls would react. They might be really happy to find out they're sisters.'

Another sigh from Charlie, like he's dealing with a stubborn toddler. And she knows she's being exactly that.

'In due course, no doubt they'd be happy. But to find out like that, at the end of a long, boozy wedding.' He shakes his head. 'Things could get emotional, and not in the good sense.'

A butterfly swoops past, landing on the arm of the bench. Siobhán stares at it, thinking.

'What does it matter, though?' she whispers after a time. 'The cause of the fight – whatever its ripple effect – it's a moot point. We just need to find them.'

'Siobhán, you're the one who's been saying all day that we need to ask questions, to try to find out what caused them to fight.' He sounds frustrated now.

She lets out an irritated sigh.

'You know I'm right,' Charlie presses on, but more gently. 'If there's even the smallest chance that by understanding what went wrong between them it could lead us to where they are, we've got to tell the guards.'

The butterfly beats its wings and soars to the rose bush.

'Fuck. Fine. But Grace?'

He throws up his hands. 'Of course Grace. Luna is missing, too. She deserves to have all the information. She deserved to have all the information twenty-five years ago.'

A spark of anger flames inside her. 'Oh, fuck off, Charlie, easy for you to say. You're the one who slept with both of us without being honest. Easy for you to sit on your high horse now, talking about "deserving the truth". You're a pretty big part of this mess.'

He grabs her hand. 'Sorry. You're right, I know. And I'm sorry for not being honest back then. But right now, we need to tell everyone in there.' He points up at the house.

'Emma-Rose, too?' she asks in a smaller voice.

'I told Emma-Rose already.'

'*What?*'

'Siobhán, she's my wife. Xavi and Luna are her stepchildren. She was here when Xavi told me what happened. Yes, of course I told her.'

'Jesus. Fine. God, this is such a mess. Grace is going to kill me.'

They stand up from the bench and walk together towards the kitchen.

39

THE SANDWICHES ARE PILED high on two large serving plates in the middle of the kitchen table. Cut into triangles, spinach leaves and tuna peeping out. There's enough food here to feed triple their number, and Siobhán still can't imagine eating anything, but she appreciates the effort and manages a watery smile of thanks for Emma-Rose before remembering that Emma-Rose has just found out her new husband and his old friend share a child. Her smile falters as she meets Emma-Rose's eyes and braces herself for whatever's coming, but Emma-Rose just nods and, somehow, the nod is everything. Siobhán finds herself close to tears yet again.

Xavi has started eating, but Grace is on the other side of the room, pacing, looking at her phone.

Siobhán sucks in a breath. *Here goes.*

'Grace, could I chat to you for a minute in the living room?'

Grace's eyes are wide with fright as Siobhán closes the living-room door. It's darker in here, the east-facing windows having already lost the sun, and for the first time today Siobhán feels cold. She doesn't sit, and neither does Grace.

'Has something happened?' Grace asks in a terrified whisper.

'No, nothing's happened. I have something I need to tell you.'

Oh god. Maybe they should sit after all. She gestures towards the sectional sofa, but Grace shakes her head.

Siobhán walks over to the bar cart by the wood burner, lifts a bottle of gin, puts it back down. She turns to face Grace, who is standing by the coffee table in the middle of the living room, eyes like saucers, hand over her mouth, waiting.

'This is something I should have told you a long time ago. Twenty-five years ago.' *Rip off the plaster.* 'OK. So . . . there was this night out for someone's thirtieth and Charlie was there and he was sad about his split with Xavi's mum and we'd had a lot to drink and the party was boring and we snuck off and went back to mine and one thing led to another, and you weren't seeing him yet, or at least, I didn't know you were.' All of this comes out in one long breath of words. Siobhán pauses, waits for a reaction. Grace's hand is still over her mouth.

'I'm sorry,' she continues, speaking more slowly now. 'I had no idea you two were talking, starting something. He never said.' She watches for Grace's response, not sure what to expect. But Grace keeps her hand over her mouth and Siobhán can only see her eyes. Wide and dark and confused.

'It was a one-night thing,' she adds hurriedly, suddenly realizing Grace might think it was more. 'Maybe an itch both of us always wanted to scratch, and then that was it. Scratched and never to be repeated.'

'Except . . .'

'Except then you told me you guys were seeing each other.' Siobhán's back is against the wall, for the small comfort its solidity brings. Grace is still in the middle of the room, eyes on Siobhán. 'And I didn't want to admit what happened. How awful would that have been – "Oh, you're in a new relationship? I slept with him a few weeks ago." You see that, right?'

Grace stares. Doesn't speak. But surely she understands,

Siobhán thinks – no real friend would rain on the parade of a new relationship with that kind of news?

'And then you told me you were pregnant.' Siobhán remembers that moment so well, remembers the light bulb going on when Grace said the word 'pregnant'. The sudden realization that the nausea she'd been feeling might not be a bug. The sick feeling buying the test. The shock when she saw the result. The shock and the flutter of excitement. The two things she knew within minutes: she wanted the baby, and she'd never tell Grace. She draws in a shuddery breath, continues her confession. 'I did a test right after you told me. I was pregnant, too. And then you guys were moving in together, and I'm so sorry, but surely you can see there was no way in the world I could tell you this new love of your life was the father of my child, too?'

Grace's eyes are huge and round with horror. 'You still should have told me.' A whisper. 'No matter how hard.'

'Maybe. But at the time, I panicked. I didn't want to ruin things for you, and it was easier to say it was a one-night stand.' Which it was, of course. The easiest lies are the ones that are closest to the truth. A one-night stand with Charlie. A different one-night stand two months earlier, with Aidan from Australia, a man Grace had never known or known about, who became the dad of the story.

Silence now. Grace's hands cover her face, her head shaking slowly. Siobhán waits, standing by the wall still, her feet buried in the soft deep-pile rug. The tick of the clock is the only sound inside the room. Outside, a mower starts up, a car revs. Still Siobhán waits.

When Grace pulls her hands away from her face, her skin is pale, her eyes are pools of hurt.

'What were you thinking?' she whispers. 'How could you keep this from me?

Siobhán sucks in a breath. Grace hasn't heard, hasn't understood any of what she's said. Grace, who she never, ever wanted to hurt. Grace, who is flawed but generous to a fault. Loudly obnoxious, quietly kind. Grace, who'll tell the world she's on a wait list for a new Mulberry while anonymously making huge donations to Sightsavers and Fighting Blindness. Grace, who'll fund a school library to get her daughter out of trouble but just as quickly fund a women's refuge, a drug recovery scheme and guide dogs for the blind. Grace, who has no patience, no tolerance, no boundaries, no filter. Grace, who has always been there for Siobhán. Grace, who was there in the delivery room when Ré was born, because Siobhán didn't have anyone else.

'I'm truly sorry. But Grace, think about it – I didn't do anything bad to you. I kept the secret for good reasons.' Again, that little thought hits – did she sleep with Charlie on purpose, knowing he and Grace had chemistry, and is that the real reason she's never been able to tell Grace? It's guilt she'll have to live with, and it won't help now.

'If you think about it, it worked out, right? You had the husband, the big house in Killiney, the lovely childhood for Luna?'

'That's not what I'm talking about.' Grace's voice is low, on the brink of tears. 'You're supposed to be my best friend. You kept this from me for a quarter of a century.'

Grace's face is paper-white. Siobhán moves towards her. She flinches, steps back, holding up her hands, shaking her head. 'No.'

'I did it for *you*, Grace. I kept it from you for your sake, for the sake of our friendship.'

Grace shakes her head again. 'If you're lying about the biggest thing in your life, I don't even know who you are.'

'Grace, please.' Siobhán reaches for her hands, but Grace steps further back, then sits on the edge of the sofa.

Siobhán tries again. 'Maybe now is not the time to thrash this out . . . with the girls missing . . .'

'Now is exactly the time.' Grace's tone has an edge. 'You let *hours* go by without telling me this critical piece of information. I . . . I don't know which is worse, that you kept it from me for twenty-five years, or for all of today.' Tears spill over and she swipes at her cheek.

'Honestly, it wasn't even on my radar today,' Siobhán says. Or at least, it wasn't until an hour ago, when she remembered what Ré had asked her last night about the concert . . . but it's not going to help to mention that right now to Grace. 'Like, I don't think about it ever. I've been talking about Aidan from Melbourne for so long, most of the time I believe he really is Ré's dad. The lie becomes the truth.'

Grace tilts her head, assessing something.

'So why are you telling me now?'

And suddenly Siobhán feels scared. Not of Grace, of course not. But the enormity of this secret. The idea that Ré may have found out last night. The suggestion, however unlikely, that it has something to do with why the girls argued. Is this all down to her misguided attempt to protect the friend she loves most in the world?

40

'Why, Siobhán?' Grace asks again, eyes narrowed. 'Why are you telling me this now?'

The living room feels cooler still, and Siobhán rubs her hands up and down her goosebump-studded arms, aware of Grace's eyes drilling into her.

She lowers herself into her reading chair by the window, usually her favourite spot in the room. Now it feels uncomfortable.

Deep breath. 'Because Xavi told Charlie he said something last night when he was dancing with Ré.' Siobhán swallows against a tightness in her throat. 'Charlie said they were raised like brother and sister, and we wonder if Ré picked up on it.'

'Wait, please don't tell me Charlie knew all this time?' There's real anguish in Grace's voice now, and Siobhán feels every inch of it. How had she thought she could get away with this?

'No! Absolutely not. I never told a soul.' She pitches forward on her chair. 'For *you*, Grace. You have to understand, all of this was for you.' A beat. 'But Charlie suspected. He hinted at it over the years, and I brushed him off. I guess he felt strongly enough to intervene when he thought Xavi and Ré were getting close at the wedding last night.'

Grace blinks. 'Wait – you think Ré said it to Luna and things got heated?'

Siobhán shakes her head. 'Charlie wondered that, but it just doesn't make sense. If Ré said it to Luna and they discussed it, why would either of them get mad?'

'I don't know, but you should have said it earlier to the guards, that they're sisters.' Grace's mouth twists over the word 'sisters'. 'It could matter.'

'Maybe it would matter in a good way,' Siobhán says in a small voice. 'Maybe they're less likely to hurt one another if they know they're sisters.'

Grace just shakes her head.

Back in the kitchen, Charlie and Emma-Rose are huddled together at the island. Charlie is rubbing his temples again, and Emma-Rose is rubbing his back.

'Charlie, are you OK?' Siobhán walks towards him.

'I'll be fine. It's just another aural migraine. I don't usually get two so close together.'

'Aural migraine?'

'It's a migraine with no pain – just flashing lights in my peripheral vision, but it's hard to see,' he explains.

'Caused by stress,' Emma-Rose adds.

A little flag goes up in Siobhán's memory: Ré sitting in the pool house on Friday morning, rubbing her eyes, unable to see properly. Siobhán had thought she needed the optician. Was it an aural migraine? Maybe they're genetic? Triggered by the stress of Marrakesh, or whatever else is going on? God, poor Ré. All Siobhán wants is to hug her.

'Xavi's gone out for some air,' Charlie says, his hands still at his temples, his eyes closed.

Siobhán swallows. 'Does he know?'

Charlie opens his eyes. 'It's only fair when the rest of us know.'

His gaze swivels from Siobhán to the kitchen doorway, where Grace is standing.

'Grace . . .' He gets to his feet, steadying himself with one hand on the island.

'Don't, Charlie.'

'I didn't know.'

She steps forward, just inside the door now. 'Maybe you genuinely didn't know Ré was yours, but you slept with my best friend when you were texting me, asking me when I was going to give in to a date. Remember all that?'

His head dips low. 'I know. I have no excuse. I'm sorry. We were young, I suppose . . .'

'Not *that* young, and we were friends, all three of us. How could you do— Oh, for fuck's sake, who even cares?' Grace throws up her hands. 'We just need to find them.'

Emma-Rose is on the other side of the kitchen now, listening to all of it, her eyes flitting from Charlie to Grace. She shakes her head slightly, to herself almost, and Siobhán picks up on it.

'Emma-Rose?'

'I'm so sorry.' Her skin flushes. 'I didn't know . . . and I . . . I told Xavi and Ré they were a cute couple. I'm sorry, I had no idea they were brother and sister.' Her eyes dart around the room. 'And then, later, I said it to Charlie. That's why he went over when they were dancing – because I said it would be cute if they got together.'

Siobhán waves Emma-Rose's apology away. 'You couldn't have known. But . . . was Luna there when you said it?'

Emma-Rose frowns. 'I'm not sure, I can't remember now. Sorry.'

Grace lets out an exasperated sigh. 'We need to get on to O'Connell to let her know this latest news and get back to finding the girls.'

*

O'Connell is furious. Absolutely *fuming*.

Pressing the phone close to her ear, Siobhán walks out to the hall and closes the kitchen door.

'It doesn't really change anything, though. They're still missing, and we still don't know where or why.'

'Well, based on Charlie Caine's net worth, it certainly gives one of them a motive for murder,' O'Connell snaps.

It feels like a slap. The phone almost slips from Siobhán's hand, and it takes her a moment to gather a response.

'No,' she says after a moment, quietly. Then stronger. 'No! It absolutely doesn't.'

'Why do you think people kill people?' O'Connell carries on before Siobhán can answer. 'Domestic violence. Alcohol-fuelled arguments. And financial gain, inheritance.'

'No way. They're twenty-four. They're not thinking about inheritances. And I mean, there's Xavi, too, and just . . . no. Ré isn't even into money.'

'And Luna?'

Siobhán is shaking her head.

'Siobhán?' O'Connell asks.

'No. She's maybe more into money than Ré, but that's not it. One of them is not going to do something to the other over money. I'm sure of it.'

Silence on the other end of the line tells Siobhán that the detective is not sure of this at all.

41

The day of the wedding

RÉ STARES AFTER XAVI as Charlie steers him, weaving between guests on the dancefloor, and on into the kitchen.
You were raised like brother and sister. It's inappropriate.
And unless her mother has genuinely mixed up her concerts, Aidan cannot possibly be her dad. And now it seems oh so clear. Of course it's Charlie. Charlie, who has always been good to her, included her, treated her like part of the family. Generous, kind, welcoming. A father figure. Her actual father. Charlie, who she's known inside out her whole life. Charlie, who likes good suits and smart shirts and red wine. Charlie, who loves golf and rugby but can hold his own in conversation about football and GAA. Charlie, who only reads non-fiction, and only political and sports biographies. Charlie, who says his favourite food is Japanese, but really, it's the Kung Po chicken from his local Chinese takeaway. It's always been Charlie. *Jesus.* A wave of dizziness sweeps over her, and she looks for somewhere to sit.
'Are you OK?'
Luna. Strands of hair stuck to the side of her face. Skin glistening from dancing. Eyes slightly glazed, eyeliner smudged. Still beautiful. Always beautiful. Her half-sister. Wow. Does she

know? *Slow down, slow down.* It might not even be true. Maybe Charlie in his alcohol blur really does think it's inappropriate. Because Xavi is his son or because Xavi is older or because Xavi is Luna's brother . . .

'Ré? Are you OK?' Luna repeats. Her pupils are huge. One strap of her dress slips towards the cusp of her shoulder.

'Yeah, I need to sit down. But first I need a very large gin.'

'OK, I know a great free bar,' Luna says with a tipsy wink. Taking Ré by the hand, she leads her to the cocktail bar. The dimpled barman and the Scottish manager are both on duty, pre-filling glasses of red wine.

'I thought the bar would be slowing down by now,' the Scottish guy says with a grin, 'that I might be sending Robert home. No fear of that!'

'Not with us,' Luna replies. 'We're party people.'

'What can I get you, ladies?' asks the barman they now know as Robert.

Luna does the ordering. 'Two very large gins, please.'

As he pours, she whispers to Ré, 'He's quite cute. What age do you reckon – mid-thirties?'

Ré nods absently.

'And the Scottish one isn't bad either, though way too old. And clearly taken by my mother.' An eyeroll. 'Emma-Rose is not going to be pleased.'

'Would Charlie mind, do you think?' Ré says, his name feeling strange in her mouth.

'God, no,' scoffs Luna. 'It's so long since they split, they're really just good friends now.' Luna turns to lean against the bar, wobbling slightly in her heels. 'And we're literally here at his wedding. It would be a bit rich.'

'It's nice the three of you get on so well.' Ré isn't sure where she's going with this. What does she think Luna is going to say?

Yes, we get on well, but I've always felt there's a missing sister in the equation?

Their drinks are ready – double Dingle gins with Fever-Tree and a slice of cucumber in each. Robert smiles as he hands them over, deepening his dimple. Luna tips the tonic into each glass, thanks Robert and shimmies her way through the dancefloor, with Ré following just behind.

'Let's sit for a bit,' Luna says over her shoulder, and walks carefully around the perimeter of the pool. At the far end, she lowers herself on to a lounger. One of the gins wobbles, and a little drips on her dress.

'Here, sit on that one,' she instructs Ré.

Ré does as she's told and takes a long swallow of cold gin and tonic as soon as Luna hands it to her.

'Better?' Luna asks.

Away from the speakers and the moving bodies on the dancefloor, it is better, yes. The pool, lit by night lights, sparkles just beyond their loungers, the water lapping gently at the sides. Ré takes in some deep breaths and another sip of her gin. She really shouldn't say anything about Charlie. She should wait to speak to her mother. This is not the time or place. She's had too much to drink, and so has Luna. *It can wait. It can wait.*

'I think Aidan's not my dad.'

Luna's head snaps up. 'What? Why?'

She fills her in – the concert date, her mother's evasiveness.

'But maybe she really did forget which concert it was.' Luna takes a long swallow of gin. 'Why would she lie?'

Stop now. Don't say it.

'Because maybe my real dad is someone closer to home.'

'What do you mean?'

Ré lets it sit in the air between them for a moment. Waiting for Luna to figure it out.

'Like, you mean someone we know?'

'Yep.' Ré crosses her ankles, studying her boots. Waiting.

'Who, though?' The words come in a breath of excitement. Luna lives for gossip.

Again, Ré stays quiet.

Luna stretches a foot across the divide between the loungers, nudges Ré with the toe of her sandal. Ré recognizes the sandals – a pair of gold Jimmy Choo heels that belong to Grace. She's seen them before. When Siobhán had panicked over footwear for an awards dinner, Grace had sent those same sandals to Siobhán's house in a taxi. It was Ré who met the taxi man with his delivery, and his bemused expression still makes her smile.

'Oh, come on, this is major goss,' Luna prods. 'Spill.'

'I think it's Charlie.' Ré immediately regrets it. What is she doing?

Stunned silence greets her from the other lounger. It's dark down here, and she can't see Luna's face. She can hear her breath, though. And the beating of her own heart.

'I don't know for sure. Just something your dad said when Xavi and I were dancing. That it was inappropriate.'

Luna laughs. 'Oh my god, Ré. That's because he's older and he's my brother. Jesus. That's where your brain went? That my dad is your dad?'

'Yeah.'

'You are *hilarious*. This is one of the funniest things you've ever come up with.' She laughs again, but it's tinged with a brittle edge.

'It sounds mad because it's out of the blue and we've known each other our whole lives,' Ré says. 'But if you take a step back and look at it objectively . . .'

'What, Aidan might not be your dad, therefore the only remaining conclusion is that it's Charlie Caine?'

'Well, no, of course not.' Ré's throat is suddenly dry. She lifts her drink, but there's only ice left. 'It's just that my mum was friends with Charlie since college. He and Grace were introduced to each other by her.'

'I know that. I'm still not joining the dots here?' Luna has adopted a haughty, condescending tone.

'I mean, it's not beyond the realm that my mum and Charlie might have had a thing at some point. And we know your mom and Charlie weren't together very long when they found out she was pregnant with you.' This is a story Grace tells often, usually with a romantic spin – Charlie picking her up and swinging her round, proposing on the spot. Maybe if Charlie took a minute before proposing to people, he wouldn't be on his third wedding, Siobhán had said to Ré, the last time the story came up.

'Eh, still a bit of a leap.' Luna pretends to take away Ré's glass. 'Maybe you've had one too many of these.'

Ré forces a smile.

'Listen, I get it,' Luna says in a gentle but patronizing tone. 'You've never had a dad, and if you're worried Aidan's not actually your father, it makes sense to try to grab hold of someone solid, someone who's been a kind of father figure. But you'll see when you sober up how crazy it sounds. And honestly, it feels a bit weird to me. So maybe we should talk about something else?'

Shit. She'd wanted an answer, hoped Luna might shed some light. Maybe even be excited at the idea that they could be sisters.

But Luna isn't ready to process that her best friend might have a claim on her dad, and who could blame her? This is huge. To go from beloved only daughter to . . . not only daughter. It's too much, and Ré shouldn't have said it. And yet, sadness creeps in. And the first sting of rejection. Her friend is not rushing to welcome her into the family. Her friend is not excited that they might be sisters. Understandable. But sad, too. And maybe Luna just needs some time to let the idea take root. Maybe the thing to do is let it lie for now. To try again later when it's sunk in.

'You're right,' Ré says, forcing light into her voice. 'Let's talk about something else.'

42

Luna decides they need one more glass of champagne each to round off the evening and gets up to go to the bar.

Ré sits quietly in her absence. The pool glitters white-gold under the lights and the music is lower now – maybe because she's adjusted to being a little away from the dancefloor, or perhaps the DJ has been asked to turn down the volume. A subliminal message to the guests that it's time to finish up. Ré has no interest in getting back on the dancefloor, no wish to bump into Xavi or Charlie.

Luna returns with two oversized wine glasses filled to the brim with champagne.

'Figured we may as well go big or go home.'

'Cheers,' Ré says, trying not to spill the drink as she takes it.

Beside her, Luna arranges herself on the lounger again, legs crossed at the ankle, sky-high sandals still in place, her face illuminated by her phone screen as she scrolls and sips.

'That's weird,' she says, and Ré turns to look.

Luna's frowning at her phone.

'What's weird?'

'Oh, nothing. Just a message from my friend Laura.'

One-handed, with her drink still in her other hand, Luna begins to type, but then she puts down her phone.

'I'm too tired to reply.'

'What was weird about it?' Ré asks.

'It doesn't matter.'

Ré rolls her eyes. This is what Luna does. Brings something up, then gets all coy. Makes Ré feel small for asking. 'Nobody can make you feel small' – that's what her therapist used to say. And it's true, but also not always. Luna has the power to make Ré feel small.

And it's this thought that makes her say what she says next.

'Oh! I nearly forgot – I was talking to Jasmine. We made peace.'

Luna turns. 'You did?'

Ré warms to her theme. Luna won't like that Ré and Jasmine connected, made up without including her. 'She's actually lovely. Really fun, really easy to talk to. We might stay in touch, meet for a drink.' It *could* be true. 'We bonded over our—' Ré stops. Luna might not want to hear that they bonded over a mutual antipathy towards her new stepmother. 'Over our sore feet.'

Now that's lame, no pun intended, she thinks, smiling in the darkness.

'Well, if you didn't wear those clumpy boots to dance, your feet wouldn't hurt.'

Says the woman wobbling in her six-inch heels.

'It was nice, though. It reminded me how well we got on back then, how fun she was before it all went wrong.'

'Yeah, I still don't trust her,' Luna says. 'And it's awkward that she's here. Hopefully, after tonight, that's it, I'll never see her again.'

Jasmine's words come back to Ré. *I think Luna was perfectly happy to cut contact.*

Ré takes a long swallow of champagne. 'You did like and trust her back then, though, right? I mean, you were sad when we weren't allowed to talk to her?'

'I feel like maybe I'd outgrown her.'

Ré hears the little intake of breath. This is a tell that Ré knows well: when Luna says something she wants to sound casual but is anything but, she does a little self-conscious inhale at the end of her sentence.

And Ré can't help pushing a little.

'She said I should ask you about it, actually. Why you were happy to cut contact?'

'I wouldn't trust a word that comes out of that girl's mouth. She's still trying to deflect blame ten years on.' Luna swings her legs off the lounger and, with a little stumble, gets to her feet, champagne in hand. 'Anyway, I'm going inside to the pool house.'

Ré has known Luna her whole life, and she knows this tone, this faux dismissiveness. Luna is hiding something. Ré gets up to follow.

43

Now

SIOBHÁN DISCONNECTS HER CALL with O'Connell and walks towards the kitchen, her mind rolling over what the detective had said about Charlie's net worth. Should she say it to the others? When she walks in, they're mid-conversation, throwing around ideas about what to do next, so she leaves the – plainly preposterous – topic of inheritance and financial gain for now.

Grace looks up at her. 'I think we should call to Jasmine and ask her more about the argument she heard.'

Grateful that Grace has spoken to her, Siobhán replies with more enthusiasm than the suggestion warrants. 'Yes! She might have remembered more. Emma-Rose, would you have Jasmine's address?'

Emma-Rose is standing by the kettle with her head in her phone, and looks up now. 'Sorry, I missed that – Ben is texting me about his van. The guards haven't told him if they're done with it. Did Detective O'Connell say?'

'No, but I imagine they'll need to hold on to it . . . there was evidence the girls had been there. I'm guessing maybe more blood.' Siobhán swallows.

Emma-Rose's eyes widen. 'I'm so sorry.' Gone is all of this

morning's dismissiveness. And now Siobhán finds herself wishing for it, wishing for the time when Emma-Rose might have been right – when they might just have been partying elsewhere. 'OK, I'll let Ben know,' Emma-Rose says quietly. 'And sorry, you were asking me something else?'

'Would you have Jasmine's home address? And her number, so we can make sure she's there.'

They take Grace's car, travelling in silence through Sandycove and Glasthule towards Blackrock. Jasmine's flat is in a pretty two-storey block of apartments near Seapoint beach, and Grace pulls into a parking space close to the main door. She hasn't said a word for the entire journey and, after an initial attempt to apologize again, Siobhán hasn't either. Every bit of friction between them today – Grace's lie about the mugging, even Luna's text – it all pales in the shadow of Siobhán's huge betrayal.

'It's number thirteen,' Siobhán says, getting out of the car. Grace doesn't respond, but gets out, too.

The small car park is quiet, only half full on this sunny Sunday afternoon. Most people are at the beach, Siobhán supposes, or at barbecues or on walks. And it sears her now, a desperate wish to have that life again – to do something as normal as going for a walk. She presses number 13 on the keypad and a click tells her Jasmine has unlocked the front door.

Number 13 is on the first floor, right at the back of the building, and Jasmine is waiting for them there, the door already open. She looks different now. The dress has been replaced with a grey marl T-shirt and white tracksuit bottoms. Her hair is scraped back in a ponytail and her face is free of make-up. Her smile is unsure, brief.

'Come in. No news?'

Siobhán shakes her head and steps into the narrow hallway. Grace follows, and Jasmine closes the door, then ushers them down to a surprisingly spacious living room, where she gestures for them to sit.

'You wanted to see if I could remember anything more about the argument?'

Siobhán nods and sits on the couch, while Grace takes a seat on a nearby armchair.

'Can I get you any tea or coffee?'

'No, honestly, we just want to chat, and then we'll leave you in peace.' Siobhán manages a small smile. 'You have a beautiful apartment,' she adds with autopilot politeness.

'Thanks. I'm only renting, but I'd really like to buy it someday. It's lovely and quiet and near my mum.'

'How is your mum?' Siobhán asks.

'She's good, always busy with work and friends and golf.'

'It must be eleven years since your dad died? Twelve?'

Jasmine nods. 'Almost thirteen.'

How had they not been more compassionate, Siobhán thinks now. They hadn't known Jasmine at the time her dad died, but they'd heard about it later when the girls became friends. And still Siobhán had called the guards. And still Grace had told the girls to cut contact.

'You were so young.' Siobhán's eyes brim with tears. It barely registers, on this day where everything makes her cry.

'Yeah. My mum was brilliant, though, even when I was putting the heart crossways on her.' She plucks a gold tea-light holder off the mantelpiece, twists it in her hand.

'Jasmine, we shouldn't have been so hard on you back then,' Siobhán says. 'You were just reacting to circumstances.'

'I appreciate you saying it, and I'm sorry, too, for what I did. It was a horrible breach of trust.' Jasmine puts the tea-light holder carefully back on the mantelpiece. 'I don't even know what I thought I was going to do with the credit card. I never used it, you know that?'

'I know.'

'I did neck the meds, though.' Jasmine grits her teeth. 'Sorry.'

'And sold the Chanel watch, one assumes,' Grace says under her breath.

Jasmine shakes her head emphatically, addresses Siobhán. 'I never took the watch. I wouldn't do that. I'd seen it; Ré had told me it had huge sentimental value. I would never have taken it.'

Her eyes flit to Grace.

There's an awkward silence as Siobhán tries to come up with a response.

'I guess if you were drinking a lot and taking pills, you might not remember, but if it's gone, it's gone, and it's not why we're here, we should—'

Jasmine holds up her hand. 'You're right, it's not why we're here, and I promised myself when I saw you all on Friday that I wouldn't do this, but I need to say it. If you want to know where the watch ended up, you need to speak to Luna.'

Grace rears up immediately. 'Excuse me?'

Jasmine nods, her face white. 'I can't stand here in my own flat and continue to take the blame. I told the guards Luna took the watch, and they obviously didn't listen. Luna wasn't averse to a bit of shoplifting herself, and she was a magpie for shiny things. Those diamond earrings you thought you lost at the beach, Siobhán?'

Siobhán nods, mouth open.

'She took them, too.' Jasmine looks from Grace to Siobhán. 'Don't you remember the other things that happened back then? When Luna was caught with someone's AirPods and another girl's brand-new iPhone in her locker?'

'That was down to bad influence,' Grace says through gritted teeth.

'Well, that's easy to say,' Jasmine says tightly. 'And I imagine if I had kids who were caught red-handed – remember, the school literally searched her locker and found them – I'd say the same.' She folds her arms, glares at Grace.

Siobhán sits quietly listening. Jasmine has a point: Luna did get in trouble for stealing, even if Grace claimed it was a misunderstanding. The school would have expelled Luna if Charlie and Grace hadn't helped refurbish what is now called the 'Gill–Caine Library' in Rathwood Park School.

Jasmine continues. 'Luna took the watch.' Four words, enunciated slowly, carefully and very clearly.

'So easy to push the blame on her when she's not here,' Grace hisses. 'I'd like to see you say it to her face when she's back.'

Jasmine nods, two spots of red in her cheeks now. 'No problem. I would have done ten years ago, if anyone had given me the chance. It suited Luna quite nicely that you made her cut contact with me.' Her voice gets louder, but she stays calm and firm. 'And she had no qualms about posting on Snapchat, telling people I'd been questioned by the gardaí, that the vice principal's niece might be expelled, until someone – you, maybe?' – she raises an eyebrow at Grace – 'made her take it down. I lived it. Believe me when I say I'm long over it. But I won't stand here and have you accuse me of doing something I didn't do.'

Siobhán lifts her hands. 'OK. We all need to take a minute.' She gives Jasmine a small nod. A message that says *I hear you*. That says – she realizes now – *I believe you*.

'I think . . . I think this is a topic for another day, when we find the girls.' Siobhán looks at Grace, then at Jasmine. 'Luna can speak then. Fair?' She doesn't wait for a reply. 'Let's get back to why we're actually here. Please?'

Jasmine, still at the fireplace, nods.

Grace sits back in the chair without replying.

'Jasmine,' Siobhán says, 'can you think of anything else about last night?'

'OK.' Jasmine's voice is still tight, but she looks like she's trying to help. 'I've been going over what I heard.' Her heels are on the hearth and she rocks backwards and forwards slightly as she speaks. 'The thing that keeps jumping out is the word "Marrakesh". I definitely heard that. And it's clouding everything else in my memory now, if you know what I mean?'

Siobhán nods. 'We've since discovered there was a mugging in Marrakesh. Does that help?'

Jasmine purses her lips. 'Maybe . . .' Her eyes go to the far wall, or somewhere in the middle distance, and Siobhán and Grace sit quietly while she thinks.

'Now I feel like I *did* hear the word "mugging", but I wonder am I just thinking that because you've said it?'

'It's possible.' Siobhán has a crystal-clear childhood memory of a time she got lost on a beach on holiday in Spain and was found by police – the beach part was true, the police part imagined.

'Like, it might not be real at all,' Jasmine says thoughtfully, 'but now I feel like I can hear Ré's voice saying something about a mugging, and then' – her face lights up – 'yes! Something about an email?'

44

The day of the wedding

THE DOOR OF THE garden house shuts in her face. Ré steps back, startled, sloshing champagne over the rim of her glass on to her wrist. Maybe Luna didn't hear her get off the lounger. Maybe Luna didn't see her right behind.

But it's more likely that Luna just doesn't want to talk.

This is what she does. Small things. Never anything to warrant an accusation. If asked about the door, she'd say she didn't realize Ré was just behind her. Like forgetting to tell Ré about plans. Like overlooking her texts. All easy mistakes to make. Unless they go on for a lifetime.

And Ré puts up with it. When they were in primary school, it confused her when Luna suddenly left her out. By secondary, she could see it was deliberate. Luna never did anything often enough to break the friendship. Just every now and then when she was irritated. Or – as Ré began to see in college – to test how far she could push Ré. To be a little bit mean to a point where Ré reacted. Then nice Luna was back.

After college, they finally went their separate ways. And for the first time in her life, Ré felt free, out from under Luna's push–pull power. They never fell out, but there was a distance.

A natural distance, because London is big. A social distance that suits Ré. But here they are, back together. And here Ré is, facing a closed door. She pushes it open and steps inside.

The sound of running water tells her Luna is in the bathroom. Getting ready for bed or avoiding further talk? Ré goes into the bedroom and pulls the curtain across the glass doors, standing for a moment to look out. The doors face out to the back of the garden and the laneway beyond. It's dark and almost eerie, and apart from the thud of music, there's little sign that there's a wedding party in full swing. She draws the curtain fully across, walks back to her bed and flops down, again sloshing champagne from her glass. *Idiot.* Maybe she should go to bed. It's been a weird day, and she's drunk and exhausted. She checks her phone, but there's no reply from Aidan. It's late now anyway: she'll have to wait until morning. With practised ease, she removes her contacts and puts on her glasses. The tap is still running in the bathroom – Luna seems to be taking even longer than usual. Something is clearly bothering her. Something about the Jasmine conversation? Ré goes back over her exchange with their former friend – her own apology, followed by Jasmine's. The ghosting, and Jasmine's response:

Let's just say I think Luna was perfectly happy to be asked to cut contact.

And something else, just before they were interrupted:

But if you think about it, what would I have done with—

With what? Ré sits up on the bed, thinking, looking around the room. Her eyes fall on the bedside table, on Luna's velvet jewellery pouch. One necklace and one pair of earrings have spilled out on the night stand. Everything else is inside.

Luna the magpie. Luna who barely escaped expulsion for stealing.

Luna took the watch. Of course she did. It's so obvious now. That's what Jasmine had been about to say. *What would I have done with your mother's watch?*

Ré stares at the night stand, thinking. And then she sees something that turns everything upside down.

45

Now

SIOBHÁN AND GRACE ARE back in the car outside Jasmine's building. Grace turns the key in the ignition and switches on the aircon but doesn't start to drive just yet. The seat burns hot under the backs of Siobhán's legs as the late-afternoon sun beats down and she tries to order her thoughts.

Jasmine possibly heard something about a mugging and something about an email. And it could have been either girl's email, either girl's voice she heard.

She turns to face Grace, who is staring straight ahead, hands gripping the steering wheel.

'I think we need to access their email accounts.'

'Yeah.'

'We can check with the guards to see if they can get in on Ré's phone. It wouldn't be password protected there once the phone itself is unlocked. I don't know how we'd get into Luna's email, though.' Siobhán pauses to think. 'You'd have to try on your phone, since we don't have hers. Would you know the password for her email?'

'No.'

'Would she have any go-to password? Like, Ré uses Dublin111

for absolutely everything, no matter how often I tell her to come up with something better.'

Silence.

'Grace?'

'No.'

Oh, for fuck's sake.

'Grace, come on. Our daughters are missing. That's where our focus should be. I'm sorry I didn't tell you about Charlie.'

No reply.

'Remember what you said outside the Egans' – when you felt I was blaming Luna, because of the text? Well, same goes here: once we find the girls, feel free to never speak to me again. But for now, let's work together. Please?'

Grace lets out a shuddery breath.

'OK, fine.' She rubs her hands on her lap. 'I don't know her passwords for individual email accounts, but her iPad PIN is 9999.' She turns to face Siobhán. Gives her a small smile. 'They're as bad as each other. Hacker's dream.'

'OK! So if we had her iPad, we could access whatever apps she has there. Oh.' Siobhán's elation dies. 'I guess it's in London.'

Grace shakes her head. 'She left it in my house when she was home two weeks ago. If we charge it, we'll be able to get into her email apps.'

'OK, let's do it.'

Siobhán leaves a voicemail for O'Connell, explaining what Jasmine had heard, suggesting she check Ré's email for Marrakesh references.

Grace reverses out of the parking spot and turns in the direction of Greystones.

*

Even though the guards have already checked Grace's cottage and confirmed the girls aren't there, as Grace pushes open the heavy front door, Siobhán can't help holding her breath. Desperately wishing to find them here. Desperately scared of what might lie inside. But there's nothing. Just Grace's big, bright kitchen-living room and the sea view beyond. So different to Siobhán's Dalkey home, and yet very much the same. Just like Grace and Siobhán, different but the same. Just like the girls – or so she always thought. Did she and Grace push their daughters together from the start? Of course, it had dawned on her over the years how awkward it would be if the girls fell out. She'd even said it to Ré, jokingly: *If you're going to fall out with any of your friends, please make sure it's not Luna.*

Joking, but also, very much not joking.

Grace throws her keys on the kitchen table and turns to face Siobhán, shoulders slumped. She, too, must have hoped they'd somehow be here. It's quarter to five now, more than twelve hours since the 999 call.

'I'll grab her iPad. It's in her room.'

Siobhán nods, and Grace makes her way across the kitchen to the open staircase.

Luna had sworn she'd never stay in the Greystones cottage after her mother sold their Killiney house – it was too far from Dublin city centre and all her friends, she'd said. Grace had nodded; she understood. Then she decorated the second bedroom in the pinks and whites Luna favoured, put in a brand-new double bed and a cute freestanding wardrobe, and filled the room with Carolyn Donnelly cushions and Cloon Keen candles. Sure enough, Luna, earning OK but not amazing money as a junior accountant, soon found she was more than happy to stay in Greystones. However far out from the city centre, it beat sleeping on friends' couches or paying for expensive hotels.

Grace comes back down, iPad and charger in hand. Wordlessly, she plugs it in beside the kettle and, together, they wait by the worktop. Within a minute, it's up to 2 per cent. Grace powers it on.

With visibly shaking fingers, she begins to swipe. Too quickly at first, missing the screen with the familiar Gmail app. Yahoo, too. She swipes back, her breathing fast, and hits the Gmail icon. It opens immediately, straight into Luna's inbox. Siobhán cranes her neck to read over Grace's shoulder.

An email about a college reunion. Her Aer Lingus check-in reminder for her flight back to London tomorrow. Grace puts her fist to her mouth, as though holding in a sob. Siobhán keeps scanning the inbox. A receipt for teeth whitening. An email from her credit card provider about an unpaid bill. A confirmation of a hair appointment last Thursday. That must have been for the wedding. Back when everything was OK. Back when the big concerns were which nail colour to wear and how to get the blow-dry to last from rehearsal dinner to Day Two lunch. The Day Two party they should be at right now. Grace scrolls, and both of them read, scanning dozens of life admin emails. The only personal emails are from Emma-Rose, letting her know about staying in the pool house, and an old friend from secondary school, someone called Lauren, who has just moved back from Spain and seems to have reconnected with her recently.

'There's nothing here that jumps out,' Siobhán says quietly when they're back to January. 'Nothing about Marrakesh, nothing that would cause an argument. Try Yahoo?'

Grace does, murmuring, 'She only uses this to sign up for newsletters to get discounts in shops.' And indeed, the entire screen is full of retail newsletters and digital receipts. There's nothing here to help, unless Luna's shopping habits are relevant – Ganni, Acne Studios, Zadig & Voltaire, Odd Muse. Siobhán raises an eyebrow. No wonder her credit card company has been in touch.

'Is there anything else we could check while we're here?' Siobhán asks. 'Social media?'

Grace swipes and taps the Snapchat icon, but it brings up a password screen.

'Maybe it logged her out on the iPad while she's been using it on her phone,' Siobhán says.

Grace nods and tries Instagram. This time they are led straight into Luna's account. The first photo on her grid is the Marrakesh art shop, then one of a Christmas tree in London, then a beach bar picture from last summer – Luna and Prisha with cocktails in hand. Grace tries Stories, but Luna hasn't shared anything from the wedding there.

'I could check her DMs?' Grace says tentatively, and Siobhán hears the unspoken uncertainty.

'Definitely.'

Luna's DMs are not quite as sporadic as her posts, but Instagram doesn't seem to be her preferred mode of communication. Presumably, like Ré, she mostly uses Snapchat. The most recent DM is from a week ago, responding 'thanks babe x' to someone called LoopyLu who had written 'gorge dress' in response to a photo. Grace slides quickly through ten more DMs, but there's nothing of any interest.

'What about Theo?' Siobhán asks. 'Would she have chatted to him on here?'

Grace puts 'Theo Hogan' in the search bar. His account is private, and Luna is not a follower.

'Is that weird?' Siobhán asks. 'Surely they followed each other if they went out together?'

'I think she unfollowed him when they broke up . . .'

Siobhán thinks again of the Polaroid they'd found in Theo's room. *Was that just this morning?* She pulls it out of her pocket as Grace continues to look through DMs. Is it summer in the Polaroid, in which case, according to the nose stud, it really does seem like Ré was with Theo when he was going out with Luna? Or could it have been *this* summer, long after they'd broken up? Ré is wearing a black sweatshirt with GRMA on the sleeve. This doesn't help – Ré wears the same type of clothes all year round. And Theo's in a burgundy Nike T-shirt. If he's anything like the men she knows, he might wear a T-shirt in the depths of January as easily as the middle of July. She slips the photo back in her pocket, the damning nose stud branded on her brain. Surely Ré wouldn't go behind her best friend's back like that? Then again, do they know their girls anywhere near as well as they believed they did?

A thought strikes her.

'I have one more idea – what if we try her photos? Would Luna have her cloud here?'

Grace scrolls again and finds it. When she clicks in, the photos hit like a punch to the stomach. So recent. So innocent. A different lifetime, but also, yesterday.

The dancefloor at the wedding, Charlie and Emma-Rose dancing.

The bar, the dimpled barman side by side with Ben, pre-pouring red wine.

Grace chatting to Ben, her smiling face close to his.

Ré dancing with Xavi.

An arty shot of a margarita against a blurred background.

For a moment, Siobhán can't speak. What she wouldn't give to go back twenty-four hours. To take Ré home, to stay in Dalkey, to hold her and keep her safe. Safe from whatever was done to her. Or safe from whatever she would do.

Grace is scrolling back further, and Siobhán sees why now – she's gone to April, to Marrakesh. The iPad screen fills with sunshine-lit brightly coloured photos of markets and food stalls and food. A glittering blue pool in what must be their hotel. The four girls bunched together for group shots – some selfies, some taken by someone else. Luna, tanned in string tops, her hair piled high on her head. Ré, pale in her staple black, arching a brow. The obligatory legs-on-lounger shot, dozens of times over, as Luna worked to get it just right. Book balanced on her knees in some, drink in hand in others. Luna doesn't really read fiction, Siobhán knows, but she often grabs Ré's books for a photo. Daytime sunning. Night-time drinking. Pouting faces. Grinning faces. All taken before the mugging, perhaps. Grace scrolls quickly forward again, letting out a sigh of exasperation.

'I was sure we'd find some kind of clue. This whole journey's been a waste.'

'It's not a waste. It's better to do something. And we could have found—' Siobhán stops. 'Hang on, Grace.' She points at the iPad screen. 'What's that?'

46

The day of the wedding

RÉ STARES AT THE night stand, at the earrings and the necklace that have spilled from Luna's velvet jewellery pouch. In the bathroom, the sound of running water stops.

She sits up straighter on the bed, wincing against an oncoming headache, and reaches to pick up the necklace. She'd know it anywhere. The Tiffany crescent-moon necklace Grace had bought Luna for her twenty-first. The one that had been stolen during the mugging in Marrakesh. So how is it here?

The bathroom door unlocks.

Luna steps out, wine glass still in hand.

'I think the champagne has caught up with me,' she says. 'I'm gonna sleep.'

Ré holds up the necklace.

'Where did you get this?'

Luna's face creases in bewilderment. 'My mom. You know that.'

'Yes, but it was stolen, in Marrakesh.'

As Ré watches, dawning realization creeps over Luna's features. She puts a hand on the door jamb.

'Oh, yeah. I forgot to tell you. They found it and sent it back.'

Ré hears the familiar intake of breath at the end of the

sentence. Luna's tell. She is thinking on her feet, and thinking badly.

'What? The police caught the guys?' Ré asks, playing along for now.

'Yeah.' Luna's mouth is set; her eyes flick to the side. Ré knows this look, too. Luna is getting behind the lie. Fully committed.

'That's weird. I'm in contact with the police liaison guy there. He literally emailed me last week.' She rubs her temple as her headache intensifies. 'I wonder why they didn't tell me they'd caught them?'

An airy shrug. 'Maybe they only caught the ones who attacked me, got my stuff back. *God*, I'm in bits, I've *got* to sleep now.'

'I'll ask them,' Ré says, in her own faux-casual tone. 'This all seems very odd.'

She pulls out her phone.

'What are you doing?'

'Emailing them.'

'It's, like, three in the morning. And you're drunk.'

'I can still write an email.'

Ré clicks into her Gmail and finds that, despite her protestations, the champagne haze is indeed making it difficult to find the email, or even focus on subjects and senders.

'By the way,' she says as she searches, 'I know you took my grandmother's watch. It was never Jasmine.'

'What the fuck?'

'I don't know why we never put it together before.' Ré is still using the same casual, conversational tone, quietly enjoying the shock on Luna's face. 'You were caught with a stolen phone in your locker not long after.'

Luna puts a hand on her hip. 'I never took that iPhone. Or anything.'

SUCH A NICE GIRL

'You're a magpie for things that aren't yours and you're a narcissist who takes what you want.' Ré can't believe she just said that. She's going to regret it tomorrow. But right now, she *really* wants to tell Luna exactly what she thinks.

'I may be a magpie,' Luna concedes, 'but I'm not stupid enough to steal a phone and hide it in my *own* locker. If I needed a new phone, I just had to ask my dad.' There's a slight and probably deliberate emphasis on 'my dad'. 'You're way off, Ré.'

'Whatever.' Ré is focusing on her inbox, on the unopened email from Marrakesh. It hits her now – is Luna actually telling the truth about the necklace? Maybe the email is not, as the subject suggests, just CCTV footage – maybe it's also to tell her they caught the guys? And for the last two weeks, she's ignored it, afraid of reliving the mugging. She goes into the body of the email, bypassing the video clip for now.

One step at a time. The words are blurry; she squints to read.

Dear Ms McKenna,

Further to my previous email, I am sending you a CCTV video clip in which you will see the two men who we believe robbed you. Unfortunately we can only see them from behind and there are no identifying features. As you are aware, we have not yet apprehended these men, but we are glad to have this footage (it is from a restaurant on the same street). It may help prompt a memory for you, something that may in turn help us. Please do contact me if you think of anything that will help us identify the perpetrators.

With my best wishes,
Mohamed Idrissi
Sûreté Nationale

A cold feeling spreads through Ré's stomach. So they categorically have not caught the men. Certainly not two weeks ago, when this email was sent, and surely if they had in the meantime, there'd have been a follow-up communication. Ré looks up from her phone, the movement making her headache worse. She watches her friend as she rummages in her suitcase for a tube of something then returns to the bathroom to apply it to her skin.

Why is she lying?

'Who from Marrakesh sent you the necklace?' she asks.

'I can't remember his name now,' Luna says from the bathroom, after a pause. 'One of the police guys we were talking to that night.'

'And they just put the necklace in the normal post and sent it? A four-thousand-euro piece of jewellery?'

'They sent it by courier.' Luna turns from the bathroom sink, looks out through the doorway. 'What's with all the questions?'

Ré stares at Luna, and Luna stares back.

'Oh, nothing. Just wishing I could get my grandmother's ring back, too.'

Ré clicks on the file in the email and presses play.

47

Now

SIOBHÁN'S FINGER IS STILL pointing at a spot on the iPad screen, but Grace has scrolled further on. 'Grace, slow down, go back – I just noticed something.'

'What?'

'Go to the photos of Luna in your garden. Her visit was two weeks ago, right? When you had the barbecue for Charlie and Emma-Rose?'

Grace nods and scrolls back up.

There.

A series of photos from a bright sunny afternoon in Grace's garden. A pre-wedding informal get-together with Charlie and Emma-Rose and some close friends. Luna is there, smiling for the camera. One shot posing with Charlie and Emma-Rose, another with Xavi, a third with Grace, cheek to cheek. A glass of champagne in her hand. A dusky-pink dress that sets off her tan. Light grey Birkenstocks. Hair in glossy waves. Pearly smile. Silver hoop earrings.

'I don't get it. What's wrong?' Grace asks.

'Now scroll down. She went out that night? After the barbecue?'

'Yes, she met some friends in Dún Laoghaire.'

The next photos are all taken in what looks like Haddington House in Dún Laoghaire, at the picnic tables at the front of the hotel. A group of people Siobhán doesn't know, with Luna at their centre. Still in her dusky-pink dress and her silver hoop earrings, but with something else now, too.

'Look.' Siobhán points. 'She's wearing her Tiffany necklace.'

Silence as Grace stares.

'Wasn't that stolen in Marrakesh? That's what you told me earlier.'

'Yes,' Grace says slowly. 'I don't understand.'

More silence now.

'Did she only pretend it was stolen? Would it have been some kind of insurance thing?'

'Oh, come on.' Grace runs a hand through her hair, frowning. 'She'd hardly do that. She knows she can come to me if she needs cash.'

'It's weird then, right?'

'Maybe she lost it and didn't want to admit it so pretended it was stolen?' Grace says hesitantly. 'And found it again later?'

'Maybe. It's just . . . odd. And when we know Marrakesh is something they argued about. It makes you wonder, doesn't it?'

Grace's eyes narrow ever so slightly. 'I don't get what you mean?' Her tone has a sharp edge now.

'I'm just thinking aloud. Marrakesh was a . . . a source of disagreement, and now we can see that the expensive necklace Luna said was stolen wasn't really stolen. And if she wasn't wearing it at the barbecue but did have it on when she was out with her friends, it almost seems like she's deliberately hiding that she still has it.'

'If she was trying to do that, why would she wear it at all?'

'Well, she wouldn't have imagined us here, looking at her iCloud photos . . .' And, Siobhán adds in her head, Luna does what she likes, with zero fear of consequences. That's how she's been brought up.

'Come on, Grace.'

With sudden and shocking force, Grace slams the iPad on the counter. The screen cracks, a neat, jagged line down the centre, but it seems not to register. She throws up her hands, and stalks to the other side of the kitchen.

'Grace . . .'

'No!' Grace shouts. 'All day you've kept on about Luna. "Luna must have done something."' She mimics Siobhán, screwing up her face, bobbing her head side to side, and oddly, it is this that stings more than Siobhán could have imagined. 'And to be honest, Siobhán, it's a *lot*. It's a fucking lot. And it's not getting us anywhere, all this blaming.'

Siobhán stares open-mouthed at her best friend.

'I . . . I'm not *blaming*. Grace, I'm trying to work it out. I—'

'I need some air.' Grace steps out through the front door and closes it behind her.

Siobhán phones O'Connell, who promises Siobhán they've already looked at all of Ré's email and social media apps on her phone, that they'll look again. She has Ré's phone in her hand right now. It's hard to tell if the detective is just humouring her, trying to get her off the call. Siobhán asks if O'Connell can phone her back when she's looked at the emails, conscious she's pushing it now, but desperate, too.

'It's a live investigation,' O'Connell reminds her, sounding as though she's forcing herself to be patient. 'I can't necessarily give you information about what I find.'

Siobhán looks up as the front door opens and Grace comes back in.

'But she's my daughter – don't I have a right to know?'

'She's an adult, and she's a missing person, so no, anything we find is confidential until we deem it otherwise,' O'Connell says. 'I'm sorry, Siobhán. But believe me, it's in the girls' interests that we follow procedure.'

Siobhán says a weary goodbye, ends the call and tries Abbey next. Of course, Abbey doesn't pick up. Ré never answers unknown numbers either.

She types a text:

Abbey, this is Siobhán, Ré's mum. Did she say anything about getting an email linked to what happened in Marrakesh?

Dots. Abbey is typing.

Yes, she said she got an email with the subject CCTV, which she assumed would be footage of the mugging but couldn't bear to watch. So she hasn't opened it yet.

Grace has moved to sit at the kitchen table now, head in hands. Fight gone out of her, perhaps. Siobhán walks over and nudges her, nods towards the text on her phone. 'Look at this.'

Grace squints to read. 'OK. What does that mean?'

'I don't know. But it's an email and it's about Marrakesh, and that's what Jasmine overheard. And the necklace wasn't taken, and . . .'

'And what?'

'I don't know . . . Look, let's go over everything.'

Grace huffs out some kind of response that might be an exasperated 'OK'.

Siobhán pulls out a chair and sits.

'We know that they argued about Marrakesh and that Ré may have discovered they're siblings.'

Grace nods. Siobhán continues.

'We know Jasmine's presence may have been a bone of contention, if Ré knew or found out that Luna took the watch and that she let Jasmine take the blame.'

'I don't believe for a second that Luna took the watch,' Grace snaps.

Siobhán closes her eyes. *Deep breath.*

'Well, put it this way – Jasmine says she did, and if Ré thinks the same, whether it's true or not, that might have caused a problem.'

'Fine. We also know that Ré was seeing Theo behind Luna's back.'

Touché.

'But possibly after they broke up,' Siobhán counters.

'Which is almost as bad.'

'Yes. OK.' Siobhán gets up and takes a notebook and pen from a bookshelf by the glass doors, raises her eyebrows to ask Grace if she can use them.

Grace nods. Siobhán sits back down.

She writes four words:

Jasmine
Siblings
Theo
Marrakesh

She reads them aloud then chews on the pen before remembering it's not hers.

'If we could just get into Ré's email ... I mean, wait, we probably can.' Siobhán sits up straighter. 'Assuming she uses Dublin111 for that, like she does everything ...'

Grace nods, looking unenthusiastic. Exhausted.

Undeterred, Siobhán goes to her own email app, logs out of her account and types Ré's address in the sign-in screen and 'Dublin111' in the password field. But a message on the screen tells her it's sending a four-digit code to her phone ending in

7544, which is, of course, Ré's phone. Not only can she not get in, she has also now alerted the guards to what she's trying to do.

It's dead end after dead end – every time they find something new, they hit a brick wall. She's about to suggest driving back to Dublin when her phone rings. O'Connell.

'Was that you just now, trying to get into Ré's email?'

'Yes . . .'

A sigh. 'I'm begging you, just let us do our job. When you do something like this, we don't know if it's Ré or someone else linked to the disappearance. It's a waste of our time chasing it down.'

Siobhán feels her face heat up. 'I'm sorry, I didn't think of that. And I'm not trying to be difficult. I genuinely believe if Grace and I have all the information you have, we can help.'

'I'm about to send you something. Could you have a look and come back to me?'

'Of course.' Siobhán's skin prickles. *What's coming?*

O'Connell hangs up and, seconds later, a video file arrives on WhatsApp.

Siobhán clicks in and presses play.

48

The day of the wedding

RÉ LEANS CLOSER TO her phone to watch the video, her stomach churning at the memories it brings back, her head pounding. A busy street in Marrakesh, viewed from up high. The camera must be near the rooftop of the restaurant. Pale pink buildings line the narrow, busy street. Pedestrians and motorcyclists weave around each other in both directions. A café. A red Coca-Cola umbrella. A stall selling fruit.

And there they are.

Oh god.

Ré sees herself, sees Luna. Ré in her blue sundress and Saltwater sandals. Luna in her white broderie anglaise top and denim shorts. Walking together, tired, she remembers, after hours of rambling. A crowd coming from the opposite direction – six or eight people clustered. Ré and Luna separated in their midst. And then it happens. Two men. Two horribly familiar men steering Ré towards a narrow side street. The camera doesn't stretch that far, and she can't see what happens next. But she doesn't need to. They said they had a knife. She never even saw it and wonders now if they were lying. And she wonders why she didn't hold out, resist. But in truth, she's not that brave. She's not the kind of person to take on two men on her own. She's a five-foot-two girl in unfamiliar territory in a two-against-one situation. Cowering against a wall on that dark, empty laneway, she handed over her phone, her money, her grandmother's ring. She doesn't need CCTV to remember this. To relive this. She relives it every other night when she's trying to fall asleep.

Onscreen, the pedestrians and motorcyclists continue up and down the street, oblivious to what's going on a few feet away. Meanwhile, Luna's on a different side street, facing two other men. How easy it had been to separate them. Divide and conquer. But then she spots something in the corner of her phone screen. Luna. Luna in her white top and denim shorts. Luna coming out of a shop, a plastic bag in her hand. Luna looking around. Luna disappearing inside a café beside the laneway. Coming back out. Moving to the laneway. Standing facing away from the camera now, looking up the narrow side street where Ré – back-then Ré – is being robbed. And Luna pulls back from the entrance to that narrow side street and flattens herself against the café wall. And then she hurries away in the opposite direction. Offscreen. Out of sight.

49

Now

SIOBHÁN LOOKS UP FROM the video. Meets Grace's eyes.

'Luna wasn't mugged.'

'I . . . She said she was. Maybe they'd let her go at that point?'

'We just saw her come out of a shop. With a bag in her hand.' Siobhán is speaking slowly, but she can hear the tightness in her voice, the barely controlled rage. 'While Ré was being propelled up that side street, Luna had popped into a shop.'

Grace's mouth is open, but no words come. Her hands twist on her lap.

'And then,' Siobhán continues, 'she looked into that street and she saw my daughter being robbed and she walked away. She fucking walked away.'

Grace's eyes widen. 'I honestly don't know what happened . . .'

Siobhán stabs the screen. 'You just saw what happened. Will I play it again? Here.' She hits play, holds the phone up to Grace's face. 'Look! She left her.' She's shouting now. 'She left Ré to deal with those men on her own!'

Grace stares in horror, shocked more, Siobhán realizes, at her reaction than what's on the video. Because this never happens. Siobhán does not lose it. She does not shout. And not at Grace, not at her best friend.

And now the next part of the puzzle slips into place. 'Oh my god, Luna claimed she was mugged to cover up, didn't she. Did you know she made it all up?'

'Of course not! Jesus, no!' Grace pulls back in her chair, putting distance between herself and Siobhán.

'*Anything* could have happened. What if they'd raped her? Killed her?' Siobhán is on her feet now.

'They didn't . . . it wouldn't . . .'

'You don't *know* that!' She bangs the table at the last word.

Grace jumps, eyes startled.

'Luna stole my watch.' Siobhán's jaw is clenched, her fists are clenched. 'She let me blame Jasmine.'

'That was ten years—'

'I'm not *done*!' Siobhán roars. 'She left Ré when she needed her, then lied about it.' Bits of spittle fly out of Siobhán's mouth, and she's vaguely aware of Grace putting a hand up to wipe her face. 'There she is in a photo, happily wearing the necklace she's told everyone was stolen. What did she say – her phone wasn't taken because she had it in her pocket and not in her bag? For fuck's sake, that's not how muggings work. How did you not wonder at that?'

'Siobhán, I . . . You're not being fair.'

Now the red mist truly descends. Siobhán has spent all day keeping the peace, backing down, playing nice.

'Being *fair*? We are way beyond fair. Luna hurt Ré. She had a knife, and she hurt Ré.' She takes a gulpy breath. 'Luna's a liar. A manipulator. And now she's done something to Ré.' Siobhán can hear her breath, fast and angry, and, in an echo of their earlier confrontation, the ticking of a wall clock. Only now the roles are reversed.

'Well, if Ré did see the clip,' Grace says, shouting, too, 'doesn't that mean that *Ré* was the angry one? That *she* lashed out?'

'She wouldn't . . .'

'Of course she would,' Grace snaps. 'I'm the one you confided in, remember? When you were looking for a therapist?'

'That wasn't—'

Grace cuts her off. 'I was there, don't forget. I saw her rages. Losing it over tiny things. You told me you thought there was something wrong with her. She's unpredictable, a loose cannon, and you know it.'

Siobhán's mouth drops open. 'You're the only person in the world I told that to, and it's a fucking shitty thing to throw it back in my face.'

'But doesn't this video mean that Ré is the one who had reason to be mad? That Ré has done something to Luna?'

'This is so you,' Siobhán says, ignoring the uncomfortable truth of Grace's words. 'You'd say anything to suit your own narrative. You're a selfish, self-absorbed, pushy, grabby dramaqueen narcissist, and Luna is exactly like you. So just fuck off.' Siobhán is aware that this is not the most mature way to win the argument, but she's far beyond caring.

Grace stares at her, mouth open, eyes wide. Siobhán has never spoken like this to her, and in the midst of everything, there's satisfaction in seeing Grace's shock.

She waits for the retort, ready to fight, ready to get more out of her system. Hours – or maybe years? – of built-up resentment. But Grace just picks up her keys, turns on her feet and opens the front door. When she slams it behind her, a framed print slips from the wall and crashes to the floor. The sound of a car engine draws Siobhán to the front window, where the low evening sun blinds her momentarily. With one hand shielding her eyes, she watches in disbelief as Grace reverses, turns, and speeds out on to the road.

50

The day of the wedding

'You left me.'

It comes out so quietly Ré barely hears her own words.

Luna is at the full-length mirror, plaiting her hair, her back to Ré.

In the reflection, Luna's eyes flit to hers.

'What did you say?' Still she doesn't turn around.

'You left me on my own in Morocco that day. You weren't being robbed by two other men in the same gang. You were in a shop. And you saw me, and you left me.'

'What are you talking about? Don't be ridiculous.' Luna is slurring.

Ré lets out a slow breath.

'That's why you have the necklace.' She scoops it up from the night stand. 'It was never gone.'

Luna laughs, high-pitched and strange. 'Oh, come on, Ré! What? You spot the necklace and decide just from that I made the whole thing up? That's a leap.'

Ré gets to her feet. Her boots are hurting, but it barely registers. She shoves the necklace in the pocket of her dress and walks across the bedroom towards her best friend. Her lifelong frenemy.

'Not a leap. A video.'
Luna whirls now. Lets go of her half-done plait.
'What?'
Ré holds up her phone, presses play.
This time she doesn't watch the video, she watches Luna's face.
Luna opens her mouth. Closes it again.
Then she turns away. Looking in the mirror, she resumes plaiting her hair. She does not watch the video.

This, more than anything, is what gets to Ré. That Luna left her is bad. That Luna lied about it is worse. But this – ignoring her, treating it as . . . as nothing . . . Her breathing speeds up and an all too familiar veil descends.

Without thinking, she thumps Luna, hard, on her shoulder.
Luna spins.
'What the fuck? Did you just hit me?'
'Don't turn away from me! Answer me. What if they'd hurt me?'
'Oh, get a grip, Ré. You were mugged. It happens every day. No need to make a drama out of it.'

Breathing hard, Luna turns back to the mirror again. It's deliberate; she's trying to get at Ré, and Ré is absolutely here for that. She grabs Luna's plait, yanks her back around to face her.

'What the fuck! I am not staying in this room with you. Get out of my way.'

'No!' Ré is properly roaring at her now. 'You are the most selfish fucking bitch I've ever met. It's all about you, always, you self-absorbed fucking cow.'

Luna's eyes flash. 'Oh, because you'd never do anything bad. Ré McKenna, Little Miss Perfect, such a nice girl. It's all bull, and you know it. You were just as bad as me with Jasmine. And now you've decided my dad is your dad. But *I'm* self-absorbed? Take a look in the mirror.'

'Do not push this back on me. Of all the things you've done

to me over the years, this is the first time I can see it objectively with my own eyes.'

'Oh, shut the f—'

Ré cuts her off with a slap across the face that shocks both of them.

Her hand stinging, her whole body shaking, Ré holds up her phone.

'I've seen this, and now everyone we know will see it, too.'

51

Now

SIOBHÁN STARES AT THE disappearing tail lights of Grace's car as Grace's words echo in her ears.

Doesn't that mean that Ré has done something to Luna?

What if it's true? *It can't be.* Either way, she needs to let the guards know. She phones O'Connell, tells her she's looked at the video, what it means. O'Connell has picked up on this, she says. She'd recognized Luna, understood what it meant about the mugging. One of her colleagues is making contact with the Moroccan police.

O'Connell advises Siobhán to go back to her house, to rejoin the others. She'll come by when she can, to regroup. Siobhán doesn't tell her that she's been abandoned in Greystones by Grace, that she has to call a cab to get back to Dalkey.

When the taxi pulls into Siobhán's driveway, she's surprised to see that Grace's car isn't there. Her anger has receded now, with guilt and defensiveness vying for first place. Maybe Grace just needed to let off steam, drive around. Siobhán doesn't really want to face her, not after everything they said. Though . . . not speaking doesn't feel great, either.

Inside the house, she goes straight to the kitchen to tell Charlie what they've discovered, and that Grace needed some time on her own, which is technically true. Charlie fills the kettle as she speaks and, suddenly, Siobhán really wants tea. The comfort of a hot cup on her hands, the familiar taste. She still hasn't eaten. Emma-Rose's sandwiches are curled and dry, sitting in the middle of the table.

Xavi's gone to pick up a takeaway for everyone, Charlie tells her. She nods. The thought of food is unappealing, but they're running on empty.

She asks if Emma-Rose is upstairs, and Charlie says she's gone to pick up some groceries, to stock Siobhán's fridge. He excuses himself to check messages, stepping outside to the garden.

Siobhán watches him walk across the lawn. The sun is lower in the sky, and it feels ominous, somehow. If it gets to dusk, gets to dark, and they're still missing . . . on TV, they always say the first twenty-four hours are critical in any missing-person case. She puts her hands on a kitchen chair to steady herself as another wave of dizziness threatens.

Outside, down by the bench at the end of the garden, she sees Charlie lean over, as though peering at something on the ground. What has he found? A wave of anxiety swells through her, and she rushes outside, then she's running down the lawn towards him. What is it? She wants to call his name, but no words come. She's just running. Closer now. He hasn't turned to see her. Maybe he didn't hear her. She slows, taking him in. One hand rests on the back of the bench, the other covers his mouth. His head is dipped, his shoulders shake. He's not looking at anything, Siobhán realizes as she draws level. He's crying. *Oh god. Charlie.* She's never seen Charlie cry. Not in the three decades she's known him. Good-humoured, upbeat, cheerful Charlie is sobbing. All this calm holding-it-together act – that's what it's been, an act. For them, she realizes, for her and for Grace, and now Siobhán thinks she might break down completely.

She goes to him, puts her arm across his shoulder and hugs him.

We'll find them. She doesn't know if she says it out loud or in her head. *We'll find them.*

Back inside the kitchen, Charlie gives Siobhán a quick, sad smile and continues making tea. Closing his eyes briefly as the kettle comes to a crescendo, he winces, and his hand goes to his temple.

'Another aural migraine?' she asks.

A nod. 'Never gotten three in a day like this.'

'Well, there's never been a day like this.'

His phone pings as he pours boiling water into the first cup. He squints at the screen, swaying slightly. 'It's hard to read when I have these goddamn things.' Then his brow furrows.

'What is it?' Siobhán asks.

'Emma-Rose got a message from her tenant about an ongoing black-mould problem and they mentioned that they're actually back in China.' He looks up. 'She hadn't realized. She says she's going to her house in Stepaside now, in case the girls are there, and asked me to let O'Connell know.'

Siobhán freezes. Is this it? Is this where they are? Although, the girls would hardly know the tenants were away, if even Emma-Rose didn't? It's still worth checking, Siobhán decides. 'Luna knows the house?'

Charlie nods, winces. 'She's been there. Back when Emma-Rose and I were first dating. Emma-Rose used to have us over for dinner.'

'Would she have a key?'

'No.' Charlie is rubbing his temple again. 'And to be honest, this all feels like a long shot. I'm going to tell Emma-Rose to leave it.'

'Long shot or not, it's something.' She opens Google Maps. 'Do you know her Eircode?'

He can't remember the postcode but calls out the address, and she enters it on Maps. Zooming out, the app shows that the house is at the end of a laneway off a back road in Stepaside. A remote countryside area with houses spread quite far apart. Near the Dublin mountains, and little else. They wouldn't have needed a key, Siobhán thinks. If the girls broke a back window, no one would see.

'I'm going to go there. Charlie, tell Emma-Rose I'm on my way, and remember to phone O'Connell. And . . . and text Grace.'

'I should go with you.'

'No, you stay here until you feel better – I'll phone you straight away if there's news.'

Siobhán has one eye on Google Maps as she hurtles along a narrow, winding road towards the Dublin mountains. A text pings through from Charlie. She doesn't slow down to read but gets the gist of it – Emma-Rose hasn't replied to his text, nor has Grace. He's left a message for O'Connell.

Google Maps tells her that her destination is on the left. Siobhán drives through a gateway and up a tree-shrouded driveway. Dusk is setting in, and there's an eerie, ominous feel to this remote setting – it really is the middle of nowhere. Maybe she should have brought Charlie. More than anything, she wishes Grace was here.

At the top of the driveway is a small white bungalow, with Emma-Rose's silver Range Rover parked at the front door.

The car appears to be empty. Emma-Rose must be inside the house. Siobhán slows to a stop at the top of the driveway, switches off the ignition. Other than the Range Rover, there's no sign of life. She swallows, takes a breath and gets out of the car.

She circles the Range Rover, towards the front door. It's ajar, just an inch. She pushes it carefully, her pulse accelerating, and steps inside. Silence. Emma-Rose must be somewhere in here, but – her heart sinks – she must be on her own. If the girls were here, there'd be noise. Wouldn't there? Her heart hammers in her chest. There's still some light in the sky outside, but the hall is dark, windowless. All the doors are closed. There's a tang of lemon in the air, as though the house has been cleaned. Lemon, and something else, something metallic. Siobhán steps forward, her eyes trained on what must be the living-room door. Then she stumbles. Trips over something on the ground. Reaching for the wall, she manages to stay upright. What is on the floor? She hunkers down, heart in mouth, stretching to touch whatever it is. Hair. Oh Christ. She yanks her hand back. It's a head, a person.

Someone lying face down on the hall floor.

52

Siobhán lets out a scream. She stands, fumbles for the light switch, but somehow, even before light floods the hallway, she already knows who it is, who's lying on the hall floor. The blonde bob, the Celine tracksuit. She feels her neck for a pulse. Nothing. Just blood. *Oh god, the blood.* There's blood everywhere. It's on Siobhán's hand, it's on the carpet, it's all over Emma-Rose's head and body. And it hits her now that that's what she's looking at. A body. There's no question, Emma-Rose is dead.

Siobhán is crying. Grabbing for her phone. Trying to call an ambulance. There's no way any doctor can help, but it feels like the right thing to do. After three failed attempts to hit the numbers, she gets through to emergency services. Trying hard to steady her voice, she asks for an ambulance and gardaí. It comes out in a whisper, but the phone operator seems to understand. She gives the address and hangs up. She's still on her knees, and now she realizes she's holding Emma-Rose's hand.

Emma-Rose, who was alive and making tuna sandwiches in her kitchen just a few hours earlier. Emma-Rose, who was deeply annoying for much of the weekend but today she made them sandwiches. Far too many sandwiches. This makes Siobhán cry even harder. What are they going to tell Charlie? His life partner, his third-time-lucky, the bride he married just yesterday. Dead. Murdered.

SUCH A NICE GIRL

Murdered by who? Not by one of the girls. No way. This is something bigger. Gently, she lowers Emma-Rose's hand to the carpet, lets go. Something on the floor catches the light from the bulb above, sparkling from beneath Emma-Rose's shoulder. Siobhán stares. A silver chain. A familiar crescent moon. Luna's. The girls have been here. Or maybe . . . She stands slowly, staring at the closed doors. Maybe they're still here.

53

Siobhán steps slowly through the hallway, taking in her surroundings. A narrow table with a ceramic bowl of silk flowers sits under a mirror but, otherwise, the hallway is empty. There is no sound from any of the rooms, and Siobhán feels a fresh flash of fear. The desperate need to find Ré mingling with the outright terror of what might lie behind these closed doors. She reaches a hand towards the first handle, a room just beyond where Emma-Rose lies, then stops, realizing she's about to contaminate a crime scene. She pulls the sleeve of her sweatshirt over her hand. She'll be in trouble with O'Connell for this, but if the girls are here, if they're hurt . . . Holding her breath, pushing down fear, she turns the handle and pushes the door. A living room. Brighter than the hall, a large window to the front letting in evening light. Two couches, a fireplace, a TV. No indication that anyone has been here. She steps out and moves down to the next door, most likely the kitchen.

The kitchen shows more signs of life. Two cereal bowls stacked upside down on the draining board. A box of granola on the countertop. Wrappers beside it – protein bars. Nothing else. She goes back out and turns down the longer part of the L-shaped hallway, where the bedrooms must be, and moves towards the first door on her right, again using her sleeve to turn the handle.

Inside is what looks like a child's bedroom: a single bed, a desk, posters on the walls. No sign of disturbance.

The next door is on the left and isn't quite closed. Siobhán pushes it slightly, enough to peer in, then pushes it wide. Another child's room, this time in a riot of pink. There's nobody here.

At the final room on the right-hand side of the hallway, Siobhán hesitates, then takes a sharp breath and turns the handle.

54

IN THE MIDDLE OF the room is a double bed. And in the middle of the double bed, there are what look like blood-soaked bandages. Siobhán stares, her heart in her throat. There's no question this time. It's not pizza sauce or nail polish or blush. Strips of gauze, red and brown with blood, thrown on the bed. Immobile for just a moment, Siobhán runs into the room and over to the far side, checking the floor, under the bed. Nothing. Nobody. But someone's been here. It's definitely blood. Emma-Rose? That doesn't add up. If she was killed in here, and dragged out, there'd be blood along the hallway. So . . .

She moves back towards the door, staring at the blood, then out to the hall. It feels wrong to leave, disloyal. But fingerprint care notwithstanding, she's potentially contaminating evidence.

Quickly now, she rushes to the front of the house, blinking back tears as she steps past Emma-Rose and out through the front door.

A garda car pulls up behind her car, and O'Connell emerges, looking furious. Sirens in the distance tell Siobhán more guards or maybe the ambulance are en route.

'Out of here. Now!' O'Connell roars at her. 'Get in your car and wait for me there.'

How will she tell Charlie, Siobhán thinks, staring through the car windscreen as gardaí file into the house. A sob lurches in her chest, and she rests her head on the steering wheel. She won't have to tell Charlie, she realizes; the gardaí will do that. And they'll have to question her, about finding the body. A new thought dawns. Will she be a suspect? A prickle of fear takes hold. Of *course* she'll be a suspect. However ridiculous it seems to her that she – nice, law-abiding, never-so-much-as-a-speeding-ticket Siobhán McKenna – could have killed Emma-Rose, the police don't know that. Fuck.

Her head is still on the steering wheel when a rap on the window startles her upright. O'Connell. Siobhán rolls down the window.

'Where did you go inside the house?' O'Connell asks, her voice clipped with anger.

'Living room, kitchen, three bedrooms, but I had my sleeve over my hand for the door handles and I didn't touch anything else.'

'Except the body, I take it?' She is absolutely fuming, and doing nothing to hide it.

'Yes, but I didn't know she was dead. I had to check, to help if she was alive.' A sob escapes. 'I'm sorry, but anyone would have done the same.'

O'Connell's mouth is set in a tight line.

'You've contaminated a crime scene. I understand you're worried about your daughter, but you *cannot* just barge your way into an investigation. Any conviction for tonight's murder is in serious jeopardy because of you, do you understand?'

Siobhán nods. 'There's . . . there's a necklace under her body. It's Luna's.'

O'Connell makes no reply, gives nothing away.

'What about Charlie?' Siobhán asks. 'Does he know?'

'Two of my colleagues are on their way to him now, to break the news. Who was there – in your house – when you left?'

'Just Charlie. He got the text from Emma-Rose saying she was on her way here, and he told me, and I left straight away.'

It strikes her now that there wasn't a phone beside the body. Was the text from Emma-Rose, or was someone else using her phone? Why draw people here, and also . . .

Despite O'Connell's fury, she risks asking one question. 'Is it strange the person who killed her didn't hide the body?'

O'Connell holds her gaze as she answers. 'Emma-Rose was tall. Perhaps whoever killed her wasn't strong enough to move her. Someone shorter than her.'

Siobhán's skin heats up, and O'Connell continues to stare. Is this supposed to elicit a response? Does she mean Siobhán? Or Ré, perhaps? For god's sake, Ré didn't kill Emma-Rose.

Finally, O'Connell breaks eye contact. 'One sec.'

She steps away from the car, makes or takes a call; it's not clear which. Then she's back, bending to the open window again.

'Where's Grace?'

'She went for a drive to get some air.'

A pause. 'Right. Obviously, you'll have to come in for questioning.' O'Connell nods towards a nearby garda car. 'Could you step out of your vehicle, please.'

55

THE QUESTIONING IN THE station is more intimidating than Siobhán expects. She's never had any dealings with the guards before, but today, sitting in an interview room, she gets a sense of what it must feel like to be a criminal. Answering the same questions over and over – what time she arrived, what she did inside the house, how the body looked. Two gardaí, or maybe they're detectives, write everything down, recording it, too, and they take a sample of her DNA, giving her a kit to swab her cheeks and under her tongue.

It's dark when the interview finally comes to an end. Her car is still in Stepaside, but nobody offers her a lift there, and she doesn't ask. The Uber app tells her a driver will pick her up in three minutes. Then home. Home to Charlie and the news he's been given. Home to a house without Ré. And . . . the thought strikes her now, where is Grace?

Charlie is in Siobhán's living room when she gets back, sitting on one of the sofas, staring straight ahead. Two gardaí keep him company – one on the opposite sofa, the other standing by the fireplace. Charlie is pale and hollow-eyed and barely reacts when Siobhán enters the room.

There is nothing to say. Nothing that can help or make this better. She goes to him, takes his hand, and they sit wordlessly as he continues to stare straight ahead. And now a tear spills out, trickles down his cheek. Siobhán feels her own eyes well up again. Christ almighty, how have they ended up here?

The garda by the fireplace – Siobhán realizes now that it's Garda Stephanie Harrington, who was at Charlie's house earlier – leaves the room and returns with two mugs of tea.

'Mr Caine, if you're up to some questions, it would really help us find out who did this,' she says, placing the teas on the coffee table.

Charlie nods.

'Could we see the text your wife sent?' she asks.

Charlie picks up his phone and reads in a voice that's almost robotic: '"Tenant just replied about the guy coming to sort the black mould – tenant says they're actually back in China so guy can come whenever. I didn't know that. And now I'm wondering about the girls? Long shot, but I'm going to go and check, just to be sure. Don't have that police woman's number, can you send it to me or let her know to go there? Love you HUSBAND!"'

Charlie's voice breaks on the last three words, and a sob chokes from Siobhán's throat. Garda Harrington is quiet for a moment, giving them space, perhaps.

Then she puts out a hand to take his phone. 'So I can see it myself, send a screenshot to Detective O'Connell, OK?'

Charlie nods, just as the living-room door bursts open and Xavi comes in, two Saba To Go carrier bags in his hands.

'There you are. Sorry I took so long; I called to a pal who used to hang out with Theo, to see if he had any ideas about where the girls might go. And then traffic was hell, everyone driving home from the beach.' He holds up one bag, looks at Siobhán. 'I just got five different things, I wasn't sure what you guys like. I got pad Thai for Emma-Rose and a red curry for you, Dad.'

Siobhán opens her mouth, closes it. Is she supposed to tell him his new stepmother is dead? Charlie is immobile. Harrington steps forward.

'You must be Xavi? I'm Garda Stephanie Harrington. Let me help you with the food. Let's go to the kitchen for a minute.'

Now Xavi seems to pick up on the atmosphere. On his dad's catatonic state.

'Dad? Did something else happen?' He looks at Siobhán. 'Is it the girls . . .?'

'Come.' The garda steers him gently by the elbow.

The male garda speaks now, addressing his words quietly to Siobhán.

'Emma-Rose wasn't Xavi's mother, is that correct?'

Siobhán nods.

No, not Xavi's mother. Just slightly neurotic, somewhat self-absorbed, generally irritating Emma-Rose, who died trying to find their girls.

56

CHARLIE STANDS.

'I think I need to be alone for a bit. I might go and lie down.'

'Are you sure? Maybe you're better off being around people?'

A headshake. 'Later, maybe. But for now—' His voice cracks. He pats her hand. 'Thanks, Siobhán. I'll come down if I need anything.'

He starts to walk towards the door, then turns to her again. 'Grace?'

'Not back yet.' Siobhán's stomach turns with anxiety. The fight with Grace feels so long ago. And Grace has no idea Emma-Rose is dead. Where *is* she? A frisson of worry takes hold.

Charlie walks out of the room, and Siobhán hears him climb the stairs to her guest room, the room he was supposed to share with Emma-Rose tonight. She gives it a minute, in case he changes his mind, then gets up to follow Xavi into the kitchen, leaving the other guard doing something on his phone in the living room.

As she walks, she texts Grace.

Sorry about earlier. I know this isn't the time to fight. Something's happened (not the girls) I think you should come back here x

In the kitchen, Xavi is sitting on a high stool at the island, his eyes wide with shock. Harrington is making tea for him.

He looks at Siobhán. 'I can't believe this.'

'I know. I'm so sorry, Xavi.'

'Thanks, but it's Dad who—' He shakes himself. Pushes back the stool. 'I need to go in to him.'

'He's gone up to lie down,' Siobhán says gently, taking a stool beside him. 'He asked for some time on his own.'

Xavi lets out a breath, looking slightly relieved.

'You . . . you saw her?'

A nod.

'She . . . How did she die?'

Oh god. Is Siobhán supposed to tell him?

Garda Harrington steps in. 'We can't give details yet, as the investigation is ongoing.' She's impossibly young, with beautifully applied make-up and butter-blonde hair tied in a short ponytail. As young as Ré and Luna, maybe.

'Was it an accident?' Xavi asks, in a way that suggests he's clinging to hope more than expecting a yes.

'We're investigating,' Harrington says, in what sounds like a Cork accent, spooning a teabag into the bin.

'So it has something to do with Ré and Luna.'

'We don't know.' She places a very milky tea in front of him.

'But Emma-Rose was found in her house,' Xavi says. 'The one she rents out?'

Garda Harrington nods.

Siobhán watches as Xavi puts two and two together.

'Wait – is that where the girls have been hiding?'

An image of the blood-soaked bandages flashes through Siobhán's mind, followed by a roll of nausea.

'We don't know,' Harrington says. 'Can you tell me anything that might help?'

It's not clear if this rather broad question is a distraction tactic or if Garda Harrington really wants Xavi to answer, but either way, she takes out a notebook and pen and waits expectantly.

'We were here,' Xavi says. 'My dad, Emma-Rose and me. Just waiting and worrying, you know? Grace and Siobhán had gone out to meet with Jasmine.'

'Jasmine is?'

'Emma-Rose's wedding planner.'

Siobhán wonders if Harrington already knows this and just wants to get Xavi talking. Or maybe she doesn't. Maybe there isn't a big database of up-to-the-minute investigation info available to all gardaí, the way she imagines there is.

'OK, go on?' Harrington prompts.

'We got hungry. That sounds bad, I know.' Xavi flashes a guilty look at Siobhán. 'We were so worried all day none of us had eaten properly. I said I'd get takeout for everyone, and she was going to get stuff for the morning. Bread, milk, and so on.'

He stops, looks at Harrington, wondering perhaps if any of this is what she needs.

Harrington glances up from her notepad.

'Go on?'

'We left around the same time. I . . . I was kinda happy to get out of the house, to be honest. People think all actors are extroverts, but I always need some time on my own. So I drove around a bit, then called to a pal who knows Theo before I started thinking about where to pick up food. Emma-Rose took her own car; she was going to SuperValu in Dalkey.'

'OK, and?' the garda prompts.

Xavi lifts up his hands. 'That's it. That's the last time I saw her.'

'And going back to the girls, is there anything you can tell me about last night?'

He shakes his head. 'I wish I could help, but I already told the other guard everything.'

'Xavi, do you have any theories yourself as to what went on last night? You heard their argument, I believe?'

'Yeah, but I'd had quite a few drinks, and I don't really remember . . .'

Siobhán thinks of the piece of paper in Grace's cottage. The four words she'd written: Jasmine, Siblings, Theo, Marrakesh.

She clears her throat, addresses Garda Harrington. 'I wonder if Jasmine said anything about knowing Ré and Luna at school?'

The garda nods for Xavi to answer.

'Jasmine told me about it herself when we were chatting.' A small smile. 'It's funny, because the hardest part for her wasn't seeing the girls or you,' he says to Siobhán. 'It was Emma-Rose – she's not easy to work for. God.' His face crumples. 'And I agreed with Jasmine. I feel bad now. I called Emma-Rose a Karen. Sorry, I know Grace and Luna hate that,' he says to Siobhán. 'Emma-Rose was hard work, but she was far nicer to me than I was to her. And in fairness, who wants their twenty-eight-year-old stepson still living in their house?'

A curious expression crosses the garda's face. She notes something, and Siobhán can't help wondering what.

'And about being siblings,' Siobhán says to Xavi, 'obviously, that was news to you today, but looking back now, is there anything at all to suggest Ré guessed it last night?'

'I wish I could say. But after Dad sent me inside, I wasn't talking to her again.' He pauses, as though considering something. His face reddens slightly. 'And Siobhán, just so you know, there was never anything . . . We were just having fun.'

Siobhán shakes her head. 'I know, don't worry. I get it. And when we find the girls, you and Ré can bond as new siblings and laugh about all of it.'

They will never laugh about all of it. Not with Emma-Rose dead. But they have to keep going.

'And then Theo – did you know he and Ré were seeing each other? There was a message to Theo on Ré's phone last night, saying "Luna knows."'

'Oh. I didn't know that. I met Theo once when he was going out with Luna. Seemed like a nice enough guy.' A shrug. 'But I wouldn't know about Ré and him.'

'There's a photo,' Siobhán says, taking it out of her pocket. She lays it on the island.

Garda Harrington steps closer, a look of intense interest on her face, and Siobhán wonders now if she's in more trouble for not handing in the photo.

'We know it was taken some time since last July, because Ré's nose is pierced.' She points at the nose stud. 'So it's either while Luna and Theo were together or after they broke up.'

Xavi picks up the photo. Takes a long look. The room is quiet. Harrington puts her notebook on the island and leans in closer again, craning over Xavi's shoulder.

'In case this has any bearing on the investigation, I'll need to take it,' she says, reaching a hand out.

'Wait—' Xavi runs his thumbnail across Ré's face in the photo. The nose stud disappears.

'It was just a speck of dirt on the photo,' he says, looking around. 'So maybe it's not recent after all?'

57

Siobhán stares at the Polaroid. If it wasn't taken in the last twelve months, then they no longer have concrete evidence that Ré was with Theo in the last year and they've been putting a lot of stock in a misleading photo. It was this that pointed to Ré and Theo in the first instance; it was this that prompted them to ask the guards to check for texts between Ré and Theo.

That stops her cold. What about the text? *Luna knows*. If they weren't together some time since last July, then what does it matter what Luna knows?

She turns to Garda Harrington. 'I think we need to ask Theo if he and Ré were seeing each other. Would you know if anyone has managed to reach him?'

'I believe my colleagues are still chasing,' Harrington says. 'I'll check.'

Along with a hundred other things they're chasing, though. And maybe like every other Gen Z'er she knows, Theo's simply not answering calls from unknown numbers.

Siobhán grabs her phone, calls Abbey.

As it's ringing, the doorbell chimes, and Siobhán gets off her stool, phone clamped to her ear.

'It's fine.' Harrington waves her back to her seat. 'My colleague will answer. It might be Detective O'Connell.'

The call connects. 'Did you find them?' is how Abbey answers.

'No, but could you phone Theo?' She throws a glance at Harrington, wondering if she'll object, but her face is neutral. 'He'd have your number in his phone, right? He'd answer?'

'Sure. What do you need?'

'Ask him to phone me. It's urgent, please. Abbey, was Ré seeing him while he was going out with Luna?'

'What? No! Not that I know of, anyway. Is that why you need to speak to him?'

'Yes, please just get him to call me. Tell him it's an emergency.'

As she disconnects, the kitchen door opens, and Grace appears in the doorway. Her face is pale, her eyes are red-rimmed. The pristine T-shirt she put on this morning looks grubby now, her hair dishevelled.

'I got your text,' she says in a small voice. 'I'm sorry, too. Is there news?'

'Where have you been?' Siobhán doesn't know if she wants to hug her or shake her. It's only now that Grace is safely back that she realizes she was scared. Afraid something had happened to her. Like to Emma-Rose.

'I drove around, everywhere I could think of. Places Luna goes. Pointless, I know, but I had to try.' She looks at Garda Harrington, at Xavi. 'What is it? What's happened?'

Siobhán tells her. All of it.

Grace takes a seat, moving as though she's sleepwalking, drops her head into her hands, shoulders shaking.

And then Siobhán's phone lights up with a call.

58

'Hello? Theo?'

'Hiya, yeah, this is Theo. I'm really sorry, I didn't know what was going on. I was asleep. I'm so, so—'

Siobhán cuts him off. 'Were you seeing Ré? Were you in a relationship?'

Garda Harrington whirls, pointing at the phone and the surface of the island. Siobhán lays the handset down and puts it on speaker.

'Um, yeah.'

Fuck. OK. OK. All information is useful, even when it's not what she wants to hear.

She looks at Harrington, wondering if she wants to take over, but Harrington nods for her to continue. Maybe they'll get more information from Theo without putting gardaí in the mix.

'When did you two get together?' Siobhán asks.

'Like, two years ago, maybe? It was short, just a few weeks. We had fun, but I don't think she saw me as boyfriend material.'

A shiver runs across Siobhán's skin. 'Not more recently than that?'

Grace sits up straighter, on high alert now.

'No. Summer two years ago, at Electric Picnic,' Theo says. 'We were chatting for a few weeks before she went to London.

London was the reason to knock it on the head, but I knew she wasn't into anything more serious.'

Siobhán steadies herself with a hand on the island, meets Grace's eyes.

'And did Luna know about it?'

'Yeah, course. It's how I met Luna, actually. Through Ré, at her going-away drinks before she moved to London.'

Siobhán frowns. 'So, wait – the text you got from Ré last night, saying "Luna knows" – what did that mean?'

'I have absolutely no idea.'

For a moment, it's as though all the air has left the room. The four of them stare at the phone.

'Hello?' comes the faraway voice.

Siobhán blinks. For hours now, they've been assuming the text and the Polaroid are linked. *This doesn't make sense.*

She starts to speak again, but Harrington interrupts.

'Theo, this is Garda Stephanie Harrington. I'm looking into the girls' disappearance.'

'Oh. God. I didn't know there was anyone else there.'

'That's fine, just a few more questions. Are you certain you don't know what Ré meant in her text?'

'No. I hadn't heard from her in ages, and I didn't even see the text until a short time ago.' Theo sounds suddenly a little defensive, the effect of speaking to a guard, Siobhán supposes. 'I'm in Canada, the time difference, I was out late, slept late . . .'

'Are there any secrets you and Ré shared, anything she could have meant other than a relationship?'

'Honestly, no. We haven't seen each other in ages.'

'OK. My colleagues may be in touch, so please keep your phone on.'

'No problem, and good luck. I'm so sorry.'

Siobhán ends the call and looks at Harrington, Grace and Xavi.

'If it's not about a relationship, what does the text mean?' she asks to no one in particular and all of them at once.

Xavi sits up straight suddenly.

'What if she didn't send it at all?'

Siobhán's stomach twists. Instinctively, as soon as the words hit air, she knows he's right.

'What do you mean?' Grace asks.

'The message makes no sense; Theo doesn't know what it means.' Xavi's eyes are bright, his whole being energized. 'But it made you two think it was all part of the argument. Along with the other stuff. A reason to fall out, to fight, for one of them to lose it, to grab a knife.' He slips off the stool, looks around at all of them. 'But what if Ré never sent the message. What if it was someone else. What if there was a third person there last night?'

59

SUDDENLY, EVERYTHING LOOKS DIFFERENT. Like seeing the same scene through another lens. Like a drawing you turn upside down and it's actually the right way up. *What if there was someone else there?*

Siobhán catches Grace's eye. She feels it, too. It makes sense. Unless . . . unless they're both grasping at this straw because it means their daughters are innocent? It's a lot easier to believe someone else did this . . . But also, it might just be true. And it has to be worth exploring, if only to test it, to rule it in or out.

She looks to Harrington, expecting scepticism, but finds her with her phone to her ear.

'While we have no evidence to suggest third-party involvement, this new information from Theo Hogan is interesting,' Harrington says. 'I'm going to let Detective O'Connell know.' She steps away, and Siobhán hears her leave what sounds like a voicemail.

'She's going to call by,' Harrington says when she returns.

'Do you need us to wait for her?' Siobhán asks. 'Before we talk about it, I mean?'

Harrington shakes her head. 'Let's thrash it out now.'

Siobhán takes an A4 pad and some pens from a drawer in the island. Harrington, too, has a notebook out, and she begins to speak.

'OK. We know your daughters argued, because Xavi heard it.' She starts to write; Siobhán does, too.

Xavi nods.

Harrington keeps writing as she talks. 'The audio of the 999 call tells us that one of the girls believed the other had a knife.'

'If we think now there was a third person involved,' Grace says, 'then whichever of the girls was on the audio could have made a mistake about who they saw holding a knife?'

Harrington's demeanour is neutral. Siobhán imagines her thinking this is parental defensiveness again. Half-baked hopes. But Grace is right: it's worth considering.

'So, an intruder, who broke in?' Siobhán says, thinking aloud. 'And one of the girls thought it was the other?'

Harrington looks up. 'If it was light enough to see a knife, would it not also be light enough to recognize the person holding it – would they really mix up a stranger with a friend?'

Nobody says anything for a moment. Maybe they really are just desperately grabbing for any solution that doesn't make either girl a killer. An image of Emma-Rose's body flits through Siobhán's mind. All the blood. Who killed her? And why? Because she actually did find the girls? And what about the necklace – what does it mean that Luna's necklace was under Emma-Rose's body? . . . Should she tell Grace? She told O'Connell. That's enough for now, she decides.

The sound of the kitchen door interrupts her thoughts, and Charlie walks in.

His eyes are red-rimmed; his face is raw with grief.

'I just need a glass of water.' He walks towards the fridge, but Garda Harrington is ahead of him, already filling a glass.

Xavi slips off his stool, walks around the island to his dad, pulls him into a slightly awkward half-hug.

'I'm so sorry,' Xavi says.

Charlie doesn't reply, just nods into his son's shoulder then pulls away.

Grace is next, hugging him for longer.

'Can I do anything?' she asks. 'Do you want to sit with us for a while?'

'I . . . I think I need to sleep,' he says, his voice low and lost.

He takes the water, turns and, like a shadow of the Charlie they've always known, he leaves the room.

When O'Connell arrives, she, Harrington and the male guard talk in the hallway, then, back in the kitchen, O'Connell tells Siobhán and Grace they'll look again at the theory of an intruder. She seems less interested than Harrington in the idea that the text to Theo was sent by someone else. Harrington asks if she can hear the 999 call, and after some searching on her phone, O'Connell finds it and presses play.

Harrington looks curious when it comes to an end. She addresses Grace and Siobhán.

'You definitely don't know who it is – which of the girls?'

In unison, they nod.

She turns back to O'Connell. 'I wonder could we chat in the hall again?'

'What is it?' Grace asks. 'Just say it, *please*.'

The detective and the gardaí are moving towards the door.

Siobhán replays Harrington's words in her mind.

And now it hits her.

60

'Wait,' Siobhán calls after Harrington. 'I get it – if we don't know whether it's Luna or Ré in the audio, you think it could be someone else? Someone whispering, pretending to be one of the girls – the same person who sent the text to Theo?'

A sharp intake of breath from Grace.

Harrington and O'Connell exchange a glance. Harrington gives a tiny nod, and together they move back into the centre of the kitchen.

O'Connell, looking pensive, plays the audio again. Siobhán strains to listen objectively, to try to imagine it's someone else entirely. It's a scared, whispered voice. Probably female. Possibly Irish, more than likely a native English speaker. That's about as far as she can say. Looking around at the other faces in the kitchen, it's clear everyone is thinking the same thing.

'If it *is* someone else – then that person took the girls,' Siobhán says, her stomach gripped in a new wave of fear. 'A stranger? Someone who knows them?'

'It must be someone who knows them,' Xavi says. 'Otherwise they wouldn't know to text Theo.'

He's right. Siobhán can't help thinking Charlie has been underestimating his son.

O'Connell has her notebook out. The scepticism has disappeared from her face. Harrington has a gleam in her eye, the look of someone who knows they're on to something.

O'Connell clears her throat. 'Stranger abductions are rare, and taking two people – two adults – at once would be extremely unusual, so if we work on the assumption for now that it might be someone they know, can you tell me if there's anyone who might hurt them?'

'What about Jasmine?' Grace says. 'She has a history with the girls.'

'But I was with her all evening,' Xavi reminds them. 'We were together at the time of the 999 call.'

'Any violent ex-partners?' O'Connell prompts. 'Troublesome relationships of any kind?'

Siobhán and Grace shake their heads.

'Would either of them have been involved in drugs?'

Siobhán answers for both of them. 'No. I appreciate we sound like we're loyal mothers defending our daughters, but I promise you, neither of them has ever been in any trouble.'

O'Connell continues asking questions, and Siobhán answers, but her mind is whirring, running over everything they've seen and discovered since early this morning. It makes so much sense that there was someone else involved, and not just because she doesn't want the girls to have done this to each other. Yet the gardaí had dismissed it as soon as she suggested it this morning. Why? She knows why. Because it *looked* like one girl had attacked the other.

'What is it, Siobhán?' Harrington asks, watching her.

'Well, it's just . . . not only does it seem like someone took the girls, but actually, it's as if they worked really hard to stage it, to make it seem like the girls fought and one of them hurt the other.'

O'Connell and Harrington are listening intently. The third guard puts down his phone and walks closer to listen, too.

Siobhán continues, thinking aloud. 'Like, maybe the 999 call didn't cut off accidentally after the number forty-six. Maybe that was deliberate, so the guards wouldn't have enough information to respond last night but would have enough to connect it to my call this morning when the girls were missing.'

Silence. A silence that says they think she's right.

Grace sits up straighter. 'Oh my god – and the way the person on the call says, "My room-mate has a knife." Like they're purposely keeping it unclear.'

Siobhán nods. 'I think it was all deliberately staged.'

'But why?' Grace asks.

'I don't know. But the two of us have been driven demented all day, worrying that one of the girls hurt the other, not knowing who is the victim, who was the attacker. It makes me wonder if this is all about us?'

61

O'Connell sits at the island, notebook open. She stares at Siobhán for a moment, then at Grace.

'Is there any reason someone would want to get at you?' she asks, and Siobhán feels the tiny win – O'Connell is taking it seriously.

Apart from *maybe* Jasmine, who has an alibi, Siobhán and Grace can think of no one. They answer all of O'Connell's questions as best they can – jobs, relationships, friends. O'Connell asks about Aidan – could he have found out he's not Ré's dad?

Siobhán almost laughs. Aidan is so long gone, he's on the other side of the world, and he never thought he was a dad in the first place.

They talk through where they've lived, various stints in the US, a year in Spain for Siobhán, but there's nothing. O'Connell asks about Grace's recent inheritance – Grace acknowledges that it was covered in a newspaper, but she was estranged from her dad and can't imagine anyone being angry with her for an inheritance over which she had no say.

'What about the kidnap case?' O'Connell asks. 'The baby that was taken when you were looking after her?'

Grace shakes her head. 'She was found, though. It was awful at the time, but Arabella was found unharmed.'

Siobhán glances over. This is not entirely true. Has Grace

forgotten? Of course she hasn't forgotten. The years of donating to Sightsavers and Fighting Blindness and sponsoring Irish Guide Dogs are testament to this.

'She wasn't really unharmed, Grace. I know you hate to think about it, but obviously Arabella lost her sight.'

O'Connell tilts her head. 'OK. Tell me more?'

Grace throws up her hands. 'This all happened thirty-something years ago. I'm sorry, but there's no way it's linked to this.'

'No, wait. Think for a second,' Siobhán says. 'Arabella was in your care when she was taken. It was your boyfriend who took her, and your boyfriend who crashed the car that left her without sight.'

'Hang on, Siobhán, that's hardly something—'

Siobhán cuts in. 'Shouldn't we consider Arabella's parents?' Out of the corner of her eye, she sees Harrington searching on her phone. 'If something happened to their child, leaving them terrified, not knowing where she was, it's not impossible to imagine they might want to do something similar to you?'

'But all these years later? And they'd be old by now.' Grace shakes her head.

'OK, but didn't Arabella have two brothers who were in school when she was taken? One a few years older than her, and one a teen?'

'Yeah . . . But surely this is all a stretch?' Grace says, with what sounds like false confidence.

O'Connell intervenes. 'If you give me the details, we can at least check into the parents and the brothers to rule them out. So please, tell me again what happened?'

62

Thirty-four years earlier

THE CALL COMES ONE fine afternoon in late May as Siobhán is packing for her J1 summer in America. She's still not sure that going with Grace to South Carolina is the best idea. Everyone else from college is going to Virginia Beach – lining up accommodation in cheap rentals near the seafront, lining up work in bars on the strip. But Grace is adamant that her family's summer home on Hugo Island will be a far superior experience. She got her mom to send photos, and Siobhán has to admit, the house looks stunning. Especially compared to the caravan her parents usually rent in Kerry.

Grace's mother will be there for the first three nights, then she's off on a cruise. The most important thing to remember, Grace keeps telling Siobhán, is to make sure her mother never finds out she's dropped out of college.

Siobhán thinks she's insane, but then again, when your family has *that* much money, and you're not a fan of study, it probably makes sense. That her mother has modified Grace's expense budget to keep her on the straight and narrow was a blip at first, but then Grace found a nannying job with a rich family on Ailesbury Road, and that was the end of that problem. Siobhán cannot imagine lying to her own parents to that extent. Mrs

Gill thinks Grace goes into UCD every day to study commerce, just like Siobhán *actually* does. In reality, Grace turns up at the Bailey-Creans' house at eight every morning to look after five-year-old Bertie and his baby sister, Arabella. There's an older brother, too – sixteen-year-old Philip, born a few months after the Bailey-Creans married – but he doesn't need any minding at all, and Grace barely sees him. So the whole gig is an easy enough job, by all accounts. The mum, Judith, doesn't work but is very busy socially, hence the need for a nanny. The dad, Jonathan, is gone all day at work in a bank. So Grace has the run of the house and freedom to do whatever she wants as long as she looks after the kids. The Bailey-Creans have a housekeeper and a cleaner and, beyond her childminding duties, Grace doesn't have to lift a finger. As long as she's back to pick up Bertie from school each day at half past two, she can go wherever she fancies with baby Arabella. What the Bailey-Creans don't know is that she often takes Arabella to her own flat in Stillorgan, driving her there in her pink Mini Cooper. And it's there that she meets up with her boyfriend, Anthony.

Siobhán is not a fan. Anthony is bad news. It's pretty clear that his unusual work hours, coupled with the sporty BMW he drives, add up to something that must be less than legal. Siobhán suspects it's drugs. Anthony is slick and well groomed, charming and confident. But his 'business meetings' don't take place in offices, and on two occasions, he's had gardaí take him in for questioning. Both followed drug-related crimes in a different part of town, and Siobhán could join the dots. Of course, Grace said it was a misunderstanding, but she's not stupid. Even if she can't stretch to seeing her boyfriend involved in violent crime, she must know the money's coming from something illicit. And this is the main reason Siobhán agreed to go to Grace's South Carolina holiday home for the summer – to get her away from Anthony.

When the call comes that fine afternoon in late May, Siobhán sets aside her packing and goes downstairs to pick up the phone, assuming it will be someone for her mother. But it's Grace. Grace in a panic. It takes a moment for Siobhán to work out what she's trying to say.

'Anthony. Took her to a meeting. Someone he's meeting, I mean. I don't know what to do. Mrs Bailey-Crean rang my flat, looking for me. I let it go to the answering machine. She's freaking out that I'm not at their home. Siobhán, help me, what am I going to do?'

'Slow down. What do you mean, Anthony took her to a meeting – not Arabella, surely?'

'Yes. I had her in my flat, and I had a dentist appointment, and it took a lot longer than I thought and when I got back, he'd gone and left a note. Gone to a meeting.'

'A meeting with . . . do you mean with one of his druggie cronies?'

They never talk about this.

'Yes.' A whisper.

'Grace! What the fuck? When will he be back?'

'I don't know. He's gone for hours sometimes. What am I going to tell Mrs Bailey-Crean?'

'You have to call the police. This is fucking dangerous! You can't have a baby at a meeting like that. Those people have guns. There've been shootings.'

A whimper. 'Anthony wouldn't . . .'

'The baby could get caught in crossfire, forgotten in the car, taken by someone else – anything could happen. For fuck's sake. I'm going to call the police.'

'What are you going to tell them?'

'I'll give them his name and car make and colour and, like, they *know* him. So I'm sure they'll get the seriousness.'

'Just say he has Arabella, OK? Don't say he was in my flat?'

'Jesus, Grace, I have to give them all the details.'

'OK, just say from outside my flat, not inside. That's a tiny detail. The Bailey-Creans will go mad if I had her inside my flat. If I left her with someone else.'

'I'm hanging up now to call them.'

Siobhán is right: the gardaí do know Anthony O'Shea, and they do know Anthony O'Shea's dark blue BMW 850i, and within an hour, they've located the car speeding along a suburban road near Anthony's home. They give chase, blue lights on, and it ends forty-two minutes later when Anthony's car mounts a footpath, just about misses hitting a kid on a bike, ploughs through a garden wall and smashes into a parked car. Arabella and Anthony are taken in two separate ambulances to two separate hospitals. The Bailey-Creans are broken – terrified, shocked, struggling to comprehend. The fury comes later. When Arabella's doctor gently explains she's lost her sight. The blame starts then. Why did Grace take Arabella so far from home? Was she bringing her to her flat? Did she leave her alone, unattended outside? Grace is adamant. Absolutely not. No way would she ever leave the baby unattended. She had walked by her flat because there's a nice park nearby. Anthony O'Shea must have been watching her, knew the baby was from a wealthy family. He pulled up in his car, snatched her, lifting the entire carry-cot off the pram wheels, and drove off at speed. Why didn't she call the police immediately, they asked. She panicked, called her friend Siobhán instead. Siobhán, uncomfortable with the lie, never got quite as far as correcting the story. And Anthony, the only other person who knew Arabella had been inside the flat, that he was Grace's boyfriend and not a stranger, died in hospital three days later. Grace's secret was safe. Of course, that was the end of her tenure with the Bailey-Creans. They needed time to be alone as a family, they said, to come to terms with Arabella's sight loss. And Grace had been due to finish soon, anyway, for her summer in the US, while the Bailey-Creans decamped to the south of France. And in September, they might take another look at their childcare, they said. And that was the end of that.

63

Now

SIOBHÁN TELLS THE STORY with Grace sitting quietly across from her, head down. O'Connell's face remains inscrutable throughout, as she jots notes and joins dots. Harrington is on her phone again, maybe looking up the Bailey-Creans. Xavi listens open-mouthed. Grace says nothing. It's Siobhán who breaks the silence.

'Obviously, the entire thing was horrific, and Grace knows she made a massive mistake, leaving Arabella with Anthony, but she was eighteen, and when I think of the stupid things I did at that age, sometimes I wonder how any of us are still alive at all.'

O'Connell clears her throat, looks at Garda Harrington then back to Siobhán. 'We'll track down the family, check what they're all doing now.'

'I just found Arabella's Instagram,' Xavi says, holding up his phone. 'There's only one person called Arabella Bailey-Crean. It was easy,' he adds, perhaps registering the surprised faces.

O'Connell takes his phone, and Siobhán searches quickly on her own phone. There she is. Arabella Bailey-Crean. Arabella with a handsome dark-haired man, showing an engagement ring. Arabella and a labrador on Sandymount Strand. Arabella on holidays in Spain. Arabella on a night out in Café en Seine.

Her profile says she's a barrister, dog owner, book lover, jelly-snake addict. The only indication of her sight loss is a photo of and post about her guide dog, Cara, and a fundraising link in her bio.

'What were the two brothers called?' O'Connell asks.

'Bertie and Philip,' Grace says. 'Bertie was four or five years older than Arabella, and Philip was maybe sixteen at the time. I never really saw Philip. He was in fifth year and out with his friends a lot.'

'So Bertie would be in his late thirties,' Harrington says, scrolling on her phone. 'And Philip would be around fifty.'

Siobhán types 'Bertie Bailey-Crean' into Google, but the only results are from back when the kidnapping took place. No Instagram, no adult photos of Bertie. When she types Philip's name in, she's not surprised to find the same. They're either very private people or they're hiding something.

O'Connell walks towards the back doors, phone to her ear.

In silence, they wait, listening to the side of her call that they can hear.

'Jonathan and Judith Bailey-Crean ... Foxrock, yes. With adult children, Philip, Bertie and Arabella.'

A long pause now. The only sound the haptics on Xavi's phone as he keeps searching.

Then O'Connell speaks again.

'Ah, OK. How long ago? Right ... Sorry, can you repeat that? ... The Willowbank ... Not really ...' A glance back at the group gathered around the island. 'I'm just going outside to hear better.' O'Connell opens the glass door and steps out on to the deck.

Moments later, she's back.

'OK, I have an address for Mr Bailey-Crean, Arabella's father.' She nods at Harrington and the other guard. 'Dunleavy's an hour away, so you two come with me instead.' She turns back to Siobhán and Grace. 'The team are working on tracking down the brothers, and someone will speak to Arabella.'

'What can we do?' Siobhán asks.

'Sit tight and keep talking. Anything like this, no matter how small or unlikely, is worth following up. Ring or text if you think of anything else.' She looks at her watch. 'And I know you might not think you can, but try to get some sleep.'

64

WITHIN HALF AN HOUR, O'Connell phones Siobhán to say she's visited the Bailey-Crean home. Judith Bailey-Crean is deceased, she says, so clearly not involved. Siobhán asks how she died, and O'Connell says it's confidential but not relevant. Jonathan still lives in Foxrock, she says, in the house he bought back when the kids were small. He has early-onset dementia and a carer to assist him, but they've been able to get contact details for the two sons, and will follow up, though it will be morning before she gets anywhere.

So the parents are ruled out, but the sons are not. Siobhán googles 'Judith Bailey-Crean death', and a newspaper report of an inquest comes up – an accidental overdose of prescription drugs. Her chest tightens. That poor family.

'What should we do next?' Xavi asks, looking from Siobhán to Grace.

'We keep thinking about anyone who might want to harm the girls or us for whatever reason,' Grace says, exhaustion coating every word.

And that is what they do, sometimes out loud, together, sometimes quietly, heads down, staring at phone screens. Grace tries again to suggest Jasmine as a suspect, and again, Xavi reminds her that he was with Jasmine until late. At midnight, Xavi goes to bed. They should do the same, Siobhán knows, but how can they, while the girls are still out there? By unspoken agreement, she and Grace relocate to the living room. Siobhán curls against one side of the couch; Grace takes the other. They spend the night scrolling, talking, occasionally dozing, until early slants of daylight creep through the window.

Siobhán opens her eyes, realizing she must have fallen asleep. Stiff and stressed, she grabs for her phone, squinting. So many messages. Messages from people she knows, people she hasn't seen in years, people who have seen the appeals on social media and the news on TV. Messages from journalists covering the story, but nothing new on where Ré is. Nothing from Ré.

She realizes now that Grace is sitting upright at the other end of the couch, wide awake, as though waiting for Siobhán.

'I think we should go to speak to Jonathan Bailey-Crean ourselves,' Grace says.

'We don't even know where he lives.'

'We do. I heard O'Connell say "The Willowbank" when she was on the phone last night. I just googled, and there's only one house in Foxrock called The Willowbank – it's on Brighton Road. Let's call by and see if we can find out more about the sons – recent photos, maybe?'

'I don't know. O'Connell said to stay here.'

An irritated sigh. 'I get that the police have to do their job, but we know the girls better than anyone. And we know what happened with Arabella. There might be something the police miss because they weren't there back then.'

Siobhán bites her lip.

Grace looks at her watch. 'If you're worried, stay here. I don't mind going on my own.'

Siobhán rubs her eyes. Anxious. Hopeful. 'I'll come too.' Then she remembers her car. And where it is. She swallows. 'But first can we go to Stepaside to pick up my car?'

*

The Willowbank is an imposing Edwardian house set back from the road with a dusty green Mercedes parked in the gravel driveway. The front door is opened by a tall man with a shock of dark grey hair and pale blue eyes. He smiles broadly, revealing dimples in both cheeks, but his eyes are confused. The face of a man afraid he knows them and won't recognize them, Siobhán thinks, remembering her own mother at the same stage.

'Hello there,' he says, his accent plummy, his greeting designed to keep his options open.

Grace takes the lead. 'Mr Bailey-Crean, I'm Grace. I used to work for your family years ago – I wondered if we could come in to talk to you for a few minutes?'

The smile fades. 'Ah. The lady who comes here to make the tea, and so on, she's told me not to let people in, I'm afraid.'

Siobhán takes a step back from the doorway. 'Of course, we understand.'

Grace throws her a look. 'We'd only take a minute of your time, and it's very important. It's just, our daughters are missing and we think you might be able to help.'

His eyes film with what might be sorrow or a distant memory.

'Goodness. Well, the lady should be here any minute, and maybe she can help.'

She – the carer, presumably – will quite rightly send them packing, Siobhán thinks.

'It's you we need to speak to,' Grace says. 'And you don't need to worry, I'm not a stranger. I nannied the boys. How *are* the boys? Philip and Bertie?'

Grace omits Arabella's name, Siobhán notices, maybe to avoid reminding Jonathan of what happened back then.

'You know Philip and Bertie?' He beams. 'You should have said. Come in, come in.'

Grace doesn't hesitate. And Siobhán, feeling guilty for taking advantage of an ill man, but not enough to stop, follows, too.

He leads them to a beautiful old-style sitting room decorated in rich reds and golds. It's like something from a film, like stepping back in time.

'Sit down, sit down.' Jonathan gestures to a red-and-white-striped sofa. 'Now, what was it we were talking about when I last saw you?'

Siobhán opens her mouth to explain, but Grace cuts in.

'Jonathan, we heard the police were here last night, asking about your sons, and we wanted to ask some questions, too, if that's OK?'

A cloud of confusion passes over his face. 'Of course, yes.'

'Do Philip and Bertie live nearby?'

'Well, yes, indeed they do. Now, I don't have my notebook with all my addresses, but the girl who makes the tea will be able to tell you. She deals with all that kind of thing.'

Siobhán's heart goes out to him.

'That's great. I'll ask her to find the notebook when she gets here,' Grace says, her eyes on something to the right of Jonathan's armchair. Siobhán follows her gaze and sees a long mahogany sideboard, its surface covered in ornaments and framed photographs. A bride and groom that must be Judith and Jonathan. The same couple with a baby – Philip, presumably, born a few months after they were married. Then another, where Philip looks to be about ten, holding a newborn. Bertie. Some photos of the boys together, then one with the two boys and another newborn. Arabella.

'Would you have any photos of Philip and Bertie that are more recent?' Grace asks, nodding towards the sideboard.

A helpless look washes over his face. Grace gets up and walks to the sideboard, picks up a photo of the boys aged roughly thirteen and two.

'I'd love to see what these guys look like today?'

'Oh. Goodness. Yes.' He glances around the room, and Siobhán's eyes follow his. But there are no further photos.

'Maybe an album somewhere? Or photos on your phone?' Grace holds out her hand. 'I could have a look?'

Siobhán squirms but doesn't object.

Jonathan pats down his pockets. 'Gosh, I can't find my phone. I wonder if the girl took it?' He looks towards the hall.

On cue, they hear the front door open and close, and a small, dark-haired woman appears in the living-room doorway.

'Is everything OK?' she asks in accented English. 'Jonathan?' A polite but wary smile.

'Yes, these nice ladies know Philip and Bertie.'

Grace jumps in to explain. 'I used to nanny for the family. I've known Jonathan a long time.' A brief smile, an attempt to reassure. 'Our daughters are missing, and the police were here last night to see if Jonathan could help in any way. We wanted to ask, too.'

The carer's smile drops. 'I am so sorry to hear about your daughters. I saw this on Facebook.' She clears her throat. 'However, I do not think Mr Bailey-Crean can help with this, and it is now time for his medication.'

Siobhán stands. 'Of course. We'll go.'

Grace stands, too. They thank Jonathan, and the carer walks them out to the hall. At the front door, Grace turns.

'Sorry, we didn't introduce ourselves. This is Siobhán, and I'm Grace.' She extends her hand, and the woman takes it.

'I'm Camile.'

'Camile, we're trying to find Jonathan's two sons, or a photo even, to see what they look like today. It's really important. Do you know them?'

She shakes her head. 'I know his daughter. Arabella. I have not met the sons.'

'So they don't live in Dublin?'

She nods vigorously. 'Oh, they do. They live in Dublin. They don't visit.' A small, coded smile. 'Only the daughter visits. The sons are too busy working. All the time.' The tiniest eyeroll now.

'What do they do?' Siobhán asks.

'Philip runs a business, and I think maybe Bertie helps him. Or Bertie is just too busy with life . . .'

'What kind of business does Philip run?' Grace asks.

'It is a catering business.'

65

Siobhán and Grace look at each other.

A catering business.

'What is it called?' Siobhán asks, urgency making her breathless.

'Oh, I'm sorry. I do not know details. But this is what Arabella says. They are so busy working, and so on, they can't visit. You could ask her?'

Camile moves past them to open the front door. 'I do not wish to be rude, but I must . . .' She gestures back towards the living room.

'Of course. Thanks for your help.' Siobhán steps outside, and Grace follows. Camile closes the door gently behind them.

'Oh my god, do you think Ben could be Philip Bailey-Crean?' Grace has one hand over her mouth.

They're standing by Siobhán's car, still in the Bailey-Crean driveway, trying to process what they've just heard.

'The age fits,' Siobhán says, her mind racing, trying to put pieces together. 'From what you remember of Philip, could it be him?'

Grace lifts her hands helplessly. 'I saw him so little, and it was more than thirty years ago. He could be, I guess . . .'

'Although Ben is Scottish, and Philip Bailey-Crean is Irish, so maybe not?'

Grace frowns. 'True. Or Ben was putting on a Scottish accent?'

Siobhán pulls out her phone to call O'Connell. It goes to voicemail, and she leaves a message, then continues thinking aloud, pacing beside the car, her feet crunching on gravel. 'Ben had access to the garden house. He could have gone there at some point, could have knocked over the lamp, made it look like the girls fought.'

A movement at the house catches her eye, and she glances over to see Camile at the living-room window, perhaps wondering why they're still there.

'What about the 999 call?' Grace says. 'Even though it's whispered, I feel like it's a woman's voice?'

'Maybe because we thought all along it was one of the girls, though,' Siobhán counters, still pacing. 'When someone whispers, it's hard to tell. It could have been a man?'

'And it was Ben's van that was stolen.' Grace's eyes widen. 'He could easily have taken the van himself, then reported it stolen, acted surprised.' Grace glances over to the window where Camile still stands, and opens the car door. She nods at Siobhán, an unspoken *let's go*. 'Although, he can't drive at the moment, so maybe not.'

Grace has a point, but there might be some explanation, Siobhán thinks, slipping into the driver's seat. The story with the missing keys from the catering kitchen – that came from Ben. He could have staged it. Something else strikes her.

'Grace,' she says, as they close the car doors, 'we've believed all along that one of the girls took the other at knifepoint. But with a third person involved, maybe it wasn't a knife? Maybe whoever took them drugged them, spiked their drinks, and who could do that easier than someone involved in the catering?'

'Oh god.' Grace shakes her head. 'If Ben did this . . . He didn't seem . . .'

'It adds up, though, and he was helping Robert at the bar at the end of the night,' Siobhán says. 'I'll try O'Connell again.'

O'Connell still doesn't answer, so Siobhán leaves another voicemail, then she googles Sage Catering and phones the number that comes up.

'Sage Catering, Tara speaking, how can I help?' says a chirpy female voice.

'Hi, I'm trying to track down a man called Ben who worked at my friend's wedding.' Conscious of Camile's gaze, she puts the phone on hands-free and begins to turn the car. 'He was really good, despite a broken ankle, and I wanted to thank him personally, but I didn't catch his surname.'

'Oh. Ben Wilson. Yeah. Didn't know about the broken ankle.' The woman's tone has flattened. 'Sure. I'll pass on the thanks.'

Siobhán and Grace exchange a look.

'Would you be able to let me have his number so I can thank him myself?' Siobhán tries, edging her way on to the main road.

'I can't give out personal numbers, and he's busy today at another wedding so couldn't answer anyway.'

Her clear lack of enthusiasm prompts Siobhán to push.

'He's *so* good at his job, he must be very popular.'

'Yep, he's absolutely brilliant,' Tara says, in a tone that suggests he's entirely the opposite.

'And the guests loved his Scottish accent.' Siobhán winces at her own clunkiness as Grace nods approval.

Tara sighs. 'They always do.' Nothing more seems to be forthcoming.

Siobhán says goodbye as she stops at a red light and glances at Grace.

'He really is Scottish, so maybe not Philip Bailey-Crean after all?'

Grace nods slowly, unconvinced. Siobhán feels it, too. They're on to something.

As Siobhán pulls away from the lights, she can't help thinking about Tara's response. There's something niggling her about the conversation. She runs back over it, trying to figure it out, while Grace googles 'Ben Wilson'. When they pull up outside Siobhán's front door, Grace shows her the LinkedIn profile that's come up. The picture is that of the person they met at the wedding. Charming, warm, friendly Ben from Scotland.

Grace zooms in. 'This is definitely Ben, but is it also Philip Bailey-Crean?'

'Maybe.' Siobhán turns off the ignition. 'I keep thinking there's something more to Tara's response, but I can't—'

That's when it hits her.

66

'Grace, why didn't Tara at Sage know anything about Ben's broken ankle?'

'What?'

'I was so focused on the Scottish accent question, I completely overlooked the other thing she said – she didn't know about the ankle.'

Grace's mouth drops open. 'That *is* odd. Call O'Connell again.'

Siobhán phones the detective, turning it over in her mind as she waits for O'Connell to answer. How is it possible his employer wouldn't know about his injury? More to the point, how easy would it be to wear a boot and fake a limp and say you can't drive – and exclude yourself from suspicion?

'Siobhán. What is it?' O'Connell sounds impatient.

Siobhán puts the phone on speaker. 'Ben Wilson. The catering company didn't know about his broken ankle, and now we're wondering if he faked it. Maybe he did something to the girls? Then faked the emergency call?'

A sigh down the phone. 'We've spoken to Mr Wilson and excluded him from our inquiries.'

'Oh. Are you sure?'

'I'm sure. He was at home by the time the girls disappeared.'

Grace jumps in. 'He lives alone, though, so is there any proof he was at home?'

A pause. 'I shouldn't be giving you this level of detail, but if it eases your mind, I can tell you we have Ring doorbell footage that shows Ben Wilson was at home by 2.30 a.m. and we know Jasmine and Xavi heard the girls arguing around three. And I've just heard that initial voice analysis tells us the 999 caller was almost certainly female.'

Oh. Siobhán deflates.

'Maybe whoever you spoke to at Sage got mixed up – look, Siobhán, I have to go, but I've made a note and I'll chase it up.'

She disconnects.

Siobhán looks at Grace. 'I still think this is weird. Like, when it first happened, it would have affected his ability to do his job, surely? He'd have needed time off, so how could Sage not know?'

Grace nods. 'There must be some explanation. And the police are busy with everything else – it's going to take them ages to follow up on something minor like this. Let's go to see the woman at Sage.'

Sage Catering is based in Deansgrange Business Park, and when Grace and Siobhán arrive they're greeted by Tara, the receptionist who spoke to Siobhán on the phone. She's a well-dressed woman in her early forties, with thick black shoulder-length hair and deep red lipstick. She's joined by a woman with a glossy pewter bob who introduces herself as Caroline, owner of Sage.

Siobhán starts by explaining to Caroline and Tara that their daughters disappeared from a wedding catered by Sage.

'Oh, my goodness, I'm so sorry.' Caroline gestures for them to sit on a plush couch in the foyer. 'How can we help?'

'We wanted to ask you about Ben Wilson,' Siobhán says. 'The police have ruled him out of having anything to do with the disappearance—'

'Oh, thank god.' Caroline puts a hand to her heart. 'Ben's such a nice guy. He would never be involved in anything like this.'

'Well, yes,' Siobhán pushes on. 'We're confused about one thing – Tara, you mentioned you didn't know he had a broken ankle?'

Tara is still behind the reception desk. 'Oh, sorry, I'm only back today after my holidays.' She looks at her boss. 'Does he have a broken ankle?'

Caroline nods. 'He does. He fell off a bar stool a couple of weeks back. Oh dear, is that why you're here? I'm sorry.' She nods towards Tara. 'She's been off, she wouldn't have known.'

Disappointment washes over Siobhán. Another waste of time.

Tara clears her throat. 'Hm. I wouldn't put it past him, just to say.'

'Tara!' Caroline's tone sharpens. 'This is serious. These ladies aren't talking about a bad date, they're talking about a disappearance.'

Tara tosses her hair, turns to her computer, mouth turned down. 'Mm,' is all she says.

'A bad date?' Siobhán prompts.

Tara swivels back towards them. 'Let's just say, Ben doesn't treat women very well.'

Something ticks inside Siobhán. A warning. A red flag. 'Can you tell me more?'

'Tara,' Caroline warns.

'Well. I asked him to go for a drink, and he said yes. It went well, but when I asked if we could do it again, he said we were better as friends.' Her expression is petulant, almost childlike. 'Then he basically ignored me. So much for being friends.' She makes air-quotes, turns back to her keyboard.

Caroline is shaking her head. 'Tara, I don't think this is the kind of thing they're looking for.' She turns to Siobhán and Grace. 'I'll walk you out.'

'Sorry about that,' Caroline says as she walks them to the car park. 'Tara's tricky. She's my best friend's daughter, I hired her as a favour, and I can't do anything about it now.'

Siobhán looks at Grace. Mothers and daughters and friendships. That's a dynamic they understand.

'Ben is a good employee, and to be honest' – Caroline glances behind, lowers her voice – 'I suspect Tara has been driving him demented. I mean, borderline stalking him as a result of their one date. And woe betide any other woman who catches his eye.'

'Oh, awkward,' Siobhán says, wincing.

'I know. I'd fire her if I could, for Ben's sake and for mine.' A grimace. 'She's a godawful receptionist, too. But anyway, that doesn't help you. I'm sorry.'

Siobhán's phone rings just as she pulls into the driveway, squinting against the mid-morning sun.

O'Connell.

Her stomach drops, just as it does every time the phone rings now.

'Hi,' she says, sounding breathy and hopeful and terrified. 'Did you find something?'

Beside her, Grace waits, wide-eyed.

'I wanted to pass on some reassurance to you about the Bailey-Crean brothers. I know you were anxious about this – we tracked them down.' The sound of a car horn interrupts O'Connell briefly. 'They're CEO and COO of an international catering firm called PBC that does food for prisons and detention centres. Bertie is in Madrid for business, and Philip is on holiday in Dubai right now. Neither of them was anywhere near Dublin this weekend.'

Siobhán frowns. 'Are you sure?'

'Certain. I'll message you their pictures. You'll see for yourself that neither of them is Ben Wilson, and neither of them was at the wedding. OK?'

Siobhán and Grace lock eyes. Another wild-goose chase.

O'Connell finishes the call, and two photos arrive on Siobhán's phone. Both handsome men, one around fifty, one in his late thirties. Two complete strangers.

They're back to square one.

When they walk into Siobhán's kitchen, they find Charlie staring at his phone, his face ashen. Xavi is by his side, his hand over his mouth.

'What is it?' Siobhán asks in a panicked whisper.

With a shaking hand, Charlie holds out his phone.

67

Siobhán takes the phone from Charlie. The screen is open on a text message:

CHARLIE. DO NOT CONTACT POLICE. THIS IS YOUR ONE CHANCE TO HAVE THE TWO GIRLS RETURNED. DO NOT FUCK IT UP. NEXT TEXT WILL BE INSTRUCTIONS TO PAY.

Siobhán's legs go from under her. She sags against the wall and slips slowly to the kitchen floor. Beside her, still standing, Grace is frozen.

Siobhán's mind whips and tumbles over the text, the words, the meaning. A kidnap. After all this, it had nothing to do with anything. Nothing to do with Jasmine, with Marrakesh, with Theo. Nothing to do with the girls finding out that they're sisters.

'Did . . . payment instructions come?' she asks.

'Not yet.' Charlie sits on the floor beside her. Visibly shaking.

'Do you think the person knows they're both your daughters?' Siobhán asks, her voice hoarse, her head swimming.

'Maybe . . . I don't know.' Charlie rubs his temples.

'It could be someone who knows Charlie has money and would pay for both girls to be safe,' Grace whispers. 'It might have nothing to do with being sisters. Oh my god. What if they hurt them?'

'We need to phone O'Connell,' Siobhán says.

'No!' Grace is no longer whispering. 'Slow down. You saw the text. No police.'

Siobhán closes her eyes. They *have* to tell the guards. This is too big. The police deal with this kind of thing; Siobhán and Grace are just ordinary people. What if they get it wrong, make a mistake?

Charlie is nodding at Grace, his eyes wide and scared. 'I agree. We can't rush into telling anyone outside this room. We need to find out what they want first.'

'We *have* to tell the guards, this is too—' Siobhán is interrupted by the sound of a text on Charlie's phone, followed by a second beep.

Charlie looks briefly, then holds out his phone for the others to see. The first text is just a long string of letters and numbers. The second, a set of instructions.

TRANSFER 1,000,000 EUR IN CRYPTO TO THE ABOVE ETHEREUM WALLET. WHEN IT ARRIVES, YOU'LL GET AN EIRCODE FOR WHERE THEY ARE.

'How do we know if they're still . . .' Siobhán can't say the word.

Charlie understands. He starts to type.

You need to prove that the girls are OK. Let me speak to them.

The next text is an image. A close-up of Ré, her cheek bruised, blood crusted on her mouth. Siobhán stares, sick with terror. Another image. Luna this time, eyes wide in horror.

Oh god. They really didn't do this. This was done to them.

Another text.

THEY'RE ALIVE FOR NOW. BUT NOBODY KNOWS WHERE. IF YOU DON'T PAY BY 12 MIDDAY I HAVE NO REASON TO KEEP THEM ALIVE. I HAVE A PARTNER WHO WORKS FOR THE GUARDS. HIGH UP. IF YOU CONTACT ANYONE THERE I'LL KNOW IMMEDIATELY.

Another image pings through. Luna again. A thin serrated blade against her neck. Something like a . . . hacksaw?

Oh Jesus.

Charlie stands, scrolls on his phone. 'I . . . I can scramble the money,' he mutters, pacing. 'I should have enough between the business accounts.'

'Won't the bank limit how much you can send?' Xavi asks.

'I have a 1.6 million daily limit for paying suppliers. They'll call to verify, though, and I don't know a thing about crypto.' He runs a shaking hand through his hair. 'How the fuck do I send crypto?' Xavi slides off his stool, walks over to his dad. 'I can help – I know how. You need to create an account first; use Coinbase.'

'What?' Panic is emanating from Charlie like a physical force.

'Dad, think of this like business, like any other deal.' Calm and calming. 'I'll do it, if you like. Then you can buy crypto using your business debit card, and send it – let me see?' He looks at Charlie's phone. 'They're asking you to send to an Ethereum wallet. So you set up Coinbase, buy Ethereum and send it to that wallet.'

'OK.' Charlie exhales, visibly trying to steady himself. 'What will I say if the bank calls to verify?'

'Just say your broker advised you to buy Ethereum, that it's about to go up in value. It's a legitimate thing to do. Lots of people invest in crypto.'

Charlie nods, his expression a mix of surprise, gratitude and relief.

Siobhán, still sitting on the floor, listens to their exchange, dazed, shocked. They can't seriously be doing this, can they?

'Guys, we have to tell the guards,' she says. 'We're not equipped to deal with this ourselves.'

'You saw the text.' Grace hunkers down beside her. 'He'll know if we tell.' Her voice drops to a scared whisper. 'He'll kill them.'

Siobhán *has* to make them understand. The gardaí are the experts. 'What if we do something wrong and make everything worse?'

Charlie shakes his head. 'Grace is right. It's too big a risk to tell them.'

'It's too big a risk *not* to tell!' Siobhán raises her voice. 'And this thing about a partner high up in the gardaí – how do we know that's true?'

'We don't, but I'm too scared to take a chance,' Grace says. 'I just want Luna back.'

'Me, too.' Charlie clears his throat, his eyes glistening. 'I just want both of them back.'

Siobhán stares at them. She could tell O'Connell. They can't stop her. Her phone is in her pocket. All she has to do is pull it out, call the number. And still she sits there, on her kitchen floor, motionless. Making the call is the right thing to do. But a huge part of her wants the decision to be taken out of her hands, wants Charlie to send the money and get the girls back. Her next action or inaction will make things better or worse, and there's no way to know which. Life or death . . . The person *must* be lying. They don't have someone high up in the guards. *But what if they do?* Another ten seconds tick by, and Siobhán doesn't take out her phone. The path of least resistance wins out. She doesn't make the call.

68

Xavi is on Charlie's phone, tapping and scrolling. 'Dad, I need your driver's licence for KYC for a Coinbase account. Do you have it with you?'

Charlie pulls his wallet from his back pocket, slides his driver's licence out and passes it to Xavi. His hand is still shaking, but he's calmer now.

'OK, that's pending approval,' Xavi says after uploading a photo of the licence. 'You should have an account in about ten minutes.' Xavi clears his throat. 'Is there some way to make sure the person keeps their word?'

'I don't know how we'd do that,' Charlie says. 'I think I need to make the transfer and pray.'

'OK, but what if you send it and he—' Xavi stops. 'If he doesn't hold up his end of the bargain?'

'I honestly don't know, I've never been involved in kidnap before, Xavi,' Charlie snaps.

'There's no harm in asking,' Xavi pushes. 'Just write, "We need reassurance you'll keep your side of the bargain," and see what they say?'

'OK,' Charlie relents. He types something on his phone, then holds it out for the others to read.

Siobhán squints at the screen.

Preparing payment to buy currency but need assurance/proof that you'll let the girls go unharmed.

They wait.

The message arrives seconds later.

I HAVE NO NEED FOR THEM ONCE I'M PAID. AND I DON'T HAVE TO GO IN PERSON TO LET THEM GO SO THERE'S NO RISK FOR ME IN GIVING YOU THE ADDRESS. OTHER THAN THAT, YOU JUST HAVE TO TRUST ME.

Charlie looks at Xavi, eyebrows up.

Xavi nods. 'OK, I guess that's all we're going to get.'

Charlie looks around. 'So I'm gathering the funds to make the crypto purchase?'

Grace nods. Siobhán hesitates, then nods, too. He goes back to his phone.

Siobhán pulls herself off the floor and moves to sit at the island, head in hands. Something is bothering her. Something they've overlooked. Her mind tries to grasp it but misses each time.

Charlie looks up from his phone. 'OK, there's enough in the business current account; it's ready to buy the crypto.' He addresses Xavi. 'How long will it take to complete the transaction?'

'It could be immediate, but for a higher amount, maybe longer,' Xavi says, and Siobhán's stomach turns at the thought of sitting here, waiting, hoping the transaction goes through, and waiting for a reply from the kidnapper. *Kidnapper.* How on earth is this happening? And why them? Charlie is wealthy, but there are higher-net-worth people in Ireland who could pay a lot more than a million euro. And now she's back to wondering if it's someone they know. Someone who had access to everything.

Charlie and Xavi sit together at the kitchen table, as Xavi

does most of the work to complete the crypto purchase. On his son's advice, when the bank calls to verify the transaction is real, that Charlie isn't being scammed or robbed, Charlie says in a stilted voice that his financial adviser told him Ethereum was going up in value and now is a good time to buy. To Siobhán's ears, he doesn't sound terribly confident or credible, but she's hearing everything through the filter of abject terror. The bank asks security questions and, finally, as they all watch over Xavi's shoulder, the transaction goes through. Xavi pastes the Ethereum wallet number from the text into the recipient field, and they sit in silence at Siobhán's kitchen table, all looking at their own phones but waiting for a text on Charlie's. When it comes, all four of them jolt in their seats. Charlie's phone is already in his hand. A sharp intake of breath tells Siobhán the message is from the kidnapper. But it's not a message. It's a video.

69

CHARLIE LAYS HIS PHONE in the middle of the table and presses play on the video.

It's Luna. She's speaking, her voice shaking. Siobhán looks over at Grace, her hand over her mouth, her eyes huge. As one, they lean closer to listen.

'Mom, Dad, he says you have to pay or he'll kill us. Please can you make it happen. It's real. He has a knife, he really will kill us. But we haven't seen his face.' A sob. 'We don't know who he is, he's wearing a balaclava. So if you pay, he'll let us go. I know he will. I believe him.'

Where's Ré? Siobhán screams silently at the video. *Why is it only Luna onscreen?*

The clip comes to an abrupt end, and Charlie immediately presses play again. Grace walks away, her head in her hands, her shoulders shaking. But Siobhán stays. They need to watch again; they need to know as much as possible.

Luna's eyes look bruised, though it's hard to tell in the low lighting. She's sitting on a floor, it seems, against a plain-coloured wall. It's difficult to make out the exact colour – cream or off-white, maybe. A wall flecked with peeling paint, a faded rusty water stain. Siobhán's eyes roam the screen, looking for more. A metal bracelet circles Luna's left wrist. A handcuff. The other end looks like it's attached to something. A radiator valve,

Siobhán thinks. To Luna's right, on the floor, is an item of clothing. Or a blanket, something pink. That's it. A wall. A radiator. And something pink that blocks them from seeing the floor. The video ends again.

Charlie picks up the phone, types a message. 'I've replied to say we've made the transfer. He should be able to see it on his side.'

'What if there's something wrong with the transfer?' Grace says. 'What if he thinks we're bluffing, that we've called the police, that they've stopped us from paying?'

'I . . . I don't know. All we can do is hope.'

Xavi takes Charlie's phone to look, then goes to his phone to check the Coinbase and Ethereum terms and conditions.

'I'm pretty sure it should be there,' he mutters. A pause. 'It is, it's there now for sure. The person should be able to see it.'

And then another text pings through on Charlie's phone.

70

Heart pounding, Siobhán leans in to read the text.

GIRLS LOCATED AT D18 XF92. NO POLICE. I HAVE CAMERAS ON THE HOUSE. IF YOU BRING POLICE, I'LL KILL ALL OF YOU IN YOUR BEDS, THE GIRLS TOO. I KNOW WHERE YOU LIVE. I CAN GET INTO YOUR HOUSES. I KNOW ALL YOUR SECRETS. SO UNLESS YOU WANT TO END UP LIKE YOUR WIFE CHARLIE, NO POLICE.

Christ. Siobhán looks up. Charlie's face is frozen, staring at the phone. Her mind goes back to Emma-Rose, her lifeless body, her smashed skull. Because of them, all of them.

Grace is typing on her phone.

'The Eircode is for an address in Stepaside.' Breathless, panicked words. 'Not far from where Emma-Rose's body was found.'

Charlie flinches visibly at her blunt words, but Grace is already on her way to the door. Siobhán follows; Charlie, too.

'I'll wait here in case the guards come by. If they do, I'll say you've all . . . gone out for air or something,' Xavi says. Then sombrely, quietly: 'Good luck.'

Eircode D18 XF92 is a house. A house in a housing estate. A normal eighties housing estate with semi-detached homes and a big green and a warren of cul-de-sacs. Google Maps brings them to number 39, and they pull up outside. It's a little run-down, in need of paint. The grass in the front garden is overgrown, and there's an old blue Peugeot in the driveway. Siobhán turns off the engine, and the three of them get out of the car. Her legs are shaking. What do they do next? Just walk up and try to open the door?

'Look,' Charlie whispers, pointing at a security camera above the porch, trained on the front driveway.

'We didn't bring police, so we're not doing anything wrong; we're following instructions,' Siobhán says, stepping forward into the driveway. 'It doesn't matter if the camera captures us.'

At the front door, they stop. How will they get in? The door is weathered, white paint peeling off, but sturdy nonetheless. There's no window in the hall, no way to see what's inside. Grace steps across to the living-room window and peers in.

'Nobody in there,' she whispers.

'I say we try around the back,' Charlie says, 'and then break a window if we—'

He stops abruptly when the front door swings open.

71

THEY'RE GREETED BY THE startled face of a blonde woman in her thirties with a baby on her hip.

'Oh! God, you gave me a fright. Sorry, I'm just heading out,' she says to Siobhán and Charlie. Then her eyes go to Grace at the living-room window and her expression switches from friendly to wary.

'What's going on?' She takes a step back, pulls her baby closer. 'We have a neighbourhood watch group, just to say.'

Siobhán holds up her hands. 'No, we're not . . . We're looking for our daughters. We were told they were here.'

The woman shakes her head, her eyes anxious. 'You have the wrong house.'

Fuck. Fuck. Siobhán looks at Grace. 'Did you type the Eircode wrong? Fuck! Charlie, what's the Eircode you were sent?'

He already has his phone in his hand, text open. 'D18 XF92.' He looks at the woman, speaks clearly and calmly. 'We may indeed have the wrong house. Could I just ask, is that your Eircode?'

'Yes,' the woman says, starting to close the door. 'But there's nobody here except us. I really need to go. I'm . . . I'm not comfortable with this.'

Siobhán is crying now. 'It's the girls on the news. Luna and Ré, the missing girls. We're their parents. We were given this address.'

The woman's eyes widen, soften. 'Oh my god. I'm so sorry. I saw it on social media, the appeal. They're not here, though.' She pulls the door wide again. 'Come in, look around for peace of mind. But you have the wrong address. There's nobody here but us.'

They do, of course they do – they search the house, but they already know, this woman is not a kidnapper, this woman with a baby in a normal house in a normal estate is not holding their daughters for ransom. It takes less than ten minutes to check all the rooms. They congregate outside on the street by Siobhán's car, trying to get their heads around what's just happened. The woman stands in her doorway, unable to help, but unable to close the door and abandon them, it seems.

'He lied.' Charlie is pacing the footpath, texting.

'What are you writing?' Siobhán asks.

'Asking for the real address. That's all I can do. Maybe it was a mistake, a typo.'

'We have to tell the guards now,' Siobhán says, panic making her voice sound strange to her own ears. She waits for the other two to object, but they don't. 'Charlie, send me the video of Luna. I'll forward it to O'Connell. The texts, too. And I'll let her know the address is wrong.'

'Why would he lie?' Grace says, anguished. She lowers herself on to the small stone pillar at the end of the driveway of number 39. 'What does he have to gain?'

Siobhán has no idea. If money was the aim, then why not give them the real address? Or is this still about torturing them . . . the whole staging thing, making it look like the girls did something to each other . . . Why bother with all of that if it's solely about money? That's what's been bugging her, she realizes now. A stranger kidnap doesn't tally with the attempts to make it look like one of the girls did this to the other.

Her legs are weak, and she leans against her car, outside this stranger's house, trying to think straight.

Her phone rings, and she answers without looking, expecting O'Connell, bracing herself for fury. But it's not O'Connell; it's Tara from Sage.

72

'Hiya, Siobhán? this is Tara. We spoke at Sage earlier. So . . . I'm just calling you back about Ben.'

Something electric goes off inside Siobhán.

'What is it?'

'I know Caroline said he's great, blah, blah, and I know she thinks I'm just pissed off that he didn't want to take things further but, honestly, I do *not* trust that guy.'

Siobhán deflates a little. Is this something real, or just, as Caroline suspects, the rantings of a jilted love interest?

'Go on?' she says anyway.

'Well, I was curious about why he was so nice on our date but didn't want to go out again. I couldn't help thinking there was more to it.'

Siobhán's deflation deepens. 'Look, Tara, I'm sorry, but I—'

'So I followed him.'

'Oh . . .'

'Not in a *bad* way. I'm not a stalker.' Caroline's words come back now. *Borderline stalking.* 'I just didn't trust him, so I wanted to see, you know, where my gut feeling was coming from. Anyway, I followed him home and saw where he lives.' There is only the slightest hint of defensiveness when she says this. 'He always goes on about his little flat, how it's tiny but he loves it, blah, blah. But *actually* . . . he lives in this luxury apartment down on Charlotte Quay.'

Siobhán hears the unspoken *ta-dah*, but is underwhelmed. 'OK . . .' is all she says. A tall woman with a small white dog walks past, looking at them strangely. Charlie is pacing up and down the footpath, still on his phone, and Grace is sitting on the pillar, watching Siobhán, listening to her side of the conversation.

'Isn't that strange?' Tara goes on. 'It's nothing like how he describes it. And no *way* he's paying for it on the shit money they pay us here – no offence. So I was thinking drugs. But then when you were worried about your daughters, I wondered if it's something else.'

'I just . . .' Siobhán isn't sure what she just. People are entitled to their private lives. Not everyone shares personal details with work colleagues.

'I'm telling you, it's suss. I asked him the next day at work where he lives – casual like – and he said a tiny flat on Gardiner Street. I mean, we all know Gardiner Street – it's mostly backpacker hostels. He's really going out of his way to hide that he lives in this fab apartment somewhere else entirely.'

Grace is straining to listen, frowning. *Who is that?*

Charlie is still pacing, still texting.

The woman with the baby has quietly closed her door.

'Even so—' Siobhán tries.

'He has a secret income, I'm telling you. I followed him to a restaurant one night. Saw him ordering champagne for his girlfriend. That's not on his Sage wages, I can tell you.'

'His girlfriend?'

'Oh, like, I didn't know he had a girlfriend when I asked him out,' Tara adds hurriedly. 'I'd never do that to another woman. And maybe he only met his girlfriend after our date – who knows.'

Siobhán puts the phone on speaker, holds it towards Grace. 'Are you sure he has a girlfriend?'

'Yeah. She's fucking gorgeous, too, excuse my French. Tall, blonde, fab clothes, cute little gap between her teeth that I'd say she could well afford to fix – rich bitch, you know? Only thing letting her down was the tattoo – didn't love that, but that's a me thing.'

Gap between her teeth. An alert lights up in Siobhán's brain. 'Tattoo?'

'Yeah, wouldn't be to my taste,' Tara says. 'Small thing on her shoulder, a little blue butterfly.'

73

EVERYTHING FREEZES. THE WORLD around Siobhán begins to swim. *Butterfly tattoo on her shoulder.* It's Grace who says it out loud.

'Emma-Rose?' She stares at Siobhán, stands up from the pillar. Charlie stops pacing.

Tara carries on, oblivious. 'Oh, do you know her? Maybe that's her name – I wouldn't know. He obviously didn't tell *me* he had a girlfriend. Now that I think about it, I bet he was seeing her when he went out with me. Fucking men.'

Charlie comes closer, eyes on the phone in Siobhán's hand.

'Ben and Emma-Rose?' Siobhán's body is like lead, trying to take it in.

This makes no sense. If Emma-Rose was with Ben, then what was she doing with Charlie? Or was it an affair with Ben – something that started during the wedding planning?

'Tara, when did you see them together?' Siobhán touches Charlie's arm in a fruitless attempt to ready him for whatever's coming.

'Like, four months ago?'

Charlie's face drops, and Siobhán feels every inch of it.

So not a recent affair. *What is going on here?* Questions ricochet through Siobhán's head. Why would Emma-Rose marry Charlie if she's with Ben? Money? And isn't that what they thought when Emma-Rose first got together with Charlie ... that she was a gold-digger? But then what does it have to do with the girls, the kidnap ... It can't be coincidence. Was Emma-Rose involved? A new thought strikes Siobhán: could it have been Emma-Rose who made the 999 call? Ben was safely at home by then, his own Ring doorbell giving him an alibi. If they were working together, Emma-Rose could have made the call to emergency services, made the calls to Siobhán's phone, sent the text to Theo, driven the van to the Egan house, then taken the girls to her own home in Stepaside. She had access to the house, she might have known the tenants were away, pretended she didn't ... Emma-Rose, who had access to every part of the house and grounds all weekend. Access to bedrooms, gardens, pool house, conversations.

Emma-Rose is involved. Emma-Rose *was* involved. Emma-Rose is dead.

Grace is on her phone, calling O'Connell. Siobhán barely registers what she's saying. Why would Emma-Rose be involved in hurting Ré and Luna? She likes Luna. Doesn't she? Why would she marry Charlie if she's in a relationship with Ben? Her brain is going around in circles. Going nowhere. Was it all a long game, all for money? And why is she dead? Who killed her?

A car rolls past, a driver wearing sunglasses, a huge dog with its head out the window. The driver stares at them, these three anxious strangers in a sleepy suburban estate. Siobhán looks back at number 39. Why were they sent here? And who sent the texts?

'The guards are going to search Emma-Rose's house in Stepaside again, look into her background,' Grace says, ending her call. 'They took it seriously.'

Siobhán nods, still speechless. Emma-Rose and Ben. How?

Why? And if Ben's not in fact a Bailey-Crean brother, where does he fit into all of this? On her phone, she googles Foxborough Foods, Ben's father's business. The articles that come up are just as Ré described – headlines about slum landlords and abuse of staff and poverty and rats. There are follow-up articles, too, about the demise of the business, the what-happened-next pieces, and Siobhán notices that about half of them were written by one person – a journalist called Kim Brogan. Siobhán knows Kim's name, follows her on Instagram – she's gone freelance in recent years, writing mostly sharp observational lifestyle pieces. Without stopping to think, Siobhán goes to Kim's Instagram and DMs her, explaining she's a parent of one of the missing girls, asking if she knows anything about Ben Wilson, the son who blew the whistle on Foxborough Foods.

Kim's reply comes through quickly.

Hi Siobhán, I'm so sorry about your daughter. I saw the appeal. Happy to help however I can. So, you have it the wrong way around – Ben Wilson wasn't the whistleblower. He was running the company. His dad had handed over the reins and his brother was taking a sabbatical in the States. Ben ran things his own way – got rid of existing staff and replaced them with newly arrived immigrants. Paid them less than half of minimum wage, piled them into overcrowded rentals. Horrific. His brother moved back unexpectedly and found out what was going on. His father and brother cut ties with him, but it was too late for Foxborough – they went under. Don't quote me, but Ben Wilson cares only for himself and will do whatever it takes to get what he wants. Obviously, I'm not qualified to diagnose, but I'd say Ben Wilson is a sociopath.

74

CHARLIE LOOKS CATATONIC. Frozen in place, standing beside Siobhán's car, slack-jawed and pale. Grace grabs his shoulder, shakes him, begins asking frantic questions about Emma-Rose – how *exactly* she and Charlie met, what he knows about her life before this. Charlie's voice is dazed when he tells her. They met at the golf club, just over four years ago. She'd been hired to organize a fiftieth for his friend, David Kearns, Jasmine's uncle. Siobhán had known that Charlie and Emma-Rose met at the golf club, but not that David Kearns was the common link. She wonders now, did Emma-Rose know their history with Jasmine all along? Did she hire her as a wedding planner on purpose – to stir things up? But why?

Three tween boys troop past with a football. Siobhán tries to give them a reassuring smile. They must look odd, standing here on this footpath, on a sunny Monday in suburban Dublin. Maybe they should drive, go somewhere, before the neighbourhood watch people get antsy.

Charlie is still answering Grace's questions. He and Emma-Rose met for a drink soon after David's fiftieth. They hit it off. She liked all the same things he liked – Formula 1, golf, eighties music, Indian food, Mediterranean holidays, non-fiction books. Siobhán and Grace exchange a look. Neither of them has ever heard Emma-Rose express an interest in Formula 1 or golf, and the only thing she ever read was her phone.

They had dinner, Charlie says, and met again two nights later. It was fast, but it felt right, he tells them, his face drawn with shock. Siobhán tries to process it. Could Emma-Rose really have done all of this for money? And if so, why kidnap the girls when all she had to do was marry Charlie and be rich for the rest of her life?

Grace asks about Emma-Rose's background, if there's any conceivable crossover with Ré, Luna, Siobhán or herself?

Siobhán's mind races. Could Emma-Rose be related to the Bailey-Creans – perhaps to Judith, who had died by accidental overdose, or Arabella, who had lost her sight?

She pulls out her phone to google, listening to Charlie's answers as she does.

Emma-Rose grew up here in Dublin, Charlie says. It had mostly been just Emma-Rose and her mother – for many years they lived in her childhood home, then they moved together to a flat in Dún Laoghaire. Her mother died last year. Siobhán remembers that from their dinner conversation on Friday night. Her dad left when she was a baby, Charlie says, and her brother died when she was a teen. That stops Siobhán.

'She didn't mention a brother when we chatted on Friday night.'

'She never talks about him,' Charlie says. 'She didn't even tell me. I was searching for a safety pin in her dresser one morning and found a photo of Emma-Rose as a teen with a guy a few years older than her. I thought it was an old boyfriend, and teased her about hiding the photo. But she got desperately upset, bawling crying, saying he was dead and it's not funny, and this was soon after her mother died, so I should have known better than to tease her. And it turns out it wasn't an old boyfriend, he was her brother. She said he died when she was a teenager and she didn't want to talk about it ever again.'

'What was his name?' Grace asks.

But Siobhán already knows his name. The only name that makes sense of everything. Anthony.

75

Siobhán's throat is so tight it hurts. Her mind whirls over all of it, tapping and spinning and hitting on snippets of conversations, knowledge that's sitting there, just under the surface. Pieces she didn't put together. Emma-Rose, her name, her business—

EROS. 'Charlie, her business name, EROS – it's her initials, isn't it?' She knows the answer already. She's always known Emma-Rose's name, she just never paid it any attention.

'Yeah. Emma-Rose O'Shea.' He's still leaning against the car, like he's unable to hold himself up. 'What is it? What's going on?'

'Anthony O'Shea was Emma-Rose's brother. Oh my god.'

Charlie, ghost-faced, looks from Siobhán to Grace. 'Did you know her brother?'

A small nod from Grace seems to be all she can manage so Siobhán tells Charlie the same story they told Xavi last night. How Anthony – a criminal, a drug dealer – had taken baby Arabella to a 'meeting'. How she had called the gardaí. How Arabella had been saved. How Anthony had not.

Charlie shakes his head, dazed. 'But surely even the most loyal sister could see that he brought it on himself? I mean, if he kidnapped a baby, it was always going to end badly?'

'It wasn't a kidnapping, though.' Siobhán's voice is quiet.

'That's what the parents and the gardaí thought. But Grace had left him minding Arabella.'

'OK.' Charlie seems to be searching for the right words. 'But even so . . . he was a criminal, and he did something criminal. He still brought it on himself. Emma-Rose . . . Emma-Rose must have understood that.'

'I suppose people might feel that there's a big difference between selling drugs and putting a child in danger,' Siobhán says. 'The inquest found that he had abducted a child and the ensuing garda chase led to his death. That's worse than being a drug dealer, to most people, I'd imagine.'

'Even so . . . it doesn't add up.' Charlie is resolute. 'He should never have taken the child. He brought it on himself.'

Grace looks up now, pulling her hands away from her face. She turns to Siobhán.

'There's one part of the story I never told you.'

76

Thirty-four years earlier

GRACE JIGGLES THE BABY in her arms, trying to shush her tears. No wonder Judith Bailey-Crean hired a nanny. *She* can lunch in peace while Grace does all the hard work. Arabella's mewling pierces her ears, making her wonder yet again how something so small can be so loud. If it keeps up, she's going to have to leave the café, she thinks, staring longingly at her untouched coffee. A woman at the next table smiles in sympathy.

'It gets easier, I promise.'

Miraculously, Arabella stops crying.

'There you go. The little dote. She looks just like you!'

'Oh, she's not—' Grace's explanation is cut off when a figure in the café doorway catches her eye. A familiar figure that makes her heart leap and her stomach flutter. He steps inside, staring at her, his mouth hovering towards an unsure smile.

'Grace.'

Anthony.

'I thought it was you.' He shakes his head. 'Wow. It's so good to see you. You look great.'

Grace smiles. She does look great. The heartbreak diet suits her cheekbones, it turns out.

He steps closer, leans towards Arabella.

'She's beautiful.'

This catches her off guard. Anthony had never struck her as the baby type. Quite the opposite, in fact, bearing in mind he'd dumped her the minute she told him she was pregnant. And at this stark memory, the bubble bursts.

'Well, I'd better get her home,' she says curtly, scooping Arabella up to her shoulder. It would be time to collect Bertie from school in an hour. It takes everything she has in her to remain calm and poised. Almost a full year since she's seen him, and he still turns her legs to jelly, like Kiefer Sutherland in *The Lost Boys*. A vampire is an apt comparison, Siobhán always says.

'Could I walk a bit of the way with you?'

She should say no. The man broke up with her because she was pregnant. He is an asshole of the highest order. He doesn't even know about the miscarriage. He never checked on her, never wondered. He is the worst kind of person. And yet . . . well, what harm could it do to let him walk with her for a bit? It's a free country.

Anthony asks if he can push the pram, and she's so surprised she lets him without a word. He asks where she's living, and she tells him it's still the same flat in Stillorgan. And then comes the apology, just as they reach his car. He should never have left her, he'll never forgive himself, and it's only now that he sees the baby he realizes what he's lost. Or almost lost he says, posing it as a question, as he gets into his car.

'Maybe I can see you both again?'

She nods, confused but pleased, and it's only as he drives away that it hits her. He thinks Arabella is his. Her laugh is so loud it startles a passing dog walker. Of course he thinks the baby is his. If her pregnancy had continued, their baby would be just a month older than Arabella. Who knew quintessential bad boy Anthony O'Shea would turn to putty over a baby? She smiles all the way back to the Bailey-Crean house.

That night, he phones her flat. Asks if he can call by tomorrow morning. Against her better judgement, she says yes, but suggests meeting in the park. She'll have to tell him Arabella isn't his. And she really does intend to tell him. But he turns up with a giant stuffed elephant for the baby, and pink roses for Grace, and she doesn't have the heart. That's the version she tells herself, at least. That she doesn't want to burst his bubble. The truer story is that she doesn't want to burst her own bubble. This kind, soft, attentive version of Anthony is one she hasn't seen before. He never brought her flowers, never asked to meet during the day. It was all about nights out and drinks and a pretty American on his arm. This is different. Good different. And it's hard to make herself put a stop to it. Too hard. So she doesn't.

He asks if he can visit her at her flat. Her single-girl flat with no sign of an infant occupant. She puts him off for a couple of weeks, but in the end, it's easy to leave a few of Arabella's things lying around the small living room – a muslin cloth, a bottle, a teddy.

And seven weeks later, when he's visiting her flat on a warm afternoon in late May, she asks if he could watch Arabella while she goes to the dentist for an emergency filling. And she's gone longer than she intends. And she comes home to find a note. Anthony's taken Arabella to a meeting. And Mrs Bailey-Crean is ringing the phone in the flat. And in a panic, Grace phones Siobhán.

77

Now

'OH JESUS, GRACE.' Siobhán stares at her friend. 'Anthony took Arabella with him that day thinking she was his own child? That he was taking care of his own daughter?'

A quiet nod.

Charlie, still leaning against the car, looks from Grace to Siobhán, mouth open, face grey. The woman in number 39 opens her door and peers out, then closes it again.

Siobhán steps closer to Grace.

'All those headlines about the drug-dealer kidnapper snatching the baby of the wealthy Bailey-Crean family – *he thought he was her dad?*'

This time Grace doesn't move her head at all.

'Jesus Christ, Grace! What the fuck were you thinking?'

'I wasn't thinking. You know how I felt about him.' She sinks back on to the pillar at the gateway to number 39. 'I was devastated when he dumped me, and stupidly in love, and then he turned up again, and it was just . . . nice. It was easy and nice. And he kept coming to see me, and I suppose I knew deep down he was coming to see Arabella, really, and if she wasn't his, that was going to be the end of it. I didn't think it would do any harm . . .'

'Are you off your head? Not do any harm? Letting someone

believe a child is theirs? Is yours?' Siobhán is just about conscious of a woman in a garden two doors up staring, picking up her phone.

'I know. I was eighteen and stupid. Come on, Siobhán, you know what I was like back then. A mess.'

'Not a *mess*. A rich, entitled narcissist who made up rules to suit herself. How could you do that to him—'

Charlie interjects. 'OK. OK, but Anthony was a convicted drug dealer, he was hardly pure as the driven snow.'

'Yes, but he didn't deserve to die, and I called the guards on him. Jesus Christ.'

'Is that why you're so angry, because you think you caused his death?' Grace's voice is infuriatingly gentle.

'No!' *Maybe.*

'He died because instead of stopping when the garda car signalled, he sped up,' Grace says. 'That's why he crashed, that's why he's dead, Siobhán.'

'He's dead because you lied to him and then you let that lie linger after his death. Newspapers called him a ruthless, cold-blooded kidnapper. He thought she was his own child!' Siobhán's glance goes to the woman two doors up again; she's definitely calling someone now, but Siobhán can't stop herself. 'And look where we are – if we're right, and Emma-Rose was Anthony's sister, this is why Ré and Luna have been taken. Grace, what have you done?'

Charlie lifts his hands. 'I . . . I'm still trying to take this in, but we need to focus on the girls, on finding them. And maybe knowing Emma-Rose was involved, we can look again at where they might be? It might narrow it down?'

He's right; of course he's right. Siobhán lets out a shuddery breath.

A man pulls into the driveway of the house beside 39. He

gives them a curious look as he locks his car and goes slowly into his house, glancing back a number of times. The woman with the baby is watching them from an upstairs window and the woman two doors up is still in her garden. Siobhán suggests they get into the car; the others nod. Grace sits in the back, with Charlie in the passenger seat, and Siobhán drives a little way down the street towards a turning point at the end of the cul-de-sac. Once the car is parked, she turns to the others.

'If Emma-Rose and Ben were together, and this was a long time in the planning, that changes everything, doesn't it?' She throws an apologetic look at Charlie. 'I think we have to explore the idea that Emma-Rose engineered meeting Charlie at the golf club in the first place. That she'd been keeping tabs on Grace and me and knew Grace shared a daughter with Charlie.'

A slow nod from Grace. No response from Charlie.

'And if we look at what happened this weekend – for the longest time, it seemed as though the girls had fought and one of them had hurt the other, or worse.'

Or worse. Siobhán swallows.

'And we looked at what might have caused the fight, not realizing someone else was involved. Two other people. Ben and Emma-Rose.'

A dog walker goes past, looking curiously at the car.

'Keep going,' Charlie says.

'But then we found out Ré wasn't seeing Theo. That . . .' It suddenly hits her. That was Emma-Rose's mistake. She sent the text to Theo from Ré's phone, believing that they'd really been together when he was seeing Luna, but Emma-Rose was wrong about that. 'And that's when we started to suspect a third party was involved.'

'But why is Emma-Rose dead?' Grace asks, and Charlie briefly closes his eyes, pain crossing his face.

'And assuming the text was from Ben,' Siobhán says, 'why did he send us the wrong address?'

'Because the girls saw him at the wedding,' Grace says quietly.

Siobhán swallows. Oh god, that's it. The girls must know who he is, despite what Luna says about a balaclava in the video. Ben doesn't know that she and Grace have worked it out, because he doesn't know that Tara was stalking him, that she's told them about him and Emma-Rose. So as long as he doesn't let the girls go, he thinks he's safe. Only his link with Emma-Rose puts him in the frame at all, and without Tara, they'd know none of this . . .

'There's no way he's going to let them live,' Grace whispers.

Siobhán's chest tightens.

They call O'Connell to pass on the discovery and every detail they know about Ben and Emma-Rose, then the three of them go back over all of it again, growing ever more frantic. Where might Emma-Rose have access to apart from the house she rents out, and what about Ben's luxury apartment? The video of Luna doesn't look like it was filmed in a luxury apartment, Grace points out. The wall behind her looked stained, decrepit. That's when Siobhán decides to play the video again, to look and look, frame by frame, until she can find a clue to where it's filmed.

And then, finally, she sees it.

78

THE PINK ON THE floor beside Luna. A piece of clothing, she'd thought, when the video arrived on Charlie's phone. Or a blanket. Maybe deliberately there to obscure the floor. But now, paused on a frame near the end of the video, she takes a screenshot and zooms in. It's not clothing, it's not a blanket. It's a pink feather boa.

She turns to Charlie. 'Emma-Rose. Her business stuff – her props for parties, where did she put them? A spare room in her grandparents' house, that's what she said, I think?'

'Oh my god, that's it.'

Grace jolts to attention. 'What?'

'When Emma-Rose's grandparents died, the house was left to rot while her cousins fought over the inheritance,' Charlie says.

Siobhán nods, remembering. Emma-Rose was talking about it on Friday night.

'It's quite dated, a bit run-down,' Charlie says. 'But it's sturdy and dry and not in use. That's where she put the stuff from the pool house.'

Siobhán is still looking at the screenshot as Charlie talks. At the pink feather boa. Luna's wrist, chained to a radiator. Except . . . she zooms in further. *It's not*. One handcuff bracelet is locked around Luna's wrist. The short chain leads to the radiator pipe, where the other bracelet is looped over the radiator valve. Not around the pipe. Over the valve. There's nothing to stop Luna from taking the handcuff off the radiator. Nothing to hold her there. So why is she . . . The idea of what this might mean is almost too much. Is Luna faking the video? Pretending to be chained to the radiator?

'Siobhán, we need to go there,' Charlie says urgently.

She shakes herself, glances at Grace in the rear-view mirror. Grace meets her eyes. Siobhán opens her mouth to say what she's seen. But maybe she's wrong. And maybe it doesn't matter. All she knows is she needs to go there, to send the guards there, to find Ré.

'Do you know how to find the house?' Siobhán asks Charlie, turning the key in the ignition.

'I do. It's near her own house in Stepaside,' Charlie says. 'Not far from here. Give me your phone. I'll text the address to O'Connell and put it in your Google Maps.'

Siobhán pulls out of the cul-de-sac and on to Kilgobbin Road.

'Which way, Charlie?' she shouts.

'Left.' A sharp intake of breath. 'Oh my god. The Eircode of the grandparents' house. D18 XJ92. It's just one letter different from the one we were sent. He tried to send us there but got it wrong. A fucking typo.'

They see the smoke before they turn into the laneway. Siobhán speeds up, swerving to a stop at the front of the small L-shaped bungalow. Thick black smoke plumes into the afternoon sky from somewhere at the back of the apex roof. She jumps out of the car, running towards the front door with Grace right behind her.

'Call the fire brigade!' she yells back to Charlie. The front door is locked and, despite its ancient paintwork, doesn't budge when she and Grace push against it. Charlie tries, too, then the three of them together, but it won't move. The windows at the front of the house are boarded up. Charlie tries pulling off the plywood, but it's fixed tight.

'Is O'Connell coming? And fire services?' Siobhán asks, breathless, panicked.

'On their way. But—'

Siobhán finishes the sentence in her head. *But it might be too late.*

'There's a back door,' Charlie shouts, running around the side of the house. They follow, tripping over brambles in the overgrown garden. Out back, they can see the source of the smoke. The roof is smouldering; a fire in the eaves, maybe. Or any given room at the back of the house – there's no way to know. The smell is overpowering. They have to get in. The girls are here; Siobhán is sure of it. The windows at the back of the house are dirty, hard to see through, but not boarded up. Charlie tries the handle of the back door, but it's locked. Putting a shoulder to it does no good either. Siobhán looks around frantically for something to smash a window. She picks up the largest stone she can find and hammers it against one of four panes of glass in what might be the kitchen window. The glass breaks. She does the same with the pane beside the first one. Then the top two. Now she pushes at the wooden cross of the window frame, calling for the others to help. With a creak, it gives way and topples to the floor inside.

Siobhán goes first, crawling on to what turns out to be a kitchen sink, then dropping on to the floor. The smoke billows, momentarily choking her. Grace has followed her in, and now Charlie is heaving himself through the window frame, too. Siobhán doesn't wait – she pushes the door to the hall. The smoke makes it almost impossible to see but, as her eyes adjust, she can make out something on the hall floor. It takes another moment to compute. It's not a thing. It's a person.

79

SIOBHÁN RUSHES FORWARD TO the prone body, stumbling on a hole in the floorboards but righting herself before she falls. If this is Ben, she'll take her chances. Her hands make contact with thin fabric, warm skin. They're alive. But whoever it is doesn't move. Is it Luna? Or Ré? It's not Ben; the person is too small. And they're not responding.

'Help me!' she calls to Grace, looking for some way to grab the girl, to lift her. It's Luna; she knows this without knowing it. 'Come on, grab her!' She feels around to get purchase and her hand brushes against something. Something wooden, heavy. A wooden beam, like something from a ceiling. Maybe that's what hit her. She hooks her hands under Luna's arms and pulls, but something is stopping her. Grace is beside her now, trying to lift Luna's legs.

'Her foot is stuck,' Grace yells. 'I . . . I can feel . . . there's a hole in the floorboard and the heel of her sandal is caught inside it.'

Oh Jesus. Siobhán tries to see beyond Grace, through the smoke. Is Ré here somewhere, too? Or somewhere else entirely? Grace is still trying to free Luna, with Charlie just behind her.

'Got it!' she shouts, and Siobhán almost falls backwards when Luna's body jerks free. Together she and Grace carry Luna. Siobhán has her upper body; Grace has her legs. Siobhán shouts at Charlie to get the front door open; the smoke seems to be worse at the back of the house. Charlie sidles past, opens the front door. He holds it back, waiting for them to go through, then follows them outside to blessed daylight and cleaner air. Siobhán collapses on scrubby grass, laying Luna on the ground. Her eyelids flicker. But her eyes don't open.

Siobhán shakes her. 'Luna, where's Ré? Is she in there? Please tell us.'

Luna's eyes flicker again. Her lips move. 'Bedroom.'

Siobhán thinks of the video. The handcuff. The staging. Can she trust Luna? She has no choice.

'Which—'

Her words are cut off by an explosion. A shower of debris peppers Siobhán as she hunches on the ground, shards of wood and plaster raining down. Shielding her eyes, she looks back. The smoke is thicker than ever, but she sees it now; the roof has blown off the house.

80

'Ré!' Siobhán screams, gets off the ground, runs towards the house. Charlie is flat on his back, stunned or unconscious, hit by debris, his forehead bleeding, but Siobhán can't stop to help. Grace is ahead of her, already running through what's left of the front door. Thick black smoke blinds Siobhán, and the heat is unbearable. The kitchen at the turn in the hallway is alight, flames roaring towards the ceiling. Grace runs past it, racing down the corridor that houses the bedrooms. A cracking sound behind Siobhán tells her something heavy has fallen. She doesn't look back; she follows Grace towards the first bedroom, but Grace is already coming back out, her mouth and nose covered with the front of her cardigan. She runs into the next bedroom. When Siobhán gets there, a second later, Grace is on the floor lugging someone. Ré. *Oh god, it's Ré.* Unconscious. Or . . . or worse . . . It's hard to see – smoke stings her eyes and obscures her vision – but Ré is sitting on the floor, her back against what looks like a radiator, her eyes closed. Grace is on her far side, has her arms hooked under Ré's and is trying to pull her up. Siobhán bends to help, but something's stopping them. It takes another moment to understand. Ré's wrist is caught. Tethered to a pipe, a radiator pipe down near the floor. Just like Luna in the video. And maybe she can . . . Siobhán tugs at the handcuff, trying to slip if off the top of the valve, but it's not the same as in the video after all. The handcuff bracelet is below this time, secured around the pipe that goes into the floor. Not staged. Real. Siobhán pulls, trying to yank the pipe free, her daughter's hand free, but nothing happens. The smoke thickens around them; the heat presses against her skin. The roar of the flames seems louder now. Has it spread to the hall? A wave of heat hits her, then a billow of smoke. Siobhán pulls the neck of her T-shirt up over her nose and mouth, but it slips straight back down. She tries again to pull Ré's hand free, but nothing gives. Grace, still hunkered, looks up, meets Siobhán's eyes through the smoke, then looks towards the doorway. The heat is intense, the crackle terrifying, the flames too close . . . Grace stands, her eyes panicked and desperate and desperately sad. Her glance goes down to Ré, then one last time back to her best friend. *I'm so sorry*, her eyes say.

Siobhán nods. With every cell, every fibre, she wants Grace to stay, to help. She doesn't want to be left alone to figure this out. But the pipe's not coming free from the floor. The cuff's not coming off Ré's wrist.

Go, Siobhán tells Grace from inside her mind. *Leave*. A sob rises in her throat. *I forgive you for leaving.*

Then, head bent low, Grace runs from the room.

The smoke stings Siobhán's eyes and scratches her throat, making her cough more and more as it thickens. She can't breathe in properly. There's not much time left. She puts every ounce of strength she has into pulling the radiator pipe from the wall, but it's clear it's no good, it's not coming free. Ré is slumped forward in her sitting position, oblivious. Unconsciously breathing in toxic smoke. Unaware of how close they are to the end. And Siobhán knows without a single doubt that, terrified though she is, she won't leave her. She'll fight until her final breath to free Ré, and when it's time to give up, she'll close her eyes and hold her daughter. She won't leave her to die alone. All the things she's done wrong, all the things she's done right, all the questions she's asked of herself, all the guilt, the second-guessing, the worrying, the overthinking – none of them matter now. It's just down to this moment, this final moment, and not leaving her daughter to die on her own.

With a whimper of terror and one last jolt of strength, Siobhán pulls at the handcuff, the pipe, her daughter's wrist, but it's still not giving. For the last twenty-four hours, they've been talking about grasping at straws over and over, and this is it, now, the final grasp. She pulls one more time at the handcuff, willing the pipe to come away from the wall, but it's no good. It's no good. She can't free her. It's over. Coughing, she sits, back against the wall, side by side with Ré. She wraps her arm around her daughter's shoulder and buries her face in her daughter's neck. *I'm here. I won't leave you.*

Something hot, something metal, glances suddenly off her shoulder. She lifts her head, and it's so hard to see now through the smoke, but it's a metal rod, and it's Grace. Grace, standing over them, with a long, metal rod. Her cardigan sleeves over her hands, pressing down. What is she doing? It takes a moment for Siobhán to understand. She's using the rod to leverage the radiator pipe away from the wall. Scrambling to her knees, Siobhán reaches to join her, to pull down on the rod, only half aware of the metal's heat on her hands, and then there's a cracking sound and some give, and it's working, it's worked, they've done it. The pipe has come away from the wall. Siobhán is on the floor again, feeling around with her hands to pull the handcuff free of the pipe. Grace is already hunkered down by Ré, hooking herself under one of Ré's arms. Siobhán goes to Ré's other side and does the same. Together they stand and, blinded now by smoke, they move in synch, heads down, Ré's feet dragging behind her, out to the hallway. Someone else is there – Charlie on his way in. Grace is gesturing, pointing, telling him to go back out. That they have her. They run through what's left of the house, flames licking the walls, the ceiling. They run, and then they're there, outside once again in the air.

Beautiful air, and strong arms, and Charlie is pulling her further away, pulling her on to the ground, and Ré is in her arms, and Grace collapses beside her. They lie there, coughing, choking, breathing. They're alive. She's alive. Ré . . . Ré . . . Siobhán sits up. Turns to her daughter, prone on the ground beside her. That's when she notices the blood. Blood all over Ré's neck and arms. And maybe on the dress, but she can't see because the dress is black, the dress she wore to the wedding . . . Is it old blood, from whatever Ben and Emma-Rose did in the pool house? Or something new?

Luna is coughing beside them, trying to sit up. Grace's arms wrap around her, her hands red raw, branded by the metal pole. Charlie is calling an ambulance. Sirens in the distance tell them O'Connell is more than likely already on her way.

'You need. Ambulance. Ré,' Luna is saying. 'He cut her. Stabbed her, left her in the bedroom.'

Oh god. A stab wound.

A faint pulse at her daughter's neck tells Siobhán that Ré is still alive. Frantically, she feels around for the wound. There. Her stomach. Wet with blood, the dress ripped, skin split. Blood still coming.

'He wanted it to look like I did it,' Luna is whispering. 'Like I was faking. Faking being tied to the radiator. He left a wooden beam beside me. You were supposed to think it fell. On me.' She stops to catch her breath. 'While I was waiting to be rescued.'

'Oh god, we got here just in time,' Grace says, looking back at the house, now engulfed in flames.

'I know.' Luna is crying. 'He sent an Eircode.' A ragged breath. 'One digit wrong. You'd find me dead, and it would look like I wanted to be rescued but fucked it up.' A whimper and something that sounds almost like a strangled laugh. 'As if I would. As if I'd send the wrong fucking Eircode.'

Another gulpy breath. 'I'd go down in history – the idiot girl who faked everything then caused her own death. The Darwin Award goes to me.'

Siobhán cradles Ré, pressing on the wound in her abdomen because that's what they do on TV, and it sounds so stupid to think that, but what is she supposed to think. Nobody prepares you for this. No amount of first-aid training teaches you how to stop the blood when your daughter's been stabbed. More hands press on top of hers. Grace. They lock eyes, both crying. As the siren draws near, Siobhán presses and hopes.

81

Three days later

SIOBHÁN FEELS RÉ'S FINGERS move in her hand.

'Hey, I'm here.' Siobhán sits forward in her chair, closer to the bed. 'Are you feeling any better than earlier?'

A grimace. 'Yeah. A little.' Her voice is hoarse. Siobhán pours water from a plastic jug and holds the cup to Ré's lips. Ré takes a small sip, then another. She raises her hand to hold the cup herself, winces, and lowers it again, changing her mind. It hurts to bend her elbow, she'd told Siobhán earlier, because of the drips. One in each arm, and something called an arterial line in her wrist. Nasal prongs in her nose and an O2 probe on her finger. Siobhán is trying her best not to react to all the machines and drips and beeps. It's reassuring, but also disconcerting.

'Did . . . did Luna get discharged?' Ré asks, when Siobhán puts the cup back on the locker.

'She did. Grace took her back to Charlie's. She had a concussion from where Ben hit her, but that was it. You got the brunt of it.'

'Because Ben wanted it to look like Luna did it all. Did they find him?' Ré asks, just as a nurse pulls back the curtain. He's checking fluids, he says as he does something to a bag attached to one of the drips. All good, he tells them, and slips back out.

Ré is in a four-bed high-dependency unit, quieter than a bigger ward, and Siobhán is grateful for this, as well as the regular checks from medical staff. She tries not to think of something going wrong in the middle of the night. That's what all the machines are for, she reminds herself, as she watches Ré's heartbeat on a monitor.

'They arrested Ben in Málaga Airport,' she tells Ré when the nurse has gone. 'He got on to the flight in Dublin no problem – his passport matched the name on his boarding pass, but Málaga Passport Control picked up that it was counterfeit.'

Ré gives a small nod. 'And Emma-Rose is dead.'

'Yeah.' Siobhán isn't sure how she feels about that. What Emma-Rose did to the girls and what she planned to do was horrific, and if Siobhán was given the chance, she'd strangle Emma-Rose with her bare hands, but that's why victims don't get to dole out justice. Emma-Rose should be alive and facing prison.

'Do you have any lip balm?' Ré asks. 'My lips are in bits.'

Siobhán rummages in her bag and pulls out a tube of Scorch Cherry Rose.

'I knew one day your business would come in handy,' Ré says, carefully applying the lip balm, wincing again when she moves. 'How's . . . how's Charlie?'

'Not good. Still processing. I can't believe his wedding was five days ago . . .'

'Mum . . . there's something I need to ask.'

Deep breath. 'Yes. I know, and yes, it's Charlie. Ré, I'm so, so sorry. I should have told you a long time ago.'

'OK.' A small smile twitches at the corner of Ré's mouth. 'You know I met Aidan, my not-dad from Melbourne, and hung out with him over a few months?'

Siobhán's mouth drops open. Another nurse interrupts, this

time checking Ré's catheter, and Siobhán has to wait a moment before she can hear the full story – how Ré has been meeting up with Aidan.

'Oh my god, Ré, I'm so sorry. I had no idea. If I'd just told you the truth, none of this would have happened. Jesus, I'm—'

Ré cuts in. 'I may be high on painkillers when I say this, but Aidan is lovely, and I'm glad I met him, and I think you should meet him again, too. Come to London with me.'

'Well, one step at a time.' Siobhán nods towards the wires and monitors and drips. 'Let's get you well enough to get out of hospital first. Is Detective O'Connell coming back later? She said you were pretty sleepy this afternoon.'

Ré nods. O'Connell had been in for about an hour while Siobhán had gone home to wash and change.

'Do you feel ready to talk some more to her? I know she's confused about what Emma-Rose's endgame was, and Ben's, and what happened between them.'

'Yeah, I know. And I do want to talk to her while I can still remember. Some of it is hazy, and I'm afraid I'll forget. It's like trying to remember fragments from a really drunken night out.'

'Do you feel like you can tell me?'

Ré nods and takes a deep breath.

82

The night of the wedding

'Oh, shut the f—'

Ré cuts Luna off with a slap across the face.

She holds up her phone, the video onscreen.

'I've seen this, and now everyone we know will see it, too.'

Luna puts her hand to her face, her mouth open in shock.

Ré's hand is stinging. She stares at it, then looks at Luna, who now has her face in her hands and is rocking back and forth.

Is she crying? Or just drunk? A whole day of drinking hasn't helped any of this, and Ré, too, is feeling blurred, fuzzy and exhausted. Did she really just hit Luna? Fuck.

'OK, Jesus, sorry, Luna. I shouldn't have hit you. But you saw me being mugged and walked away.' Sorry comes out as 'shorry'. How is she slurring this badly?

Now Luna looks up, swaying slightly. 'I'm sorry, too.' All the bluster has gone out of her voice. 'I went to get help. I wish I'd gone into the laneway, and I feel like I always thought I was the kind of person who would, but turns out I'm not.' 'Turnsoutimnot' comes out as all one word. Luna's slurring, too.

'But you said you were mugged.' Unexpected tears threaten, and Ré grits her teeth, holding them back. All she wants to do is lie down.

'I saw a policeman and grabbed him and tried to explain what was happening.' Luna takes a sip of her drink, blinking slowly, her eyelids remaining half closed. 'He thought I said *I* was mugged. We tried to find you, but we couldn't.' She touches Ré's arm. 'Then I found you later, near the hotel, remember? The police already thought I'd been mugged, too, and it seemed like the easiest way to explain why I'd disappeared, why I hadn't gone up the laneway to help you.'

'Are you insane?' But Ré can already feel the fight going out of her. Fuck. How does Luna always do this, always win her back?

'A bit. I'm really sorry. But I did get help. Like, if you get more CCTV, you'll see me coming back, dragging the police guy by the arm. I didn't go to you in the laneway, Ré, and I'm really sorry about that, but I didn't leave you.' She reaches again to touch Ré's arm, wobbles a little, puts her hand to her head. 'God, I'm so locked. I really, really need to sleep.'

Ré's shoulders drop, all fire gone now. 'Yeah, I need sleep, too. I don't think I can even get out of this dress.'

She flops on to her bed and closes her eyes. Luna has done the same. Neither of them has turned off the light, and Ré doesn't have the energy to get up.

'I'm sorry, Ré.' Luna's voice is muffled with drowsiness. Ré doesn't reply.

Sometime later – seconds or minutes or more, she doesn't know – she hears the door open. Didn't she lock the door? How could it be opening? Did they forget? Did she forget? Luna is going to kill her for this. She tries to sit up, to see who's coming in, but her body is like lead. There's a voice, a whispered, urgent question and a whispered, urgent answer. And then she's out cold.

When Ré wakes, she has no idea where she is. Her mouth is dry, her throat is sore, and her head hurts. How much did she drink last night? Fuck. She's sitting, not lying. Sitting on a floor, on what feels like a thick, soft carpet. She tries to get up, but she can't. There's . . . there's something holding her back. What's going on? Ré tries again to move, and nausea roils in her stomach. Something is holding her. Something on her wrist. She manages to open her eyes, wincing at the headache that immediately gets worse. A metal bracelet. On her wrist. Not a metal bracelet – handcuffs. She's handcuffed to a radiator pipe. She's on a floor. Her lip is throbbing and she can taste blood. And . . . and her leg is bleeding. What the hell is going on? She tries to think back. The wedding. The dancing. Xavi. Sitting with Luna, and that's it . . .

Voices now. Instinctively, she closes her eyes, dips her head as though asleep.

A woman's voice. Familiar. Snappy. Talking to someone else. She strains to listen.

'I can't stay long. I've said I'm picking up flowers, so I'll have to arrive back with actual flowers.'

Emma-Rose! Ré opens her mouth to call out, to ask for help, but the next words stop her cold.

'I am still fucking furious, though. What the hell were you thinking, putting drugs in their drinks?'

Drugs? Ré looks at her hand, at the cut on her leg.

Another voice now. A man. But further away. No, not further away, on the phone.

'I told you this last night – to make it easier to subdue them. If we just walked in and started cutting them, it'd be a bloodbath.'

Cutting? Ré looks at her leg, focusing for the first time on a dart of pain throbbing there.

'But you know that was the plan.' Emma-Rose again. Closer. Clearer. 'And by changing it, you've messed everything up. Every fucking thing. Do you know how many years I've put into this?'

'It doesn't make that much difference.' The man's tone is petulant. And his voice is suddenly familiar. The Scottish accent. Ben from the catering team.

'Of course it does! If the girls were found dead in the pool house but both with Rohypnol in their systems, who's going to believe a drunken fight broke out between them, that no one else was there?' Emma-Rose is closer again. And again, some primal self-preservation instinct guiding her, Ré hangs her head, closes her eyes, holds her breath. 'Obviously, if they've been drugged, someone else was involved, and then they are *victims*.'

Emma-Rose did this . . . Emma-Rose and Ben from the catering team . . . Another thought strikes now – where is Luna?

'I know, and I'm sorry. I didn't think it through.' Ben's voice is smooth, even. He does not sound sorry.

'Now we have to wait god knows how long for the drug to leave their systems. I've googled, and I'm getting mixed results. This is a shitshow.'

'Wait, where did you google?' There's a slight edge to his voice now.

'On the pay-as-you-go phone. I'm not an idiot.'

'You know, there's a silver lining to this,' Ben's tinny voice says. 'The fact that they're still alive. We could ask for a ransom?'

'No!' It's so loud and so near, right outside the door. 'If it's a kidnap, they're victims. And they cannot be victims. They need to be dead, and they need to be killers. Drunk girls who got in a fight and wound up dead.'

'OK. Fine.' Ben's tone is tight. 'Just throwing it out there. Calm down.'

'As soon as the drugs are gone from their systems,' Emma-Rose says, 'we end this.'

83

Now

'And then a few hours later' – Ré sucks in a breath – 'Ben killed her.'

Siobhán stares at Ré, the shocked silence punctuated only by beeps from the heart monitor.

'Oh my god, Ré.' Siobhán squeezes her daughter's fingers, then, feeling the O2 probe, loosens her grip. 'Did you see it happen?'

A tiny headshake. Her mouth is tight; her eyes glisten.

'I heard.' Ré clears her throat. 'I was in a bedroom at the front of the house – Emma-Rose's house, the one she rents out. They were just outside.'

'What happened? If you're OK to talk about it?'

Ré nods. 'Ben was in the house. Not in the room with me, and I don't think in with Luna. She was in a different room, but I heard her roaring and shouting.' She smiles. 'She's fucking brave, for all her faults, you know that?'

'So is Grace, for all her faults,' Siobhán says softly, thinking of her friend running into a burning building to look for Ré.

'I heard a car and started shouting, thinking it was someone who might rescue us, but it was Emma-Rose.'

Siobhán nods. This must have been when Emma-Rose supposedly went to get groceries.

'Ben went outside to talk to her, and they argued. She was saying it was time to end it, to kill me and Luna.' A tear slips out now. 'God, Mum, it was . . . I can't even explain.'

'Don't. Leave it, it's too much.'

'No, I'll tell it. I'll deal with the feelings later.' A small smile. 'With many hours of therapy. Ben kept saying to hold off, that rushing into killing us wasn't a good idea. Like he was talking about some, I don't know, decision to renovate. And Emma-Rose was adamant that she wanted to kill us right then. Fucking psychopath.'

Siobhán squeezes her hand. Ré winces as the O2 probe presses against her fingers, and Siobhán shakes her head in apology, begins rubbing the back of her daughter's hand instead.

'I heard Emma-Rose tell him to get out of her way.' Ré takes a deep breath. 'She said something like, "If you won't help, I'll do it myself, now *move*."' He was still telling her to slow down, to stop, to think about things for a minute. That if she killed us, there was no going back, no way to ask for a ransom. He talked about killing two birds with one stone. That she'd have her revenge, and they'd both have money. She laughed then. Said she didn't need money, she had Charlie. In sickness and in health.'

Siobhán winces. *Poor Charlie.* 'And this was all outside at the front door? So she was trying to get inside, and he was barring her way?'

'That's what it sounded like. His tone was pleading, hers was . . . resolute, I suppose, but also kind of breathless with effort. Like she was trying to push past.'

It plays out like a film in Siobhán's head as Ré describes it. Emma-Rose determined to see her plan through to the end, to avenge her brother. Ben determined to get something out of it for him. Ben, who was stronger and bigger. Ben, who no doubt understood he was surplus to requirements now that she was married to Charlie and about to have her revenge. That his income from Emma-Rose might not last for ever. Kim Brogan's words come back. *Ben Wilson is a sociopath.*

'The thing is,' Ré says, 'even with Ben's talk of a ransom, I clung on to the idea that he was doing it for *us*. That he'd had a change of heart. That he stopped her in order to save us. So being really, really honest, when I heard her shout, then the thud and the silence, I was glad.' She looks at Siobhán from under wet lashes. 'Is that awful?'

Siobhán kisses the back of her hand.

'Not awful. Human.'

'And then it turned out he wasn't doing it to save us. He just wanted the ransom. He killed her to stop her killing us for one reason only – money.'

'You know he sent us photos of you and Luna?'

The curtain twitches, and Siobhán looks up, but this time no one comes into the cubicle.

'Yeah, he came in and took the picture. He told me if I stayed quiet and behaved, and if Charlie paid, we'd be let go. I heard Luna. She was shouting, saying she didn't believe him, he was going to kill us anyway because we knew who he was. He didn't answer that.'

Siobhán points to Ré's lip. 'Did he hit you, for the photo?'

Ré touches her mouth. 'No, I woke up with a split lip. I think it might have happened in the van.'

'And after the photo, after Emma-Rose was killed, Ben took you to the other house? The place we found you?'

Ré nods. 'He took us separately, Luna first. I think he didn't want us to be able to talk to each other, or maybe he was worried he couldn't control the two of us at once. And he was right.' Her voice hardens. Resolute. 'We would have managed it between us, to do something, to escape, maybe.'

'I have no doubt.' Siobhán runs her hand over her daughter's hair, her cheek.

'Then he came back for me. Clipped the handcuff to the handle above the car door. Emma-Rose's body was on the ground, her head all smashed in.' A shudder. 'I saw him take her phone and text something.'

The text from Emma-Rose, Siobhán guesses. The text that drew them to Emma-Rose's house and her body.

'He drove me to the other house,' Ré continues. 'And locked me in a bedroom. Another radiator, but this time a really old, wrecked house with bare floors and boarded-up windows.'

Siobhán nods.

'And then the worst bit.' A visible swallow. 'The next morning, he came into the room I was in. And he had a knife. Just a normal knife, not like something you see in a horror movie. A long, sharp knife you see in any kitchen. I was terrified. And he reached for the handcuff, and he looked kind of sad, and for a minute I thought maybe he was coming to free me. But he wasn't. He was checking it was secure. He said he was sorry, but it had to look like it was all Luna all along. I was terrified, but I told him Luna would never agree to it, she'd never say she killed me, he was insane.'

Ré coughs, and jerks forward to cough again. Siobhán holds a cup to her lips. She sips, then carries on.

'Ben said she wouldn't be able to say anything. It would look like she put everything in place so she'd be rescued, then died in the fire. The fire she set herself to make the whole thing look authentic. To burn evidence. To burn me, having already killed Emma-Rose because Emma-Rose found us.'

Siobhán blinks. 'Oh my god. So it would look like Luna did all of it?'

'Exactly, which keeps Ben completely out of it.'

'And then Luna supposedly killed you?'

A nod. Ré's eyes glisten.

The curtain is pulled aside, and this time a cheerful man appears bearing a tray of food. A dinner plate with turkey and salad. A smaller plate with bread and foil-wrapped butter. A plastic tub of some kind of yellow substance that might be custard.

'Compliments of the chef,' he says, placing the tray on a mobile table that he pulls in front of Ré. She wriggles to sit up straighter, thanks the man, but doesn't reach for a fork. It's hard to tell if this is down to lack of appetite or lack of culinary appeal. The man disappears again through the curtain.

'You should eat,' Siobhán tells her.

'You know what I'd love?'

'Go on.'

'Libero's fish and chips.'

'I'll see what I can do, but maybe give this a go for now.'

Ré picks up a fork and pierces a cherry tomato but doesn't go as far as eating it.

'What I'd really like is fish and chips with Luna and Grace, sitting on the grass near Sandycove beach.' Her voice cracks a little. 'Remember we used to do that?'

Siobhán nods, squeezes Ré's hand.

'Mum, could you ask Luna to come in? I really want to see her.' Ré's eyes film with tears. 'He nearly did it. Ben nearly killed us both, and you'd all have thought she did it.'

'I know, I know.' Something strikes Siobhán. 'Why did Ben send the wrong Eircode?'

'The same reason he left her unconscious but didn't kill her – because if he killed her, the police would be looking for someone else. He had to make it look like Luna did it but her plan went wrong. And if Luna really did set it all up, she'd have covered her tracks.'

Siobhán nods slowly. 'So in this fictional version of events, the guards would believe Luna staged it to look like someone else was responsible? A kind of double bluff on Ben's part?' She frowns, trying to get her head around it.

'Yeah. The narrative would be that Luna set the fire, sent an address and waited to be rescued.'

'But sent the wrong address.'

'Yes. It would look like she ended up dying in the fire she set herself.'

Siobhán nods. She'd fallen for it herself – the video with the handcuff looped over the top of the radiator valve. The wooden beam beside Luna when they found her unconscious.

'And presumably Emma-Rose made the 999 call, keeping it deliberately unclear, but if Ben's plan worked, we'd have assumed it was a legitimate call from you.'

Ré nods. 'Exactly. Emma-Rose and me would look like victims, Luna would look like a killer.'

'And Ben would be completely outside of all of this, beyond suspicion,' Siobhán says. 'The police wouldn't be looking for anyone else.' If Tara hadn't followed him and seen him with Emma-Rose, none of them would ever have known this . . .

'He said that Emma-Rose would get what she wanted, and that was important to him, even though she was gone. That Luna would look like a killer, and both of us would be dead.' Her voice breaks. 'And then he stuck the knife in me.'

84

O'Connell calls by again the following morning, looking somewhat fresher than she had the previous day. She sits with Ré to ask more questions while Siobhán goes for a coffee and some air. On her way back to Ré's room, Siobhán bumps into O'Connell and asks if she can tell her anything more, fill in the blanks.

O'Connell buys a coffee from a vending machine and suggests they sit – this is going to take some time. They move to chairs at the end of the corridor, and O'Connell begins to fill her in based on what they've put together.

'We found tracking apps on Luna's and Charlie's phones. Emma-Rose was reading their messages, tracking their locations. She was following all of you on all of your social media accounts for years, but under the name Laura.' O'Connell sips her coffee, winces.

Siobhán remembers the profile picture – the starfish brooch on green velvet.

'Grace's and Ré's accounts are mostly private, but yours is public, for your business, and Luna's accounts are public, too. Luna had been corresponding directly with "Laura" for years, having met her in a Dua Lipa fan group on Snapchat. She believed she was someone her own age from Galway.'

Siobhán waits while a floor-cleaning machine is pushed towards them, then away again.

'How long has she been spying and integrating herself into our lives?'

'Since the day she found out the truth about why Anthony died.'

Siobhán shakes her head, trying to take it in.

'So everything with Charlie, that was all engineered?'

'Yes.'

Poor Charlie. 'And Ben? Was he a crime partner or a life partner?'

'Life partner.' O'Connell, a glutton for punishment, it seems, takes another swig of coffee. 'It seems they met through their respective jobs in catering and event management five years ago, soon after Ben's family cut ties with him.'

This floors Siobhán. The Emma-Rose they knew for the last four years is a made-up person.

'And he didn't mind her being with Charlie? Marrying Charlie?'

'He was all for it, it seems. Eyes on the prize, the prize being money, when Emma-Rose and Charlie would later divorce.'

Siobhán frowns. 'How do you know all this?'

'Ben's phone.' O'Connell sets her half-full coffee on the floor between her feet. 'He destroyed Emma-Rose's pay-as-you-go phone, but in his arrogance, he didn't think he'd be caught, and still had his own phone. We got a lot from the messages between them. From what we've been piecing together, the idea to wind her way into Grace's life, all your lives, was more important than anything to Emma-Rose. Ben was fully supportive of her revenge plot, but it's clear his motivation was money.'

O'Connell clears her throat. 'Where they diverged was on the girls. It looks like Ben played along but tried to convince her more than once to ask for a ransom. And we're also reasonably sure that while she needed Ben to help with holding the girls hostage, she didn't necessarily need him beyond that. It looks like she was perhaps planning a life with Charlie.'

'You got all of this from the phone?'

'No, Ben is talking, too, though trying to push the blame on to Emma-Rose, trying to say he was afraid of her, pressurized to do what he did.' O'Connell arches a brow. 'From what we know of Ben, especially from speaking with his family, it seems highly unlikely Ben is afraid of anyone.'

'And Ré and Luna's evidence will count for a lot, too, I imagine.'

'Two against one.'

Two against one. That prompts an uncomfortable memory. Grace and Siobhán's word against Anthony's – Anthony, who was dead and couldn't speak up. Two against one.

'Anthony O'Shea didn't kidnap the baby.'

'We know that now. And there'll be a fresh inquest. But Siobhán' – O'Connell touches her arm, looks her in the eye – 'he was a convicted drug dealer. His nice house in Stillorgan came from the profits of selling heroin to desperate people who had neither the money to pay for it nor the willpower to say no. He may have been doing what he thought was a good thing that day, but he wasn't a good person.'

Siobhán nods. Perhaps in recent days, she and Grace have paid for what they did.

'How did Ben manage all this with a broken ankle?' she asks O'Connell.

'It wasn't broken. He wore the boot to help place him above suspicion. He was just the nice Scottish guy flirting with Grace and serving up drinks.'

'That's how he drugged the girls?'

'Yes, those last two glasses of champagne had Rohypnol in them.'

'And he did that to keep them alive so he could ask for a ransom?'

'Exactly. Emma-Rose's plan was to kill them there and then in the pool house.'

Siobhán winces.

'Sorry, that's hard to hear, I know. But yes, she wanted to make it look like they argued and fought and one of them picked up a knife and both of them wound up dead. You'd never know which girl had started it, but they'd both be in the newspaper headlines.'

Something dawns on Siobhán now. 'Ré told me she spotted Luna's Tiffany necklace on the night stand and that's when she suspected the mugging never happened. Did Emma-Rose do that – put the necklace there?'

'Yes, it was in the safe in her room and, according to Charlie, she took Luna's jewellery out of the safe and said she'd drop it to the pool house because Luna had asked her to. Luna hadn't asked her to.'

Stirring the pot. Provoking. Setting the stage for a fight.

'We assume,' O'Connell continues, 'that Ben put the necklace under Emma-Rose's body to make it look like Luna was responsible for all of it.'

Siobhán thinks about that now: finding the necklace, crying in the hallway, holding Emma-Rose's lifeless hand. Emma-Rose, who had wanted to murder her daughter.

'The sunglasses, the call about the house on Kill Lane, the "I messed up" text – that was Emma-Rose?'

'Exactly.'

'And same for the calls the night of the wedding?'

'Yes. Ben says Emma-Rose called your phone and texted Theo's from Ré's, then used the desk phone to make a 999 call so you wouldn't know which girl it was. Emma-Rose was like a . . . a puppet master. Pulling strings, pitting the girls against each other so that when we looked into their deaths there would be a trail of real and staged clues.'

'Because they really did argue. About Marrakesh and Jasmine and Ré's suspicion that Charlie was her dad.' Siobhán remembers something else now. 'It was Emma-Rose who provoked that, too – she told Charlie they looked like a cute couple.'

'Yes. The mistake she made was the text to Theo. She genuinely thought Ré and Theo had been with each other at Electric Picnic last summer, when he was already seeing Luna. Emma-Rose overheard one of your daughter's friends, Kayla, on the bus, talking to someone on the phone, and messaged Ben to tell him that she had another string to pull. But when we asked Kayla and Ré, it was Electric Picnic the year before, which was before Luna and Theo ever met.'

'So that was her mistake. And that's what made us realize someone else was involved, not just the girls.'

'Exactly.'

'The puppet master pushed things too far.'

85

Twenty-four years earlier

EMMA-ROSE SEALS THE CARDBOARD box with masking tape, writes 'Charity' on the outside, and sets it in the corner of Anthony's room. She sighs. There's so much left to do. And her mother's not able. It's not a physical problem, but a kind of mental inertia that prevails still, ten years after Anthony's death. A paralysis, an inability to move on. And of course nobody around here is prepared to let her move on.

Back when it happened, when Anthony died, their neighbours didn't care about his chosen profession, or the smashed garden wall or the parked car. But they did care about the twelve-year-old boy who swerved his bike to avoid Anthony's BMW when it mounted the footpath. The boy who toppled over the handlebars, landing hard on his back. The boy with life-changing injuries. The promising footballer who didn't walk for two years after the accident. Emma-Rose is not convinced about the promising footballer part. But it doesn't matter what Emma-Rose thinks. The boy's parents were the heart of the community, still are. Influential, liked by some, feared by all. For Emma-Rose's mother, the result was the same either way – messages on her phone, graffiti on her door and, worst of all, complete ostracization. *I blame the parents,* everyone said. *If he'd been properly brought up, this wouldn't have happened. That family – they brought it on themselves.* Loud whispers at the shops. Cold shoulders at mass. Anonymous notes in the door. *You should kill yourself,* they said, *and save us the bother.* And one cold winter morning, that's exactly what she tried to do.

Her mother, unable to claw herself out from under her black clouds of grief and ostracization, had somehow had the wherewithal to transfer the house to Emma-Rose, and to quietly dispose of most of her belongings. That's the part that breaks Emma-Rose's heart. Imagining her mother clearing out her life, knowing what she was going to do, carefully saving up her prescription Diazepam. If she had just taken the goddamn medication every day instead of hoarding the pills and taking them all at once . . . Emma-Rose sits back on her heels as anger and grief threaten to engulf her. But horrific as it was finding the note on the bedroom door, on some level, Emma-Rose understands.

Losing Anthony was unbearable for her mother.

Dealing with years of torment and gossip and shame pushed it beyond unbearable.

Emma-Rose found her. Cradled her, called an ambulance, saved her. And now they'll move together to a small flat in Dún Laoghaire, away from the whispers and memories.

Into a fresh start. Eventually, she might even launch her dream business, work for herself. One step at a time, though. For now, it's about clearing this room.

Down on her hands and knees, she pulls out the bottom drawer of his bedside table. A mishmash of notebooks, pens, chewing gum and chocolate greets her. Anything linked to his business was taken by the guards ten years earlier, but still, part of her doesn't want to touch the notebooks. Who knows what could be inside? It's not poetry, that's for sure. In the end, she tips the drawer into a bin bag without touching anything. But when she slides the drawer back in, something stops it from fully closing. Something trapped at the back. She still doesn't want her fingerprints anywhere near her brother's written correspondence, but she also cannot bring herself to leave the drawer unclosed. Reaching in, her fingers brush against something. She pulls it out. An envelope. White, large, stiff. Curiosity trumps caution, and she opens the unsealed envelope. Inside is a card. A pink cradle, a cherubic baby, text that reads 'Welcome to the world, baby girl!' With rising confusion, she opens the card to find her brother's familiar handwriting, all in uppercase, as usual:

DEAR ARABELLA,

I WASN'T THERE FOR YOUR BIRTH, BUT I'LL BE THERE FOR YOUR EVERYTHING ELSE.

LOVE, DAD

Emma-Rose sits back on her heels, her mind reeling. Arabella was Anthony's baby? But that can't be. Surely. There's something else still in the envelope, she realizes, and tips that out, too. A photograph. Three people. Anthony, with one arm around a woman and one arm cradling a baby. The woman is someone Emma-Rose knows. Someone she's seen in newspaper photos. An image burnt on to her mind back in those awful days when Anthony was hooked up to machines. The hours she and her mother sat by his bedside before he died. The gossip, the police, the journalists. Leaving school, hiding away here in this house for what felt like years. Until her mother couldn't take it any more. The woman in the photo is called Grace Gill. Just two years older than Emma-Rose. The woman who was minding baby Arabella when Anthony kidnapped her.

Emma-Rose eases herself off the floor, thinking. There's a new internet café in Stillorgan shopping centre. Maybe it's time to pay a visit. To search online for Grace Gill and Siobhán McKenna, the women who pushed her mother to the brink and killed her brother.

On that day, and on the next, and in all the early years of her searches, most of what Emma-Rose finds is related to the original news story. Articles about the kidnap, the chase, the inquest. But bit by bit, the information superhighway does its stuff. Through the dawn of social media, Emma-Rose slowly puts a picture together, and it's addictive. Looking at their beautiful lives is like pressing a bruise. It hurts, but it's impossible to stop. And soon, the jigsaw pieces of their lives fall into place. Where they live. Where they work. Who they hang out with. Where they socialize.

Then there's a picture posted one night in July 2012 – Grace and Siobhán out for dinner in Hartley's in Dún Laoghaire, two streets away from Emma-Rose's flat. Their gleaming smiles, their not-a-care-in-the-world faces, do something to her that night. Maybe because they're so near – living their best lives with expensive cocktails and Michael Kors bags just a stone's throw from where she sits in her tiny kitchen, her mother asleep in her tiny bedroom. Emma-Rose picks up a framed photo of Anthony, one of six her mother keeps on the windowsill above the sink. His knowing grin, his beautiful face. He was no angel, she knows that. But he didn't deserve to die. And her mother didn't deserve this half-life she's living. Without thinking, she grabs her keys, rushes outside and gets into her car. Within two minutes, she's on the street opposite Hartley's. She waits, watching. Half an hour goes by, and now she's angry that they're in there drinking and making her wait. What is she going to do when she sees them? She has no idea. But then . . . there they are. They're out on the street. She starts the car. They cross the road. She pulls out. Accelerates. Grace turns, her blonde hair lit up in the headlights, a look of shock on her face. And it's this that stops Emma-Rose. She swerves, avoids the women and keeps driving, breathing hard. What was she thinking? If she'd run them over, they'd be victims. She'd be caught. They'd be martyrs. She'd be in prison. Another taint on her family, another life ruined, and Grace and Siobhán anointed for ever. Emma-Rose is not going to prison for these two. She'll find another way.

Photos of the children appear from time to time. Luna and Ré. Moon and star. That makes Emma-Rose want to throw up. But names notwithstanding, the children are interesting. It strikes her that destroying Grace and Siobhán is not about literally killing them. Losing their children would bring them pain that lasts a lifetime. She fantasizes about grabbing the girls and pushing them off rooftops, right in front of their mothers. Her waking dreams are savage and soothing all once. But for now, they're just dreams. She needs to take her time.

A position comes up in Rathwood Park Secondary School. The moon and star girls go to the primary school and will no doubt go on to second level there. Emma-Rose applies and, within a month, she's left her retail job and is working in Admissions in Rathwood Park. Behind the scenes. Waiting for the girls. And then they come. Though one almost doesn't – Emma-Rose enjoys the phone call from Siobhán McKenna checking on the application form. Enjoys telling her she has no form for her daughter, the form she fed into the shredder as soon as it arrived. It would have been even better to tell her it was too late, she'd missed her chance, but then how would she keep an eye? And she wants to keep an eye.

In their mid-teens, the moon and star girls begin posting

online, too. Emma-Rose follows all of it, inhaling content in greedy swallows. Witnessing every moment, every movement. Luna's posts about Jasmine, the vice principal's niece, quickly taken down a day later. But not before Emma-Rose had seen them. Luna's bragging posts about Grace buying her vodka. A little word in the ear and a call from the school counsellor leaves Grace red-faced and Luna complaining and oversharing online. Again.

Emma-Rose sees everything and stores it away. All of it. Charlie, the marriage, the divorce. Xavi. The two ex-wives. The girls growing up. Moon and stars. It still makes her want to throw up.

Her behind-the-scenes world in Admissions gives her access to everything. It's easy to hide a stolen iPhone and AirPods in Luna's locker, easy to whisper third-hand information about where to search. The Gill–Caine Library irks her every time she passes it, and when she leaves to set up EROS, that's one of the things she doesn't miss. Meanwhile, her mother wastes away in the tiny bedroom in the tiny flat, unable to emerge from her fog of grief and shame.

Emma-Rose meets Ben when she least expects it. Her laser focus on the four hasn't left room for men. It consumes her, spiralling higher as each year goes by, as proximity grows. But this Scottish charmer nudges his way in, and for a while, at least, she's distracted. They meet at a wedding – of course – she'd planned it, he'd catered it. They're six months into their relationship before she tells him about Anthony and her mother. He understands. He more than understands. And – she notices – his eyes light up when he googles Charlie Caine and his net worth.

And then opportunity, finally. A fiftieth-birthday party at the golf club and a drink with Charlie.

She talks to Ben; he gives his blessing. More than that – he gives encouragement.

After that, it's easy. Dinners at hers, dinners at his. Getting to know Xavi and Luna, and eventually Ré, too. And Grace and Siobhán. The women who lied.

Tracking apps. Eavesdropping. Quiet coffees at Indigo Bean. Befriending Shiva, Prisha's mum – swimming in Seapoint, as her new friend 'Sonia'. Hearing everything, knowing everything. And all roads lead to one place – the wedding. Her wedding.

Again, she isn't sure how Ben will take it – her marrying Charlie. Too far? But he actively encourages her. After a divorce from Charlie, her half will be Ben's half, too.

Emma-Rose has found she quite likes Charlie, so she pushes that idea away for now. She'll figure that part out later.

But one October morning, everything changes.

Another note on a bedroom door.

Again she cradles her mother, again she calls an ambulance, but this time, she can't save her. This time, Emma-Rose is too late.

And Grace and Siobhán? They barely notice. They're both away on holiday, neither at the funeral. Oh, they text. *Sorry for your loss. If you need anything, just let me know.* Broken-heart emojis. And that's it. They literally caused her brother's death and her mother's suicide, and it means nothing to them. And that's it for Emma-Rose, too. She's had enough.

The wedding is her moment.

Both girls in one place, for the last time before Luna moves to the States. A whole day of drinking. Arguments. High emotions. Violence. Or so it will seem.

She knows about the mugging – she'd heard Luna on the phone to her mother. She knows about Jasmine. She'd told Charlie to ask in the golf club for wedding-planner recommendations and waited for David Kearns to recommend his niece. She'd guessed Ré and Luna might be sisters, though she didn't know for sure. The closeness between Charlie and Siobhán, their long friendship, and little things Charlie and Ré had in common: passion, hyperfocus, determination, scattiness. And then the aural migraines Ré started to get after Marrakesh. Telling Charlie they make a cute couple is like throwing a grenade that confirms her suspicion.

And she knows about Theo. Or thought she did. She'd heard Kayla on the bus, talking about 'Theo and Ré getting together at Electric Picnic'. Luna couldn't go to Electric Picnic last August, and Theo must have cheated on her there. A little part of her almost felt sorry for Luna.

It all teed up perfectly and would have gone without a hitch if Ben hadn't put Rohypnol in their drinks.

And that was no good. They couldn't be victims. They had to be culprits. Tainted for ever, just like Anthony. Neither mother knowing who started it, who attacked who. The wider public hearing about two drunk girls getting in a fight. Two dead girls who brought it on themselves. But now the Rohypnol had ruined everything.

She believed Ben at first that he hadn't thought it through. But of course he had. He'd done it deliberately so she couldn't end it in the pool house as she'd planned. So she'd have to wait for the drugs to leave their systems. So he'd have time to convince her to ask for a ransom or, failing that, to send the demand himself.

And by the time she understands this – in the hallway of her house in Stepaside, seeing the truth in Ben's eyes, in the brick he holds above his head and slams down on hers – it's too late for Emma-Rose.

86

After

SIOBHÁN WHEELS HER CASE through Terminal 2 Duty Free, stopping to quietly admire the Scorch Cosmetics concession. The woman working there doesn't know who she is but is knowledgeable and helpful when Siobhán browses lip glosses and primers. Box ticked, mood lifted, Siobhán walks onwards to Butlers for a cappuccino and an almond croissant. Ré texts to say she'll meet her at her hotel at midday and that she's booked lunch in the bar where she first met Aidan, her not-dad. Ré's real dad is starting to do OK, to come out the other side, though it took months for Charlie to process what had happened. Siobhán has a sense that he's pushing down his feelings about Emma-Rose's betrayal; it can't be easy knowing she targeted him. What he *has* done is taken a step back from work. He's letting some of his very capable management team do the jobs they were hired to do, and he's bought himself a pub in Blackrock. He offered Xavi the opportunity to manage it, but Xavi politely declined, opting instead to invest as a silent partner. To Charlie's surprise, Xavi's property consulting business is going well, with numerous high-net-worth clients who *don't* just want to click on a website to find their dream home. The acting, always his first love, is still not paying the rent, but it doesn't need to any more.

Charlie is splitting his days between Caine Construction, pulling pints in his new pub, and spending more time with his three kids.

Therapy is helping, too. Therapy is helping all of them.

Siobhán is finally coming to terms with her guilt over what happened to Anthony. Grace . . . well, Siobhán isn't sure what to think. What she did, letting Anthony think he was Arabella's father, it's hard to fathom. They haven't stopped speaking, they're still technically friends, Grace is still fun, she's still the first person Siobhán wants to tell when she has a problem or wants to call when she needs a night out. But, she can admit to herself now as she finishes her cappuccino, she's also been putting a little distance between them. Instinctively, not intentionally. A little breathing room. Their friendship isn't what it used to be, and Siobhán's grieving that, too, despite instigating the distance. Has Grace noticed? She must have. She hasn't said anything, but maybe she's allowing Siobhán her space.

Tipping her cup into the bin, she pulls her suitcase across to W. H. Smith to pick up a book for Ré. A woman and her small daughter browse the picture books. There's some kind of argument in play – the daughter wants chocolate and is stamping her foot, arms crossed. The mother is resolute, even when the wails start. The crying gets louder; the woman's face reddens. Siobhán remembers those toddler days and sends what she hopes is a smile of solidarity to the woman. Her eyes roam the chart wall, looking for something for Ré. Once upon a time, back when the girls were small, she'd have picked up a book for Luna, too. Back when they did everything together. Back when she didn't understand that just because she and Grace were best friends, it didn't mean their kids must also be best friends. Ironically,

Ré and Luna are getting on perfectly well, enjoying the novelty of being sisters. Younger people, Siobhán thinks, are quicker to fall in and out of friendships. To hate and love in quick succession. To forgive and forget and move on. Maybe she could take a leaf from her daughter's metaphorical book, she thinks, as she pays for the actual book, remembering Grace running, without hesitation, into a burning building to rescue Ré. The burns on her hands from gripping the metal curtain pole. Grace's own daughter lying concussed on the ground outside while Grace was inside doing everything she could to save Siobhán's daughter. Grace, who, for all her flaws, has had Siobhán's back for thirty years – at the school gate and at her shop openings, there when she needs a shoulder to cry on, a listening ear, or a taxi bringing high-heeled shoes. It's always been Grace.

So, maybe.

For now, she'll focus on London. On seeing Ré for lunch. And then later, dinner for three, on Ré's insistence, with Aidan, the man who is not Ré's dad but is, according to her daughter, very lovely indeed. The mother and toddler are outside the shop now, wails subsiding as the woman crouches and pulls her daughter in for a sob-soaked hug. Siobhán smiles at her again and puts the book in her bag. She checks the board and walks towards her gate, on to the next chapter.

Epilogue

July 2001

The music is already playing – is she late? It's not a Robbie Williams song . . . Oh, of course. There's a warm-up act. Something she would know if she was a regular concert-goer. Something she would know if she'd come to this with a group of friends, like everyone else, instead of on her own. Is she mad to do this? No, she decides. This is all part of getting out there, saying yes, trying new things. Though, as she shuffles forward in the line for the turnstile, listening to the babble of chatter in front and behind, it does start to feel a bit lonely . . . No, chin up, it's Robbie, it's Lansdowne Road, it's a beautiful summer's evening, it's going to be epic.

And once she's inside the stadium she really starts to feel it. The atmosphere, the anticipation, thousands of people out for a good time. Even on her own, it feels like being part of something bigger, a collective energy. A good time to be alive, a good time to be young. She has a ticket for the stands, which is maybe less fun than being down in front of the stage, but dancing on her own in the crowd had felt like a bridge too far when she bought the ticket. The people seated beside her are a group of work colleagues and once they realize she's on her own, they begin to include her. Not in an overt or condescending way. A subtle, generous way. They all work in UCD; lecturers,

EPILOGUE

she thinks. One guy is on sabbatical from Australia – going home in a couple of days. He's nice. Friendly. Good-looking, too, with his twinkly eyes and easy smile. They all have drinks already, and the Australian – Aidan is his name – offers to go to the bar to get her one. She's seen the queue at the bar, though; she can't ask him to do that. She goes herself, leaving her denim jacket on her seat, nudging past their knees to exit the row.

At the bar, the queue is deep but moving quickly. A couple in front of her turns to chat. They're dating secretly, they tell her. They met at work and don't want their co-workers to know. An affair? she wonders. The girl must see it in her expression. 'Not for any bad reasons,' she explains. 'We just wanted to keep it to ourselves for a while.'

The guy nods. 'I reckon everyone knows, but it's become a thing now, to keep it secret.' He stretches a hand. 'I'm Damien, by the way, and this is Andrea.'

She smiles and shakes his hand, marvelling at how easy it is to chat to people here. The couple turn towards the bar to put in their order, then wave as they walk away with their beers.

She watches them go, become lost in the crowd, and feels light and fizzy and energized. For the first time in a long time, she thinks actually, you know what, it would be nice to meet someone. And looking at the sea of thirty thousand people, maybe tonight's the night that kind of magic could happen. Her mind goes back to Aidan, the handsome Australian, and she steps towards the bar to put in her order.

She's back at her seat, sipping her beer, chatting to the group of lecturers, and then there he is on stage, Robbie Williams himself. Rapt, she watches, sings, stands, dances. Her neighbour's beer sloshes over her jeans and she doesn't care. The atmosphere is electric. It's everything. She is on top of the world.

EPILOGUE

Aidan and one of his colleagues are going to the bar.

'Would you like a beer?' he asks her in his lovely straight-from-*Home-and-Away* accent.

Is he being polite? Is he hoping she'll say no, so he doesn't have to wrestle an armful of plastic pint glasses through the crowd? Or does he really want to buy her a drink? She's never been good at this. Remember, she thinks, this is the time to say yes, to try new things.

His friend taps his shoulder. 'Come on, Aidan. I'm gasping.'

Aidan raises his eyebrows in question one last time and she shakes her head. He's just being polite, she decides.

'I'm good, thanks.'

Aidan never comes back.

When she plucks up the courage to ask his remaining colleagues, they say Aidan and his friend were making their way towards the pit to dance.

Oh well, she thinks, it wasn't meant to be. Nevertheless, a little seed of sadness takes root and the rest of the concert isn't quite so buoyant. She's not quite so high on life and possibilities.

As she's leaving the stadium, she sees him one last time. He's kissing a dark-haired woman. She can only see the back of her head, but she's probably far prettier. And still she wonders as she exits on to the street, *What if?* What if she'd said yes to the beer? She'll never know. Emma-Rose turns left and makes her way home.

Acknowledgements

This book was inspired by the uniquely anxious feeling I used to get when a minder at creche/pre-school called to say, 'There's been a little incident.' And, let's be honest, it was usually a biting incident. And in that moment, I used to have a desperate hope that my child was not the biter but the bit*ee*. Then, of course, I'd feel guilty for thinking that, but with those small, everyday transgressions, it was easier to be the victim.

What if, I wondered, on a train to Cork in 2023, it was something bigger than a biting incident? That's what this book is about and, as always, it took a whole team of people to whip it into shape:

Thank you to my brilliant editor, Finn Cotton – this is the fifth book we've worked on together and at this point I can hear his comments in my head long before I send him the first draft, which makes everything so much easier.

Thank you to my superstar literary agent, Diana Beaumont – you have changed my life – and thank you to my TV and film agent, Leah Middleton – you have also changed my life!

Thank you to all at Transworld and Penguin UK: Anna Carvanova, Becky Short, Jen Porter, Sarah Day, Vivien Thompson, Grace Smillie, Tom Chicken, Phoebe Llanwarne, Deirdre O'Connell, Mathew Watterson, Eleanor Rhodes Davies, Cara Conquest and Nekane Galdos.

ACKNOWLEDGEMENTS

At PRH Australia and New Zealand, thank you to Kate Hoy, Taryn Burges, Jess Malpass, Grace Howe, Dot Tonkin and Janine Brown.

Special thanks to Richard Shailer for the cover design for *Such A Nice Girl* and all the beautiful matching covers.

And huge thanks to Penguin Ireland – to the superstars with whom I work directly: Leonor Araújo, Sophie Dwyer and Kate Gunn, and the wider team, who are an amazing support and always fun to hang out with – Michael McLoughlin, Patricia Deevy, Cliona Lewis, Carrie Anderson, Finn Roche, Nicole Carey and Lorna Browne.

Special thanks, too, to Jessica Regan, audiobook narrator and all-round amazing person. I hope you have to read this out loud in the audiobook acknowledgements. Don't laugh, now!

Thank you to Lucy Hugo, my very, very good friend, who hosted me in her house when I was working on this book – I had the BEST time (and thank you, Kate, for agreeing to giving up your bedroom, though I don't know if you had a choice!).

Thank you to Gill Purdue, who messaged me at a crucial point and got roped into helping with a plot idea.

For Garda information, huge thanks to Sinead for the details (keep writing!) and to Richie, Ciara and Rachel for the quick-fire rounds.

On the personal side, thanks to all the people who are willing to have nights out with me to distract me from plot problems – Dad and Eithne, Nicola and Gareth, Elaine and Simon, Dee and Kev, my Sion Hill best-friend-forever, Eithne McGrath, my hp gang, my salon gang and the brilliant Irish writing community.

Thank you to the wonderful readers and reviewers on Instagram for your incredible support, especially Sinéad Cuddihy and everyone in the Tired Mammy Book Club. Long live the

ACKNOWLEDGEMENTS

Christmas lunch. Thank you, too, to the members of BookPunk for all your kindness, always.

Lots and lots of love as always to Damien, Elissa, Nia, Matthew, and of course, Lola. And kids, sorry for sometimes wishing you were the bitees.

Finally, thank you, dear reader, for choosing this book.

About the Author

Andrea Mara is a No.1 *Sunday Times, Irish Times* and Kindle bestselling author, whose books have sold more than one million copies across all formats. The TV adaptation of her 2021 book, *All Her Fault*, aired in November 2025 to huge critical and audience acclaim, with Sarah Snook (*Succession*) playing the lead. It became the most-watched TV show in America during the first week of its release. Her most recent novel, *It Should Have Been You*, won Irish Crime Novel of the Year at the 2025 An Post Book Awards. It was a No.1 bestseller in Ireland for six weeks, and a Top Ten *Sunday Times* bestseller in the UK. Her book *No One Saw a Thing* was a *Sunday Times* No. 1 bestseller and has sold over half a million copies. Andrea lives in Dublin with her husband and three children. You can find Andrea on Instagram @andreamaraauthor